THE VEIL CHRONICLES, BOOK I

TEMPEST

C.J. CAMPBELL

Iron Stream Media
100 Missionary Ridge, Birmingham, AL 35242
ShopLPC.com

Cover design by Megan McCullough

Iron Stream Media serves its authors as they express their views, which may not express the views of the publisher.

This is a work of fiction. Names, characters, and incidents are all products of the author's imagination or are used for fictional purposes. Any mentioned brand names, places, and trademarks remain the property of their respective owners, bear no association with the author or the publisher, and are used for fictional purposes only.

The poem on page vii is from R. A. Stewart Macalister, ed. and trans., *Lebor Gabála Érenn: The Book of the Taking of Ireland*, part IV (Dublin: Educational Company of Ireland, 1941), 213. Public domain.

Library of Congress Control Number: 2021940541

ISBN: 978-1-56309-446-0
Ebook ISBN: 978-1-56309-454-5

PRAISE FOR TEMPEST

Secret agents, ancient orders, shadow societies, and Irish folklore—all woven into a world you'll never want to leave. C.J. Campbell is an incredible storyteller, and *Tempest* is a stunning fantasy you'll never want to put down. Book II, please!

Tosca Lee
New York Times best-selling author

Tempest immersed me in a world of hidden identities, alternate dimensions, special giftings, forbidden love, and a secret rendezvous that includes brownies. Campbell's characters feel tangible. They are relatable and endearing but also slap-worthy at times. I loved watching Lexi grow comfortable in her own skin, buck stereotypical heroine tropes, and embrace who she was made to be. Dear reader, be warned: You will be begging for Book II!

Kristen Hogrefe Parnell
Award-winning author of *The Revisionary*

Remember to breathe. I said these words to myself time and again while reading C.J. Campbell's impressive debut novel, *Tempest.* This is not a genre I typically pick up, but I'm so glad that, this time, I did. I have now been swept into another world, experienced emotions I'd not felt in far too many years—wounded pride, renewed dignity, youthful passion, loathing, fear, courage, confusion, understanding—all within the pages of *Tempest.* Whatever Lexi felt, I felt. What she saw, I saw. Her experiences became my own. I read until I forgot I was reading. I simply *became.* Bravo! Bravo! I anxiously await Book II!

Eva Marie Everson
Multiple award-winning author of *Dust*
President, Word Weavers International

Prepare to enter a world where nothing is at it seems. Campbell slows time as her characters are spun into a new life and a forbidden love that appears unresolved even to the last page.

Bethany Jett
Award-winning author and novel junkie

The fact that this book is not yet a movie is a crime. I don't think I've ever fallen in love with characters so quickly. *Tempest* is flawlessly crafted and steeped in magnificent lore we don't see often enough in fiction. The story, the dialogue, the descriptions—everything is expertly executed. It's the perfect swirl of realism and myth to whisk you away to another world. From here on out, every C.J. Campbell book is an auto-buy.

Hope Bolinger
Author of the award-winning
Blaze trilogy and *Dear Hero* duology

C.J. Campbell's debut novel is brilliant. Both emotional and passionate, *Tempest*'s scenes played out in my mind like a movie. I devoured every page. Themes of brokenness, identity, and discovery weave around epic battles between good and evil, mortals and myths. Might I suggest strapping on a sword before diving into the world of *Tempest*? You just might need it!

Josie Siler
Award-winning author
Vice President, Broken but Priceless Ministries

From the first few pages, I needed to know how this one would end. Campbell did not disappoint—Tempest is a proven winner. Don't miss out on this fun-filled adventure.

Victoria Duerstock
Multi-award winning author and avid reader

This story is for all who believe in the impossible.
Who see magic in everything.
Who pour out love despite pain.
Who find the light even in the dark.
The dreamers.

It is God who suffered them, though He restrained them—
they landed with horror, with lofty deed,
in their cloud of mighty combat of spectres,
upon a mountain of Conmaicne of Connacht.
Without distinction to discerning Ireland,
without ships, a ruthless course
the truth was not known beneath the sky of stars,
whether they were of heaven or of earth.

Poem from *Lebor Gabála Érenn*
(*The Book of Invasions*)
The story of the Tuatha Dé Danann
from the *Book of Leinster* (c. A.D. 1150)

THE CALL

My life depends on how fast I can pack. In three minutes, I can fit all I own into one battered case.

It's a pathetic sight, me and my suitcase huddled in the back of my parents' rusted Ford Focus. There's nothing glamorous about life on the run. Hollywood gets it so wrong.

I roam a hand over the scuffed plastic shell of my faithful case. My fingers trace the collage of travel stickers I've collected over eighteen years. Four countries, twelve cities, and seventeen homes have led to this rather enviable collection. It's my map of memories, proof that I've lived.

The newest edition is a Canadian flag vinyl I bought an hour ago at a border service station. It's stuck next to a "Welcome to the Sunshine State" sticker. We spent one glorious year in Cedar Key when I was thirteen. I loved it. Loved the sun and the heat. It always felt light and bright—a far cry from the long, dark winters of Scottish Highlands or the concrete jungles of English cities. But then we fled north, far into Canada, where light and warmth don't often visit. I rub a thumb over the fading sunshine sticker. Maybe we'll go back.

I smile at the memories, then glance out at the spits of rain that streak the backseat passenger window. The inky night sky is shrouded. Not one star glints, not even a glow of moonlight. My smile falters.

"Do you think we can go back to Florida?" I shoulder between the gap of the driver and passenger seats. Mother glances up from organizing our array of forged passports, and I pout for added impact. "I'm sick of the cold, and they've got the best beaches."

Her brows pull into a mock frown. "We've talked about this, Lexi. We've a safe house secured in Niagara County. You'll like it. Lots of rivers and the lake."

I give a dismissive shrug. "I'm just saying that for a woman of your age, you look good in a bikini."

"She's got a point, Marie," my father says, never taking his eyes off the road.

"A woman of my age? What's that supposed to mean?" Mother uses an American and an Irish passport to consecutively smack his arm and bop me on the forehead.

"It's a compliment." Father snorts with laughter at her feeble attempt to cause injury. "Besides, we all know who's the swimwear model in this family."

A pause of befuddled silence ensues. He points a thumb at himself. "Me, obviously."

Mother rolls her eyes so far back they almost disappear into her skull. I snicker and tap my head, twirling a finger, indicating he's crazy. She hides laughter behind a fake cough all whilst Father mews his injustices at our poor opinion of his physique. In fairness to him, he's fit for an ex-army dog in his mid-forties, but he's maybe not Speedo's next centerfold.

That said, I'm not one to talk. I've never worn a swimsuit—never will—not with a body and face like mine. An anomaly in my blood caused a catastrophic mutation. Born half-blind and disfigured, though I do have one interesting characteristic—bulletproof immunity.

Father catches me looking at my reflection in the rearview. The playfulness vanishes from his eyes, and in its place, worry, concern, panic, fear . . . always fear.

"You hungry, sweet pea?"

I nod, despite the fact that I can't bear to face another drive-thru. Thirty hours of near constant travel has made me appreciate the comforts of a home-cooked meal.

"There was a sign for Chinese takeout a while back." Mother shifts in her seat to face us. "I don't think we've had Chinese food since we left Calgary."

She starts to tap the screen of her cell phone—consulting Google for directions. Her platinum bob hangs limp around her drawn face. There are lines around her mouth and dark shadows under her eyes. Worry is taking its toll. Each time we leave another home, her navy eyes twinkle less, and each time I perceive this change, I wonder how much longer she can take it.

"Don't." Father's fingers envelope the cell phone in her hand. She surrenders it to him without hesitation, though her shoulders inch upward and her lips purse.

"It's been three days since the call." Her eyes dart to mine, expression tight.

Ah . . . that call.

The thing with bulletproof immunity is that it's rare—one in eight billion, to be exact, and the thing with being that rare is it puts you on a wanted list. I don't know the exact details of which secret world-government agency it is that's after me, but I do know they've been relentless about it since my birth. Sometimes they almost catch me.

Three days ago, they nearly did.

They called. We were at the store. Things were good, peaceful even, and then Father's cell phone rang. We don't get many calls from outside our happy bubble, and I knew by the sick pallor of his skin that I could kiss Calgary goodbye.

Four hours later we were on the road, headed for a new life in the States . . . or maybe somewhere else? I'm past caring. Everywhere starts to look the same after a lifetime of this.

"There's a sign for a shopping complex." I point at a neon sign that not even I can miss. "We can get food and new phones, because I legit can't live without Snapchat." I heave a dramatic sigh and flutter a hand around my head. "This was made for filter fame."

This does the trick. The tension between my parents evaporates and they both chuckle. I grin, triumphant in the knowledge that my little self-deprecating jokes are still enough to make them smile in this endless game of cat and mouse.

Father veers off the highway to follow the directions for a twenty-four-hour Walmart. Or Target. Or whatever. So long as it sells chocolate and caffeine, I'll survive the rest of this trip. I can live without a phone—I've no one to text—but my parents can't. It's their only way to keep tabs on friends-turned-foes, and with their current cell numbers identified, we'll need new ones.

We pull off the freeway, rolling into a somewhat quiet lot, parking up near the gas station and farthest point from busier amenities. There are a few late-evening shoppers pushing carts burdened with groceries, but most of the activity hives around a Burger King and—score—a Starbucks.

"Caffeine money?" I hold out a hand to my father before he lets himself out of the car.

"Lexi, you have an addiction." He reaches for his wallet. "You need help."

"I need a double-shot latte," I say, eyebrow arched.

"And where does it stop?" He stretches me a twenty. "When does a double turn into a triple? Or, heaven forbid, you move to espressos? You need to take control." He shakes his head at the smirk on my face. "It's a lost cause. Fine. Get me one too. We shall all be addicts together."

"Drama queen." I roll my eyes and snatch the twenty.

He chuckles as we step out of the car to join Mother, who's tapping out an impatient tune against the car roof.

"You're insufferable." She shakes her head at him but smiles despite herself, looping an arm around my waist to pull me close. "Never fall in love," she whispers in my ear. "They're all idiots."

The two of us giggle at Father's expense, but he's too busy scrutinizing the gas prices to care. Mother takes his arm and verbalizes her sympathies at the outrageous prices. I observe them, and for a moment, I think that sometimes we're so normal, we could be any family. But then I catch a glimpse of myself in the window. The ragged, thick welt that cuts across my left eye and half of my face curls around my neck like a noose. I swallow the lump wedged in my throat because I know I'm the thing that doesn't fit.

"We'll just be in the store, sweet pea. Straight back to the car after you grab the coffees, 'kay?" My father hands me the keys. He pauses to let that hand cup my disfigured cheek. "Smile, sweet pea. We're safe. You don't have to worry."

I catch his hand in my fingers and smile for him. "I know."

"The usual for me, please," Mother says, before I can ask.

"One double-shot latte and the usual, coming right up." I stick a thumb up in the air and yank my hood up against the rain, then march for the sweet salvation of roasted coffee beans.

The dim light in the coffee shop creates a wonderful ambience, but it isn't great for the partially sighted. I catch my toe on the threshold of the front entrance and nearly take out an innocent barista carrying a tray of used mugs. With a huff of an apology, I straighten my oversized spectacles and keep a keen eye on the tile floor all the way to the bar.

Things don't get much better at the service counter. The barista almost drops the cup when he takes in my face. He's so repulsed, he can't even remember the name I give for the order. The whole exchange is awkward, but I try to remember to smile, to be polite, and to even inquire as to his day. Mother encourages this. She says that people only understand one kind of beauty, and it's our job to show them that beauty exists in everything, even in one-eyed, swamp-monster runaways.

Once the coffees are made—at speed and with little eye contact from Barista Boy—I pay and ignore how he takes the money from my scarred hand between his thumb and forefinger. He sticks the three cups in a quad-holder and puts the change in the spare space. I duck my head and dart for the door.

Not every person reacts like this; most have the common decency to pretend not to notice, or they just pretend not to notice me. But now and again, there's an ignorant individual who manages to knock my fragile confidence down a peg—Barista Boy is one of them.

Within the safe haven of the car, I let one tear trickle free, then scrub it away before taking a long, satisfying sip of my latte. The rich, velvety liquid coats my tongue and warms my insides. In an instant, I'm in my happy place, and all thoughts of the barista vanish.

Who needs therapy when you can drink coffee?

I slide into a slouch and make a happy hum of approval with my next slurp. Resting my head against the window, I close my eyes and listen to the rain pound. The earlier spit has given way to a deluge. This is close to my idea of bliss—coffee, quiet, and the rain.

Between the beats against the car's chassis, something vibrates. A noise so out of place in the lullaby of rainfall that I sit bolt upright.

Another buzz, and a shiver spider-walks my spine. I squint in the dark, chest so tight it's impossible to breathe.

A light illuminates the driver's side compartment. The sound the plastic makes with the third buzz rattles my very bones. I shove my coffee cup into the holder and squeeze my upper half through the gap between the seat and door. Fingers outstretched, I grapple for my father's cell phone that blurs to life for the fourth time. Once in my hand, I clutch it to my chest and curl into the darkness of the backseat, as if the shadows might somehow protect me.

The screen illuminates for the last time. I peek at the number, but it's listed as unknown. My heart bangs so loud that I'm afraid it will shatter my ribs. There's no one outside, at least not that I can tell, but that doesn't mean anything.

A car pulls into the space opposite, the garish headlights flood the backseat. I gasp and throw myself onto the floor, pulling Father's jacket over my head. Each second that ticks by feels like an eternity. My breath comes in quick, startled pants, and I shut my eyes to pray. Not that I'm overly spiritual, but right now I'll try anything.

"Please, please don't be them," I mouth, fingernails biting into the plastic of the phone. "Keep my parents inside, please."

The lights die and doors slam. A second later, feminine laughter bounces around the empty lot and heeled shoes clatter past the car. Relief rushes through every vein in my body until I'm limp as a fish.

"Thank you," I whisper and rub a hand down my face.

I toss off the jacket and heave up onto the backseat. It takes a full minute before my breathing regulates and I no longer feel my pulse in my ears. All I can do is stare at the phone screen, at the unlisted number, and contemplate what it means.

As if in answer, the phone buzzes in my hand again. I almost drop it, ready to nosedive to the floor, but morbid curiosity keeps me glued to the spot.

It's not a phone number this time, but a text.

A simple sentence that reads: *You can't protect her forever, Fred. They'll come for her. She'll need us. T.*

I stare and stare, afraid to blink in case it disappears.

The questions flash one by one in my mind until they're nothing but a hum of panic. Protect me from whom? Who's T, and why will I need him? What's coming?

My palms are slick with sweat, and I'm not sure I'm breathing. It's a struggle just to hold on to the phone and remain upright.

The door handle rattles. I launch at the door, ready to hold it shut, ready to scream until my lungs give out. I'm not going anywhere, not with T, not with anyone but my parents.

"Sweet pea? It's me." My father's voice shatters the delusion. I drop back against the backseat and press the lock release on the key.

"Lexi." Mother swings open the back passenger door and pauses. Her eyes widen at whatever she sees in mine, and a heartbeat later, her arms circle me. "Love, what is it?"

"Who's coming for me?" I blurt out, voice hoarse and rough.

She glances between me and the phone. Her nimble fingers work the old, silver cell out of my grasp. She studies the message for a second, then hands it straight to my father; a look of sheer fury passes between them in the exchange. "No one." Mother grips me tighter, folding my head under her chin; her lips graze my crown. "No one is going to touch you."

Father reads the message, his face a hard mask. A second passes, and he drops the phone on the ground, smashing it with the heel of his boot. He slides into the front seat and starts the engine, then gives Mother a silent nod, and she slams the door closed behind her.

"Who-who is coming?" I push for an answer as those tears start to trek my cheeks. Mother's hold on me turns viselike. "Why wouldn't you be able to protect me?"

Father twists in his seat, his blue eyes bright and fierce, illuminated by the dash lights. His whole presence alters so much that it's not my father in front of me but a trained killer. I know he has a past, I just never ask about it. I don't want to know why he carries guns and knives the way I carry art supplies and paintbrushes.

"No one will touch a hair on your head," he says in a voice laced with promise. "No one is coming, and if they even try, it'll be the last thing they do."

"Fred, you'll scare her." Mother rocks me a little too fast to be soothing, but I cling to her anyway. "Love, no one is coming. That message was just meant to scare us."

Father doesn't correct her. Instead he sinks his foot on the gas pedal until the car squeals out of the lot. We disappear into the night and speed toward a new safe place, except I don't feel so safe.

There's a new kind of frantic fear in my parent's eyes. Shadows nip the corners of our happy bubble like ice claws. They tickle the back of my neck and run a chill down my spine—a warning.

Something's coming.

FREEDOM

Three weeks and five days have rushed by since the call. I'm starting afresh, going by Lexi Danu—the surname an ancestral throwback on Father's side. Wilson, New York, is our new home, and a short drive south brings me to my chosen place of hiding—Niagara Community College.

Droves of students mill around a campus parking lot. I watch them from the safety of the passenger seat, Mother at my side in the driver's. They're like honeybees, all energy and focus. It's the perfect place to hide in plain sight. At least that's how I argued my case. Father didn't buy it, but I figure if something terrible is after me, then I'd like to fulfill some bucket-list goals before it's too late. A semester of college has topped the list for a while now.

So here I am, first day of the new, brave me, except the digital clock on the dash flashes 8:33—if I don't rally courage now, I'll never get out of the car. Mother watches all of this with an almost smirk.

"What?" I pull a frown. "I'm not stalling, if that's what you think."

"Yeah, whatever, you're totally stalling." She cackles and twists in the seat to arch a knowing eyebrow. "So what is it? You were all for this adventure thirty minutes ago."

"Thirty minutes ago I didn't feel so . . . exposed." I dare a glance at the tall campus building. "What if I make a mistake? What if someone notices?"

"Honey." Mother leans forward, our brows colliding. Strands of her platinum hair tangle with my copper curls. "You won't make any mistakes, and so what if you do? What's the worst that can happen? We move?"

I blurt out a nervous laugh and shake my head. "That is the worst. I don't want to be the reason we move again."

"Stop it." She plants a kiss to my cheek. "If moving keeps you safe, then I don't care where we go, so long as we're together." She slouches back into the seat and begins fishing in the pocket of her oversized cardigan; the black fabric almost swallows her tiny frame whole. "Now, these occasions call for presents."

"Presents?" I balk at the tiny box she procures and shoves under my nose. "What's this for?"

"It's not every day your daughter goes off to college." She grins in the most mischievous way. "Your father and I wanted to wait and give you this when you were ready."

"Ready? For what?" I ask, only partly interested, as I rip off the green ribbon.

She wafts her hands about. "I meant older."

I pop open the box and gasp at the beautiful piece of jewelry set against black velvet. "It's a locket."

"Oh, it's more than a locket." She takes it from the box and gestures for me to turn so she can fix it in place, which I do. "This particular locket was a gift from a very special friend of ours. He wanted you to have it someday, so you'd have something to remember home by."

"A friend? From Ireland? You've never mentioned him." I straighten in the seat and examine the intricate, vaguely Celtic pattern engraved in the gold.

Mother sighs. "Didn't seem right." Her slender hands stroke the lengths of my hair. "He died not long after you were born."

"I'm sorry," I say, surprised at the tears that well in my eyes for this stranger I never met, and more so that I meant so much to him that he'd leave me such a precious gift. "I'd have liked to meet him."

"I'm positive he would've loved that too." Mother presses another kiss to my temple. "Maybe next time we move we can go home. Answer some of your questions about where you came from, eh?"

"Are you serious? You think it's safe to go home?" I pull away, my gaze torn between her and the locket I've just opened. Inside reveals miniature pictures of both my parents. They look younger, happier in ways, and Father wears some kind of official uniform I don't recognize.

"I don't think it's ever going to be safe for you, love." That same weary sigh has crept into her voice, but she smiles despite it. "But you're stronger than I could've dreamed, and if you can survive a semester of college, then you'll survive just about anything life can throw at you."

At that, we both laugh, and I toss my arms around her neck for one last cuddle.

The clock flashes 8:49, and I'm aware that the parking lot is less crowded. Mother gives my arm a squeeze and nods toward the campus entrance.

"Go on, love. You deserve this. Enjoy every minute of it."

Mother has always been behind the college idea. In her mind, the very reason they've run all these years is to give me a normal life full of normal experiences. It's because of her that I won my case for this opportunity.

It's because of her I'm alive.

One last shared look and her smile widens. Her eyes glitter with an unwavering confidence that bolsters mine. She mouths an "I love you," and I blow her a kiss before opening the door.

I can do this.

It's not that I'm immune to people gaping, it's more that I don't blame them. I'd stare too. It's natural, but it doesn't help my anxiety. I might puke, and there's a chance I'm lost. So, so lost.

Clustered beside a water fountain, a trio of preened college girls catch my approach. I slow and start to smile, but I see disgust and pity war on their faces as they try to direct their attention elsewhere. A little crestfallen, I return my attention to the campus map I hold in my sweaty palms. Amidst the fuzzy lines and awful grayscale, I decipher that I need to follow this corridor left to a staircase in the main mezzanine. I quicken my steps and make a sharp turn. Then smack straight into cold leather.

"Watch it." A mountain of a man towers over me.

"Sorry."

"Are you blind or something?" He shoves me out of his way and into the nearest wall.

My right palm collides with the rough brick in my attempt to gain balance whilst the other grapples to keep my spectacles on. In the disorientation, it takes a moment for the sting to register in my splayed right hand.

Oh no.

Heartbeat hammering, I lean into the wall, sensing the cut on my palm, the hot stickiness of blood already pooling there.

No, no, no.

I take a steadying breath and glance over my shoulder. Apart from Mountain Man—who's long gone—I'm mostly alone. And any passersby are far too engrossed in their own world to notice mine. I twist to rest my back against the wall and obscure my hand and the wall it rested against from view. That was close. Too close. I curl my cut hand into a fist.

Another quick scan of my surroundings and I ascertain it is safe to pull my fist from behind my back. I unfurl tight fingers to reveal a perfect, unscathed palm smeared with intertwined blotches of purple, gold, and silver. Bulletproof immunity comes with weird, but pretty, blood. I check the wall— no bloodstains. I loose a breath, then fish Mother's embroidered handkerchief from my pocket and scrub away all evidence from my hand.

A blur of black and gold zooms by.

"Hot wheels coming through!"

I yelp in surprise and stagger—avoiding the wall this time—and follow what my slow vision pieces together as a wheelchair rocketing with unrestrained speed. The chair comes to an abrupt halt, and the fuzzy blob operating it does an elegant turn, then comes wheeling back. A cheerful face greets me.

"New girl, right?" The golden-haired boy's smile widens.

"Uh . . ." I fiddle with my satchel strap.

Did he see? Fifteen minutes in, and I make this whooper of a mistake. Think. Think of an appropriate excuse. It's paint. Yes, that's totally plausible. I'm an art student after all. Except I don't have any paint on my person. Great.

"Dude, can you hear? Cause it's cool if you can't; I know sign language."

To my utter horror, he begins to sign out words.

"No, no, I'm not deaf." My shoulders inch upward. "Yeah, I'm new, I just didn't realize others knew that I was new, y'know?"

"There's a lot of confusion in that sentence." He tilts back in his wheelchair, balancing with a confident smirk. "I'm Connor, by the way. Founder and president of the school's disabled students' voice, not that anyone listens. But hey, gotta fight the good fight, right?"

"Uh."

So maybe he didn't see. I think I'm going to hurl for real now.

"You don't have much to say, huh, new girl?" Connor quirks an eyebrow and runs a gloved hand through his golden hair. "So, where you headed? Can I be of assistance to the fair lady? I'd say hop on, but apart from the glaringly awful innuendo, it's probably against school policy, or socially unacceptable."

I cringe and start to scuttle down the packed hallway. "No, I can manage."

"Suit yourself."

Less than three minutes later, I glance back to find Connor there. "I said I can manage." I jab a finger at my left eye. "I'm not completely blind, nor am I deaf, and I don't need assistance—thank you very much."

"Fire . . . nice." Connor crosses his arms about his broad chest. A second later, and he rolls his eyes. "I wasn't following you, merely happening along the same path. Thought I'd be a gentleman and introduce myself. S'cool though. We can be strangers."

"Oh." My panic fades in the face of Connor's complete obliviousness. "S-sorry." I drop my gaze. "I, um . . . well . . . I'm a little uptight."

"Uptight? Girl, you're so tightly wound your shoulders touch your ears." His eyes glint with a warm tease. "So, are we strangers or new hall-walking acquaintances?"

"Maybe somewhere in the middle." I offer a half-smile.

"Some of the greatest friendships started as hall-walking acquaintances."

I suppress a sigh. This boy has trouble with silences.

"Can't think of any right now, but I'm sure it can be Googled," he says. "So apart from 'new girl,' what do I call you?"

"Friendly hall-walking acquaintance."

Connor keeps one eyebrow raised.

Fine. "Lexi."

He beams in victory. "I don't know many Lexis."

We engage in a brief staredown until I garner, by Connor's continued grin, that he isn't going away.

"So where you headed then?"

"The Art Department."

"Me too."

Wonderful. Why did I encourage this? Can't a girl have an anxiety attack in peace?

"You know"—Connor taps the wheel of his chair with a wince—"since your new hall-walking acquaintance has mobility issues, perhaps we should avail ourselves of the elevator?"

"You made up the term 'hall-walking acquaintance.'"

He pulls out that charming grin again. "Yes, and see how easy you forgot that, actually, I'm not walking—I'm wheeling." Connor rolls around in a little circle. "It's all a matter of perception and attitude, and you're far too serious. Come on, the elevator is prehistoric, and I don't have all day." He turns and wheels away.

The elevator is a safe bet, and if I'm going to blend in, I figure I'd best be pleasant. No need to draw attention by being rude. False alarm. Crisis averted. I square my shoulders and take a deep breath. I can do this.

The elevator still hasn't arrived by the time I stomp up to him. He blinks and pulls a quizzical frown. I ignore it and stare at the red light around the up arrow.

"It's okay to be nervous on your first day. What are you, a freshman? Being new is hard enough, let alone joining late. If you feel like you wanna puke or hide in a closet, there's a study room for us special students. Room 53—the librarians will give you a key and probably extra credit for visiting a library."

I laugh. Unintended, but it morphs from a silent snigger to a hearty cackle. I'll give it to the boy—he's determined. "Thanks," I say between chuckles.

The elevator door opens. Connor winks, gesturing me in first.

An ungodly groan echoes as the door shuts behind us and the mechanical box clunks upward. This machine is nowhere near safe. I flinch at a loud *thunk*, then scramble to say something—anything—that will distract from these unhealthy noises. "How'd you know I was new?"

"I'm secretly a century-old vampire who's been watching you sleep for weeks." Connor doesn't crack a smile.

"Nah. You're too cheerful being in close proximity to a human. I think you're the obligatory werewolf."

"You know your vampire fiction." He shakes his head. "It's a bit cliché that I'd be the vamp. Okay, I'm actually Superman."

"A telepath of another persuasion would make more sense."

His eyes narrow. "Just because I'm in a wheelchair doesn't mean I have to play the weirdo. I could be Superman."

"Seriously"—I point a finger between us—"we can play this game all day. But how'd you know I'm new?"

He deflates a little. "If I admit this, you're not permitted to repeat it."

Fingers drumming against the metal wall, I shoot him a bored look.

"My dad—foster dad—is head of the art faculty. He said a new student joined, and he might've hinted you were, y'know, not like the rest of these privileged mortals."

"You mean disabled?" I raise both brows. Interesting take. Maybe he struggles with being in that chair more than he lets on? "You were waiting on me?"

"Well, I was loitering around the front hall anyway. And you were the only kid dropped off by her mother. I made assumptions." He gives a sad smile. "I'm the welcome committee." He waggles his hands, showman style. "Yay!" After an awkward moment he drops his hands and grimaces. "I didn't want to make it forced. No one likes creepy welcome committees."

"No, creepy isn't good."

The elevator door bangs open, and light shines around the grimy third floor button.

"End of the corridor, last door on the left." Connor gestures in the general direction. "Professor Donoghue, head of faculty, he'll see you straight. And say hi to Dad for me."

"I thought you were headed this way?"

"Yeah, I lied." He cringes and steeples his fingers. "I'm a Humanities major, second floor . . . or the library. Look me up, new girl."

"Library. Room 53, right?" I say, with a fondness I didn't anticipate.

"You got it." Connor gives me a thumbs-up as the door closes. "Seriously, it's got free coffee. It's like Starbucks only without the flavor. You'd be mad to miss out."

"Okay." I strain to watch him disappear behind steel doors. "Thank you."

"Anytime, Lexi."

Wow. I think I just made a friend. Or maybe I have been adopted by a Connor? Either way, this day just got a teensy bit better.

3

THE SILENT GARDENER

Professor Donoghue—or Paul, he keeps reminding me—is a pleasant, albeit eccentric gentleman in his late fifties with salt and pepper hair, bushy eyebrows, and an overhanging brow that seems more brooding than any should.

"These are good." The professor pores over each snapshot of my creations with such intensity, I think his eyebrows will meld into one bushy line.

"Thank you." I fidget, glancing around the cramped faculty office that smells like mildew and stale coffee.

"Forgive the ignorance"—Professor Donoghue leans back on the rickety chair, eyes narrowing—"but how do you manage such detail? Such subtle color in your creations?"

Perplexing, how people assume sight is the key sense required for art. Not everything is perceived visually. Like coarse bark under hand, or the roar of the ocean as it collides with rocks, or a hug that warms the heart. Sometimes the soul feels more. But a college lecturer doesn't need to hear these philosophical rants.

"It's just the one eye that causes me trouble." I point to the horrible mess on my face. "The other one is okay, and I use a magnifying glass for the intricate things."

The professor nods. "I'm excited to see what you'll bring to the table." He stands and outstretches my portfolio to study at a distance. "Your style is reminiscent of old Celtic design. Is that an ancestry interest?"

I blink. An uneasy nervousness starts to churn in my gut.

"Apologies." He chuckles and straightens his spectacles. "It's a specialty of mine. You can take the man out of Ireland, but you can't take Ireland out of the man, eh?"

"You're from Ireland?" Recognition slips through. Mistake.

A stipulation of my parents—never, ever tell anyone my birthplace.

"Indeed." Professor Donoghue beams. "Well, the accent is tempered by many years in Europe. Can't blame you for not catching it. But you have that Titian hair and ghost-white skin. Don't tell me there isn't some Irish blood in you."

My eyes bug and I flounder for an answer. "Not that I'm aware." I snap my portfolio away. Smiling like something deranged. "Just a fleeting interest. Celtic art, that is. I'm much more intrigued by nature."

"Ah, yes, I can see that." The professor's shoulders sink, and his cheeks flush a little.

The queasiness ebbs. I don't think I need to worry; after all, the majority of Niagara County is of Irish ancestry. It's just a coincidence, there's nothing out of place, and for the sake of my nerves I've got to stop reading into things.

"Well, there's nothing left to say except welcome, Miss Danu." He circles the desk with a kind smile and guides me out. "You have your campus map and list of classes?"

"Yes." I jut out a hand to give his an awkward shake. "Thank you for the opportunity, Professor."

"Not at all. The college could use some of your fresh talent."

"Uh . . . yeah, thanks." I twist and grab the door handle, lurching it back so fast it collides with my face. "Ouch. S-sorry."

"Heavens, are you all right?"

"Great." I squeeze through the gap and gesture to my eye again. "Bad depth perception. Oh, shoot, I forgot . . . your son—Connor—says hi."

The professor gives a brief chortle and bobs his head. "Don't let that mischief-maker get you into trouble." He wags a finger. "He looks more innocent than he is. Did he tell you about library room—"

"Fifty-three." I nod. "Yeah, I heard it's special-needs friendly."

"I don't know about that." Professor Donoghue shrugs. "But it does a mean cup of coffee, and the view is delightful."

Hmm, perhaps it's worth the trip, if only to satisfy my caffeine addiction.

By early afternoon, I've visited my classes, met my tutors, gathered my schedules, and familiarized myself with the campus. After one o'clock, I'm free to study or book studio time.

I stop by a vending machine and buy a bag of M&Ms and bottled water, then decide to investigate the infamous library—if just to find the free coffee.

True to Connor's word, when I arrive in the library, the overzealous staff are keen to show me around the bright, airy, two-tier space stocked with shelves and tomes and extra study rooms. One of which, I'm told by the talkative librarian, is Room 53. As I follow the jolly middle-aged lady, who rarely pauses for breath, I find myself peering through shiny glass at the various folk who occupy these tiny offices. Some, I reckon, are underpaid and overcaffeinated educators trying to eat their lunch in peace. Others, small groups of students either messing around on the presentation they need to prep or taking it far too seriously. No in-between.

But when the librarian and I reach the steps to the lower level, she starts insisting we use the ramp all the way across the library. She's so embarrassed at herself, it takes me several minutes to assure her I'm perfectly capable of navigating steps. She seems to assume I'm downplaying my visual deficit.

We take the steps, and by the time she shows me to Room 53 she's so flustered that I need to politely shut the door in her face. Not to be intentionally rude, but there's only so much secondhand embarrassment and unnecessary apologies I can stomach.

After a morning filled with artificial light, it takes a few moments to adjust to the shocking brightness flooding in through the long glass wall at the back of the room. A table sits in the center with standard library chairs, a few computers, and the fabled coffee machine. Grinning, I lope toward the mechanical barista and drop my satchel and jacket on the nearest chair. Positioning myself up close, I snag a card cup from the stack, then squint at the various buttons. The screen is cracked, and my limited eyesight struggles. With a huff, I smack the cup on the counter and scowl at my new nemesis. I loathe being defeated.

Making a mental note to advise Connor to lobby for a new self-service beverage machine, I glide to the glorious sunshine beaming through the glass. I take the M&Ms from my pocket and snaffle them with little restraint, then peer down on a horticultural pavilion.

They grow stuff here?

I examine the courtyard as best as my limited eyesight allows, studying the various tubs and raised beds dotting the allotment. My imagination springs to life with the prospect of what I could find hidden in the compost. What could I glean for my ceramics?

A sharp knock vibrates the glass. I jump and let out a strangled squeak.

"Afternoon, new girl." Connor sits opposite the glass with a carton of seedling planters in his lap, breeze ruffling his hair. Wheeling back, he snorts a laugh and leans forward to slide back the . . . window? No, a patio door.

"It's a pretty inconspicuous door." Connor wears an understanding grimace.

"Yeah. Thanks." I roll my eyes. "The coffee machine isn't suited to half-blind new girls either." I cross my arms. "I'm somewhat unimpressed by Room 53, Connor."

"A fact that I sorely regret." He twists his chair toward the garden. "But we have a fabulous view. Why don't you walk around, and I'll fix you a cappuccino?"

"However, the customer service is outstanding." I giggle. Stepping outdoors, I inhale the earthy scent of growing life.

"I live to serve." Connor flashes me that roguish grin. "Oh, and don't mind the gardener. He doesn't speak much."

He wheels himself into the room, leaving me to meander in peace. I place a hand on the wooden edge of a raised bed, letting it guide me around the uneven turf. My eyes might fail me, but my other senses rarely do.

I never feel more at home than around nature. I like to think there's a connection between growing things and life itself, a poetic symbolism of our attachment to nature. As we tend, toil over, and love the earth, it thrives, nourishing us in turn. I feel, with my silly artistic mind, like the soil thrums around my fingers. Like a pulse where it cradles life.

I pause by a large, empty bed. The soil is rich, ready to receive life, and I can't help my grin. I could make a pot for holding soil like this, score and glaze it with the many colors in my mind's eye—browns, oranges, yellows, and blush. I knew this place would inspire me.

My parents will be so pleased to know about this.

An almighty smash echoes from behind.

I let out a shrill yell. Clutch my chest and spin to face the shattered ceramic. People have got to stop startling me like this. Ugh.

My eyes wheel, the good one working overtime to pick out the shadows too far on my left. Then, I catch the outline of a man hunched over the shards of a large terracotta pot.

"Oh my gosh . . . are you all right?" I rake a hand through my hair. "Here let me help."

We lurch toward the ground at the same time. With another resounding thud, we butt heads. Why did I think it was safe to be allowed in public?

"Ow." I rub my head. "I'm so sorry." I sit back on my heels to survey the damage.

The man shrinks back, holding his brow in a twisted hand, and shakes his head.

I stare at his gnarled, arthritic hands, wondering how he works with such deformities.

When he lifts his head, a stubbly beard hides his angular jaw. Dark hair falls onto his long, tangled eyelashes. His face is youthful—he might only be a few years older than Connor. Yet at first glance he is like an old man, crippled and bent out of shape.

I lean forward and begin piling the lumps of broken pot to the side. My embarrassment of injuring him leaves me at a loss for words. That old, deformed hand stretches toward mine. He gently grips my wrist, stilling me. With a guilty sigh, I chance a peek in his direction.

He presses his free hand to his chest, tapping his thumb and index finger to his sternum. A small, encouraging smile spreads across his cracked lips.

"M-mu-mm . . ." His face contorts as he wrestles with the words. He sighs and shakes his head, then points to the broken shards, brow furrowed.

I blink a few times until the metaphorical penny drops.

"Oh, your fault? I mean, no, I startled you." I tug at my hair. "I'm Lexi. I'm new. I mean, new to here. I was, um . . ." I gesture to the raised beds behind me. "I was admiring your work. Mister . . .?"

And then I wonder why I am asking his name? He can't speak.

Thankfully, he seems to find humor in my ineptitude. He points to the label on his overalls, where a small patch reads: KILLIAN HUNTER ~ GROUNDSMAN.

I grin and outstretch my hand to Killian. "Nice to meet you, Killian."

He gives a timid smile and awkwardly grips my hand. Then he drops his gaze, retracting his hand, a slight blush hiding underneath that stubble.

"Killian—Oh, wonderful. Would you look at this mess?" Connor wheels up the stone path with a thunderous expression. "You could have hurt someone."

Killian stiffens, his eyes still glued to the ground.

"It's not his fault. He was just doing his job, and I startled him."

"I know." Connor stops and points to the broken pot. "What have I told you about lifting heavy things with those hands?" He sighs and glares at me.

I feel like I'm in the middle of a family domestic.

"Honestly, I keep telling him to wait and I'll help carry the big pots, but does he listen? No. Stubborn as a mule, that one." Connor finishes his gripe with a loud tut.

Killian pulls himself to his feet, joints clicking.

I flinch. Poor boy. "It was just an accident." My voice is little more than a murmur, my sympathy pulled toward the silent gardener.

Killian bows his head, though his hunched stance makes every move painful to watch. He's not deformed. Or stupid. Or wrong. His body fails him in the same way my eyes fail me. I think behind that damaged façade is an articulate young man. But we'll never know how intelligent he is if others continue to speak for him.

Killian takes the seedling planters that remain nestled on Connor's lap, gaze still downcast, body still stooped, expression still sad. I wait until he leaves before I face Connor, who I assumed would know not to be so patronizing. His apologetic gaze already waits as he holds out a cup filled to the brim with frothy caffeine.

"You thought I was a jerk to him?"

I lift the cup and quirk an unimpressed eyebrow. It's not my place to draw judgment on people I've just met, but I am taken aback.

"It was an accident. I startled him."

17

Connor nods. "Killian is a good guy. He lives with us, do you know that? He works around the house. We fixed him up with a job here too. Dad knew his parents before they died. Says he owes it to the boy to look out for him. He's kinda like a brother to me." He drums his fingers on the arm of his chair. "He wasn't so genteel when he first started working here, though. The college was going to get rid of him. Kids were goading him." Connor's expression tightens, his jaw flexing as he stares off into nothing, or perhaps an unpleasant memory. "It wasn't a fair situation. But ol' Paul has a heart for helpless cases, so he put him in charge of the 'Going Green Project.'" He looks around. "As you can see, it's flourished under his care."

"Oh." I'm embarrassed that I tarred Connor as misunderstanding. I roll the cup between my hands. "He seemed pleasant enough to me, even apologetic. I think he communicates fine if given the time."

"Don't we all." Connor gives a sad chuckle and shakes his head. "This world never has patience for the likes of us. No offense."

"I know exactly what you mean." I give an appreciative bob of my head. "Not everyone is bad, though. Professor Donoghue seems very understanding."

"He does, he's great. I'm lucky." Connor grins, tilting his chin toward Killian. "Without the support of my foster dad, I wouldn't have fared much better. People can be cruel."

"Well, I often feel the same way." And I don't really want a deep conversation with someone I've just met.

"You know, I'm shocked Killian was so friendly with you. He's usually unresponsive to new people." He flashes me a grin. "You must have a way with people, Lexi."

I snort back a laugh. I barely get to communicate with people, let alone have a way with them.

"Too serious and lacking in self-confidence. You have issues, new girl." That endearing, mischievous glint lights his eyes.

He twists his chair and looks me in the eye. "You don't need eyes to truly see others." He gestures to himself. "You don't need legs to keep up with the world. And you don't need to be articulate to speak volumes."

An understanding smile lifts my face, and Connor's echoes the same.

"Sometimes I don't think the problem lies with us. I think the shortcomings lie with those thinking they know what we're capable of. Or not. I guess."

I squirm. This boy is far too expressive. Still, he's right. "Well said."

Connor grins. "Well, that's enough of my rambling wisdom for one day." He backs away with that rogue smile. "I gotta head to a seminar. Can't really bail on classes when your dad works here. But see you around?"

"I'll see you again, Connor." I lift my cup in a salute. "Thank you for the hospitality."

"Anytime, new girl." He winks and wheels off with a truckload of unwavering confidence. I'm envious.

I loiter, peering around at the garden, feeling at a loose end. I guess I should have Mother come get me. She's probably on standby anyway.

Peeling my phone from my back pocket, I trudge along the flagstone path, away from the uneven ground where I'm not likely to fall flat on my nose.

I scroll through the enlarged text screen menu, and my thumb hovers over Mother's number. Not far away, Killian carefully piles the pot shards in a small shed. He drops a piece, and a spasm of pain draws a whine from him.

"Killian—" I rush to help, spying how he nurses his crooked hand and the way he nervously searches for something to tend a wound.

He lurches away from my approach with a fearful cry.

"Wait, I'm not going to hurt you." I remember my embroidered handkerchief. I slip the soft material from my jean pocket, regretful that it's about to get ruined.

"Nn-no!"

"Don't be silly." I grab his wrist, making to dab at the blood that pools at the crease in his clawed palm. "We have to stop the bleeding and take you to the nurse."

His face contorts to a scowl, and he wrestles with my grip. I hold tight. With an aggravated growl, he pierces me with furious eyes.

I glare at him. "Fine. Have it your way." I wrestle my ruined handkerchief from his hand. "It's your fault if that cut gets infec—"

I stare in horror, and wonderment, at the unblemished skin of Killian's palm. There's no cut. But, I saw the blood.

"Anomaly." Breath gets caught in my throat as I snap my eyes to Killian. How?

Killian pulls free. "Nn-not." His face crumples with the drained expression my parents have worn my whole life. White as a ghost, he outstretches his bloodstained hand with no wound and pleads with his eyes.

I open my mouth, but words don't come. Are there more people like me? Out here? Running? Maybe I'm not so one-of-a-kind after all.

Killian walks away without a backward glance, leaving before I can give him my word that I'll never utter his secret. The hairs on my arms begin to stand, and a familiar, eerie shiver runs along my spine. I crumple the stained handkerchief in my hand, then shove it back in my pocket. I take a deep breath and scan the garden; there's not another soul here. I'm overreacting. I need to get a grip. I have to let Killian know that he's safe. I don't want him to run because I interrupted his peaceful existence. I couldn't live with myself if I ruined this for him.

I hurry back to the library room and rummage through my bag, producing my sketch pad and pen. Ripping a sliver of paper off the front sheet, I grip the pen, pausing to still my shaking hand, then write.

I'll never say a word. Your secret is safe from them!

Folding the note, I walk back across the garden, along the beds, and toward the shed. The door is closed now, and when I feel around for a way in, it seems locked. With a sigh, I step back and scrunch my nose. Maybe I can put the note in one of the seedling planters, or somewhere safe on the raised beds. I turn to put my plan into action but collide with a metal table instead.

"Ouch. Stupid contraption . . . Who left you there?" I rub my hip, withholding a tirade of curses.

Hobbling around the table, I spy a clump of dark-green material. Gardening gloves . . . or mittens? They appear to have the thumb and index fingers, for pinch grip, but the rest of Killian's fingers would never fit into ordinary gloves without discomfort—these have got to be his. I stash the note inside the right glove and set them back where I found them.

A breeze rustles the leaves in the overhead trees, the force causes the boughs to sway and groan. I look up in time to see a shadow reflect on the window of the tiny shed, but when I turn . . . nothing.

"Killian?"

I'm sure it's him, but he doesn't respond. I hope he's just hiding. I hope my promise will persuade him to stay. I need to know who this Silent Gardener is, and I need him to tell me.

I'll figure a way. I'm not safe—we aren't safe—if I don't.

CURSED

The rocking chair groans as I swish back and forth on our rickety front porch. I've barely said a word since I got home. Mother thinks I'm tired, and I'm happy to let her think it. It's better than the truth.

A thrush skips up and down the blue painted railings. Half the posts are missing or slick with moss and flaked paint. This house is old and cramped. It smells of damp and rot, like the outside tries to crawl in. Oddly, it comforts me.

I listen to the little bird's solo. He appears to sing just for my benefit, skipping close enough to try and chase my blues away. His tiny eyes scrutinize the bloodstained handkerchief in my fist. He inches closer, his head cranes, and his song softens. I swear he understands.

"It's pretty, isn't it?" I whisper.

He ducks his head and hops closer as I unclench my fist to show him the dried patterns on the cloth. Purple lines twine with gold and silver in an endless swirl of glittering shapes. Normal blood doesn't dry like that.

The little bird gives a tiny trill, like the highest note on a musical scale, as he observes the pattern. The wind ruffles his feathers, and a waft of damp fills my nose. Rain.

A long, low sigh huffs from somewhere deep inside me. The thrush skitters back at the sound and flits to a higher perch to continue his quiet warble, leaving me to figure out this conundrum alone.

I guess I'm not surprised that Killian's blood resembles mine—two ugly things on the outside, two beautiful things on the inside. My thumb smooths the stiff cotton of my handkerchief where our bloodstains overlap. The evidence that I'm not alone. I almost cry. I don't know how long I've dreamed about there being more like me.

The door creaks. I tense and scrunch the material in my fist. Mother jangles the car keys like off-key cymbals. I lift my head from the large encyclopedia of ancient mythology that I've been pretending to read, and stare at her. She grins and tucks her handkerchief—the twin of mine—under the cuff of her peach cardigan. My stomach churns.

"You okay, love?" She pushes away from the screen door, leaving it open to 'let the air circulate the house' or something like that, and squints at the book. "You've been awfully quiet since we got home."

For a moment I consider telling her about Killian, about the professor and his questions about home. About the strange, crippled boy and his blood that looks like mine. But my tongue cleaves to the roof of my mouth and I say nothing. If I tell her, if she tells Father, we'll leave this place, and for the first time in my life I don't want that. I need to stay. I need to know that I'm not alone and that it's possible to live without looking over my shoulder. Maybe Killian knows who "T" is. Maybe he's got answers. Answers I desperately want. Answers that my parents won't give out willingly.

"I'm fine," I say instead, and glance back at the page that's lain open and unread for the past thirty minutes. "Just catching up on some research for a nature-inspired assignment."

She leans forward and scrutinizes the content. "Ah, now that is an interesting story." She points to an illustration of a giant man wearing an even grander set of antlers, who's covered in moss and leaves and sat by a great bubbling cauldron. "Dagda, the good god." A misty light swims in her eyes. "Others spoke of him, but I never—" She coughs and blinks away the mist. "I never taught on him."

Mother used to teach on mythology at some fancy London university before I came along. Her specialty is ancient Ireland, and it's her love of the country that led her to accept an opportunity to do field research outside Dublin, where she met my father. The rest, as they say, is history.

"Do you miss it? Teaching?" I set the book aside and truly look at her. She's wearing a blush waitress uniform for a local diner. I can't believe this is the life she imagined for herself. I can't believe she's truly happy living like this.

She smiles when she notices my frown.

"Sometimes," she says, then strokes my scarred cheek. "Then I remember that getting to be your mother is the greatest job in the world."

"Oh, come on." I swipe her hand away and stand. "I don't believe that."

"It's the truth." She links my arm with hers as we follow the garden path to the car. "Besides, the pay is under the table. No questions asked. We're safe."

"You sound so happy that we're technically fugitive criminals," I say as I yank open the car door for her to slip inside.

"I've been called worse," she jokes, or at least I think it's a joke. "I'll not be home 'til late; there's enough in the refrigerator for an omelet. Don't let your father near anything deep-fried. He's watching his cholesterol."

"Got it." I make a salute that earns a wide grin from Mother.

Her smile falters. "Love, are you sure this isn't too much for you? College, I mean."

"I'm just a little tired," I lie and shove my glasses back up my nose. "First day jitters are wearing off. Go, enjoy your shift."

"Okay." She squeezes my hand before slamming the door shut, then lowers the window. "Stop worrying, Lexi." That warm spark twinkles in her navy eyes. "If we didn't think a semester of college was safe, your father and I wouldn't have agreed to it. Enjoy it, my love. Enjoy every minute you get."

"I know, I will," I promise, realizing that she's construed my silence as worry over college and blending in, and not the fact that there's another like me. The evidence still burns in my balled fist.

I watch Mother pull out of the drive, and wave to her until she turns out of our cul-de-sac. I'm still lost in thoughts of the Silent Gardener when a ball hurtles over the hedge and whacks me on the hip. It bounces off the pavement and rolls back to rest against my out-turned foot.

A kid with grazed knees, backward baseball cap, and a missing front tooth stares in wide-eyed horror from across the street. It's likely not the ball that disturbs him, more the ugly raised welts that serpentine every inch of visible skin. The boy tracks those horrid marks all the way to my face, then takes a full step back.

"You-you drop this?" I set the ball on the pavement and roll it toward him.

He nods, but his eyes don't leave my face.

The boy bends to pick up his ball. I attempt a smile and point toward our house.

"Um, we just moved here. I'm Lexi. You must be Pastor Robbin's son, right?" I make an informed guess by the boy's scruffy appearance, and the fact that Pastor Robbin—our neighbor—has seven children who make up the majority of the noise on our otherwise quiet cul-de-sac.

The boy doesn't speak but glances back to the huddle of kids on the far end of the street. I got it, he's the one that drew the short straw. I lift a hand and wave.

"Kevin, get away from it!" A girl—his sister, I assume from their similar looks—steps forward and scowls.

It? Ouch. I know I've got a face straight out of a nightmare, but I'd like to think I'm distinguishable as a woman—female, at least. Ugh, twelve-year-olds.

"It's okay," I whisper to Kevin, slugging the hood of my jacket over my head. "You can tell them I have fangs for teeth too."

Kevin's lip twitches upward at my wink. We both turn at the same time, each of us going back to our respective places.

"My daddy says she's cursed," Kevin's sister tells the others, and I freeze mid-step. "He says that's what happens when people live in sin."

"Shut up, Tilda." Kevin's voice slithers out from behind clenched teeth, and I hear the telltale sound of the ball bouncing off something hard—hopefully Tilda's head.

"Ow!"

Nice one, Kev. See, I can totally make friends here. I have to stay here, if only to prove I'm not at monster.

Head down, I watch my footing where I trudge the three steps to our front porch and nearly collide with the open door. Geez, I forgot that was open.

"Oh, sweet pea, careful." My father bounds out of the hall, arms outstretched.

"You know I can't watch the steps and look out for potential hazards." I cup my left eye and lean against the doorframe.

My father jabs a pretend punch to my right. I giggle and dodge left.

"Ah, but your reflexes are still good." He wags a finger and winks. My father has been teaching me self-defense for years. It's been a futile exercise on his part. I've never been able to punch straight, I always lose my glasses, but heck, at least I know the basics.

"Who were you talking to?" My father must have ears like a fox.

"The pastor's kids," I say and follow his dark gaze to the cluster of kids on the corner. "They just kicked their ball into the lawn."

"Don't think I didn't hear what that li'l squirt said." Father snorts and starts toward the garden path.

I grab his arm. "They're kids; they don't know any better. It's fine."

"It's not fine," he says, hands on his hips as he glowers toward Pastor Robbin's house. "Robbin is an old contact from my defense days. He should know better."

"Please, just drop it." I bat my eyelashes for added affect. "I want to make friends here, not enemies."

He deliberates for a minute, then sighs. He nods and points toward the kitchen. "All right fine, but we're ordering a pizza for dinner. We've a first day of college to celebrate."

"Oh, Father." I paint a fake scold on my face. "What about your cholesterol?"

"Cholesterol schmesterol. You only live once." He pulls a pained expression. "Just don't tell your mother."

Dinner remains a silent, contemplative affair. Father and I sit in the cramped galley kitchen at a recycled table and chairs he found at a flea market outside

Sanborn. I sit back in the old, rickety chair, hands clasped around a cold glass of water. I brush my thumb over the condensation running down the sides.

"All right, sweet pea, you going to tell me what's rolling around that head of yours?" Father sets down his fifth slice of pepperoni and four-cheese, then leans across the table. His forehead crinkles in concern.

I could tell him about Killian, but I want to prove that my parents wouldn't lie to me. The rational part of my mind concedes that perhaps they don't know there are others like me. But something about the mysterious text, the phone calls, their contacts, it doesn't add it up. There's something off, something they aren't saying.

"Are there more of me?" I say, a little too loudly.

Father rocks back in his seat, shell-shocked.

"I mean," I say, softer now, "is there the slightest chance that there could be more people with my genetic anomaly?"

Father shakes his head, stands, and takes our plates. He drops them into the kitchen sink with a loud clank. I jolt at the sound.

"You know your mother and I don't like you talking about this kind of thing." He gives a warning glare, then cranks on the tap and begins sloshing water about the basin.

I hop up to explain. "I know, but—"

"No, Lexi, there is no one else like you out there." He scrubs the plates mercilessly and crashes them onto the dish rack so harshly I expect them to break.

"But, wait . . ." Perhaps he doesn't know. What if all these years we've been running, we didn't need to? What if there's a way to be free from whoever T is, and whoever else has been hunting us? Killian obviously figured it out.

"No, Lexi. Don't be ridiculous. You are alone. After eighteen years of us protecting you from them, can you not see that?"

I take a step back. I'm not alone, why are you lying to me?

Precariously close to tears, I say, "I'm sorry. I just thought—"

"Lexi," Father says, but I turn and head for the front door.

"Alexandria, come back."

I stop and look over my shoulder. He stands in the kitchen door, practically dwarfing it with his giant frame. Yet, for all his imposing physique, he looks ... scared.

"Someday we'll explain. I promise. I know you hate it." Father cups his hands in front of him, almost in prayer, his eyes downcast. "But the secrets keep you safe. Please trust us. When the time's right . . ."

I want to shout, accuse him, demand, "When is someday? When will the time be right?" But what's the use? So I hold my tongue. I swallow the hurt and the accusations and accept that whatever he knows is enough to put the fear of God into him. I'm probably better off without that knowledge . . . for now.

"I know, I get it." I reach for the doorknob, unsure if I can hold it together long enough to pretend this isn't tearing me apart. "I was just wondering out loud," I say and offer him a watery smile. "I'm going to read some more, 'kay?"

He returns a version of that smile. His shoulders sag and he heads back into the kitchen. My gut twists and my unhelpful mind reminds me he's only trying to protect us. I imagine I'd do the same. Still, I need answers, and Killian still exists. If my parents can't tell me, then maybe he can.

The front door is still open a crack, and the scent of fresh-cut grass and rain saturate the hallway. I drift out the door and into the deluge. I slump on the bottom porch step and crane my neck back. Each droplet splatters across my disfigured face and dribbles between the welted crevices. When I was little, I used to pretend the rain would wash all the ugliness away and make me a princess. But Robbin's kid is right, I'm not the princess. I'm the cursed monster.

With a groan, I fold over, head against my knees, and listen to the rain patter the earth. The perfect stillness between raindrops is the most peaceful sound I know. The silence steals away all those anxious thoughts until it's just me and the thrum of water.

It's between the beats of rain that something whispers in the quiet. I sit bolt upright and squint into the twilight. There's nothing but the familiar pitter-patter. Then—

A raspy hiss echoes out from between the gap in the scraggly conifers that separate our garden from the neighbor's drive.

"Hello?" I slide off the porch step and inch toward the sound, the hairs on my arms stand on end as a shiver spider-walks my spine. "Is-is someone there? Pastor Robbin?"

Something shadowy warps the pavement and slithers under the conifers. My breath halts and my chest stills. I pause to consider what exactly I'm going to do if there's someone waiting behind the conifer. If it's T, or some of his henchmen, or government scientists ready to snatch me for study, then what exactly am I going do?

There's a piece of broken concrete lodged in the dirt. I pick it up and get ready to pitch it at whatever's out there then make a break for it, but it occurs to me it might just be Kevin and his horrible siblings playing a stupid game on the freaky new neighbor. In fact, that's a much more probable explanation.

I drop the chunk of rock and stomp to the gap in the conifers. I swing into the street, fists clenched and ready to give those brats a piece of my mind, but . . . there's nothing.

That's weird. I could've sworn—

Metal crashes against the ground at the end of the drive. A small shadowy blur scurries from the scene.

The yell that wrings itself out of my lungs is enough to alert the entire street. A dog howls from a nearby yard and a car alarm begins to wail. Our front door bangs wide open and my father's heavy footfalls pound toward me. It's only then that I realize the crash is the sound of the toppled garbage can, and the retreating shadow that triggered the car alarm is a raccoon.

"What the—? Lexi, what happened?" My father stands in his slippers, wielding a short dagger from his collection. It's a bizarre sight, but one I'm accustomed to.

"Nothing, it was nothing." I wilt, both hands clapped against my chest, which has started to move again. I jab a finger at the retreating pest. "I thought something was sneaking around the house, and it was that stupid trash-panda."

Father blinks a few times before he slams a hand to his face and groans.

"I just saw the shadow. It was on my left side. It's dark, I overacted." I don't know why I feel the need to be so defensive, but I do feel like an idiot—a paranoid idiot. Thankfully he starts to chuckle and wraps an arm around my shoulders.

"This is why I have no hair left," he says. "My poor heart can't take these false alarms." I grimace, but he hugs me close and guides me back toward the house. "Come on now, sweet pea. We'll go inside and watch a movie, eh? Your choice."

I don't argue. I'm still trying to lower my heart rate. But I do pause inside the door for a moment longer. I swear I heard something. There's nothing out of place in the yard, but that eerie feeling still causes the gooseflesh to rise on my arms. I strain to listen, but all is quiet, all except the rain.

With a roll of my eyes, I straighten and slam the door shut.

5

SECRETS AND DIABOLICAL PLANS

My teeth chatter, and I squint through my fogging spectacles. Halloween's come and gone, and the early November air holds a winter chill. I've been waiting by this confounded horticulture unit every day since Killian and I met, trying to befriend him.

It's been weeks and I've nothing to show for my attempts at friendliness but a grunt and the odd scowl of acknowledgement. Connor says it's just Killian's way, that I've to give him time to warm up to the idea, but I know the truth. He's worried, like I am, that our crossing paths is no accident. I'm not giving up; he has to acknowledge this sooner or later.

My butt is numb, and I've lost all sensation to my feet. Yet before frostbite claims a toe, my crappy eyesight picks out a blurry figure ambling along the waterlogged pasture.

"Good morning, Mr. Hunter," I say, and drop from the wall.

"G-g-go a-way." Killian stops and glares at me, an expression that could curdle milk. The intensity in his dark eyes is almost threatening. I swallow.

I step back. Well, at least he speaks. That's better than a grunt.

"I . . . um . . . was wondering . . . i-if you could help me." My glasses scoot down my nose. I push them back up and recite my inward mantra to be brave.

"N-no," he replies with effort, spinning around to hobble the opposite direction.

"Killian, wait." I use this actual interaction as fuel, and veer off the path. I give chase, wobbling and sliding in the sludge. This isn't the brightest idea. "Killian, I don't want to hurt you."

Phew, he is fast for someone with twisted limbs.

"Killian, please just . . . crap!" My ankle twists in the soggy terrain, and I sprawl out on my back with an almighty crash. Brilliant.

I gasp and roll about like a hapless upturned turtle until a hand clamps my shoulder and pulls me upright.

"That got your attention." I squint at my blurry hero.

The Silent Gardener places my awful, thick-as-bottles eyeglasses back on my nose.

29

"C-c-care-ful." His soft lilt gives me hope.

"Sorry." I flush, embarrassed that he watches me with kind, almost worried, greenish-gray eyes. Maybe the gaunt shadows hanging over his features made me miss the fleeting beauty there.

"Y-y-you s-shh-ould . . ." Killian clenches his jaw, gathering his words.

"I should what?"

He pulls me to my feet with some effort. "S-s-stay ah-way." His eyes hold a pleading sorrow that I don't quite understand.

"From you? Why?" I stuff my hand in my back pocket, procuring my handkerchief evidence.

"Miss Danu?" An irritating squawk echoes over the lawn.

Scowling, I shove my precious secret back in my pocket.

"Miss Danu, are you all right?" The younger librarian jogs toward us, as fast as her court shoes can carry her. "Is this man bothering you?"

"No, I'm fine. I just fell." I try to hide my disappointment. "Lucky Mr. Hunter was here to help."

The librarian shoots Killian a warning glare. "Indeed. But what on earth where you doing on the lawn? The pavements are much safer for you, sweetie."

"Well, I was . . ." I attempt an excuse, but I have none.

"F-f-found." Killian lifts his clawed, earth-stained hand to reveal a chain.

"My locket." My hand flies to my neck. It must've fallen when I tumbled.

"Drrr-opped." Killian eyes widen, prompting me.

It takes me a moment to twig on. "Oh yes, I lost my locket when I came out here looking for materials for my nature piece." I reach for the jewelry. "I came to see if Mr. Hunter found it. Thank you so much. Honestly, you're a star."

The librarian sidles her gaze from me to Killian. "Thank goodness for your keen eyes, Killian."

He gives a goofy little shrug.

"Are you sure you aren't hurt, Miss Danu?" The librarian asks. "That was quite the tumble."

"I'm fine."

She leads me toward the pavement, prattling on about making me a nice cup of coffee to warm me up. I glance back at Killian. He stares after me; the concern in his features feels genuine. My persistence has paid off. I think we've had a breakthrough. Now, how to get a few minutes with this strange man alone.

I pour myself into the clay.

My hands meld with the delicate creation, a bowl rising from the formless shape on the potter's wheel. My lips twitch happily. When I'm creating, nothing else bothers me. Not even the Silent Gardener—and his irritating lack of answers. It's just me, water, and clay.

"Lexi? Yo, Lex. Earth calling girl." Hands clap thrice in my left ear, like a roll of thunder.

My beautiful bowl collapses into itself, and I hiss.

"Connor!" I claw a chunk of the clay to throw at him, then decide better at wasting precious supplies. "That took me forever to center."

"Don't lie, it took you two seconds." He sticks his fingers into the massacred clump and smears gray streaks across his cheek, then adds a swish down his nose. "How do I look? Like a Celtic warrior?"

"Like an idiot." I can't prevent a grin at his mussed blond curls and beaming face.

Connor leans forward in his chair and rests his chin in his hands, war paint and all. "I'm staging an inter*friend*tion. Are you aware of how long you've been tucked away in here?"

"Um . . ." I scratch my head and swivel on the stool, checking the large wall clock.

"Five hours." He frowns. "You skipped lunch. Who does that?"

"I have a deadline." I fold my arms over my rumbling belly.

"And we had a lunch date, which you bailed on." He lifts my paintbrushes from their soaking jug.

"You befriended an artist," I remind him. "Welcome to the creative life. Scatter-brained, forgetful . . . terrible friends, actually. I don't know why you waste your time."

"Good lord, you have no remorse." Connor feigns a pout.

"None whatsoever." I smirk until he flicks murky water across my face with a cackle of achievement.

"My mouth was open!" I launch to my feet, snatch a dirty rag, and attack his filthy cherub face.

Connor doubles over with a peal of infectious laughter. "Hey . . . ouch . . . say you're sorry for bailing on me."

"Fine." I toss the rag aside and sit again. "I'm sorry for bailing on you, and I promise I'll make it up to you. Now behave."

"Apology accepted." He tilts his head and grins. "And I know how you can make it up to me."

"You never said there was a proposition." I fold my arms again. "What terms are these?"

"I believe you'll find them quite reasonable." Connor snickers. "You see, Lexi, my birthday is on Friday, and it is customary to have a celebratory feast with friends. Since you are indeed a friend, and skipping out on meals, I figured you could do with the feasting."

I blink, my mouth going a little dry. My parents will not be happy about this. But I can't verbalize that. It's weird that my parents still monitor my every movement.

Connor's brow furrows, and he shifts in his chair. "You don't have to buy me a gift or anything. I just thought it'd be kinda fun. Dad would get a kick out of me actually bringing somebody home. He worries, y'know?"

"I know." I stare at my clay-caked hands, weighing up the moral complications.

"Then what's the hesitation?" He cocks his head like a confused puppy.

"Parents."

"Aw, come on, Lexi, you're eighteen. You'll be hanging out at my house with my dad. Your professor. It's hardly a drug-fueled rave." Connor's face scrunches up. "They can drop you off in my kitchen, meet Dad, and see for themselves that I'm not a bad influence."

"It's not you." I struggle to my feet, starting to pace. "They worry about my health problems, and my eyesight. I'm very accident-prone."

"I heard all about your grand fall." Connor smirks. "The librarians were concerned when you didn't show up to the library like you were supposed to. You know . . . for lunch?"

I wince. "Darn those nosey librarians. Total gossips."

"Look, I'll personally pack you in bubble wrap and Lexi-proof the house."

"You're not going to relent until I agree, are you?"

He shakes his head, a determined smile widening on his angelic face. "Killian will be there too."

"Ugh, fine. But you're not getting a present. And I can guarantee my parents will want to meet you and Professor Donoghue."

"Gawd, call him Paul, not Professor. That's just weird." Connor pulls a face, probably suppressing a victorious grin.

"He's my head of faculty. It's weird for me to call him anything but Professor." I chuckle and throw a sheet over my drying pots, then lift my satchel. I reach to lift my locket from the desk but find Connor beats me to it.

"What happened to your necklace?" He holds up the chain to inspect, eyeing the broken clasp.

"It must've broken when I fe—when I was out finding materials yesterday. Killian found it . . . that's why I fell." I cringe—I'm an awful liar.

"Told you Killian doesn't have a problem with you," Connor says, smugly. "I can fix this if you want." He gives an expectant smile. "I can take it home and have it ready by Friday."

"Which means I absolutely must come to your house to pick it up?"

"It's not like your parents could argue with that." He tucks the locket safely in his top shirt pocket.

"Not at all." I sigh and shake my head in faux exasperation. "You are diabolical, Connor."

"And you love it." He chuckles and wheels toward the door, face beaming with excitement. "Come on, Lexi Luthor, let's go manipulate your parents into loving me."

6

MASQUERADE

As Father drives our Ford onto Connor's sprawling driveway, I'm tempted to feel jealous. His house is tastefully rustic, the gardens are preened to perfection, and the lake view is stunning. Hopefully the back door will offer better opportunities to gaze upon the dark waters. There's something haunting and beautiful about the wildness of the deep on a stormy winter night.

I clamber out of the car, and my parents follow. This is routine. My parents always scout out anywhere I go, meeting the families of whomever I'm fortunate enough to visit. It never mattered much to me, before now. I always knew those friends were only passing ghosts in my lonely existence. But this is different.

"Please don't grill him," I plead for the tenth time as we congregate around the door. "He's just a boy; he keeps me company in college. Don't make him suspicious."

"I won't, I promise." Father holds his hands up and looks to Mother for support.

I roll my eyes.

"We are just going to introduce ourselves." Mother pats Father's shoulder. "We're new in town, and there's nothing wrong in being cautious. Besides, it'll be nice to speak with your teacher. What's his name again?"

"Professor Donoghue." I pinch the bridge of my nose and breathe in. If I keep conversation to a minimum, maybe they won't make a fuss.

"Donoghue? Sounds familiar." Father's brow furrows. I can almost see the cogs turning in his mind.

To evade his tirade of questions, I reach for the doorbell, but before my finger can touch the buzzer, the door rattles and my sunny-faced friend grins up at me.

"Happy birthday!" I throw my hands wide and beam right back.

"Thank you." His smile widens as he regards my parents. "Mr. and Mrs. Danu, it's lovely to meet you both. Please come in." He wheels back, giving us space to mill into his hallway. "My dad will be down in a minute. He wants to greet you before you leave. If it's no problem, he'd be happy to bring Lexi home tonight, to save you another long drive."

"That is so thoughtful." I shrug off my coat and slide Father a glare—he'd better be polite.

"Oh, it's no trouble," Mother says, tucking a strand of her platinum hair behind her ear. "Fred and I are going to visit a little restaurant we saw on the way in, aren't we, dear?"

"Yes," Father says. "Seems like we're both having dates tonight, eh, Connor?" He winks.

Heat prickles my neck and I look to Connor, who gives a suggestive chuckle. Not helpful.

"Hey, sweet pea, it's fine. You're old enough. We won't cramp your style." Father laughs at his own stupid humor. I appeal to Mother with a pained expression.

"Fred, don't embarrass them. It's rude." She bobs her head toward Connor. "Apologies. My husband thrives on being a bane with his reckless humor."

"She said it was a dinner date," Father says.

I groan.

Connor gives my hip a playful punch. His teasing yet understanding smirk relaxes me. This is okay; it's all positive. At least Father hasn't launched into his fifty questions tirade.

"Marie? Marie Crawford?" Professor Donoghue's distinctive accent rumbles down the wide staircase. He stands at the top, wearing a smart suit.

"Paul?" Mother steps around Father to stare at my professor. Granted, he's a bit overdressed for a birthday dinner—then again, I've never seen him wear anything not tweed and tailored.

"Dad, do you know Lexi's parents?"

How on earth can Mother possibly know my professor? We move so much, and it's a little farfetched that she knows him from home, but then . . . Killian? Connor said he knew his parents. My gut starts to churn; a nervous tremor radiates through me.

"Of course I know Marie. We attended the same university." Professor Donoghue's smile widens as he hurries down the grand staircase.

"From London?" I ask, shocked.

"Don't act so surprised," she says, reaching to embrace my professor whilst Connor and I exchange baffled shrugs. She steps back. "Paul Donoghue was an esteemed associate by the time I enrolled . . . I'm not that old."

"Indeed, but this is a genuine surprise." Professor Donoghue claps his hands. "It's so lovely to see you after all this time. With a family too. You must be the husband." He extends a hand to my father, who frowns as he grips his in a brief handshake.

That's not a good sign. He's already jittery, trying to decide if the connection is safe, if we should stay or go. If not for Mother's joy at seeing her old friend, I guess we'd be long out of here by now.

"Frederick, but call me Fred," Father says. "And you've met our daughter, Alexandria."

"She's a wonderful young lady and an asset to our school."

I give a bashful swipe of my hand.

He shakes his head and gestures to Connor. "My son can't stop singing her praises either, and it's great to see him with such a lovely friend. I was beginning to worry—he only has the company of our young gardener, Killian, and the poor boy is almost mute. Not that there's anything wrong with that, or with having a man friend."

"Dad, please!" Connor snaps his gaze to the professor, mouth agape, cheeks flushed.

I attempt to restrain my laughter.

Professor Donoghue rabbits on innocently. "I don't mind what your preferences are son, so long as I get grandchildren someday."

"Oh my god. Dad, shut up!" Connor covers his face, then outstretches his hands to me and my parents. "I'm not gay, okay? Really, definitely not gay."

"S'okay, son." Father pats him on the shoulder. "If you were, I'd be much more relaxed with you dating my daughter."

"Okay, no one is dating anyone," I say shrilly. "I think there's been enough embarrassment for one social occasion. Connor, why don't you give me a tour of your amazing home, and our parents can reminisce?"

"Absolutely." Connor nods vigorously and gestures for me to lead the way. "After you, m'lady."

I give a faux curtsy and glance back toward my parents. Father, although more relaxed, still seems uneasy. That nervous niggle starts to grow. I'm not ready to say goodbye. Not yet.

The house is a renovated farmhouse attached to a converted barn. It's a clash of the old world with the new. The original structure left opportunity for open living space, allowing plenty of light and easy access for Connor. As he shows me around, I plod along behind him in awe, feeling very underdressed as he plays the part of elegant host.

Most of the art and features seem vaguely Celtic, or perhaps older. Furniture is carved from trees, naturalist, like the outside wandered indoors. A bit like my home, except there's no trace of damp and the wallpaper doesn't flake.

It's only now that I consider how a simple college professor can own all this. There's a connection here—to Ireland, and mother, and secrets. He isn't just a professor, like mother isn't just a waitress, and I . . . well, I'm not normal, that's for sure. The sick knot in my stomach constricts and I feel a little faint.

The main living room at the back of the house—part of the old barn conversion—is a glass conservatory, displaying the phenomenal lake view. Even with my poor sight, the wall-to-wall windows make it easy to soak it up.

I stand there, admiring the bleak grays of the sky, the howl of the wind rushing through the rafters, and the thrumming rain as it patters off the glass. It's comforting, homey, and I envy Connor for living in such a beautiful place. Such luxuries I can never afford. Even if we did have the money to buy it, we could never stay long enough to make it a home. I will miss this. All of it.

"You want a drink?" Connor asks after a long time of me roaming around, memorizing it all.

"I wouldn't mind," I say, a little sigh in my voice. I walk beside him toward what I assume is the kitchen.

"You've been awfully quiet since our parents declared their affiliation," he says carefully.

"Seems a bit weird." I pull a perplexed frown. Pretense, for his benefit. "But weird is the definition of my parents."

Connor chuckles. "Yeah, parents in general are weird, but it's probably just a case of a small world."

The kitchen is a long room, the most contemporary of the whole house, with its industrial silver fixtures and black stone tiles. I smirk—it's such an immaculate building, so opposite of what I come from. I doubt Connor drinks straight from the orange juice carton, belches, and shoves it back in the fridge.

Connor wheels toward the fridge but pauses by a stacked wine rack. "What's your poison?"

"Chocolate milk." I hop onto a bar stool by the island counter. "One of us is still underage."

"Very wise." He gives a solemn bob of his chin. "Frankly, I don't like the taste of the stuff. Don't know how Dad drinks it. Ugh."

"You won't even have a celebratory alcoholic beverage for turning twenty-one?" I accept the glass tumbler that Connor extends. He shakes his head, and I roll my eyes. "Jeez, and you think I don't take risks."

"What can I say, I'm a bit of a coward," he says with a sheepish grin. He pulls out the milk and pours me a generous amount, then pours himself a helping too. "I know our parents did a wonderful job embarrassing us, but for my ego's sake, I hope you'll forget all of that. I don't want our friendship to nosedive."

I laugh hard. "If my parents actually believed I was dating you, they'd be inclined to lock me up."

"Well, it isn't like I can be a normal boyfriend." Connor gives a dismissive shrug. "What poor girl would want to be burdened with someone dead from the waist down?"

I run over my response in my mind. Behind his laughter and careless attitude, he's probably suffering through insecurities in silence. A feeling I understand; who can stomach looking at me?

"Hey." I stretch to grip his hand. "No talk like that on your birthday. You're Superman; you have that tragic, sexy, superhero appeal."

Connor's eyes soften, and he gives that breezy grin that makes him brighten. "Superman? I told you, I'm the telepath. Isn't it obvious?"

"Oh, make your mind up, nerd." I scrunch my nose and chug down my drink, silently praising myself for navigating that conversation away from a very dark place.

THEM

Once we finish our refreshments, Connor announces that my necklace is fixed. I offer to wait in the kitchen whilst he fetches it. In truth, I want to eavesdrop on my parents, since they're still engrossed with the professor.

The kitchen has three entrances. A small door at the other side of the room, obscured by a small cloakroom, that leads outdoors. Then the wide, open-plan entrance that flows seamlessly from the conservatory, with plenty of space for Connor to move unhindered. And then there's a small door to the far left—old timber with a latch handle, something left over from the conversion and not suitable for a wheelchair. But, from my calculations, it leads back to the front entrance hall.

Hovering near the door, I can catch faint notes of our parents hushed conversation.

My heart sinks.

Father and the professor are locked in less-than-friendly whispers whilst Mother interjects to calm them.

Father's voice is low and venomous. "If you knew who she was then why didn't you reach out to us?"

"Fred," Mother says, the strain in her voice evident.

"I wasn't going to risk exposing her," the professor whispers. "With the boy under my care, Thomas's men keep a close eye on my movements."

Thomas? Is that the mysterious T? Oh no, Killian isn't free, he's stuck here because of Thomas. Because of whoever is hunting us. That's why he's been quiet. He's been trying to keep me safe. And the professor, he's in on it. I feel sick. I'm such an idiot.

"So you're working with him, then?" Father's voice cracks, and I hear a fist slam into something hard. "Did Robbin tout? I thought that idiot jumped on the religious zealot bandwagon to get out."

"Fred, Robbin is clueless." Mother placates the rising tension with her cajoling tone. "And Thomas isn't the enemy. It was his idea and his plan that got us out of Ireland."

"But he didn't like it when we went off radar." Anger edges his hushed words, the sharpness of his comment seems to silence my mother. "And Paul is still on it."

"Some of us weren't so lucky." Donoghue's whisper rises almost to a shout, and I flinch from the door. "I didn't have a choice. My wife was dying, and I still held an elder seat. I couldn't leave."

There's a long, pained silence. I don't fully grasp the context of their argument; it doesn't make sense. Elder seat? Off radar? Now I know there's something my parents have neglected to share. Something more than just rare genetics.

Father breaks the silence. "We have to leave."

I suck in a sharp breath.

No. Not now.

"Fred, we can't. She's happy." There are tears in Mother's voice. "She's found him without any outside involvement. They've found each other. It's the sign. She's ready."

"She's not ready, she's a child!" My father shouts this time, earning him two loud shushes before he continues. "We don't know who to trust. We don't know if it's safe. We don't know anything, Marie." His voice quietens. "I'm sworn to protect her. I'd die for her. I can't let her go. Not yet."

"We don't let her go." It's obvious my mother is crying, and the sound makes my stomach flip. "We go with her."

"We're traitors, Marie." My father's voice is thick with emotion. "They'll kill us."

"Thomas will help," the professor says. "You can't ignore this, Fred. They're here, together, for the first time since the war. It's time." A pause ensues; the professor groans. "You think I want this? That boy is like a son to me. I've given him this life away from all of that. He doesn't know any more than she does. But this is bigger than us. They are far too important to keep hidden any longer."

I lean away from the door, eyes wide and head spinning. What war? My parents, traitors? What does that mean? They must've known Killian existed. They've known it this whole time. And what about Connor? What does he know? Maybe that explains all the over-friendliness. And, the text, the warning from Thomas, it's all starting to come together. Except I know I'm missing something. Something important. Something about myself.

A faint knock distracts me. In a dazed state, I amble toward the continuous rap coming from beyond the little cloakroom and the door that leads outside. I peer through the frosted window. The person's silhouette is distorted, but I'd recognize that hunched form anywhere.

"Killian?" I yank open the door. A blast of cold air and a sprinkling of rain hits me, sending a shiver up my spine, and I hug myself. Killian blinks, then grunts an acknowledgement. Carrying several heavy, wrapped bundles, he forces himself into the small hallway. I stumble out of his way, backing into the hall.

He smells of wind and rain, but the earth clings to him in that weird way unique to him. Like he's made of it, or grew up from it, like the plants he tends. Dropping his cumbersome bundle in the corner by a large wicker basket, he removes the plastic mesh, revealing a pile of cut logs. Soundless, he neatly stacks each log, unconcerned by my presence but intent on maintaining avoidance.

I clear my throat. Loudly. I need to tell him about what's happened. He needs to hear the conversation unfolding in the other room.

Killian twists his head to peek at me with a raised eyebrow. For a very long, silent minute, we stare at each other.

Connor's wheels swish on the polished floors. "Lexi? Lexi, where the heck did you go?"

Killian bolts out of the little hall and into the kitchen, and I slink out after him. He points a thumb my direction with a questioning grunt.

"Oh, hey, you made it." Connor grins at Killian. "Dad's got company with Mr. and Mrs. Danu at the moment. Told ya Lexi would come."

Killian pauses, shoulders stiff. I hang behind, my hands twisting in anxious circles as I glance at the door that leads to the hall, then back to Killian. Does he know?

"What's wrong?" Connor asks, eyes darting about the kitchen. "Did I miss something?"

"No." My response is much too fast, and I paint a strained smile on my face to divert from my obvious nerves. I'm aware of the slight possibility that Connor may know nothing, or—everything—so I ask for the one thing I need, and then I can figure out what to do next. "Did you get my locket?"

"Oh, right, yeah, sorry. Killian distracted me." Connor fishes around in his pocket and presents me with my locket. "Cleaned it up too. I hope you don't mind."

"Of course not. Thank you," I say, and mean it, despite the anxiety that crawls all over my skin and causes my stomach to twist into knots.

I reach out and retrieve the necklace from Connor. As promised, the oval locket gleams as though new. The engraved shamrocks and yew branches are more pronounced now that the gold isn't so dull. The delicate clasp seems intact under my touch. When I look back at Connor, he beams, delighted with my approval. I don't know what it is about him, but he doesn't feel like a threat. I don't think he knows. He's my friend, or maybe I just want him to be innocent because he's my friend. Oh, god, this situation is so messed up.

"It's perfect." I finally say, then look to Killian. My eyes swim with tears at the realization that he understands more than he can tell. "Thank you, Killian, for finding it. I would've been devastated if I'd lost it."

"N-n-no ne-ed." The sorrow and strain in Killian's features softens, but his brow furrows. His deep gaze searches mine. His body tenses when he reads the fear there.

"Would you look at you, getting all flustered around a girl." Connor snickers, leaning back in his chair.

My eyes widen at the insinuation. Connor shouldn't have noticed the prolonged gazes between us and construed them as attraction. I'm being careless. This is dangerous. We need to get out.

Killian growls his disapproval, and Connor tilts back his head to let out a peal of laughter. The sound is so happy and oblivious. This is all wrong. None of this is right. I can barely smile, let alone return laughter, and he knows; he's starting to sense my distraction.

Killian is the one to break the awkward trance. "M-mus-ic." He points toward the conservatory, then gestures to me. "Sh-show."

I don't quite follow his train of thought. He stares hard at me, willing me to listen, and I nearly miss how he glances to the kitchen door where our parents whisper.

"Show Lexi what you got me?" Connor asks. His cheeks pink up. "Aw, I don't think she wants to hear me play."

The penny drops—a distraction, so Killian can eavesdrop the conversation and keep Connor occupied. And keep me safe, I realize, about a second later.

"You play something?" I ask, recalling a keyboard shoved against a spare wall in the conservatory. "I'd love to hear. Show me, please?"

"Oh, okay." Connor blushes and gives an awkward shrug. "Killian got me a new music book. It's superhero movie scores for the keyboard," he says rather sheepishly.

"Ah-amaze-maze-ing." Killian pretends to bash invisible keys, then points to Connor with a thumbs-up.

"Really?" I say and twist toward the conservatory, relieved Connor follows. Killian hangs back, blending into the background effortlessly.

"Yeah, well, I guess I'm good," Connor says, as we head into the conservatory. "I practice a lot. Nothing better to do when you're stuck in a chair."

I laugh, a too loud sound. Connor frowns but doesn't comment. I've got to keep these nerves under control.

Connor parks by the keyboard where it sits snugly against the corner wall and a long, floor-length window. He starts to search through a pile of music books and sheets whilst I chance a desperate glance over my shoulder.

Distractedly, I shove a hand in my pocket and feel the small paper bag I put there before I left the house. It's a silly homemade gift for Connor. Less than an hour ago it meant nothing. Now . . . it's all I have to give.

"Hey, um," I say when I look back. Connor lifts his head. "Look, I know I said I wouldn't get you anything, and it's nothing really, just a silly token to remember me by." I almost choke on the statement. "Here," I say and hand him the package.

"Woah, shut up. I'll decide if it's silly or not." Connor unwraps the bag to reveal a clay disc on a piece of black cord.

"It didn't cost anything. I made it." I give a dismissive shrug. "It's the—"

"Sun . . . it's the sun." Connor's voice is awed as he studies the engraved pattern, painted in those bright golds and oranges that remind me of him. He looks at me, his eyes crinkling as the grin on his lips stretches. "And it's a smiling sun."

"Yes, because that's you. You're bright and happy, like the sun when it shines. It's really hard to find such friendliness, y'know?"

"Thank you, Lexi," he says quietly, holding it to his chest. "That's probably the most thoughtful gift anyone's ever given me. I don't know what to say."

"Aw, come on, don't make it weird." I punch him lightly on the arm. "Not like it's a superhero composer music book, right?" I wink at him and turn expectantly to the keyboard.

He chuckles but nods anyway. He's about to take position over the ivory keys when the whole house goes white.

A sound like a cannon boom follows.

The house rattles.

I jump and spin to face the window. A thrill of fear races up my spine. The hairs on the back of my neck stand on end.

"Scared of a little thunder and lightning?" Connor cocks a brow.

"No." I wring my sweaty palms. "It just caught me off guard."

Connor sniggers as his fingers brush the keys. A whisper of notes lull together, an eerie contrast to the brattle. But I can't focus on the music. Something doesn't feel right. Shadows loom on the lake from beyond the window. A familiar fear snakes its way into my heart, and I start to tremble. A memory of a shadow in the garden enters my mind, and with it, the whisper of other shadows and memories that've long evaded me. It's like my heart remembers something my head forgot. Whatever it is, I now understand the fear etched in my parents' faces. It isn't a good feeling.

Another strike of lightning and a bang of thunder sounds. I step closer to Connor. My fingers dig into the back of his wheelchair. He plays on, not even noticing that I don't follow his soft, melodious tune.

Killian appears on the other side of the room. His eyes wide and focused on the lake beyond the glass. He starts to walk toward me. He opens his mouth, but before he speaks, an impatient tapping echoes. I twist in its direction. It's the front door.

"Dang, that'll be the pizza delivery guy," Connor says and ceases his playing. "Guess my one-man concert will continue after dinner."

I don't answer, I just watch Killian. He frowns, following the direction of the sound too. Nothing about his manner comforts me.

More tapping.

"Dad!" Connor throws both arms up in exasperation and starts to swivel the wheels of his chair. "Dad, get the door. We're starving."

"It's okay, I've got it," my mother's voice calls.

"Mother." I breathe her name and notice the urgency in Killian's face. He doesn't need to say another word. "No! Stop!"

Both Killian and I move in tandem. I'm faster though, as I race the length of the conservatory, back through the lounge and aim for the entrance hall.

Mother pauses, palm reaching for the door handle, when she stops to glance toward me. She frowns. I open my mouth to warn her, but Father shouts something that distracts her, and she turns away, putting her back to the door.

The lock clicks, and cold air blasts into the front hall.

The room turns blue with another crack of lightning. I lift my arm to cover my eyes.

"Lexi!" Mother screams.

"Mother?" I try to blink vision back into my eyes.

A howl answers. A horrible, bone-shattering, menacing, wrong sound. Like a wolf's cry, but guttural—wrong—monstrous.

More screams.

My eyes refocus.

There, in the doorway, Mother stares at me, clutching a length of metal skewering her blood-soaked belly—a sword, not dissimilar from the ones my father owns.

Crimson spouts from her lips.

Frozen in fear, I watch as Mother's body slips off the blade, like hot butter falling off a knife. With a deafening thud, she hits the ground.

The creature wielding the bloody sword howls again. A long-limbed humanoid with gray skin and a dark, tattered hood.

My eyes fall back to Mother. I can't look away. My heart is dying—it aches with each beat, threatening to give out.

My knees buckle. I brace myself for the fall. But I never hit the ground.

An arm circles my waist.

My captor forces me down, their weight pinning me to the floor.

I should struggle, but I'm frozen. Instead, I look up into gray-green eyes that lock onto mine, willing me to remember.

FOR LOVE'S SAKE

I hear the glass tinkle around me, outside of the shield Killian makes. Wind howls through the door, and I realize the windows are smashed open too. It's only then that I decipher the wind from the monster's howls.

There's a chorus of howls. Each joining the other, from every direction.

"No!" I cover my ears against the sound.

Killian drags us both to our feet, but I'm weak as jelly in his arms. I don't know where my father is, but I can hear him, along with the professor, in the din, but their words are incomprehensible.

The only thing I see is the blade, the blood, and my mother.

Her eyes.

Her starry eyes, and how all those magic stars disappeared from her the moment she left me. The moment that monster—wait, where is it? I can hear them, but I can't see them. Father? His shouts are farther away . . . outside? I need to get to him.

"L-Lexi!"

My name sounds closer now, loud and harsh. I'm forcibly shaken.

"Go!" Killian's voice is firm, and I follow his outstretched hand toward Connor. My friend is frozen in the middle of the darkened lounge, the lights blown out, making it harder for me to decipher the shadows. The utter fear in Connor's luminous face is such a contrast to the muted darkness.

"I can't." I suck in a sharp breath.

It's alarming how easy it is for my world to fall apart. Just like the fragile house of cards I always knew it to be. All I can hear are the noises, the howling, and my father's voice. My father . . .

I have to get my father.

"Lexi. What are you doing? Come on!" I hear Connor's frantic call, and I want to go to wherever he is going, for surely it's safe, but not with me there. These monsters will keep coming, and now I know what hunts me. Monsters who will kill without discrimination to have us. It's laughable to think I used to believe them to be men in white coats, or scientists brandishing official government papers. I never imagined this. This is the stuff of nightmares.

"Father. I have to leave with my father," I whisper to Killian. He shakes his head.

47

"I-I-I . . . g-get him."

Is he mad?

"Killian, protect Connor and the professor. Please." I grip fistfuls of his sweater in my hands and try to move him out of my way.

Another slice of lightning shoots across the sky. I squeeze my eyes shut, the searing pain of the flash destroying my vision, and in my moment of weakness, Killian takes advantage.

He pushes me back across the floor so hard that I fall and slide along the wood until I hit the far wall with force. The crack of my skull against the dry wall causes a burst of sooty black speckles to rain down on my already compromised vision.

More glass shatters and tinkles across the floor like crystallized rain. I barely find my eyesight, and my glasses, in time to see the remains of the last windows in pieces about my feet.

Killian only just misses the brunt of the cascade. He holds his hip in an awkward angle, a painful hiss sounds through his teeth.

"Lexi . . . ow . . . Lex." The sound of Connor's pained cry seems wrong. I only see an injured Killian.

"On your left."

I start at the command, but inch around, bracing at the twinge the movement causes my neck.

"Connor! Oh god, Connor . . . don't move. I'll help." I haul myself onto all fours.

Connor's chair has collapsed, and whatever way it's fallen, it traps him. He's sprawled uselessly on the floor. But the closer I shuffle to him, the more I'm able to see the blood dribbling from his lip.

The blood.

"Lexi . . ." He attempts to push his chair off. His crippled legs are too badly twisted under the metal frame. I know he'll never have the strength to help himself.

"Lexi, w-what's happening?"

I can't even comfort him as the shadows creep off the walls and surround us, separating us with their dreadful howls. "I can't get up. I have to get up. Where's my dad? Dad?"

I can't stop it—the black cloaked figure crawls over the chair and seizes a fistful of Connor's golden curls in bony claws instead of hands.

A strangled yell, broken in tears, breaks my voice. I scramble forward.

Too slow, I'm moving too slow.

Another shadow on the floor seems to grow into a mannish form. The creature's cape, like a rotting flag, flutters in the winter wind that roars from the broken window. The second invader kneels by Connor and runs an ashen finger along his busted lip. He smears Connor's blood on the dead flesh between his clawed thumb and forefinger. My stomach churns.

How could I be so blind?

"Let him go!" I stagger to my feet and lunge at the creatures with the biggest shard of glass I can find. The sharp edges bite into the flesh of my palm. The blood drips from my fingertips. No use hiding now.

The two creatures howl in their deafening tone, and with movements far too swift to be human, they dance out of the way. One knocks the glass from my hand and the other's claws settle around my throat.

I shriek and kick out. I thrash and fight with all I have, for I've never had more reason to do so than I have in this moment.

You are as weak as a feather here, little child of light.

The hideous hiss comes from the beast that holds me. The sound not from his mouth. No, its voice rings in my mind. I give a horrified yelp.

The soulless being before me has a fleshless face, smooth as bone, like a hollow china mask torched in the flames. The only thing that distinguishes this monster as alive is the glowing orange irises that burn out from his coal eyes and the slit-like mouth that holds a set of rotted, razor teeth. The joint of his jaw clicks in time with the rasps of air that slither out from that cracked, hideous grin. He is like a demon from my darkest nightmares. The monster from under the bed.

I see the glint of the blade as it scratches across my upper arm, slicing the skin in one long gash through my shirt. Doesn't he know that I can heal just as easily as it is for him to make the incision? Something about his cruel sneer makes me think he does.

I squeeze my eyes shut tight again, bracing for a cruel blow. How deep will be too deep? If he slits my throat, can I heal from that? Will I want to? The ambiguity of heaven would be a welcome release from this living hell.

Heat brushes my skin, and for the briefest of moments, I think the warmth means I have died, like I have fallen into a warm and golden embrace. But when the scent of petroleum and acrid smoke fills my nose, I realize I'm not that lucky.

Fire. Of course. Father, Killian, and the professor must've started a fire. Angry howls echo from another room, and this gives me courage, or at the very least, drive.

I lunge forward, fingers wrenching around the creature's skeletal throat.

"Let me go!" My lips twist and peel back to expose my teeth, and I let out a guttural snarl as I squeeze with every ounce of strength I have. My arm burns where he cut me. The heat radiates through my palm, almost like fury feeds it.

A sharp heat draws a roar from my throat, and something sparks like a current between us. The creature gives a terrific howl. A huff of air slams out of my lungs as I hit the ground with force, my glasses flying from my face. I don't need them to see that the monster has vanished and that billowing plumes of smoke lick along the walls. I stare at my blood-soaked forearm for a moment, trying to decipher what happened. But then I remember and turn in the direction I know Connor to be, only to find his chair empty and alight.

"No!" My weak eyes swirl in my head. "Connor? No, please no . . . help! Help me!" I cough into my arm as the smoke clogs up my lungs and stings my eyes. "Killian?" I wheeze, pathetic tears streaking down my cheeks.

"Lexi!'

My eyes fly open. They sting so bad that I can't see him, but I can hear him. So I crawl.

"Father?" I choke, hand outstretched through the smoky haze. "I'm here!"

"I'm coming, baby, just keep talking to me," he commands, and I obey.

I keep shouting for him as loud as my lungs can muster, until arms encircle me. I bury myself into his chest and hear his grunts of effort as he lifts me off the ground. His gait is wrong. He staggers with a heavy, left-sided limp.

We just cross the threshold of the front door when he falters. I slip from his arms as he crumples to the floor. I try to yank on his arm, push at his side, anything to get him up. Before we can give up, a second pair of hands finds us. Twisted limbs wrap around my waist again. I feel the bones creak and groan, and I give a relieved whimper. Killian's okay.

"Go. Get her to the car." Father's labored breaths sound wrong. This is all wrong.

"What are you doing? No, you're coming too," I say as he sinks down further beside us on the threshold of the burning house.

"Lexi, sweet pea, I can't." His voice is rough and gravelly.

"No, no, no, you have to." I reach for him, my hands finding his shirt, and the sticky feeling of blood through his clothes.

He jerks my hands away and strokes my cheek.

"Please . . . please, get in the car. We'll go to the hospital." I choke on my tears as I scramble to hold his hand to my face, trying to warm the icy coldness from his fingers.

"Lexi, hush now. It's too late, and you won't waste time on me."

I shake my head. He's still talking, and he got me out of that house. He isn't dying.

"Good lord, Fred." Professor Donoghue's cry is the kind of noise people make when they see something grotesque. I've heard it before. I twist in Killian's grasp to see the professor lean over us.

"She's been cut by a blood-blade," my father says, having the audacity to ignore his own injuries. "She doesn't have time; she needs help. She needs Thomas's protection." His voice wobbles and weakens. I'm tormented by the exchange, and the confusion of his statement. I'm not going to Thomas. I'm not leaving him.

"Please stay, get up, for me." I hold tightly to his hand. "I don't understand what is going on, and Mother—" My voice chokes off at the end, the memory far too fresh.

Somewhere in the confusion I feel Killian's grip on my waist tighten. It helps to curtail the tsunami of grief threatening to drown me again. It keeps me focused on the present situation.

"Your mother isn't your mother." My father's voice is quiet but edged with something painful. "And I'm not your father."

"W-what are you talking about?" I drop his hand. "Th-that isn't true. I'm your daughter. Stop this ridiculousness and get up. We've got to leave here."

"You are my daughter, Lexi." A quiet sob catches his voice, and he clutches my cheek again. "You are our daughter—at least as close to the real thing as we could ever dream of having. Whatever they choose to tell you, don't you ever doubt that."

"What? Who are they? I'm not leaving you." I struggle with Killian's grip, desperate to stay, to hold on to him as my failing eyes burn in directionless accusation. But the world is starting to fade. My arm and shoulder are numb, and I'm not sure I can stand.

"Lexi, you remember those secrets that we couldn't share."

I almost growl in agitation; now he wants to talk secrets.

"I don't care. I need you to not leave me!" I let out a weak cry, knowing for certain I'm somewhere between devastation and fear.

"This is breaking my heart, Lexi, just listen to me, one last time," he says with that paternal voice. So, for a moment, I listen.

"You're special, sweet pea. You're not meant for this world. Your mother and I were charged with your safety. We were to raise you until it was safe for you to go back home."

"Home? W-where's home? Not meant for this world? I'm confus—" I slump against him, the questions dying on my lips as my vision blurs into tunnels.

"Shhh, honey," he whispers in urgency and strokes my hair. "We don't have time. You need to go with your professor and Killian. You can trust them." Father relinquishes me completely into Killian's arms, and between him and the professor, they haul me up.

"No! You can't leave." Tears slide down my face like endless rivers. I can't keep my eyes open. I can't hold on to him. I'm going to lose this battle.

"Get her out of here, Paul. The emergency services will be en route. Someone is bound to have reported that fire by now."

"And what are you going to do?" His patience has worn thin, and the strain is evident in his voice.

"You think those are the only howlers left? They'll be coming back for her; they know who she is now. I won't let them pick up your trail." Father peels himself from the ground; an agonized whine catches in his throat.

"You'll die!" I cry and throw out a hand to him, using what little strength I have to struggle against my captors and hold on to my father.

"I'm already dying, sweet pea." His hand holds mine as his kiss brushes my cheek. "But I won't let them take you. I love you; we both loved you. Everything we did was for you. You gotta remember that, sweet pea. Please remember it for me."

"No." I shake my head, feeling my fingers slip through his as I'm hauled away. "No, please . . . don't leave him." But they don't listen, as they bundle me into the backseat of a strange car.

My heart slams into my throat, frantic sobs wracking through my chest as I reach for my father one last time. There's another howl, and the ghost of a shadow appears across the flaming building. I scream as those shadows take shape, forming into a line of five or so monsters.

"Go!" My father's roar is broken off by a car door slamming between us.

My horrible broken wail the only sound in the deathly silent car. "I love you!" I thump the glass weakly. "Daddy, I love you!"

And then the world slips into darkness.

ORDER IN CHAOS

Lights flicker on. Something plastic presses over my mouth and nose. Air blasts into my lungs.

Lights flicker off. Noise whirs in the background, but I don't have the strength in my limbs to sit up.

Lights flicker on. People are arguing to my right. Voices, accents I recognize as both Irish and American.

Lights flicker off. But it's not light, it's my vision coming in and out. I try to blink to clear the fog. My ears hurt. There's a pressure in my head, and the roar of engines. This isn't a car.

"We're one hundred miles from Mide, Bryce," a male voice with a heavy brogue calls. "Keep them heavily sedated; we'll be crossing over soon."

I know that sound. I'm in a plane.

"Wh-where am I?" I ask. My voice sounds off, torn and muffled. It's the oxygen mask. I force my hand up to pull it away, but larger hands hold it in place. "No . . . stop . . . help." There's not enough power in my limbs to fight off whoever holds me down.

Fear, or as much fear as I can muster, renders me useless. I give up, my hand falling from the mask and stretching into the nothingness. But another's fingertips brush mine. My head lolls to the side and I see him.

For a moment, Killian's eyes chase away the fear. He lies in a bed opposite mine, his features drained and weak. He reaches for my outstretched hand. Our fingers lace in a vice hold, and he squeezes.

His gaze is soft, his frown gentle, and I hear his silent command through our connected fingers.

I'm here. Hold on to me.

And as the lights flicker off again, I do what he says. I hold on with all I have left.

It hurts.

Everything is spinning.

I am going to vomit.

Weakly, I squirm with the heavy blanket that seems to be cementing me to a bed. Only it isn't the blanket's fault, but the fact that my bones feel like jelly.

I do not like this.

Argh . . . it feels like someone has whisked my brains into a scrambled mess whilst simultaneously beating my skull with a blunt object. Actually, I'm mildly afraid that something has blown the back of my head clean off. This headache cannot be normal.

"Uhh . . . is-is anyone there? K-Killian?" I cringe at the pain that shoots up my jaw and into my temple.

I squeeze my eyes tighter, scrunching my nose up and doing my best floppy fish impression to make it onto my side, just in case I really do projectile vomit. The throbbing in my head relents a little, enough to let the ringing in my ears subside.

There's a hum of low and strange voices. I freeze. Definitely not in a plane anymore. Definitely not Killian or the professor.

My senses fly out from myself in a chaotic panic. My jellied brain tries and fails to recall my last memories before I passed out.

The ash smell is gone, and in its place, the stench of medicinal fluids, like the harsh alcohol-based sanitizers that burn your nostrils. The leather of the plane gurney has been replaced by a hard bed of some description, with a spongy and uncomfortable mattress that doesn't protect my aching joints from the metal of the frame beneath.

I can't open my eyes because of the cornea-obliterating pain that threatens to burst my eyeballs. Worse than this, I can't pick my head off the bed or get my feet beneath me to make a break for freedom.

What is happening? Where am I?

My heart begins to beat a little too quickly, the frantic pulse resounding in my already overwhelmed and excruciatingly pained brain. I attempt to think around the delirious sensations, deciding quite quickly that if I don't figure this out and get my head in the game, then I'll be in trouble. Serious trouble.

It's a relief to know that even in the most chaotic situations, my mind still has the innate ability to leap to conclusions, at lightning speed, in the most neurotic manner. So far I've decided that the only possible logic remaining is that those awful monsters came back, and now Killian and I are their captives. It matters little that my common sense reminds me that I'd been sick with a fever, and likely passed out, and perhaps Professor Donoghue was able to get me to the help father spoke of. No, obviously that wouldn't happen, because Killian would still be here, and he isn't, and neither is the professor.

An icy fear sneaks into my fragile heart. Visions of my father's parting rise up. I don't want to be alone.

Please, if some divine power exists, I beg of you, don't take anyone else from me.

I give another deep and guttural sob, clutching the side of the bed that I lie on with desperation.

The voices come closer, maybe only a matter of feet now, and I gather that there must be at least two different speakers. One of them—male by the sounds of this deep baritone—argues with more conviction than the other. There is a warmth and familiarity to the tone that crackles with just the right amount of passion. I'm not overly frightened of the speaker's anger; however, his argument is met with the biting sound of a commanding woman, and that does make me nervous.

A brief silence ensues. I stop breathing and keep as still as I can, hoping to feign unconsciousness. This seems unlikely, since I gave away the element of surprise calling for Killian . . . doofus.

Abruptly, I am touched.

A cold shiver runs down my spine.

The knuckle of a curled finger runs along the length of my forearm to the hand that I have clamped around the edge of the bed. I expect the worst; the claw to my throat that will end me perhaps?

"Lexi?" The masculine voice becomes clear in my buzzing ears, and I inhale at the shock of the clarity of that familiar sound. That cannot be right. "Lexi, it's me; don't cry." The genuine care in his warm, steady voice utterly confuses me. In my shock, I don't flinch when his whole hand spreads over mine.

"Your voice . . ." I don't trust that strange, smooth, well-articulated voice.

Unable to believe my own ears, I try to open my eyes. The searing brightness burns, and I automatically groan and squint. The hand around mine moves to my forehead, and gently his fingers push away the strands of my hair that have stuck to my clammy skin.

"I know. It's a long story, but I promise it is me."

That same coaxing and genuinely compassionate tone only assures me that I'm not in imminent danger. His fingers work small circular motions across my brow where the pain feels the worst. It feels nice. Feels familiar.

"Lexi, you're safe, completely safe, so don't rush yourself. Your eyes are going to hurt."

"Killian?" I groan in utter disbelief as I force my eyes to open wider, hissing viciously at the pain. "This is a joke; you are messing with me, whoever you are. Killian Hunter can't speak. What did you do to my friend?"

I try to shove myself upward, wrestling with the imposter who is touching me and forcing my eyes to see through the blurry brightness. It feels like someone has shoved a white-hot poker through both my eye sockets.

"Woah, Lexi, easy," the stranger posing as Killian says, his hands landing on my shoulders to stop me from toppling.

I lash out and break his hold, determined to keep myself up without any help. Cupping my palm to my eyes, I try to create shade so I can see exactly who I'm dealing with.

"Stay away from me." I wince at the blurry silhouette that begins to focus in my line of vision. My suddenly very wide visual field.

"Okay . . . okay . . . I won't touch you." His perfected voice adopts a careful tone.

"My eyes!" I shut them tight again.

The clarity is startling, the colors shocking, and the lack of darkness completely petrifying. I can see?

I can see too much.

"Lexi, slowly open your eyes," he says, but instead of those softly spoken words being in any way helpful, I begin to hyperventilate.

"What's happening?" I gasp. "Where am I? Who are you?"

"You know who I am," he promises, his voice sounding close, his breath brushing against my face. "Lexi, slowly open your eyes. You will be okay. You can do this. Open your eyes and see for yourself."

Between panicked gasps, I try to rationalize that I need to see. I need to know who this man is. I have to face up to this, but suddenly I don't care for the answers to the secrets that have plagued me my entire life. Now ignorance seems much more appealing. But my ignorance, and innocence, died the moment that demon murdered my mother.

The memory sends a slice of agony to rip through my chest, and the heat that it leaves behind flares deep within. Hatred. That hate burns solidly, and the flames give me purpose. So much so that it drowns out all other fears. I take a deep breath in, the air fanning the flames in my heart, and carefully, I open my eyes.

For a long minute, all I can comprehend is the absolute crystal clarity of my vision. There are no dark patches, no torn holes of fragmented light, and no blurry edges. My sight is perfect—so perfect, in fact, that I can see everything in sharp focus.

My gaze focuses downward, toward my own hands, and I watch how my fingers flex and how my skin gleams a luminous pale glow, the scars of horrid blotched and ugly skin replaced with faintly shimmering, pearlescent veins of light. I stare in awe, and wonder if this is a dream or a deception of my new eyes.

"Lexi, are you okay?" The concern in his lilt seems genuine.

My new, keen eyes flick upward in accusation.

"Lexi, it's me."

I let out a tiny gasp.

In curiosity, I lift my fingers to touch the face only a hair's breadth from mine. A strong jaw, a chiseled and defined profile, a long but proportionate nose, and a full bottom lip that is soft to touch. His skin is as luminous as mine, but instead of being a milky white, it has a russet, golden hue. He isn't soft to touch, his skin is tough, built for a hardier lifestyle, but that familiar earthy scent fills my nose; rain, grass, and trees. It smells so natural, so comforting.

"Killian," I whisper in shock, my fingers tracing the stubble across his jaw.

He smiles, but all of my attention is drawn to his eyes, the only thing evidencing that it is him. Those green eyes haven't changed at all; they still hold a profound depth, a sorrowful, wise aura.

"Yes, it's me," Killian say, with a hint of relief.

Carefully, he returns his hands to rest on either side of my face. His brow creases in sympathy, his eyes fill with unspoken understanding. In response, traitorous tears track down my cheeks.

"What happened to you?" I say, well aware that I'm sounding quite hysterical and a bit repetitive with my overwhelmed questions. "Where are we?"

Before Killian can answer, a hand clamps on his shoulder and yanks him away. I jump in surprise and blink at the burly, military-esque man who keeps a free hand on the holster of his belt. His uniform. It's like the one Father was wearing in my locket. A hand flies to my neck. No locket. No. It must've gotten lost. This only succeeds in making me cry harder.

"Bryce! For the love of god, get your gorillas off me!" Killian levels said "gorilla" with a decent amount of loathing. "Seriously, a gun? That is cute. I am terrified. No, really, I'm shaking with fear."

"Please can I shoot him now, Bryce," the man says, his accent a thick, Irish brogue. Another uniformed man appears over his shoulder and chuckles, his hand moving to rest on the butt of a pistol tucked into the holster at his left side.

I think my heart is about to grind right out of my chest. Why are there men with guns? Why is Killian talking? Why can I see? Is no one going to acknowledge that I'm clearly a moment away from a breakdown?

"Drop it, Rory; he isn't worth the bullet."

That clipped feminine tone sounds to my left. The physique of a slender redhead stands only a few feet from my bed. She doesn't look at us as she adjusts her glasses on her upturned nose and jots something down on a clipboard.

"You heard her. Go. Sit. Take a sedative. Eat a Scooby Snack or something." Killian eyes the two men from their heads to their toes, but a second later, he scowls in the general direction of the woman I assume to be Bryce. "I'm not worth the bullet? Although, evidently, I'm deemed enough of a troublemaker to inherit a couple of incompetent, jarhead guard-mutts."

"This is what happens when you recklessly break the laws that govern our whole existence and decide to run away like a spoiled little boy," Bryce says as she lifts her head from her clipboard and arches a defined eyebrow. "You end up with babysitters."

"I came back, didn't I?" A divot forms between Killian's eyebrows.

Even though the contents of this argument should be cause of alarm for me, all I can focus on is the amazing sound of Killian's voice and how incredible he looks. I can't quite make it all fit. Where is the crippled young man? Where are the arthritic, gnarled hands and the hunched, twisted back?

"Yes, and one has to wonder why."

I stare at Bryce, watching as her lips purse and her whole demeanor shifts defensive.

"I swear, for so-called intelligent humans trained by the Order, you really lack insight." Killian shakes his head and returns his apologetic gaze to mine. "She needed me, and she needs her own kind. I wasn't about to let her be dragged into this alone."

My own kind? Dragged into this? "What are you talking about?" I direct the question to Killian. "Did you know this would happen? Did you know those—those monsters—were going to attack us?"

"No!" He looks genuinely horrified by the accusation, the divot deepening as his features contort into more of a frown.

"Those are excellent questions, Alexandria," Bryce says, acknowledging me for the first time—and completely freaking me out by how she knows my name.

She strides toward the bed and points her silver pen at Killian. "Do you know your friend here is thought to have dealings with the creatures that attacked and killed your custodians?"

"That's a lie!" Killian bounces to his feet and steps into the unperturbed woman's space. "Don't fill her head with the Order's deceitful misrepresentations of my character. I protected her. I did what I could to keep her and her guardians alive, which is more than you and your precious agents can claim to have done for her in eighteen years."

"And this, dear Killian, is why you're ordered to be kept under guard at all times." Bryce clicks her fingers toward the two uniformed men waiting in the wings. They bounce forward and flank him; one secures some kind of crystallized metal shackle to his wrists whilst the other grabs his upper arm. I instinctively lurch forward to defend him.

"Lexi," Killian says, keeping his eyes trained on the red-headed woman. "Lexi, you can trust these people; these are the people your father wanted you brought to."

"What are you doing to him? Where are you taking him? I don't want him to go." I begin to sob as the men pull him toward an exit.

"It's all right, Lexi." Killian's eyes lock with mine and fill with all that deep-rooted, soulful sorrow that I never quite understand. "I promise we'll see each other soon."

"Killian Hunter, you sound like you've developed a conscience." Bryce gives a disbelieving snort. "Perhaps several years outside the protection of our system and you eventually see the merits of it?"

"I see no merits in a cage!" Killian lunges forward. The two soldiers grunt and grapple to hold him in place "I wasn't born to bow to the lesser blood of bygone kings."

"But you were born," she interrupts, and he pales, a dead silence hanging between the pair of them, "to a human father of that bygone blood, no less. I would be careful of offending your paternal kin, Killian. We are the only family you've got."

The two beefy guardsmen roughly pull a livid Killian out the door, and I can't tell if he didn't respond to Bryce's comment because he was hurt by it or if he was concerned that he might hurt her because of it. None of this makes sense, but no matter how many times I close my eyes and reopen them or how often I painfully pinch the skin of my forearm, I can't wake up.

The woman named Bryce turns to face me, her manner turning a little softer at Killian's departure. The stress lifts from her shoulders as she comes and perches primly at the edge of my bed. She wears her hair in a soft bun. The overgrown wisps of her fringe frame her heart-shaped face, which is dusted lightly in freckles. I'm momentarily amazed that I can make out all her tiny flaws with ease. My eyes seem to scan and document the finest of details without me even trying. It's surreal.

I decide that she must be a woman in her mid-thirties, younger than my mother, but she lacks any kind of femininity or maternal charm. She is professional, rigid, and admittedly a little intimidating.

"Apologies, Alexandria. This is not how I envisioned our first meeting," she says diplomatically, in her elegant, vaguely British accent. She folds her lean hands over her lap and tilts her head, seeming to ponder her next statement. "I would like to offer my sincerest sympathies and express my horror at the ordeal you were subjected to. I cannot imagine how confused you must be, or how upset you are. However, it is my wish that I can be of assistance."

I blink a little spastically at her clinical tone and can't help but compare it to the genuine warmth of Killian's. It's not that I sense deception from this woman, it's just that I felt safer with Killian. Maybe that's just the familiarity of him, and perhaps I shouldn't use that as a benchmark for trust. After all, how well do I actually know him?

"Well, that all sounds terrific because I have a lot of questions."

Crossing my arms about my chest, I attempt to stress my impatience, but I still end up squinting in response to my horrendous headache. Bryce gives me a rather irritating sympathetic grimace, which I can't help but take as condescending. I scowl. "Why don't you start by explaining exactly what is going on."

SEEDS OF TRUTH

Try as I might, I can't quite keep up with the words tumbling from Agent Bryce's lips.

It's funny. I find I'm transfixed by the elegant line of her ruby lip liner, a shade darker than her lipstick. Or she has a little tuft of barely noticeable downy hair at the sides of her lips. My new eyes don't have any difficulty understanding these tiny details, yet I can't understand what she is telling me.

"Alexandria, do you comprehend what I'm saying?" she asks in her forthright manner, the higher decibel of her voice shocking me back to reality.

I wince and look around the sterile room that reminds me of a small laboratory. A cold prickle runs down my spine. I always imagined crazy scientists coming to kidnap me when I was little, and now I'm not so sure this isn't a nightmare.

My new eyes roam the sparse room looking for anything offensive or things that might point to sinister intentions, but I see no large needles or invasive medical equipment. There is only Bryce and I, sitting on a hastily made plinth bed with a large, mirrored window on the wall facing us. I assume the mirror to be a two-way observation window, and every so often I scowl at it, hoping to let the observers know that I'm well aware of their watching.

"Alexandria?"

"No," I answer in a hesitant whisper, and lean away from her rigid frame. "I stopped being able to listen when you said we were in Ireland. I was an ocean away the last time I was awake."

"I understand this is extremely disconcerting for you, Alexandria, but—"

"Lexi. Stop saying my name like that, like I've done something wrong. You don't know me, so stop assuming how I must be feeling."

"My apologies, Alexan—I mean, Lexi." Bryce fidgets with the pen in her hand for a moment before shaking her head.

"And stop apologizing." I hug myself, suddenly feeling exposed in this cold room. "You aren't sorry that I'm here."

"You're correct about that," Bryce says, but this time her voice is a little softer, a little more hesitant than her previous professional tone. I frown at the change in her approach; it makes me suspicious. "We are more than relieved to have you returned to us, Lexi. You have no idea how rare and special you

61

are to us . . . to the world . . . both the physical and the Veiled. We assumed we had lost you when your custodians ran after the attack on your life as a baby. We thought you had been seized and lost to us, another failure on our part."

"They weren't just my custodians, they were my parents." I feel the tears sting my eyes and a choking lump form in my throat. I blink back the scalding heat and look away from this woman, her sympathetic gaze enough to push my wavering sanity over the edge.

"I understand your attachment to them." Bryce's hand hovers over mine as if she thinks an affectionate gesture will make me more pliable. "However, the truth of the matter is that Agent Danu and Agent Crawford were elite members of the Order of Kings, and they were selected to be your assigned guardians . . . not your parents."

"Shut up!" I shove myself off the bed to get away from this rambling woman.

The tears I have tried vainly to prevent from falling burst forth in a ridiculous torrent. I hate the conflict that rages inside me right now. Why did they have to leave me alone? If they really cared about me, why didn't they try harder to stay with me?

I feel so foolish, so betrayed, like I don't even know who I am. I feel every emotion at once and all of them hurt, so with nothing else to do, I crumple onto the floor. Drawing my knees to my chest, I cry my ravaged, broken, torn-to-pieces heart out all over again.

Bryce, clearly panicked by my theatrics, leaves the room with a resounding *click-clack* of her heeled shoes. Perhaps she is rushing to get a strong sedative again. The same sedative they must've given me to keep unconscious whilst they body-hopped me across the Atlantic. Of all the times I dreamed about coming home to Ireland. Of all the stupid fairytale, happy-ever-after crap I created in my mind about being in the heart of my homeland, I never imagined it would be like this.

My parents are dead, the one kid who had the patience to befriend me is probably held captive somewhere by monsters you only hear about in movies, and the only other soul I know is apparently a felon. This is not the life I imagined. These are not the truths I expected to discover. I would rather be killed by that shadowed demon than face this terrifying existence alone.

A horrible and ghoulish sound escapes me. It sounds inhuman, and I feel inhuman. There is nothing familiar to me. Never did I expect that I would miss my imperfections. Never could I have envisioned a day that I'd crave them. I desperately desire something familiar, something normal, anything that isn't twisted and changed.

It takes several long minutes for me to register that someone has entered the room. When I do, I freeze, wary that it will be Agent Bryce with an oversized needle to send me back into the darkness. But it isn't the stern and professional redhead; it's an aged man, who sits hunched in a wheelchair. The irony of the image only makes the tears stream down my face all the more. I don't bother to mop away the evidence.

"Professor?" I lean forward. "What happened to you?"

"Oh, it's nothing a morphine patch and a stiff drink won't fix." He chuckles humorlessly, his watery eyes filled with the same deluge that is flooding mine. "Afraid one of the howlers sank their claws a little too deep." He pauses, and the two of us watch each other. "I know it's pointless to ask, so I won't bother inquiring to your current mood, but I thought you could do with a familiar face. Honestly, I could do with one too."

I nod to his statement, spluttering out a sound somewhere between a groan and a sarcastic laugh. The professor wheels his chair toward me, awkwardly banging into things and cursing when he can't angle the chair right. His struggle only brings images of Connor to my mind, and I look away.

"I thought you might need some filling-in since you blacked out pretty soon into our impromptu transatlantic trip." He parks his chair up close enough to me so he can speak easier.

I scowl at his statement, but he only nods in unspoken understanding.

"Where's Connor?" I say, but the pain that floods his entire face is all the answer I need. "They got him, didn't they? Those monsters. Is . . ." I struggle to say the words. "Is he dead?"

"No." The professor shakes his head. "Abducted. Taken by those who have hunted you both since birth." Tears drip down his cheeks, but he scrubs at them with his sleeve. "He's alive, that's all that matters. We'll get him back."

I nod, unsure whether to believe him. I start to cry. Hard. Again. It could've easily been me instead of Connor. I wonder how much the professor wishes that to be true.

"It should've been me." I sob into my hands. "I'm so sorry. It's my fault. I should never have come to your house."

"Nonsense!" The professor's thick hand collides with my back and gives it a firm shake. "Now you listen to me, Lexi. You won't talk like that. I don't think like that. I'm relieved that I at least saved you."

We sit in silence for a long moment. I stare up at him, scrutinizing his every expression to see if it's a lie. But it isn't. His face remains open and sad, no anger or bitterness in sight. He's a better person that me.

"You had a serious wound on your arm. Killian was able to administer some natural medicine to draw out the poison," the professor says, putting an end to our silence. "But your body took such a beating, it was inevitable that you were too exhausted to fight the fever." Professor Donoghue points to my gauze-dressed forearm. I frown and poke it, cringing when it stings a little. "Ah, ah. Let it be, lass; don't agitate it."

Screwing my face up, I snap back at him. "That I remember. Why don't you tell me something I don't know."

He nods. "By now, I'm certain you have figured out that you've been lied to regarding your identity."

I can only stare at him.

"I won't dredge up the issues right now, but let me say this: Marie Crawford was a wonderful and compassionate woman, and if she said she loved you, then she meant it. I don't believe for one minute that their decision to keep you in the dark about the Order and your true self was a malicious and selfish act. They must've had a reason, and I promise you, Lexi, I will do everything I can to find out what that was."

"What is my true self?" I ask, eyes darting up to pierce his, almost willing him—no, daring him—to tell me the truth.

The professor holds my gaze for a long moment.

"It is a complicated answer." He clasps his hands together. "For it depends greatly on how you see the creation of the world."

"Try me," I say through a rigid smile, because this day could not be any more insane.

"Very well." He nods, then glances away. A moment passes before he returns his weighted gaze. "You, Lexi, are what is left of a divine race able to move within the realms of the physical and the realms of the unseen. History has called your people many things—angels, lesser gods, giants, the Watchers, the fair folk, elves, jin, and other queer things. But the truth is, you exist, and whatever your origin, you are an endangered species."

My eyes widen and my mouth goes dry. I want to call him a mental case. Except something rings true, and it certainly explains the monsters.

The professor continues, blatantly ignoring my shocked expression. "What I know to be fact is that many millennia ago, a supernatural race ruled Ireland. History calls them Tuatha Dé Danann, but, simply, they were celestial and not of this physical and mortal world. They were not all good, as mortal knowledge tells us; some were of the darkness, and they sought to cause strife and destruction in the mortal world, preying on the weakness of mortal hearts. However, there must always be light to fight the darkness, and those of your kind that defended mortals waged many wars on the evilest of their kin. Guardians of Creation, aligned with good kings of Ireland, the ancestors of my Order. The Order that now protects you."

I giggle, feeling a tad hysterical.

"You think I'm crazy, don't you?" the professor asks, and I continue to stare. What am I supposed to say?

"It's okay, Lexi. I wouldn't have believed it either if I were you. But it is the truth, or the truth insofar as I understand it. I never told Connor what he was either. I knew his response would be similar to yours. Still, I knew one day I would have to. But with each passing year, I struggled to find the right words. And now . . . well, I regret not finding them."

"But, how?" I pause, my hands outstretched like I'm trying to make this fit. I squeeze my eyes shut and inhale. "Connor was crippled and in a wheelchair, and I was an ugly, deformed, blind girl. We are not angels or gods. It's absurd."

"Your kind placed a curse on themselves so that none would venture back into mortal lands without suffering." Professor Donoghue answers me with a completely straight and serious face. "If they did, their bodies would fail them, and they would become like the weakest of men. Their beauty would be lost in the eyes of mortals, their powers diminished, and only those with the knowledge of the Order would be able to decipher their true identity."

"Then, you knew what I was?" I haul myself to my feet and shove his hand from my shoulder.

"Yes," he says with a sad nod. "But I knew you didn't."

"How?" I shoot him an accusatory glare.

Professor Donoghue's shoulders sag under some tremendous burden, but he meets my gaze nonetheless. I take a shaky step back as he speaks.

"Because, Lexi, apart from Connor, and perhaps Killian to some degree, you are all that is left of your people."

HOMECOMING

The sun's rays magnify to treble their strength where they burn through the car window. My eyes squeeze shut; a pain shoots across my forehead and nestles under the skin of my temple. I groan.

Agent Bryce shuffles in her seat beside me. She clears her throat, and with a click, a dark mesh shield moves down over the rear windows. The barrier creates appealing shade for my sensitive eyes, but I look away. It doesn't feel right that the sun should be shining.

"We're nearly there. You'll be home soon," Bryce says. I swallow back the bile and sarcasm I feel wedged in my throat. This will never be my home.

The journey through the Mide Estate has been long. Or at least felt it, judging by the length of time I've been cooped up in this ridiculously ostentatious car. Apparently, the clinical room I awakened in is only part of the air base and protective barracks of this mighty and mysterious estate. I'm not to live there, thankfully.

Professor Donoghue did warn it would be a long drive. The estate is huge; some crazy multitude acres of forest, rivers, and even a shoreline. Bryce did prattle something about "if you lived here a decade, you still couldn't explore the sprawling beauty of the landscape." I didn't want to burst her bubble, but I have no intention of adventuring. Killian is right, this all feels like a fancy cage. Some kind of special enclosure to keep an untamed beast in. Perhaps I'm the prized endangered exhibit.

The car rolls off tarmac road and onto gravel. The skittering and spitting of the debris knocks the underside of the car, and I can't help but smirk. That surely isn't good for the expensive paintwork.

"We're here." Bryce pats my knee.

She catches the hard look I give her where I flinch from the cheerful touch. I hate this assumption that a few kind words will fix everything. My parents are dead, and I'm a million miles from anything familiar. What exactly is there to be cheerful about?

A still, small voice in the back of my mind reminds me of Connor and of the sacrifice my parents made so I could live. My father wants me here, and being here is probably my only hope to save Connor. If these are the only reasons that keep me going, then they will have to do.

I rub my sensitive eyes again; the itch has subsided, but too much light seems to set them off burning again. Bryce tells me that it's just my body adjusting to how it's supposed to be and that it may take me a number of weeks to feel anywhere near normal. I feel like reminding her that normal to me was being blind, scarred, and ugly. Normal is not being this superhuman whose reflection is so utterly alien that I don't even want to look at it.

I curl my arms tighter around myself, dipping my chin into the oversized gray sweater. Tears settle on my lashes.

The car rolls to a stop and I suppress the urge to look up. The driver exits the car; his footsteps crunch along the fine pebbles before he clicks open the passenger door. A flash of sunlight and heat brushes across my skin. I recoil.

"Miss?"

A hand is outstretched under my line of sight. I study the arthritic and age-spotted skin of the older gentlemen. His gnarled fingers remind me of Killian, and for the hundredth time today I struggle to reconcile my memories with this new reality.

I haven't seen Killian in well over five days. I wonder what they did to him, and would they put me under guard too? I glance to Bryce and acknowledge the fact that perhaps she is my guard.

With a huff, I extend my hand and take the driver's as he guides me out of the car. I squint a little, giving my eyes time to adjust, and step into the bright courtyard.

"Welcome home, Lexi," Bryce says, the humor evident in her voice as she steps out of the car to stand by my side. "Impressive, isn't it?"

A tiny gasp escapes me, and I swallow, taking in the huge expanse of the sprawling mansion. Its sheer size casts an imposing shadow over the entire courtyard and probably most of the quarter-mile drive.

The symmetrical gray stones of the fascia are both haunting and majestic. The elegant and shining windows are so numerous that I have to crane my neck both ways just to take in the width of the whole building. I count at least four floors, but there must be basements and attics. I even consider that this is more of a palace than a mansion, but then again, what do I know of royalty and noble houses? Clearly very little, I admit, as I stand small and shivering under this ominous shadow, dressed in nothing but borrowed sweatpants and an oversized sweater. I can't feel any more like a worthless orphan in this moment. Nonetheless, I follow Bryce as she leads me up the numerous marble steps to the entrance, with its Roman-style columns and high polished windows. The doors are already thrown open in welcome, and a handful of uniformed staff stand in the shadows, wide-eyed and staring at me like I'm some kind of wonder. I watch them like they watch me—wary and perplexed by their presence. My momentary preoccupation with the existence of servants is halted when I enter the opulent entrance hall.

A chandelier that could be the size of my entire house back in Buffalo hangs from the center ceiling above. Paintings of exquisite taste dress the walls, and I note how the hall splits off into two long corridors, running the length of each wing. My gaze slowly lifts upwards, my whole head tipping back as my strengthened eyes pick out the tiny details of the painted ceiling. Some kind of heavenly realm is depicted above the domed foyer. A paradise of light and beauty; certainly no place on earth, that's for sure.

Everything is polished marble framed in gold or sumptuous mahogany. It's like I stepped into another era altogether. Yet again, I'm reminded of my complete inferiority. Wrapping my arms around myself, my shoulders inch toward my ears, and I resist the urge to fade into a dark corner.

The rustle of silk and the clack of heels alerts me to the entrance of someone new, and I immediately snap my head upward. A slender figure appears at the top of the grand staircase. The woman, perhaps in her forties, dressed in a long silk skirt and matching blouse, appraises me from the safety of the top step. Her painted lips remain pursed, her hard, hazel eyes unreadable, and for the most part she carries herself like a lady of importance. I shrink back as she descends the staircase.

"Welcome, Lady Alexandria." The woman's accent is unfamiliar, and I'm certain the look on my face tells her just how ignorant I truly am.

I half choke and stare wide-eyed at Bryce. "L-lady?"

"I suppose a lady is not quite the title you deserve, is it?" the woman says before Bryce can offer up a better explanation. "Forgive me, but I'm afraid we don't know how to appropriately address an immortal Celestial."

"I-I . . ." My fingers lift to my temple and rub the tension there. "I would prefer if you didn't call me that . . . at least until such things can be proved."

"Oh, my, my." The woman smirks, her eyes lighting a little. "You have spirit. Forgive me. I don't often articulate well what I mean. I forget that all this is a surprise to you."

"Understatement of the century." I ignore Bryce's nervous cough. "And who, exactly, are you?"

The woman gives the tiniest smile and lifts a slim hand to smooth her perfectly curled bob. She slinks a little closer and offers me the same hand. "I am Lady Margot, Countess of Domnaill, and it is an honor for me to finally make your acquaintance, Alexandria."

I take her hand in a firm grip and shake it. She gives a slight grimace, and I make a mental note to remind myself that these people are not accustomed to uncouth commoner handshakes.

"I much prefer to be called Lexi." The countess's lip twitches in mild impatience, but she simply bobs her head in understanding.

"Very well, Lexi, if that would make you feel you more comfortable."

I nod in vigorous agreement.

"Well then, Lexi." She clasps her hands together and straightens her shoulders. "Welcome to Domnaill Castle."

Oh shoot . . . so it is a castle. Great, now I need a castle to protect me.

RUINS

Domnaill Castle is truly something to behold, yet for all the architectural beauty of this place, its cold. Then again, everything in Ireland is cold.

I stand by the slender window that overlooks the main courtyard and watch the rain splatter off the glass. The raindrops are thin, like a fine mist that pours from the heavens. It never stops raining here, except for brief moments of captured sunlight that never seem to last. I like to think the sun abandoned me here, like everyone else.

I touch the heavy, silvery-blue drapes that dress the wide lounge windows. The comfortable apartment I've been assigned has three rooms: this leisure space, a spacious bedroom, and my own private bathroom. It's bright, airy, with powder-blue walls, plush furniture, and silver accents. It's feminine, opulent even, except it feels cold—empty—even with the embers crackling in the pretty fireplace lined with floral tiles. The warmth never seems to reach me.

A wind blows against the castle walls and the windows rattle. A downdraft howls through the dimly lit fireplace My heart seizes in my chest. Each time the wind blows I hear the howl of them. Those murderous monsters.

Sucking in a breath, I pull the heavy woolen cardigan around my shoulders. I draw the heavy drapes across the window to block out the day, then back away, almost colliding with the round table by the fire. It's set with fine crystal and a dinner plate piled with food, but I can't stomach it. Instead, I hurtle through the double doors to my bedroom and slam them shut.

I storm across the expanse of mahogany floor and throw myself on the obnoxious four-poster bed—much too big and cold for just me. I claw the goosedown pillow to my chest and ignore the creak and groan of the old mattress springs.

I want to cry. I want to scream. But nothing ever seems to escape my lips other than painful gasps for air. I'm suffocating on these disrupted memories and all the lies. What's worse is the numbness that follows. The hours of staring up at the thick, patterned drapes that overhang the bed, trying to fit the past week into my tiny, overwhelmed head.

The most disconcerting part is that I'm not human, although the irony is, I guess I always knew that. I just didn't grasp the magnitude of the truth.

My brows furrow as I trade the descriptions of what I am in my head, but nothing makes much sense. In the end I stick with Celestial because it seems to encompass the general theme.

I roll onto my belly and groan. My head throbs with every spinning thought, and blatant hunger pangs. A handful of maids bring me my meals throughout the day, but I scarcely even acknowledge their existence. I barely touch the food. Bryce has called in twice to check on me, but, again, I try to keep my conversations with her under two syllables if I can help it.

As immature as it sounds, I really just want to be left alone. I don't want to engage with anyone, I don't want to talk about my feelings, and I certainly don't want any more truth revelations. So, at my request—or more so my defiant demand—I have been allowed this time to grieve undisturbed.

Bryce did moodily advise me this evening that my period of grieving would not be allowed to stretch on indefinitely. When the earl arrives back from his business trip, I will be expected to meet with him. I assured her if she continued to pester me, I'd consider stretching it out. This did not go down well. But what could they do to me that hasn't already been done?

Hauling the heavy blanket over my head, I curl my knees into my chest and grip my pillow tight. With another weary, tearless rasp, I close my eyes and pray for a dreamless sleep.

I wake suddenly, with a jolt.

The monstrous face in my mind's eye dissipates the minute I open my eyes. I shove myself up from the bed, cursing loudly as I go.

Planting my feet apart, I drape my arms over my knees. After a few moments of calming breaths and a stern reminding that it was just a nightmare, I lift my head up and push my fingers through my hair. It must be late at night, for the castle seems quiet, with nothing but the howling wind still sending a chilly draft through these lonely rooms.

I listen to the eerie sound, trying to persuade my paranoid mind that it is nothing to fear. There are no monsters ready to crash though my window. But as I listen, another sound reaches my ears—water gushing through ancient pipes.

It sounds terribly loud, and for a moment, I worry that perhaps there is a leak somewhere in my apartment. I'm sure the plumbing in this place is anything but modern.

Struggling out of the bedsheets, I shove my feet into the sheepskin moccasin slippers given to me, along with a fully stocked wardrobe of clothes, by the charitable countess. I never owned a pair of slippers before. I hate slippers. But Ireland is much too cold for bare feet.

The bedside lamp barely spits a flicker before the filament bursts. The electrics and plumbing in this place are completely subpar. Then again, I guess ye old merry gentlemen had no need for bedside lamps and hot running water.

Grouchily, I tug at the ends of the jersey dress I found in the back of the wardrobe. Not for the first time I lament the complete absence of pants in my newly acquired collection of daywear. Plodding toward the bathroom, I breathe out a sigh of relief when the pull cord successfully turns the light on. But the onslaught of brightness sends a zing-like pain shooting from temple to temple, like a red-hot arrow inside my skull. I loathe these headaches.

I blink into the overly bright bathroom and note that nothing seems out of place. The old roll-top tub has nothing but a drippy tap, and the black and white checkered tiles are dry as a bone. Definitely no leaks here.

So why do I still hear water?

I march up to the far wall of the massive bathroom, each step a slap of my slippers across the tiles. The gush and rattle sound loudest here. I reach out to press my hands to the paneled wall, thinking I will find it solid to the touch, but instead it bends and warps. I pull back and frown. I don't trust my sight, not even now, so I lean into the wall and let my cheek rest on the panel.

After a moment, I feel a draft. The sound of the water through the pipes seems louder and more like an echo on the other side. My fingers fan out and creep along the crevices in the molded wall panel until, at last, I hear a hollow sounding creak, and the wall gives way.

It's a door.

A secret door.

With a bit more pressure, the paneled door gives way and provides a modest gap for me to squeeze through. It is pretty dark in there, and this is a really old building, but the more impulsive part of my mind overrides the fear.

In my excitement, I scamper back to the living room and dislodge a candlestick from one of the many brass stems of the grand candelabra set on the dinner table. I use the embers of the dying fire to get one of the creamy candles to light and then carefully use the saucer from my untouched dinner to stick it to.

Returning to the secret door, I wiggle through the gap and step into a gloomy passageway. My eyes relax from their permanently scrunched-up wince and the pain from my headache eases with the lack of artificial light.

The dark brick landing is narrow, barely wide enough to pass two people, and it smells like it has been lying empty for at least a hundred years. The musty smell fills my nose, along with swirling dust motes that I disturbed with my unexpected entrance. I cough and sneeze a few times, being careful not to let the candle blow out. The smell is hardly pleasing, but that curious spark in my heart lights, and it thrills me to feel something other than numbness, so I follow it.

I pick my way along the narrow passageway, following the echo of running water. The path slips into narrow stone steps that spiral downward. I descend them, keeping a hand on the dank wall as I go around and around. They lead to more dank passageways; I follow the one where the water sounds loudest. There are always more spiral stairs at the end of each of the narrow corridors I take, so I keep going down. Farther and farther into the castle. Every so often I find other doorways, and I can't help but try them. Most barely budge or they only open a crack. Sealed up from behind most likely.

None of this dampens my adventure, because the darkness doesn't bother me. Getting to feel my way through the shadows, relying on just my touch because my vision is limited to the tiny lick of light that the candle gives out, well . . . it all feels familiar.

It's like I've descended into the bowels of this castle. The corridors and narrow stairs seem to go on forever, so much so that I wonder will they ever end? But the water sounds loudest down a particularly drafty passage. I peer into the gloom, holding my candle aloft.

The stone beneath my feet seems wet. The chill from the ground seeps into my fragile slippers and crawls up the bones of my bare legs. I can smell the outside from here—the rain, the earth, and the strange foreign air.

Maybe I've found an escape. But where would I escape to?

My fingers trail along the stone wall as I strain into the dark. My breath hitches when I spy a light coming from a corner of the wall. A door. Like a moth to a flame, I'm attracted to that glow.

When I reach the paneled door, my thin fingers feel around the edges until I find the hinges. Then, with a little effort, I push it open.

I hold a breath, then shuffle through the small gap.

From the chill in the air and the exposed stonework, I assume I'm in the cellars. The overhead lamps with their tinny, electrical buzz start to irritate my eyes, but the artificial light here is dull. Poor in comparison to the rest of the castle. I slide up against the wall, leaving my saucer and candle in the gap behind the door so I don't forget which way I came.

Instead of a basement or some kind of store, I find a rickety and unmade bed against the wall closest to me. There is a scattering of clothes and the most tattered set of mangy old rugs I've ever seen. An electric heater is plugged into a questionable electrical socket on the far wall, along with an ancient TV.

Someone lives here? Someone inhabits this manky cell? Ugh ... it's hardly fit for human occupation.

From across the room, through an ajar door that billows steam, comes the sound of shower water. I regret my curiosity in an instant.

Right on cue, the rushing water ceases.

Yikes. Time to go before I get accused of breaking and entering.

Swiftly, I make to scramble back out the secret panel. In my panic and haste, the candle dislodges. I leap to catch it.

The candle rolls back into the annex, and I, on all fours, plow after it.

Feet pad across tiles, and someone whistles to themselves.

Oh no. Oh no, no, no.

Cringing into the stone floor, I squeeze my eyes shut and hold my breath, convinced that this somehow makes me invisible. But I don't seem to have developed a camouflage superpower along with my heightened hearing and twenty-twenty vision.

Pity.

THE TRUTH HURTS

He gasps.

I peek up, just enough to see a pair of bare legs skitter back at least three feet. And right in this moment I wish I could drop dead.

It has to be him.

"Lexi? How?"

Like an involuntary reflex, my head snaps to the sound of his voice. "Killian?" I shuffle back to rest on my legs, hyper aware that my Silent Gardener has nothing to spare his dignity but a small towel clutched around his waist.

His damp skin is flushed bright pink as he gives me the most pained expression.

I clap my hands to my eyes.

"Oh my god." I swivel my body away from him. "You're naked. I am so sorry."

"Lexi? How did you get in here?" He splutters.

"How did I get in here? How did you?" I peep between my fingers and clamber to my feet to point a directionless finger.

He curls into himself, focusing very hard on keeping the towel in place.

"Lexi, um, c-can you give me a minute?"

I'm not accepting that. He is dodging my question.

"Oh, okay, so you want me to give you a minute." I throw my arms above my head. Days of anger bubble to the surface and spew out my lips. "Well, sorry, Killian Hunter—if that is your real name—I don't think you deserve a minute. I think you better start explaining who on earth you are, and what I am, and why I woke up in Ireland looking like I had some kind of miraculous recovery. And you appear to have undergone some kind of body transplant."

"I know you must be in shock, but—"

"No buts!" I shove his chest, making him stagger. "You left me!"

"Argh . . . Lexi, stop." Killian holds out his hand. The other still working to preserve what is left of his modesty.

"Stop?" Tears prick my eyes and I shove him again. "I would love to stop. I would love all this to stop and rewind back to three weeks ago. I would stop right there and walk away, like I should've, like my parents taught me."

I jab a finger into his chest, my breathing hard and heavy. "Because at least they'd still be here. Connor too. We would never have got caught up in this nightmare."

"Lexi." He ducks as I lash out. "Lexi, just listen to me!" He catches the back of my neck with his free hand. His strong fingers knot into my hair and still my wriggling for a moment. "What happened to your parents was not your fault. What happened to Connor was not your fault. It wasn't mine either. So stop using me as a punch bag and give me a minute to put some pants on."

My cheeks burn so hot I'm convinced I've turned letterbox red. Killian didn't deserve that outburst. The tears resting on the ends of my lashes break. They slide down my cheeks, one big fat sob at a time.

Killian's aggravated features morph into something sympathetic. And that's all it takes for me to lose grip on my fragile mask. With a loud and ugly gasp, I drop my head against his chest and throw my arms around his neck.

The hand that Killian has around my neck shifts and coils around my heaving shoulder. His fingers brush my back with a feathery touch. He takes a strained breath in and tries to readjust our awkward position.

"S-s-sor-ry." I try to lean away from him and mop up my flooded face.

"No. Uh, it's fine." He blushes as I gape at him. I feel like bursting into tears all over again for being so stupid as to have a breakdown in front of a strange man.

"Lexi . . . sweetheart . . . can I please just put pants on?"

The tears brim my eyes again, and I suck in another awful gasp. Could this get any worse?

"Oh god. Please don't cry again." Killian shuffles away, and I've no inclination why that seems to make everything feel worse. He flutters his hand a little in front of my face, as if he was contemplating wiping my tears but thought better of it. "Just, um, sit here a minute." Killian clutches his towel and takes my wrist to drag me to his unmade bed. "Just sit here and wait; I'll be right back."

I nod and watch as he swoops to pick up the discarded clothes on the stone floor. He disappears into the bathroom and returns fully clothed in under a minute. Notably, he still looks at me like I'm the definition of a psychiatric test subject.

Killian perches carefully on the edge of the bed. His beautiful eyes, which haven't changed at all, roam over me with trepidation. He clasps his hands in front of him, opens his mouth, then closes it again. I persist in staring at him from beyond the cracks in my fingers, which are splayed across my face. After a contemplative moment, he reaches over the bed and tugs a blanket over my quivering shoulders. I flinch a little, but the warmth of the fleece pushes me to abandon my hiding place behind my hands. I claw the fabric around me and sigh into the fluffy cocoon.

"You eventually get used to the cold." His lips twist up into a crooked grimace. "But I wouldn't recommend runnin' about in a flimsy dress; you'll catch your death."

"And I wouldn't recommend running around butt naked." I scowl petulantly at him, his sly smirk the only response.

His lack of words unnerves me. I bundle the blanket around me tighter and eyeball him with as much uncomfortable anger as I can muster.

"In all fairness, I wasn't expecting company. How on earth did you get in?"

I squirm a little, feeling disarmed by his soft voice and lack of anger at my rather unforgivable rant-slash-emotional-outburst. After all, I did kind of break in.

I nod toward the alcove. "The wall." Killian follows my line of vision and then snaps his head back to mine with a quizzical frown. "I found a secret door in my bathroom, and curiosity got the better of me, so here I am. Surprise."

"Consider me surprised," he says, and I cringe even further into the borrowed blanket.

"I am sorry about that display." I sniff and scratch the nonexistent itch on my forearm.

"I'm sorry. I should've tried to get word to you before now." Killian's shoulders tense. "But it isn't easy when you're under house arrest and the guard mutts take shifts outside your front door."

"Oh," is my eloquent reply. He really is in trouble.

"Though, I never actually considered using the old servants' passageways." He gives an approving nod. "Then again, I didn't want to just arrive in your bathroom. Heaven forbid that you might've been in a compromising position."

The heat rises up my neck and all the way to the tips of my ears. I bring my knees up to my chest and, with a groan, bury my face there. A case of sudden amnesia would be great right now. Killian chuckles, and I can't quite decide if that makes my embarrassment less or more.

"I didn't think anyone could live this far into a dingy old castle," I say in a muffled voice, still unable to look him in the eyes. "I thought I'd find cellars or a kitchen or even an escape route. Not your personal cell."

"Oh, now, cell is a little harsh." He sucks in a sharp breath. "This is my very own dormitory. I think it is rather homey; much nicer than your fancy apartment. I quite like my lack of feathered pillows and working radiators."

"You know what? I would totally trade you." I risk a peek, relieved to find his forest eyes still twinkling with good humor.

"Nah, this has always been my pad." Killian shakes his head, those smooth dark lengths catching in his tangled eyelashes. I still can't process how much he's changed. It's like all the soulful beauty in his eyes has spilled out over his flesh, and I wonder if I could truly be as warm and inviting as he looks right now.

I know I've stared way too long when Killian waves his hand in front of my face. I jerk back a little and give a nervous cough. "So, um, you lived here before?" I fidget with the sleeves of my cardigan, redirecting my gaze.

"Yes." His eyes are still trained on me, watching my every reaction. "Same as you, only you were too young to remember. You and Connor were just babies; neither of you would remember the war."

"The war?" My curiosity is piqued. "What war?"

Killian's soft eyes harden, their shade turning almost as dark as mahogany. His jaw tightens and a mixture of anger and hurt creeps into the shadows of his perfected face. For a moment I feel like I understand that look. There are no words to explain that pain.

"Our home," he begins, his warm voice now rough with the sting of bitterness. "It was destroyed by a betrayer to the crown, and everything good and pure was wiped, save a few lone rebel survivors . . . and us."

I stare long and hard at him, contemplating many reactions. Somehow I doubt out-and-out laughter is the best route to take. Ugh, I'm sick of this dark, fairytale, fantasy story. I'm getting real tired of this, real quick.

"Lexi?" Killian reaches for me as I shove off the bed, tossing the blanket. "Don't you dare walk away from this."

At the alcove, I pause to scowl at him.

He lurches to his feet and follows me. "You know you're not human; you've known that for years."

My mouth pops open and sort of wobbles around a bit. Killian's intense gaze leaves me a little rattled, and his words hit hard, but he doesn't say any more. He strides to a wooden ottoman and pulls open its heavy lid.

"I don't know what I am supposed to believe, but believing all of this seems far-fetched." I'm both annoyed and curious that he just has his say with me and then toddles off to organize his trunk.

"As far-fetched as the monsters that killed your parents?" Killian glances over his shoulder to give me a meaningful look. "You were there, Lexi. You saw the wraiths that butchered your mother. You saw them take Connor when the evidence of what he was—what he truly is—was written in his blood. You were in the claws of one of those beasts. Tell me how you can ignore that."

"Stop!" I cover my ears as the memory of those haunting wails pierce my mind. So loud, so real, like they're in the room. "No." I shake my head, eyes wheeling around the room until I find the alcove. The cruel memories flash before my eyes, along with every sight and smell of that night. Without thought, I dash for the secret door in the wall, ignoring Killian's calls for me to stay.

In blind grief, I run, with tear-blurred eyes, with arms sprawled so as to feel the narrow walls. I just want away from this place. Away from the cold empty walls and away from the strangers who all claim to know me. I want to run as far away from this awful truth as I can go.

Making a left turn into an even darker corridor, I hear water running down the walls. I pick up my frantic pace. The damp clings to everything, but I don't care because that can only mean one thing. I'm close to freedom.

I crave the outside air like it is the only thing that can help me breathe properly. This whole castle is filled with choking dust and horrible memories.

My shins catch the concrete steps, and with a sharp cry I fall. My head smacks the stone, and a burst of speckled rain falls before everything goes dark.

SMILE

An intense light beams into my eyes. I wince and hiss, squirming away from it.

"Lexi, can you hear me?"

Oh for the love of all that is holy—it has to be him.

I groan, loud enough to alert Killian that I do indeed hear him.

"I will take that as a yes." He mercifully drops the flashlight. His fingers seem to work their way down my neck. I cringe in response. "Can you lift your head for me, sweetheart?" His tone treads a fine line between concern and condescension.

"I'm not your sweetheart." I attempt to shove myself upright but find my arms have gone dead from lying on the cold floor. The pain in my side feels like someone stuck a screwdriver between my ribs.

"Argh . . . what the—" With a useless slap, I end up back on the ground. A broad palm cushions the blow to my head.

"At least the mouth still works." Killian sniggers, and I frown in his general vicinity.

"Go away." I whine and close my eyes.

My head hurts and my ribs ache. I just want to be left alone, not berated again, especially not by him.

"I would normally, but my conscience won't let me leave you lying out in the cold." Killian slips his arms under the crook of my legs and beneath my shoulders. I give a sharp gasp as he lifts us both off the ground.

The sudden change leaves me a little disoriented, and the pain in my side spikes for a brief second. Killian relaxes his grip along the more tender spot on my ribs.

"All right, here is the plan." Killian rocks me a little. "You stay awake for me and direct me back to this fancy suite of yours, okay? Can you do that for me?" I give a weak nod and an agreeable grunt. "Good job, sweetheart."

"Still not your sweetheart," I say, though my jaw feels a little stiff and my head pounds too much for me to worry about giving him a dirty look.

"Understood."

Resting my head against his chest, I give a disapproving snort.

Though he still makes me verbalize directions, Killian finds the secret door that leads to my bathroom with ease. I assume it's his ploy to keep me talking. After all, there is a chance I have a whopper of a concussion.

After he deposits me onto my bed, Killian disappears, only to return with a cold flannel, which he presses to the tender side of my head. He speaks only once to ask my permission to let him check me over. I nod, the throbbing in my head preventing me making actual sounds.

Killian makes do with the light of his pocket torch. He flicks the light over my legs, probably looking for cuts on my shins. Though, I'm pretty certain any scrapes will be long healed. Satisfied there is nothing sinister there, he set his hands on my tender ribs, and I hiss.

"I'll be fine." I turn my face into the flannel, exasperated by his fussing. "We heal quick, remember?"

"You've been through a lot." His gaze flickers to meet mine.

We both look away in a matter of seconds, neither of us prepared to dredge up the memories. A weighted silence passes, and I get the distinct impression that Killian wants to talk. That he wants to stay and explain himself, but he doesn't really know how to go about mending the awkward gap between us. Truthfully, I don't know how to either. It's not like we had a substantial friendship before. But we have something, I just don't know what.

"I'm sorry." I pat the edge of my bed to signal him to sit. "I know you're trying to help. It's just weird, y'know? You don't look anything like the Killian I know, but you feel like him." I give a disappointed sigh. "It's confusing, and I'm not handling it well at all." I rub the aching point on the side of my head that only gets worse when I talk. "And headaches make me grouchy, and I've had a permanent one since I got here."

Killian elicits a soft laugh as he sinks down on the mattress. His smile weary but hopeful. His eyes never losing their depth of sincerity as he lifts my hand in his. The gesture takes me off guard for a moment, but I don't react, I only watch.

He holds my arm across his lap and smooths the skin with his palm. Where his touch sweeps my skin, I feel a familiar spark. It isn't painful but is enough for me to twitch back in alarm.

"Your arm was cut, do you remember?"

I nod, still a little wary.

"It was a cursed blade, and it is the only type of weapon that can wound one of us substantially enough to prevent our accelerated healing." Killian's eyes remain downcast as he gently lays his hand upon the skin of my forearm. "Most of those howlers keep their weapons dipped in a poison. It means a scratch wound will fester long enough to let poison seep into our bloodstream."

Killian draws his palm across my arm in that same sweeping motion. I feel the heat prickle the skin. This time I don't retract, and my patience is rewarded.

A vein of shimmering gold, woven with pearlescent white and deep purple, marks the skin where the wound should've been. The vein pulses with the energy flowing through it, making mesmerizing patterns so colorful that it makes me forget the uncomfortable burning sensation. My lips part, and I give a little gasp.

"There's an antidote for the poison." Killian's thumb sweeps over the burning skin, massaging it a little. "It's a type of dried clay. My mother would make it, and she never let me leave her sight without it." At that, Killian dips his hand under the neck of his shirt and pulls out a cord necklace.

The pendant shines against the dim light of the torch. It's shaped like a silver tree; the trunk and woven branches conceal a small glass vial of gray granules. The vial sits in place by a silver ring surrounding the whole tree and its roots. A small catch hides at the bottom of the glass, hidden by the roots.

"It's potent stuff." He flips the heavy silver pendant around to show me the half-filled, funnel shaped vial. "Just a pinch will cleanse the blood from poison, but to do its job, it has to weaken our natural immunity. That is why you are still feeling rotten, Lexi. The poison is still being worked out of your system. Your bloodstream is looking much cleaner now." Killian gestures to the flowing and colorful patterns below my skin. "That's a good thing. You'll feel stronger soon. Hopefully less headaches, as long as you avoid knocking yourself out."

"Hey."

Killian grins a wicked grin, and just for that I pick up a pillow and prepare to throw it at his smug face. "It's not like I did it on purpose. I fell."

"You do that a lot around me." He catches the pillow, one of his bushy eyebrows shooting up his forehead. "I'm beginning to think I make you weak at the knees."

"Wow!" Wheezing out a few chuckles, I hold out my hand and gesture for Killian to help me sit up. "That is so cheesy, I swear you can smell the cheddar."

"Yeah, I admit that was pretty bad," he says with a regrettable bob of his head.

"Really bad," I tease, but continue giggling despite myself.

"You have a beautiful smile." The humor diminishes in his eyes long enough to let me know he isn't kidding around this time.

My watery smile falters. He looks away, and I catch the tail end of a blush as he wrestles his lips apart to try and rework his statement. "I just mean that it's good to laugh."

"I guess I've nothing left to smile or laugh about."

"Maybe not now," is his surprising answer, because I half expected him to launch into one of those ridiculous pep talks.

Bryce loves those irritating rants on how my parents wouldn't want me to be sad, and that I should honor their death by living and being happy about being alive. Clearly the woman has no sensitivity or she's just plain stupid.

"Killian, I don't have an estimated timeframe to get over losing my parents, so don't get your hopes up." I drop my head into my hands and blow out a long sigh.

"Why would you ever get over that?" He almost sounds shocked that I'd even say such a thing. "You will never, ever get over that, trust me. That is one sore that never stops hurting."

"Is that not what I am supposed to do? Just get over the fact they're dead because, technically, they weren't my parents." I glare at him, daring him to challenge me.

"Oh yeah, because you're an immortal Celestial and incapable of feelings." Killian scoffs and rolls his eyes as if it is a moot argument that he's heard a million times before and is evidently sick of it. "Lexi, they raised you, and for nearly nineteen years you believed you were their blood. Heck, I say they nearly believed it."

"Don't joke about it, Killian. It was all lies." I go to get up, but he reaches for my arm and tugs me back down.

"What was a lie?" He forces me to look at him, his gaze impossible to turn away from. I can't find an answer for him, but he doesn't slacken his grip either. "Was it a lie that they loved you?"

I shake my head.

"Was it a lie that they gave their lives so you'd have a chance, because they believed in what and who you are?"

Killian's stare only intensifies until I feel exposed and too vulnerable under it.

"No, Lexi, no one throws their life away for a lie. Sweetheart, you need to stop dwelling on what they didn't tell you and focus on what they showed you."

Tears spring to my eyes with the fresh memories of both my mother and father, along with the terrible and suffocating reminder that I'll never see them again. Sometimes I blame their lies for stealing them from me, and that even an ounce of knowledge would have kept them with me. But I'll never know that now.

"They showed you love." Killian's reasoning breaks through the mess of thoughts swirling in my head, and his words are enough to make me pause.

He shoves his hand into the pocket of his jeans and pulls something out in his clenched fist. "It doesn't matter about their mistakes now. What matters is that you remember you were loved by people who cared enough to make sure you knew it." Killian finishes his little speech by pushing something cold and metallic into my hand. "And if you hadn't run off before, I would've returned this to you sooner."

I unfurl my clenched fingers and let out a strangled gasp. My free hand rises to cover my mouth to muffle the sobs. My shoulders tremor when I look up at Killian, and an overwhelming desire descends on me to hug him, or kiss him, or both.

"My locket." I sniffle. "I-I thought it was gone."

"I found it on the floor; I grabbed it before the fire started," Killian says, but before he can get another word out, I throw my arms around him. He draws me in close and lets me cry my ugly tears all over his clean shirt.

It seems so stupid to put so much sentimentality into something material, but until this moment, I thought I had nothing to remember my parents by. Everything—our house, our belongings, personal treasures—were a million miles away and probably long since destroyed. Yet, the locket survived, and inside a picture of the only two people my young heart has ever known. It's everything to me.

"I know the Order makes out your parents did something bad," Killian says once my sobs have subsided, "but I ran away from this place too, y'know. Even I know it's no place to raise a child."

"Why did you leave?" I rest my head on his shoulder.

The thought has only just occurred to me; both he and Professor Donoghue, along with Connor, left Domnaill at some point in the course of the years. Clearly my parents went rogue, like Killian, but the professor chose a smarter way to get out. Or perhaps he had the ability to relocate. Either way, something made them get out. But what?

Killian pauses a moment to consider my question, his hand still rhythmically stroking my back. I don't quite believe he's aware he's still doing it.

"I left for a lot of reasons." Killian heaves a sigh before he glances my direction. "But mostly because I was young and felt misunderstood. I was willing to take the sacrifice of the flesh to just live a moment outside these cold walls. My father was a mortal man and my mother loved him, so I had to assume that something redeemable lived somewhere in the world beyond this middle ground. It was far from perfect, but at least I was free to think and feel how I wanted."

"So if it was so much better, why did you come back here? You could've just abandoned us at the house and kept your freedom."

I watch a slow smirk spread across his handsome face. "Because, Lexi, everyone needs something to live for." I frown at his cryptic answer, and he laughs. "I spent most of my life being the only one left, and then I had Conner, and then you. I guess I didn't feel so lonely anymore. I think it is only instinct to want to be with those of your own kind. It feels right, like home maybe. I'm not losing that again."

I sit up straight, a little shell-shocked by his honesty. For the first time since my life went to the proverbial dogs and I ended up in this crazy scenario, in a place I don't remember and with people who scare the living crap out of me, I suddenly feel a smidgen of clarity. Yes, things are bad, but I'm not alone. Not really. I understand what he means by having something to live for, because I do; I have him and Connor to keep me going. I lost sight of that in my anger.

"Killian." My hand circles his. "Thank you, for saving my life and everything else."

"No problem." He grins and bumps his shoulder with mine. "We Celestials got to stick together, right?"

"Ugh, that still sounds weird."

"You know what I thought was weird?" Killian levels me with a serious expression, and I cock an eyebrow. "Mortals. No really, total freak-shows."

I resist a roll of my eyes at his pitiful attempt at humor and decide to steer the conversation in another direction. "So, you remember who you were before?" I take a breath and ignore the cynical part of my mind that is screaming that my next statement is nuts. "Before the war that separated us from our world?"

"Oh, yes." Killian brightens at the question. "I lived with my mother in the forests, on the borders of the Veiled Lands, until the war broke out. I must've been six or so; time moves differently there."

"Huh?" I fold my arms to ponder his revelations. "So, you said your mother made that antidote that saved me. Was she like a medicine woman or something? And those things that attacked us, you said they were called howlers, right? Well, how'd they get through the Veil, and are there lots of them? Like how dangerous are we talking here, should I be worried? If we traced them, do you think they could lead us to Connor?"

"Woah, slow down, sweetheart." Killian chuckles and places his hands on my shoulders to push me back toward the bed. "Let's deal with one mountain at a time. You need to rest."

"But you said you'd tell me everything," I say and refuse to move, but he's pretty strong. Instead, I end up smooshed back against the pillows.

"And I promise I will." He gives a warning look. "But I have only a certain amount of time before the guard mutts do their night watch swap, and the bigger of the two doesn't sleep on second duty. So unless you want our little secret passageways uncovered, then you best let me get back."

"Well, this is going to be a problem." I hadn't stopped to consider the implications of Killian's enforced security as a barrier to our friendship and the key to me getting my answers.

"Not entirely." He smirks as he slides off the bed and picks up his torch. "I still have to earn my keep around here during the day, and there is absolutely nothing stopping you getting up and going for a walk around the grounds. I hear the Victorian glass house overlooking the lough is particularly lovely."

"Is it now?" I slump back on the bed, raising both my eyebrows. "And why exactly should I come looking for you?"

"Well, firstly, you have to be bored out of your mind sitting in this gaudy room all day." Killian saunters confidently toward the bathroom. "And secondly, who wouldn't want to spend time with me?"

"Everyone in Domnaill, and I'm pretty sure you scared off most of those college kids back home. Oh, and the librarian wasn't fond of you either."

I snicker when he narrows his eyes at my honest appraisal.

"Touché, sweetheart," Killian says, a wicked grin settling on his lips when I scowl at the use of that irritating endearment.

"All right, tomorrow at the Glass House." I slap my hands on the bedsheets in defeat. "But you better answer my questions."

"You got it, sweetheart," he says and slinks into the dark bathroom.

"I'm not your sweetheart," I say back and toss a pillow at the door.

Only silence answers.

THE GLASS HOUSE

It takes several attempts at relaxing breathing techniques and a stern discussion in front of the mirror to get me to step over the threshold of my suite the following morning. It isn't so much that I'm having a severe case of agoraphobia, or that I don't want to see Killian, or even the fact that I've absolutely no suitable clothing. It's more to do with the fact that I don't want to make awkward conversations with Bryce.

What am I going tell her?

I've effectively hidden in my bedroom for days and suddenly I'm washed, dressed, and feeling like a walkabout. I can appreciate why she might be suspicious, but I really don't want her knowing about Killian and me. Not because I feel I'm doing anything wrong but because I feel like I'm in control for a change.

However, my concerns seem to be misplaced, for by some monumental miracle, Bryce doesn't seem too suspicious when we bump into each other at the top of the grand staircase.

"Good morning, Lexi." Her eyes light with enthusiasm. "I was just coming to see how you were this morning."

"Uh . . . good, yeah, better than I was." I squirm.

"Good, good," she says with a professional bob of her head. "Perhaps you would like to have some breakfast, become acquainted with the staff and the rest of the castle?"

"Um, well, actually, I had breakfast," I say, though it's a slight lie. I'm a little hungry but not enough to make me want to sit through a boring introduction-to-Domnaill-tour hosted by the ever-efficient Agent Bryce. That is about as appealing as watching paint dry.

"Oh. Well, if you are feeling up to it, I would like—"

"Yeah, actually, Bryce, if it is all right with you, I just want to go for a walk." I give a wave of my hand in her expressionless face. "I need to clear my head," I continue, slightly unnerved by her unresponsiveness. Maybe it's rude to cut her off like that. "It seems like a dry day, and being outside always makes me feel better."

"Right, yes, of course." She continues to nod, using that irritating professional voice. I spy a little hesitation in her features but not enough that I couldn't succeed in manipulating her.

"I won't go far," I lie again, because I've no idea how far the Glass House is from the main building. "If you want, we can agree on a curfew. It's not like I have anywhere else to go but here, and I promise I'm not going to run." I attempt a halfhearted chuckle to convince my babysitter of my rationality.

"No, I don't believe that's necessary," Bryce says with a click of her tongue. Her eyes refocus for a moment, and I cross all fingers and toes that I've won this round.

Years of bargaining with super strict parents may have just paid off.

Bryce nods after a moment of silence. "I think a walk will do you a world of good, but I think it's reasonable to request that you would be willing to have dinner with the Lady Margot this evening if you are feeling better."

Drat. Conditions. Well, it could be worse. I suppose I can stomach the posh waif for an hour or two.

"Sure, that'd be nice," I lie for the third time this morning.

My mother would be ashamed of me—if she were here. I swallow a hard lump that fixes itself uncomfortably in my throat, but for the purposes of maintaining my cover with Bryce, I paint on a watery smile.

"Wonderful, she will be delighted to have your company," Bryce says and I can't quite decide if that was a lie too. "Well, come now, I can show you the best entrance to use for accessing the gardens. We only really use the main entrance for welcoming guests."

I nod and follow her lead, making mental notes on our locations as we move through the castle.

In the light of day, it doesn't seem so confusing. In fact, the old castle doesn't even seem quite as grand or as overwhelming as it did on my first night here. Yes, it's definitely a spectacle, but the carpets and rugs seem old and dusty. Even the walls—though cleverly disguised in expensive art—look tired and aged. I guess you can dress a place up as much as you like but that doesn't change the fact that it's an old, cold, and empty dwelling with next to no cheer about it. My various homes over the years may have been pokey and poor in comparison but at least they were filled with warmth and good memories. This place just feels like a crypt.

Bryce leaves me at a back entry, which is apparently a groundsman entrance. I suppress a grin at how my specific groundsman probably uses this very entry. We say our short and awkward goodbyes, and I promise to be back in the afternoon to be ready for dinner, which she says will be promptly served at seven o'clock. I ignore the promptly bit and surmise that I shall show up whenever I am good and ready. After all, am I not some noble, supernatural member of an ancient race?

With a snigger at my childish boldness, I skip out into the frigid winter air and inhale. My lungs expand to treble in size as the cold air swirls in them and wakes me up. The cleansing oxygen mingles with my tired body and gives an injection of much needed energy. Shoving my hands into the depths of the ugly green coat I found buried at the back of the closet, I shuffle along a pebbled pathway by a walled garden.

There aren't any appropriate outdoor garments in the wardrobe Lady Margot donated to me. Even if there were, they'd hardly fit my fuller figure. Today, I decide to make do with the scruffy tracksuit I brought from the barracks.

Shuffling around the open gates, feeling a little like a vagabond, I peek up at the landscape. Even in the desolate grip of winter I can still see the beauty. Bryce is right; you could live here a decade and still find something new and interesting in its wildness.

I follow a beaten path to a river that rushes by the grounds. Beyond that, the evergreen forest embraces the whole castle. I feel a little safer with such dense acres of flora surrounding us. I can almost believe, for a second, that those dark monsters will never find me here.

This well-worn path must lead somewhere, and I gather, as I trundle along, that the groundsmen use this route often. True enough, after a seemingly long walk, I register that the path leads to a more preened and decorated series of gardens. And behold, a glorious Victorian glass house.

I pause, mouth agape.

The Glass House is something out of time, large and expanding the length of the garden. The glass windows are so highly polished that I can't see beyond the luminous reflection of the gray sky overhead. My new eyes roam over the beautifully detailed dome in the center of the structure. Tilting my head in curiosity, I wonder how exactly it has been so well maintained over the centuries. Perhaps it's a new build. If it is, then it is the most awe-inspiring replica of Victorian architecture I ever did see.

A commotion to my left has me jumping and ripping my wonder-filled gaze from the marvelous house. A strange bird has landed with little grace on the preened bush beside me. I give a soft laugh at the befuddled look the foreign bird gives. Its long neck craned and head cocked to the side, it peers just as dazedly at me as I do it.

"You scared me, silly boy." He leans back to flap his colorful tawny and golden wings, exposing his bronze feathered breast.

He gives a shrill cry, and if I didn't know better, I'd say he looks rather cross.

"You are a pretty boy, aren't you." His eyes narrow into peeved slits. "Or perhaps a pretty girl?" I offer an apologetic wince.

In response, I receive a delighted trill of twittering musical notes.

"C-c-can you understand me?" I blanch.

The bird makes more of a timid coo in answer. I give a baffled shake of my head and observe the strange bird with a shrewd eye. I don't recognize the species, not that I know the first thing about birds, but I assume she must be completely indigenous to Ireland.

Her body isn't that big, more like a common hawk or falcon, but her long and elaborately feathered tail makes her seem much bigger. Her wingspan must be fabulous.

She has a long and graceful neck, almost like a peacock, but with a sharper eye and curved hunting beak. Her feet are in proportion to her elongated body, but I see the glint of her razor-sharp talons and gather she is no gentle songbird, though she sings as sweetly as one.

"Hey." I jab a finger at her and she lurches her long neck back. "Did you follow me here?"

The bird stares in silence, tilting her head left to right before growing bored and fluttering off the hedge to perch on a low wall a few feet away.

Throwing my arms in the air in exasperation, I lament. "Great. Now you're talking to birds. Well done, Doctor Doolittle!"

"Lexi?"

"Holy crap."

With a screech, and what feels like the beginnings of a minor stroke, I spin to face Killian. My friend is brandishing a rake and is kinked up over my eloquent use of words.

"What the heck, Killian?" I gasp for breath and clutch my chest. "Way to creep, you absolute freak!"

"I'm sorry." He chuckles and holds out his hand. "I thought you heard me, and I wondered who you were talking to. Are you all right?"

"Fine. I am perfectly fine." I slouch into myself and attempt to disguise the terrible heat creeping up my neck and into my cheeks.

"I am glad to hear it," he says with a goofy shrug, his eyes glittering with humor. I'm pretty sure he'd love to say more but he doesn't—wise choice.

"I'm glad you came. I wasn't so sure you would."

"Oh please." I sniff and square myself up to him, having to stand on my tip toes to meet his gaze. "You knew I'd be here. We have important matters to discuss."

"Direct and straight to the point." Instead of leaning away from my futile attempt at intimidation, he leans forward. "I like a woman who doesn't waste time."

"Um, well." I falter at his proximity, alarmed how his confident smirk has me almost—*almost*—grinning back. He raises an eyebrow and I lose the giddiness. "You made a promise, now spill, Hunter."

"Okay, okay." Killian gives a gentle laugh as he shakes his head, gesturing toward the great Glass House. "You wanna step into my office?"

I roll my eyes in the most dramatic fashion and follow him. Killian's smile stretches as he offers me his hand when we reach the nearly indistinguishable doors. The only thing that makes them differ to the windows is that the glass shimmers, like how a rainbow looks through a bubble. I slip my transfixed gaze from the door to Killian's hand. A deep and suspicious frown settles on my face.

"You'll want to take my hand."

"Why?"

His soulful eyes soften.

"Just trust me, Lexi, this is no ordinary glass house."

Suppressing a nervous swallow, I tentatively slip my fingers into his rough and callused hands. His grip is tight and secure, and for a moment, I linger on the sensation. I feel stable when he holds me, like I'm not going to fall, or be abandoned. My world doesn't spin so much when he's around.

Gently he pulls me toward the glass but makes no move to open the door. Then, as if stepping into a mirror, his body melds through the glass.

I gasp, making to retract, but his grip tightens and his thumb runs along the underside of my hand. The tingling sensation in my palm distracts me enough for Killian to pull me through the glass with him.

Shutting my eyes tight, I hold my breath. Perturbed that I'm passing though a solid material just as easily as air.

The first thing I sense is warmth. Not humidity or a suffocating heat, but a cocooning warmth that feels so lulling and inviting.

"Open your eyes," Killian says with a gentle squeeze of his hand. "It's okay, there is nothing frightening here."

Taking a settling breath, I swallow before letting my lashes flutter open.

A gasp huffs up through my lungs and out of my mouth before I can silence it. My new eyes bulge in their sockets, and my heart accelerates in my chest.

"What is this place?" The question tumbles from my lips as I step forward, the fallen leaves and warm earth crunching underfoot.

The scene is like something from a fairy-tale picture book. Some enchanted vision from a time forgotten. A place lost in a memory . . . My memory?

There are trees growing in the same misshapen, wild pattern as any natural forest. Their roots run deep and poke out from the rich soil, like great gnarled fingers. Even their trunks are wide, giving a hint to their ancient years.

The place is teeming with flowers of every discernible shape, size, color, and fragrance, but they are all so much more vibrant and beautiful than any flower of the world. Great, big, leafy ferns splay over every corner, and the shrubbery grows dense and succulent in the shadows. Even the moss and various species of ivy seem huge and much more alive than that of their duller counterparts outside this glass haven.

"This is hallowed ground," Killian says in a reverent voice. "The last of Eden on earth, or so they say."

"Eden? Like the garden?"

Killian shrugs and gives a sort of nod. "That's what the mortals call it, but it is a poor substitute for home."

"But man was cast out of Eden."

My statement comes out like a flummoxed question, and I internally curse myself for not taking religious studies more seriously. I knew I would regret it someday.

"Man was, but we weren't." Killian chuckles darkly and gives me a knowing look.

"Wait, are you saying Eden is real, and this is it?" My jaw still refuses to tighten from its permanently gobsmacked position.

"No, this isn't Eden," Killian says as he trots toward me, shrugging off his tattered, wooly cardigan and tying it around his waist. "The Creator took Eden away from the corrupted Earth, veiled from mortal eyes and beyond their reach. This place, I believe, is the last remnant of our people's beauty from the ancient world."

"Before they were made to leave?" I suggest, dipping my chin and eyeing him curiously.

"Yes." He nods and helps me out of my coat, which is becoming slightly cumbersome in this heat. "You see, the term 'mide' basically means 'middle' in the old tongue, but it's not to be confused with the geographical region in the middle of Ireland. Mide Estate is the middle ground between Earth and the Veiled Lands. Our home."

"Huh, well that makes a lot of sense." I bob my head a little, satisfied with that account.

I explore the beautiful tree that looks like something akin to a weeping willow, a few yards in front of me. "So," I say, as I clamber up onto one of its great roots, "how do you get to the Veiled Lands? Surely we can get there because of who we are, right? There must be like a map or something?"

"You know, Lexi, it's not like the Lonely Planet publishes guides to Celestial lands." Killian folds his arms and leans on the huge root.

"Oh, shut up." I give him a gentle shove. "You know what I meant."

"It's not that simple," Killian says, with a serious but saddened look. "You can't just enter the Veiled Lands; it's sacred and protected by creation itself."

"But those *things* that attacked us, they must've gotten here somehow. It can't be that complicated."

"It's not complicated if you know the various incantations, locations, and keys required to open the gateways." Killian snorts and shakes his head at my petty ignorance, his dismissive attitude irritating me. "If I had knowledge of those things, do you think I'd still be here?"

"Why are you here then?" I snipe, my patience with these stories is beginning to wear thin. I still don't get why he bothers to help me if there is no actual way to help.

"Because, Lexi, I am only half of what you are." Hurt rips across his features. "I don't have the right or the abilities you were born with. My mother was one of the Celestial people, but my father was just a man. Don't you understand yet? I'm just as much an unwanted runt here as I am there. It was only by my mother's love, and her good favor with our rulers, that I'm allowed to live."

I shrink from his pain, instantly remorseful, and feeling a smidgen guilty that I didn't put aside my selfishness to try and consider his story in all of this.

He starts to walk away, but I slide off the trunk and tiptoe after him. "Killian, I'm sorry."

He does stop when I call, but he doesn't turn around. Instead, I watch the muscles in his back bunch up under his shirt, where he works to relax them. After a few seconds he lets out a steadying breath.

"It's all right." His voice is flat, his face turned a little toward me. "It's a sore point of discussion. It's not your fault. You didn't know."

"But I'm still sorry." I catch up with him in time to stretch my fingers out so they tangle loosely with his. "I guess I feel like if I can get Connor back then everything that happened, the fire, my parents' death, you ending up back here against your will, would be worth it, y'know?"

Killian doesn't answer, but I note how his gaze lingers on our interlocked fingers. I work to hold back the tears pooling in my eyes again.

"Like, if I hadn't gone after you for answers, or just left Connor alone, if I hadn't messed up so epically that I destroyed everything. Look, I'm sorry. I never meant for any of this to happen, and I never meant to uproot your life and get you embroiled in this disaster. That was never my intent—"

"Lexi." Killian says my name in the strangest tone, something above a whisper, but nearly like a whine. I register I'm sniffling back sobs when he turns around, his hand tightening around mine.

"This is so embarrassing," I snivel as great, watery tears start squeezing out of my eyes and running down my flushed cheeks. "I'm pretty sure this is like the tenth time I have cried in front of you."

"Do you ever not have something to say?" Killian half laughs as he shakes his head, his voice still stuck in that strange note. "None of this is your fault, and me being here is my own choice, not yours. Stop taking credit for my bad decisions."

I give a strained chuckle and sniff back a rather disgusting sob in response. He grins, but his eyes remain heavy and deep with sadness. It's a look I think I'm beginning to understand.

He brushes away a tear. "No, really, I like that my presence seriously pisses these guys off. You've no idea how satisfying it is to be a perpetual pain in the rear, but sweetheart, stop blaming yourself. You're killing me."

"I'm going to let that sweetheart slip because I really can't deal with us not talking right now."

"Jeez, you really are too sensitive."

"You have no idea."

He throws his arms around my shoulders, pulling me in for a hug. At first the gesture is awkward, but Killian is so relaxed and warm that I accept his proximity. I wrap my arms around his waist, hugging him back with just as much assurance.

I don't feel compelled to push him away, even when I feel him tuck my head under his chin. Part of me rationalizes that I crave this, and that I really just need to be comforted, because nothing good ever came of bottling things up.

"Hey," Killian says when my sobs finally subside and I can think rationally again. "You didn't come here to waste time in petty arguments and tears, you came for answers."

"Can we just rewind and start over." I make an counterclockwise winding motion with my fingers.

"Yeah, let's just chalk that outburst up to the both of us being a little stressed."

I nod along in agreement. "Thank you." I drop my gaze to my sneakers, my head bobbing dejectedly. "I'm really not the best version of myself at the moment."

"I think you are a pretty brilliant version of yourself." His eyes crinkle around the edges as he beams right back at me. I'm not sure if he's teasing me or not. So in lieu of an actual response, I just fidget.

With a smirk, he turns and walks deeper into the Glass House forest, gesturing with his chin for me to follow. I sort of watch him stride off, admiring how tall he is, and how he looks like he could easily be a young tree in this weird but wonderful place. It's like he was born out of the earth. His teak skin, his strong limbs, those eyes that seem to capture every green, brown, and gray hue of nature.

I realize that I've been staring way longer than socially acceptable when he pauses and gives me an impatient look. With a deflecting cough and shrug of my shoulders, I pick up my coat and tramp after him, determined to keep things on a lighter note.

16

DAGDA'S CAULDRON

For a peaceful few hours, I follow Killian around the Glass House, learning what I can from his fascinating memory. He explains that the house itself was only added during the Victorian era, to hide the sacred contents from an advancing society. Up until that point, there'd been no risk of discovery by the outside world.

He explains that the enchanted ecosystem keeps everything living and growing in harmony, without interference from Celestial or mortal alike. The ground is hallowed, blessed by our ancestors, and therefore no mortal can come into the garden without prior invitation. This little nugget of information has me falling in love with the protected privacy of the garden. I can cheerfully make it into a hideaway.

I get the distinct impression that Killian likes to hide out in the Glass House too. He babbles for an age about all the various plants and herbs that he has growing in this paradise. Herbalism appears to be a great passion of his, and he tries, with much patience, to teach me the different healing properties of the many species of flora in his care. It's nice to listen and watch, because it's familiar. Like he hasn't changed that much from the Silent Gardener. Only now, he can talk and tell me why his eyes light up over the growing things he finds in the depths of the rich soil.

"You really love this, don't you?" I swing lazily from a rickety old swing that hangs on the branch of a small tree, low enough to allow me to abandon my shoes and socks in favor of dipping my toes in the babbling brook that runs through this little paradise.

"I really do." Killian pokes about a patch of large leafy plants, their ginormous leaves reminding me of some kind of waxy cabbage. "It's in my blood. I am an Earth Celestial, or half of one, I guess."

"What does that mean?"

"Um . . ." He pauses and leans out of his crouch, scrubbing his filthy palms against his jeans. "Our race, they were originally designed to safeguard the balance of creation." He inspects his dirt-encrusted nails, then saunters to the water to clean them. "We have traits, or maybe powers, that are a manifestation of what element we were designed to encompass and defend."

"You are most definitely Earth." I chuckle, and he grins back at me with such delight. "Your natural green thumb is a dead giveaway."

I flick a little bit of water at him with my toe; he dodges it, but manages to splash me in return.

"I wonder what mine is."

"You'll not know until you start accepting who you are, Lexi."

Killian's words, though kind, feel chastising. He slides away from the water to kneel by me. With his arms outstretched, he takes a strong grip of the ropes that hold up the narrow bit of wood.

"What?" I grin at him, half expecting him to add a sarcastic remark.

"Have you even looked at your own reflection since you arrived here?"

He already knows the answer. I avoid mirrors at all costs. I'm pretty sure my dodgy ponytail gives testament to that sad fact.

He gives me that irritating smirk. The urge to knee him in the chest is overpowering, but before I can react at all, he tips me off the swing.

"Come on, let's get this over with."

"What? No!" I try to cling to the ropes, but he grabs both my arms and hauls me off. "Killian, seriously, I don't want to do this yet. I'm not ready. What if I don't like what I see?"

"Trust me, you'll like what you see," he says with an over-confident tone that I don't particularly appreciate.

"Okay, well, what if I say I don't want to do this with an audience." My logical argument falls on deaf ears as he pulls me though the dense foliage. "Oh come on, don't make me cry in front of you again."

"Jeez, woman, do you ever just stop talking?" Killian spins to face me, his expression a mixture of impatience and humor. "I'm going to be honest, and you're not going to like this, but Lexi, sweetheart, sometimes you need a little nudge in the right direction."

"This isn't a little nudge." I grind my teeth. "This is a full-on drop kick into the deep end."

"You're such a drama queen." Killian grabs me by the arm again and drags me to a circular, black boulder nestled directly beneath the glare of the light from the domed roof. The boulder is huge, twice the height of Killian and equally wide. Smaller stones of varying sizes wrap around it, like they prop up its smoothly rounded planes, in case it might roll away.

Craning my neck upward, I follow the light where it streams from the overhead dome and illumes the moss and ivy that grow so lusciously from the gigantic, granite rock. I tiptoe over the grass, noting how the stream I dipped my toes in seems to originate from a source deep in the rock. Not only is there one stream, but three more small brooks find their beginnings in the hidden spring.

As we get closer, I discover that the boulder is not a solid stone but a hollow rock, like a basin or well. A steady supply of crystal water fills up the deep bowl, constantly spilling over the edges and feeding the four babbling brooks that section the Glass House.

"H-how?" My hands gesture in bewildered motions as I try to search the ceiling above for a way in which rainfall could be collected.

"Isn't it magnificent?" Killian steps up onto the smaller stones and leans into the deep basin. He holds out his earth-stained hand to help me up. I tentatively take it, my wary eyes still locked with his shining ones.

"What is it?" Something about the waters reflective depths unnerves me.

"A relic of our people," Killian says with a deeply reverent voice. "The mortal poets and lore masters called it the Cauldron of Dagda."

I gasp in recognition. "The Undry!"

"Mortals and their fairy stories." Killian scoffs and rolls his eyes in mock disappointment. "This is no mere magical cooking pot. The Cauldron of Dagda sustains the life of the land. The water never runs dry. My mother told me it was because the water is pure and from the miraculous wisdom of the Creator."

"Fascinating." I rest my hands on the shiny rim of the smooth stone. "It seems reality is far more magical than I was led to believe."

"Magic is everywhere, Lexi, you just have to look." Although his statement is marked with an ominous undertone, Killian tries and fails to hide his amusement. "Come, look into the cauldron . . . you never know what it will show you."

I quirk an eyebrow at him before gently shoving him out of my way. I'm not in the mood for his boyish teasing. My legendary scowl seems enough to put him off goading me any further, and with palms raised in a peaceful gesture, he takes a large, respectable stride back.

Blowing out an exasperated sigh, I prepare for what I'll be hit with when I look. The less logical part of my mind has concocted a mash of frightening images to taunt me. Visions of a banshee, a hideous crone, or even worse, a woman so frighteningly beautiful that I'll lose myself to her.

Somewhere in the background, Killian clears his throat, making his impatience known. I resist the urge to club him with the nearest available shovel. Little nudge? Humph. I suck in a deep breath and take the plunge— metaphorically speaking, of course.

What strikes me first is how perfectly still the water is on the surface of the cauldron. It appears as reflective as the most dazzling mirror, intensified by the shaft of light streaming down from above us. The stone of the ethereal basin shimmers like a night sky, almost like I'm underwater looking up. It's so beautiful that I nearly forget why I'm here, but slowly my eyes focus, and the reflection begins to waver on the surface.

With much relief, and no small amount of gratitude, I find that my long hair retains its natural strawberry hue. Although the golden highlights seem to stand out like sunlight crowning my head. I coil a lock around an ivory finger.

It's strange that the most significant loss I feel is my missing scars. The hideous thick bands that weave around my face and body have entirely vanished. Although that fills me with a euphoric feeling, its disconcerting all the same. Those ugly welts were a protective layer; they hid me from the world. Without them, I feel exposed in a way I never have.

My skin is perfected, glowing like backlit alabaster. The curve of my lips is familiar though, and my full cheeks still blush an unsightly pink. I still think my nose is a little too squat for my face. Those little familiar flaws are a comfort.

But the one thing that frightens me, the one thing that makes me uncertain, and the farthest thing from human, is my eyes.

My once dull eyes, veiled and partially blind from birth, are wide open and glittering with a depth I didn't know they had. The pupils are a frosty cerulean gray, ringed by an intense and vibrant shade of blue that crackles through the lighter shade, making it all the more terrifying. I have precious gems for eyes, and they shine with a hard, icy intensity that flickers in every direction.

I try to reconcile myself with the reflection of my strange eyes. My fingertips hover over the water. My brow furrows in deep concentration as I trace the outline of myself.

The pad of my index fingertip taps the water. The rippling tides distort the image, and in response, I retract my hand. But as I pull away, so does the water in the cauldron.

Droplets surge around my outstretched palm, and I freeze, hunched over the rim of the cauldron. Little ribbons of water dance below the surface of my hand, like how energy pulses on a monitor. I'm mesmerized.

It dumbfounds me to watch the thin ribbons take on a more fluid form. The watery lines weave over the skin of my hand and through my fingers, trailing up my forearm in a swirling and hypnotic pattern not dissimilar to my old scars. But now, instead of ugliness, those veins glitter with otherworldly beauty.

It's then that I sense something different within myself. Something old but strong surges and wrestles from somewhere deep down in my being. The feeling is addictive.

I feel unstoppable. Dominant. Unrestrained. I'm not restricted to this fleshly body. It's nothing, just a skin that I could cast off and leave behind in favor of the coursing freeness of the water that beckons me. The feeling makes me forget where I am, what my name is. That I'm even in the presence of someone else. I'm intoxicated by this primordial state. I want more of it, but there isn't any more. There isn't enough depth, or breadth, to this measly cauldron. I want a river, a lake, even an ocean to pour myself into.

Frustration wells up in my core as I try to pull more of the current of the water to satisfy my desires. I want more . . . give me more.

"Lexi!" An urgent call sounds in my ears, distorted a little, like I'm hearing it through a barrier of water. "Lexi, you have to stop now. You have to contro—"

I stop listening.

Control? I don't want to be controlled. How dare this voice attempt to interrupt me? I'm not something to be commanded—I'm free.

My mind reminds me of those fleshly limbs; a solid form I can use to repel this irritating distraction. I lift my hand, rolling it into a fist. The water snakes around my knuckles as I draw back to strike. I feel sure of the powerful surge running through my veins. I'm certain I will be victorious. Nothing can stand against me.

Nothing but the warmth of sturdy fingers that draw around my fist like the roots of a tree.

Suddenly my cold and indiscriminating nature is calmed, warmed even. And a new desire enters my strange heart. I recognize the other spirit that holds me—not restraining, but balancing. A solid and immoveable force. Instead of frightening me or angering me, it desires me, and I it. Now, instead of craving freedom, I want more of this. But what is this?

My senses remind me again of that physical form and its limited but useful functions. As the water stops roaring in my ears and my heartbeat calms, my vision returns.

The green depths of his eyes are what I see first. That green blooms a more vibrant color. It's because of me that they do. I feel it.

The second thing I notice is that I no longer stand over the cauldron. Instead, I have this creature I desire backed against the trunk of an ancient tree. His heart pounds in time with mine, our bodies tightly pressed together, his face angled downward. His lips part to give quick and startled pants. His every inhale draws me closer, and I smile in anticipation.

"This isn't you." The words roll off his tongue like breathy music. "You aren't thinking as yourself. You h-have to s-stop."

The reluctance in his stammering voice only thrills me more. He doesn't truly mean what he says. I give an obnoxious laugh.

His fingers retract from around my fist. Slowly, and with much effort, he attempts to withdraw. I'm abruptly devastated.

"Let go, Lexi. You can let go."

But I don't want to let go. Why would I return to feeling anything more than this simplicity? Nothing hurts here. Nothing is complicated. I'm free to live without thought or emotion.

"Please don't make me hurt you," he says, and I grow impatient with his demands.

A sharp pain slams against my hand.

I yell in defiance as I back away. Traitor.

Clutching my hand, I hiss and stumble until my body crumples onto the ground. The shock of the pain is momentary, and precisely what my hijacked mind needed. With a rush of clarity, everything comes flooding back with an embarrassing sting.

What did I do?

Killian groans as he slides down the trunk of the tree, a dazed look on his face. "I guess we know what your celestial energy is bound to now."

"Water." I pant and peer at the small nick on the back of my hand that is fast fading. "It's water."

"Sweet." He starts to laugh, and I can't help my infuriated glower. I'm embarrassed enough without him adding insult to injury.

He tosses a piece of sharp flint stone at me with a pointed look. "At least we know we are compatible."

"What?" I feel my skin burn red hot from the tips of my ears to the soles of my feet.

"Don't flatter yourself." Killian huffs and stands. With a confident smirk, he saunters toward me, hand outstretched. "Not like that, sweetheart. It just means our energies are compatible and in tandem." He winks, and the heat blazing across my skin intensifies. "It means we exist peacefully together. Natural friends, so to speak."

I don't accept his hand because I'm just so mortified. I know what I felt, and it's a little more than simple friendliness. But is it real? In the clear light of day, with all my senses intact, I'm not sure what to think.

"Hey, it's okay. You did nothing wrong." Killian gives my arm a gentle rap with his fingers. I flinch at his touch but, mercifully, feel no desire to jump his bones again.

"I think some courts of law would disagree." I fume and hunch into myself, determined to a keep a cool distance between us. "Maybe I should go back to the castle, lock myself up, and stay twenty-five feet away from any water source. Clearly I've no self-restraint."

"I think I can handle your lack of self-restraint." Killian chuckles, and I let out a strangled groan as I bury my head in my hands. "And in your defense, it was my idea to introduce you to the water-filled cauldron, which, in hindsight, was not the brightest idea."

"Nice try." I stalk back in the direction we came, though pause to glance over my shoulder, albeit a little sheepishly. "But you saw or felt what I did, so don't try to make me feel any better for that mortifying display."

"Whoa, whoa, whoa!" Killian jogs in front of me, arms outstretched, hands fluttering just shy of my shoulders. "Stop that. How else did you think you were going to react? You should be proud of yourself. Delighted even. Your power came to you naturally and wasn't forced. Don't you see? That's incredible."

I don't quite echo Killian's enthusiasm, though he does make me feel less horrible about myself. He's right; I've been taken unawares with the whole water thing. But at least I know something about myself that the Order doesn't.

"I'm still embarrassed." I cringe, keeping my arms crossed over my body.

"Don't be. I'm not," he says, his trademark smile making me feel less awful by the second. "You weren't in control of your own mind, Lexi, but in time you will be. You'll be able to take command of your power before you know it."

"Really?"

"Really," he promises, and I almost believe him. "You can come here; we'll practice, every day. I promise I can teach you."

"But do we have the time?" Worry creeps into my distracted mind as I stare beyond the protective dome of Eden. "Does Connor have the time for me to learn how to grow up and be of actual use to him?"

"We'll find Connor." Killian places his hands on my shoulders. "Time is always going to be our enemy. We'll just have to work against it. Have a little faith, sweetheart."

"And the Order?" I shake out of his grasp, lifting my coat and heading for the exit with him following beside me. "What about them? They're going to want something off me—off us . . . what are they going to do when they learn about my powers?"

"Nobody can force you to do anything you don't want to do." Killian's eyes darken with that familiar sorrow. "Lexi, they don't have to know. No one can touch you here, not without your permission at least. Your parents raised you to think for yourself. They can't make you believe anything that your heart doesn't recognize as the truth."

"Does that also extend to you?" I pause at the disguised door with its shimmering mirrored glass. "Am I supposed to believe what you tell me just because we share kinship?"

Killian looks genuinely hurt by my words, but I have to ask. I have to see if he will try to force me into believing him. I have to know if I'm being played.

"What does your heart say?" He gestures toward my chest, the sadness evident in his voice.

"My heart is broken, Killian." I clutch my locket where it rests against the empty spot in my chest, which still aches just as fiercely now as it did the night my parents died. "I don't understand what it tells me anymore."

"Then learn how to listen," he says with a crooked smile. "But I promise I'll never harm you. I just want to help, if I can."

"That I do believe. You have a habit of keeping me alive." I smirk and nod toward the exit. "It's late; I gotta get back. Her ladyship requests my company for dinner."

"I'll walk with you," he says, then steps over the threshold.

I follow him, doing it without his help. I'm determined not to be dependent on it.

"Do you think that'll be a little suspicious, us returning to the castle together? Won't they try to separate us?" I trot a step behind, glad, and even the tiniest bit happy, that he didn't attempt to convince me of his trustworthiness.

"They're always suspicious." Killian shakes his head and picks up a wheelbarrow filled with tools. "Bryce has probably been keeping tabs on you all afternoon," he says whilst I struggle to keep up with his long strides. "Wouldn't put it past her to know that you've already met with me and we entered the Glass House together."

"Oh please." I scoff. "I came out here by myself. No one followed me. Not unless you're suggesting she has some kind of tracking device attached to me."

"No, not a tracking device." Killian slows his pace, his eyes narrowing on something on one of the low walls surrounding the gardens. "Just a little snitch."

"Huh? Who?" My eyes scout the darkened landscape.

Killian picks a rock from the debris at the bottom of his wheelbarrow. Before I can protest, he takes aim at the pretty bird I met earlier.

"No! You brute!" I howl as the stone smacks the defenseless bird with a hollow thud. She gives a deafening screech and tumbles from the wall to land behind a cluster of evergreen shrubs.

Shocked by Killian's ruthless actions, I jog toward the helpless animal. The bush trembles, giving away that the little critter is still alive. It takes me all my self-discipline not to hurl a rock at Killian's head for being so cruel.

But, a high-pitched, rather peeved voice echoes from the bush. "You absolute beast!"

I skid to a halt. Either the shrubs are talking or the bird really does have a firm grasp of the English language.

"Ugh. That is a direct violation of the code, Killian. Ooh, my head. You better believe I'll be telling Bryce about your barbaric behavior, you mongrel."

"Ack, shut it, Kes, you overgrown chicken." Killian stalks toward the shrubbery and attempts to wrestle something from the disturbed leaves.

"Get your grubby, oversized, tree-trunk fingers off me!" The shrill feminine voice continues to berate Killian as he yanks her free of the shrubbery.

I give a yelp in shock, pointing wildly between myself and the petite woman in Killian's grasp.

"This is Kes," Killian explains, albeit rather grumpily, and shoves the small, wild woman before me. "A subordinate race of winged shape-shifters that are under the rulership of our people. They call themselves *spiorad na spéire*, or sky spirits."

I study the woman with no small amount of fear and uncertainty. Though she couldn't be more than four foot ten with windswept coil curls that bounce about her sharp face and boney shoulders. But her fragile bird-like limbs, painted in tribal tattoos, suggest a more dangerous disposition. Her eyes remain golden, and much too fixed to be human, as she looks me over with intense interest.

"Relax, she isn't dangerous, just a sneaky little snitch." Killian returns to my side and folds his arms.

"Humph. Speak for yourself, tree hugger." She tugs at her leather apparel, which barely covers her dignity. "I'm not beyond challenging you to a brawl. I'd like a fair chance at wiping that smug smirk off your face."

"I'm trembling with fear." Killian sneers. "Bring it on, bird brain."

"You are a severe disappointment to your noble bloodline," Kes says with disgust, before snapping her overly alert gaze to meet mine. "Forgive me, my lady, but I wouldn't encourage you to keep company with this stray. He's more trouble than he's worth."

Killian scoffs. "That's delightful. Did Bryce feed you those lines, pigeon?"

"I'm not a pigeon!"

"Whoa, all right." I wave a "T" sign hand gesture between the pair of them. Can we all just take a time out for a second? Give me a minute to digest the fact that a bird just magically transformed into a person."

"My apologies for the fright I must've given you, my lady." Kes solemnly bobs her head, but I don't miss the grumpy glare she shoots Killian. He snorts in disbelief.

"It's okay." I sigh and rub my forehead in an attempt to curtail the ensuing headache. "And I'm not a lady. The only lady around here is the Lady Margot, so please just call me Lexi."

"Oh, but that isn't a proper address." Kes fidgets awkwardly, her face flushing in embarrassment. "You are my mistress. I'm bound to serve you and protect you with my life. I don't believe it's proper to address you so casually."

"What?" I groan in irritation, bringing my palm against my face with a loud slap. "I didn't ask for any servants." I bet this was Bryce's idea.

"Oh no, my lady, it is my honor and birthright to serve you." Kes's whole countenance brims with pride. "That has long been the noble custom and purpose of my people."

"Great," I mutter and glance around the courtyard. "Well are there any more of your noble friends that are going to be following me around?"

"N-no, there is just me." Kes deflates a little at my tone, her head hanging shamefully. "If my presence is at all displeasing to my lady, I can leave."

"Kes is the last of her kind," Killian says, a small hint of sympathy soaking into his indifferent gaze. "Her kind perished in protection of our noble leaders. She came here with you and Connor, and despite her being the most irritating creature on this plane of existence, she's actually duty bound to serve you."

I guess sarcasm doesn't compute with this intensely loyal and sensitive creature . . . person . . . girl . . . Ugh!

"I'm sorry, Kes, of course I want you to stay. You're very welcome to serve me." I'm not exactly sure I mean that, but the way Kes beams with happiness at my request is enough to make me feel semi comfortable with the idea.

"Oh, my lady, I promise I shall not let you down." Kes croons and folds into a deep bow.

I despise the gushy treatment. I don't believe I've done anything to warrant it, but I'll suffer it. At least until I can figure out what to do with her.

"Right, well, I have to get back." My heart sinks at the thought.

"I shall fly ahead and advise Agent Bryce of your imminent return. She will be most pleased to find you unharmed." Kes hops from foot to foot. "She was so worried this morning."

"Wait. What?" I call after Kes as she spins away from us.

In two graceful bounds—and in a blink of an eye—she easily shifts into her beautiful feathered form and swoops off in the direction of the castle.

"I told you she was a little snitch," Killian says, and I twist around to give him a horrified look. I really am being tracked.

"How long has she been following me?"

"Probably just today." Killian chuckles as he rests a hand on my back. "Calm down. She's harmless. But Spiorad na Spéire are notoriously renowned for their loyalty, and for being sticklers for the rules. The Order raised her and kept her safe. She trusts them without question. And if Bryce wants her to keep tabs on you and report back on your whereabouts, she'll do it, thinking it to be in your best interest."

"Wonderful." I turn to stalk along the beaten path, silently fuming at my newly acquired babysitter. "Why doesn't she follow you about then, huh? Why do you get off so easy?"

"She does—or did when I was younger. But I caught on to her antics and set traps for her." Killian sniggers, and I pause to give him an impressed but still disapproving look.

He only shrugs. "Besides, she'll see you as superior to me. You kind of trump all of us. Whether you like it or not, you're incredibly special."

Somehow Killian's compliment doesn't really feel that comforting. It feels more like a warning. A really worrying warning.

BURNING HEART

I sit across from Lady Margot at the excessively long cherrywood dinner table. The intimidating distance between us feels more than just physical. Everything from my lack of presentable wardrobe options to my poor knowledge on dinner etiquette and even my very presence seems out of place next to this immaculate woman.

Margot's spine is so unbearably straight, I wonder if she wears some kind of corseted contraption under her chiffon blouse and creole skirt. Her dark hair is pinned to perfection, her makeup flawless, and her every movement so controlled and achingly graceful. In comparison, I feel like a fat, frumpy elephant with too-big hands and an uncouth mouth. I've slurped my soup, dipped my bread roll, and slugged back the revolting wine like a barbarian. Under Margot's judgmental gaze, that's precisely what I've felt like. An American barbarian lacking any hint of European elegance.

Our already strained conversation plummets into nothing but cold looks and curt replies. I try to remind myself that I should be grateful, that I should be warmer toward the hospitality of this woman, but I'm beginning to get the distinct impression that I'm not living up to her preconceived expectations. There is little I can do about that.

I'm just me, just Lexi Danu, an almost nineteen-year-old orphan who apparently isn't quite so human after all. What is she expecting? Aphrodite? Some flaxen-haired Viking warrior? Jeez, I can't even manage to use a knife and fork properly without stabbing myself let alone don war paint and shake a battle axe.

Two weeks ago I was making pots—nice, colorful pots—and that's all I wanted to do. Not defend the race of men against an ancient evil of biblical proportions.

Ugh . . . Connor would be so much better at this than me.

"How is the salmon? To your liking, yes?" Margot's accented voice draws me out of my cocoon, and I realize I've been poking the fleshy, pink meat with about as much interest as this dead-eyed fish.

"I'm not that hungry," I say, but spear a piece of the steaming meat nonetheless, forcing it past my lips and making a show of savoring the extravagant meal. "It is lovely though. My compliments to the chef."

113

"Pádraig will be delighted to hear of your praise." Margot's answer is stiff, and her pursed lips close around her wine flute.

I note she hasn't touched much on her plate either. By the size of her teeny tiny waist, I imagine she doesn't ingest much but air and alcohol.

"Is Pádraig your chef?" I hope my casual attempt at conversation might make this evening a little more tolerable.

Margot merely nods, and I resist the urge to roll my eyes. This is like drawing blood from a stone.

Note to future self: Never agree to this form of torture again.

"I'll have to meet him and thank him personally," I say, but she doesn't really respond. "I mean, if my appetite were a little better I'd totally clear this plate. It's nothing personal or anything, I'm just not up to big meals at the moment, after everything that has happened, you know?"

"You will be in time." Margot barely bats an eyelash as she reclines back on her chair. "As painful as death is, it is just another passage of time. It is what Agent Crawford and Agent Danu signed up for. They knew the price of taking on the responsibility of you, Alexandria. You should be proud; their death redeemed their sullied names amongst the Order."

"Sullied?" My voice cracks around the word, like ice splintering across a frozen lake.

How could my mother and father be sullied? They were beautiful people, kind, and I loved them. I thought they loved me; I thought I was more than a responsibility. More than a death sentence.

"Alexandria." Margot breathes my name like a warning. A patronizing and entirely fake smile tightens across her jagged face. "I will not partake in this doting lie they coddled you with. You were an endangered creature, and we have all taken oaths to keep you alive. Our debt repaid to the gods, so to speak." Margot shifts in her chair, sloshing the wine out of her crystal glass as she waves her bony hand above her head. "They were not meant to treat you like a child, especially not their child. But faerie children are so beautiful, yes? Who can blame them for falling under your natural charms? They were weak, and they lost their lives by insisting on giving you this mortal life, this delusion of family. It is no matter, for you are returned to us at a prime age. All this can be rectified. It only distresses me that you did not have more competent guardians."

"Distresses you?" My hands curl into tight fists around the napkin on my lap. My heart pounds so loudly that the sound vibrates in my ears, and for a moment, I can't draw enough air into my aching lungs.

"Forgive me." Margot shrugs, her uncaring eyes betraying how little stock she puts into her apology. "I am not expressing myself well. You are not what I thought you'd be."

"And what exactly did you expect me to be?" My voice rasps out in a broken sound, my eyes fixating on the water in a crystal vase at the center of the table.

Blood boils under my skin. A pain in my chest burns, and I find myself yearning for the powerful relief of being ruled by my element.

"Not so"—Margot's well-manicured nails waver about her head as she gestures to me in disgust—"human. They softened you, Alexandria. This is not your natural state, and I find it strange. We expected to be dealing with powerful beings who could defend us. Not a little child grieving her parents. But it is no matter; you will grow up now, as you should."

She rambles on in her drunken daze, her tongue loosening and giving away her true intent. These people don't care about me. I'm just some weapon to be used for their own devices.

"Please excuse me." I drop my napkin with deliberate force, then push my chair away from the table with a horrible screech. Sliding on my cardigan, I keep my eyes on the water inside the crystal vase. It's captured essence seems ironic. Who would believe that they could possibly hold something as changeable as water?

"Alexandria!"

My name comes as an authoritative command from her red-stained lips. I freeze, my insides crawling at the insinuation of the control she lashes over me, like I'll bend to her will. But how can I? How can anything fall into willful servitude if it isn't made to feel safe, or even valued?

"Sit, enjoy our meal." The Lady Margot snaps her fingers.

My eyes flash over her, anger accumulating somewhere deep within my chest. I can't stop it. I don't want too. I just let it explode.

The crystal vase shatters.

Shards splatter across the room, along with scalding-hot water and steam.

She lets out a startled shriek as the steamy haze of burning water douses us both. Her bony hands rise to protect her precious mortal skin where it turns a vibrant pink on contact. I never flinch as the sharp crystal and hot water slap across my skin. I only glare at the lesser being that cries and howls under me.

Is this what I'm expected to kneel to?

I turn on my heels and march from the room. My mind buzzes with hatred. I feel it then—the storm inside of me.

Water is everywhere too. It surges in the pipes, it trickles down the windows, it seeps up toward the soles of my feet from the dank cellars. It's tangible, it has so much power in it, and I can release it. I can render this stupid, stone prison to nothing but rubble.

Heels clack with irritating clamor against the tiled floor. "Lexi! Oh good lord. Lexi" What happened?"

Bryce's hand reaches for mine. I lurch away. "Let me go!"

The roar in my lungs sounds like the crash of waves. She staggers at the sound, gripping my forearm in shock, but I hate that touch.

My fingers snap around her blazer collar, and I toss her so hard that she slips on the polished tiles. The force sends her into the far wall with a merciful thud. A large picture frame rattles then falls from its hook on the wall. It crashes by her side. She yelps and tucks her chin against her chest, covering her head with trembling hands.

What did I do? This isn't normal.

I don't wait to see the true extent of the damage. I'm too much of a coward for that. Instead, I take the stairs and flee the scene of my crime.

Terrified of the wrath brewing inside me, I run like the wind, streaking through the hallways like a watery shadow. The castle's many servants cower as I blow past, the horror etched on their pale faces plain to see. Only a monster causes those reactions. Maybe I deserve to be locked up, chained to iron, and kept in a tower.

Skidding to a halt by the double doors to my suite, I throw them back and retreat inside. I try to ignore the terrified voices echoing in the hallways. I cover my ears and claw at my hair. I do everything, but the terror never quells. Not in me and not in them.

A shrill squawk from behind startles me. I spin to find Kes beating her golden wings at me, talons exposed. One look at the alarm in her eyes, and I scream in frustration. She has to leave. She's not safe.

Without thought, I raise a hand and catch her about her breast. The strike sends her flailing across the room. She crashes through the doors in a plume of feathers and terrified twittering.

The glass windows shudder with each of my ragged breaths. Consumed by the rage in me, I can only watch, unable to breathe, unable to think, unable to stop it.

Another growling exhale brings on the sickening sound of glass cracking. I let out a terrified cry, then cover my ears.

The windows shatter before I can fully protect my head. A few shards scratch the skin of my cheek. The wind circulates through the now broken windows, but it doesn't matter how much I gulp down the air, I still can't breathe.

Wind howls, furniture scatters, things smash against the walls, but all I can do is hold desperately to the barest shred of my sanity . . . to my humanity . . . if I even have any of that left. It's just as much an illusion as everything else in this twisted story.

"Is this what you want? Is this what I am?" I scream into the chaos, unsure whom I actually address. "Make it stop! Please, make it stop."

But it doesn't stop, and I can't figure out how to make it. They'll have to take me out, like a crazed animal. But maybe I deserve that.

"Lexi!"

That voice. It means something.

Arms wrap around me, one secure around my waist, the other across my chest. A solid and unmovable force melds against my spine. It holds against me. It gives me form, and suddenly, I'm not spinning out of control in a dark abyss.

"It's okay, Lexi." The voice, soothing, masculine, trickles through the roar in my ears. The command authoritative but not controlling. I listen like my life depends on it. Truthfully, it probably does.

"I've got you. Don't be afraid. You've got this, sweetheart."

Killian.

I want to shout his name, but I still can't find my breath. I'm choking on the pain, but he holds me tighter still.

He gives me a firm shake. "Breathe, Lexi, just breathe." His lips scrape at my ear, his breath hot on my neck. His stubble grazes my cheek. His lengths of hair tickle me.

I trust all those little things.

He is real. He won't let me go.

Killian's palm spreads across my chest, the gentle force pushing me against his so I feel his steady breath. It rises and falls, unfazed and entirely unlike the erratic pattern of my own. I breathe in deep, matching the pressure of his hand on my chest, and like magic, my lungs open and fill with calming air.

I focus on nothing but the steady rise and fall of Killian's chest. The perfectly rooted sound of his beating heart creating a calm rhythm that makes everything slow down.

"It's okay," he keeps promising me, a tinge of exhaustion in his voice. "I'm right here. I've got you. You're safe."

"Don't let me go."

I find I'm trembling when the initial surge of energy ebbs away. It leaves me as weak and listless as the tiny droplets of rain that seep tiredly from the window ledges. It's rather unnerving how powerful water can be in one moment and how utterly still and ineffectual in the next.

"I'm not letting go, Lexi. I never stopped." He swears it, but I feel myself slide through his grasp.

Instead of letting me collapse to the ground in my exhaustion, he keeps his promise. We both fall together, or more so, he guides me to the ground, pillowing my landing. I'm a dead weight in his arms, and he gradually gives way, carefully keeping my head protected on his forearm as I lie pinned beneath him.

The two of us breathe deeply, our foreheads touching. His beautiful green eyes shine with vibrancy through the darkness of this terrible place, and I register he must've expended some power of his own to curtail the chaos of mine. I reach up my fingertips to touch his cheek.

"You didn't let go," I say, my voice all horrible and husky.

"Neither did you," he says, his voice something just above a breathless whisper.

And then I remember the plane. His hand outstretched to mine. The silent plea to hold on to him. I haven't stopped. Something cracks within me, and fresh tears gently slide down my cheeks in quiet release. He's never let go.

The horrific bang of my suite doors shatters the stillness.

"What is this?" An unfamiliar intruder shouts. "You disgusting animal! Vile heathen!"

I cringe at the words; no doubt I deserve them. That display can only be considered rabid. However, instead of burly men wrapping me up chains and dragging me off to join Killian in the cellars, I'm shocked when Killian's posture stiffens.

"Filthy dog!" Another roars.

A hard fist collides with Killian's jaw and another knots his hair and trails him off me.

I just about manage to pull myself upright in time to see two men smash Killian against the nearest wall. They rip into him with a brutal assault of punches, but he doesn't defend himself. Why won't he stop them?

"Lexi! Oh my god, what did he do?" Bryce's shrill voice splits through my ears, horror and sympathy swimming in her eyes where she kneels beside me.

"What? He didn't—" My confused gaze flits over my body, and then I see it.

My ill-fitting dress is shoved about my hips, the bust line misshapen and almost exposing my tatty gray bra. There is a bruise on my thigh, which I probably sustained from the fall, but it's nothing more than a yellow mark. Surely nothing to worry about. Except perhaps . . .

The realization hits. "No! Let him go!"

Clawing at the soaked fabric of my bust, I stagger, trembling with the concentration to push power into my jelly-like bones. Killian jerks his head upward at the sound of my voice just in time to receive another crack to the jaw. He winces in pain but says nothing of his innocence. Would they believe him anyway?

"Stop it!" I stomp toward the two men who are clearly intent on ignoring me. "I demand you stop this. He's innocent."

I reach for the closest guard's hand, but he accidentally brings his elbow back too fast and catches my jaw. With a sharp hiss, I stagger backward, clutching my face as a fluster of colorful feathers and angry chittering blows past.

Kes launches at the man, pecking him with venomous anger. He bats her away with his thick hand, but Killian's fist connects with his throat before he can do Kes any serious damage.

With an almighty thud, the guard lands on the cold floor, a hand clawed at his neck and gargling nonsense. Killian steps over the man, and Bryce lets out a shriek and calls for help. He just stares at her, like she's a complete lunatic, before he crosses the short distance to find me.

He cradles my jaw in his hand, brow creasing in worry, as he smooths back the hair from my face. I shake my head and give him a gentle smile. I'm not hurt, he doesn't need to upset himself. Apart from a dribble of blood below his lip, he doesn't look that bad either, considering the brutality of the assault. It occurs to me then how truly strong he is. It is almost frightening.

Kes hops awkwardly to my side, her wing cocked uncomfortably. I gasp and reach for her, but Killian beats me to it. He stoops down and offers her his shoulder, which she gingerly steps onto, being careful not to jostle her drooped wing.

"Oh, Kes, I'm so sorry," I manage through my stiff jaw. She chitters a little, head bobbing as if to say she's fine. She isn't angry at me at least, but I still feel incredibly responsible for her . . . for both of them.

They tried to help me, they both stuck their necks out for me tonight, and this is how I have them repaid? One with a broken wing and the other beaten senseless. This isn't fair, I'm supposed to be their leader, their protector. At the very least they should be under my care and command. Not these morons.

My father was a good and kind man, and I can almost hear him advise me in the moment. He'd remind me that life is full of responsibilities that we can either run from in fear or take on with courage. As a child, he'd bend down to my level, and with a serious stare, ask, "Are you a coward, Lexi?"

My answer was always a resounding "No way!"

So what am I going to do here?

Just on cue, the doors of my suite swing open again, and Lady Margot enters, flanked by a few more guardsmen along with an uncomfortable looking Bryce. In fairness, I don't mind Bryce. She's thoughtful at least, but I distrust her loyalty to Margot. In fact, I distrust anyone who would listen to that woman; she reeks of dishonesty and deceit. My mother always taught me to trust my instincts with people. Right now, my instincts really hate her.

"This is abominable behavior, Killian." Margot sniffs indignantly as she steps into the disarray, still protected by her men. "You expect to be given leniency, yet you skulk around my home like a thief in the night? Attacking a female—your superior?"

I'm briefly shocked at how easily these people seem to brush over my abominable behavior but hold Killian's act of bravery as an indecent assault. I frown and glance up at him; his jaw flexes, and he doesn't drop his gaze. But he doesn't speak either. I gather by the hate in his eyes that he dislikes Lady Margot as much as I do.

"I'm not his superior." I place a hand on his shoulder and glare at the woman who started this. "I'm his equal, his tribe, his friend, and unlike you all, he knows how to help me. He has my permission to come into my rooms, as does Kes and anyone else of my kind."

"And who gives you the authority to demand that in my home?" A challenging smirk settles on Margot's pinched face.

"This is not your home, Margot!"

I startle at Killian's scathing remark, mostly because he has been so silent up until now.

"This is your husband's home, and Lord Domnaill is abroad on business with the Order. No doubt informing them of the guardian queen's return." Killian's weighted gaze lands on me as he shifts his shoulders and sets his chin a little higher. "Furthermore, Lady Margot, it is written into the oaths of this order that Alexandria, as her birthright, could take command of this castle and everyone in it if she so wished."

There is a stunned silence that lasts much longer than even I'm comfortable with. Killian holds Margot's gaze with such deep contempt, and I can't help but wonder what the history is there.

"Killian." I touch his arm, tugging him a little to draw his attention back to me. "It's okay, you don't have to defend me." I give him a gentle smile and he returns his own small version of it. I know how much he is risking speaking out for me. I know how cruel they've been to him, how cruel they are, but not anymore.

"It is ironic, really, that you should trust him." Margot's dark eyes flit from me to Killian.

I scowl at her, irritated by her clipped tone and haughty indifference. I would trust Killian a hundred times more than I would her and her cronies.

"Lady Margot." Bryce interjects this time, a worry line creasing her brow. "It's not a wise time to bring that up. I wouldn't advise that to be good for Lexi's stabil—"

"Perhaps not." Margot cuts off Bryce with a wave of her skeletal hand. "But she should know who she is willing to place her fledging trust in. Who she wants to have at her side in her efforts of diplomacy."

"What is she talking about?" I ask Killian, growing panicked when he closes his eyes and buries his face in his palms.

"Killian." I wrap my fingers around his wrists. "Answer me."

"You venomous snake." Killian's head snaps up to pierce Margot with his sorrow-filled eyes. "Don't." He jabs a finger in warning, but Margot barely flinches, her dead eyes roaming over him victoriously as he buckles further under her judgmental glare.

"Do you know who he is?" Margot directs the pointed question at me, but I can only watch in panic as Killian recoils into himself. "He's the grandson of Dian, the traitor. The very being that slaughtered your tribe and landed you here. The reason you have lived in hiding; and more than that, Dian is the reason your beloved mortal parents were murdered in front of you, why Connor is captive, and why you are all alone, Alexandria. Did he tell you that?"

I can't do anything. Can't breathe again. Can't blink or look away.

He promised to help me. I thought he was good, kind. He asked me to trust him but left out the single most important thing—that he knew who and what killed my parents. I've let him comfort me. I trusted him. All along he was related to that incomprehensible evil?

What if it's all a game? What if he's only wanting to get close to me so he can kidnap me too? Or worse, find my weaknesses?

The meager contents of my stomach threaten to crawl up my throat. I work hard to prevent it.

"Lexi." Killian speaks my name with such heavy emotion. "Lexi, I'm not him. I'm not my grandfather. I'd never let anything happen to Connor." He reaches for me, but I retract. "I'd never let any harm come to your parents . . . to you."

"Get out." My thunderous glower meets his, and he shrinks from it.

"God, please." He runs a shaky hand through his hair, eyes bloodshot and pained. "You know what Connor means to me. You saw my life, why would I—"

"I don't know what to believe anymore." My cold stare only rattles him further.

"Dian was a madman. He murdered my uncle, his own son. He would slit my throat too if he could. Lexi . . . please don't look at me like that."

"Like what?" I fold my arms. "Like a liar?"

There is only silence as we exchange weighted looks. I see the hurt creep into his features, and the shame of rejection is written all over him. I find it hard to care. He can try to convince me of his good standing, of his honorable nature, but he wasn't honest from the start. How can I trust him? I don't even know him.

"Lexi, think." Killian raises both his palms in pleading, or placating, I'm not sure which. "What does your heart tell you?"

"You don't get to ask me that." I gesture to the door. "I told you to get out."

He hangs his head as his two guards flank him. They grab his shoulders and shove him toward the exit. His pride burns at being dragged from my sight. I can see his anger evident through the tightness of his jaw, but he is resigned to it, and much to my annoyance, he doesn't fight it.

I hate that he is so noble. Even with my scathing judgment, he doesn't let himself down by blabbering out his useless defense. Somewhere in my broken heart, a little voice screams that my assassination of his character is unjust. Someone guilty would not go so peacefully. I choose to ignore that voice.

Turning toward Lady Margot, Bryce, and the rest of their measly entourage, I find that I'm irritated by their smugness, though quite aware that Bryce is not smug, just concerned.

"Get out!" I say again, my seething glare meeting Margot's suddenly rather offended one. "All of you, get out of my rooms, and stay out!"

I watch as they retreat, noting how Bryce reluctantly loiters by the doorway. Her lips are pulled down in stress, and her fidgeting suggests she isn't convinced I should be left alone.

"Can I get you anything?"

I resist the urge to retaliate with a sarcastic comment. But, before I can come up with one, a thought hits me.

"Yes, actually, you can do something for me."

Bryce perks up at the suggestion.

"I want Professor Donoghue brought to Domnaill as soon as he is well enough. I trust him, and I trust him to be honest with me, which is more than I can say for the rest of you."

"The professor is under investigation by the Order for breaking the stipulations of his oath in the care of Connor," she says in her ever-efficient manner. "He is technically a prisoner."

"Then I pardon him," I say with an equally efficient tone. "And I command his immediate resettlement to Domnaill. I'll take full responsibility for him; he'll be under my care. Is that understood?"

"Yes, my lady." Bryce bobs her head and exits the room at lightning speed.

With a sigh, I glance around the shattered windows and then to Kes, who is perched on one of the broken panes, her bright eyes watching me with intense interest. I suppose she's waiting to see if I order her out of my life too, but I don't really have the heart. She, at least, has been pretty clear about who she is.

"Come on, Kes." I pick my way across the floor, motioning for her to step onto my shoulder. "At least I didn't break my bedroom."

Kes twitters and rubs her beak against my temple. It's a comforting gesture that brings me to tears. Silent, thoughtful tears that slip down my cheeks as I enter my bedroom and close the door on the shattered lounge. I'll worry about this mess tomorrow. Instead, I roll up a sheet from the bed and use it to block out the cold draft leaking through the gap.

Pity there isn't a blanket that can block the coldness in me.

MOVES

I rise early the following day. It's a dull morning, both in color and feeling, but I have my mess to clean up. I work in silence, speaking only to dismiss the two maids that come to assist in the tidying. Help is the last thing I want. Everyone has helped enough, especially that stupid, deceitful, lying, all-too-noble, and utterly frustrating Silent Gardener.

My stomach twists in sickening knots. For some frustrating reason, I keep looking toward the bathroom door, like I expect him to appear at any given moment and grovel for forgiveness.

He never does.

It's around late afternoon when I eventually clean the mess in the adjoining lounge. An old, graying groundsman appears with slats of spare wood to board up the broken windows. We work quietly, and I get the impression the old man is frightened of me. This really doesn't help my mood or my gut-wrenching guilt. On a few occasions, just to diffuse the awkwardness, I'm tempted to ask about Killian, but my pride prevents me. Besides, do I really care?

Yes.

That irritating voice from the depths of my heart squeaks defiantly. I ignore it.

I watch the dreary sunset from between the thin cracks in the wooden slats. The fingertips of my left hand idly play with the chain of my locket whilst my right thumb traces the knots in the wood, eyes squinting at the dying light. I huff out a lonely sigh.

Why am I so terrible at this? Connor would know what to do. Connor can make things better just by existing. He'd find a way to think through all of this, he'd know what to say, and he'd decipher the truth quicker than me. He's a leader, a born survivor, and I guess that's the only thought that stops me from retreating to my bed. He's out there, surviving an unimaginable hell and holding on for the sake of those he cares about.

If he can survive this then so can I.

There's a gentle tapping at the main doors to my suite, and, begrudgingly, I lift my tired eyes to acknowledge the intruder. A small hand creeps around the door panel, followed by a tawny head of wild hair and striking hawk eyes.

"Kes." I breathe in relief, glad that it isn't Bryce or another annoying maid, rabbiting on about my self-neglect.

"I can wait outside until you're finished, my lady, if that pleases you."

Kes's timid voice touches my much-abused heart. I shake my head and gesture for her to enter. "I told you that you were welcome here."

Kes gives a small smile. I wrap my cardigan tighter around my middle and hesitantly close the distance between us when she steps through the door. I note her left arm has been splinted and she holds it quite stiffly. It feels a whole lot worse now that I see the damage in her humanoid form.

Kes is quick to follow my gaze, her super sharp eyes picking up each and every one of my reactions with startling speed. "Don't worry yourself, Lady Alexandria, it isn't painful. I heal quick too. I'll heal quicker in this form . . . unfortunately."

"You don't like being so human-like?" I ask with a slight smirk.

"I'm more useful to you, my lady, with my wings and keen eyes." Kes bows her head, and I squirm at the use of the title.

"I don't doubt it." I bob my head. I need to put an end to this uncomfortable notion that she and I are not equal. "Can you stop calling me mistress or lady? Lexi is plenty respectful."

"If that is what you wish." She seems delighted that she can adjust her behavior to bring me comfort. Not exactly the desired point, but at least we're making baby steps.

"It is." I nod, forcing as much of a reassuring smile as I can muster. After a few moments of silence, which nearly teeters into awkward territory, I gesture to her arm in desperation for something else to talk about. "That's a good job. Did Bryce take care of it?"

Kes shuffles her feet, biting her thin lower lip, and darts her weirdly focused eyes downward. She blushes. She doesn't need to say who fixed her arm now. There is only one other person with the ability to administer first aid to a supernatural being, and he is in my bad books.

"Don't tell me." I stalk off toward my bedroom door. "I don't want to know. Just 'cause he fixed up your arm doesn't mean I forgive him or trust him. Or that he is even allowed in here."

"If I may . . ." Kes hurries after me, panic written all over her distressed little face. "As much as Killian and I have an antagonistic relationship, I truly do not believe he would mean you any harm. I cannot defend his choice to keep the truth from you, but for what it's worth, I believe him to be remorseful."

"Good," I say sourly, folding my arms and ignoring that inner voice that harps on about his innocence. "He should be remorseful, and if he truly wants to make amends for his grave lapse in conscience, then he can earn my trust back by staying away."

Kes slows her quick steps and eyes me up, perhaps thinking I'll crack again. She might not be wrong about that. I do feel oddly unsteady.

"Yes, well, if my lady is displeased with his presence, I can ensure he doesn't bother you." Kes squares her athletic shoulders, the muscles flexing underneath her tattooed skin. She gives a resolute nod, and her eyes sharpen to a deadly gaze. I almost feel bad for Killian. If he did try to cross the threshold of my rooms right now, Kes would maul him.

"It's all right, Kes." I give a disgruntled huff and roll my own feeble shoulders. "I'm pretty sure he won't bother us, but if he does, I've no problem telling him where to stick himself."

I'm tempted to laugh when Kes nearly giggles, but she is so determined to remain professional in my presence that she disguises it well. Maybe once she gets over this superiority complex between us, she and I will be friends.

"My la—Lexi"—Kes corrects herself when I shoot her a raised eyebrow—"I have come with news for you."

"News?" I lounge back on the bed, disguising a yawn.

"Yes," She leans forward eagerly. "Sources have confirmed that Lord Domnaill will be home sometime late in the night, and no doubt he will wish to meet with you first thing in the morning."

"Oh?" I sit bolt upright, stress creeping into my posture. "Should I be worried? I did kind of wreck his house and assault his wife."

"Nonsense." Kes flutters her hands, dismissing my concerns. "No one blames you for last night's incident. You're only now learning about yourself; no one expects you to be in control. Lord Domnaill will want the best for you. To make your life here easier."

I frown at her statement. It feels stale. The only way this earl can make my life easier is by helping me retrieve Connor and then letting me return to the familiarity of my old life. Although, I'm not stupid. I register there is no going back now.

No way back to the girl I was and no way back to what home was. The only way is forward, into the unknown, and that, in itself, is terrifying.

Bryce interrupts breakfast the following morning. I'm more than a little disgruntled when she yanks my mug out of my hand and proceeds to throw a minor hissy fit over my state of dress and wild hair. After a short lecture about the importance of first impressions, I'm forced into a much more forgiving button-up dress and sensible, black courts before being hurried out the suite doors to meet Lord Thomas Domnaill, Earl of Domnaill and caretaker of Mide Estate.

So, the infamous "T" and I are about to meet. I'm ready for it.

I'm directed through the corridors of the castle by a suspiciously jittery Bryce and a reluctantly un-feathered Kes. Our meeting room is somewhere on the first floor, behind a set of highly polished doors inlaid with gold and dripping with old opulence. Bryce, before she leaves, tells me to sit on one of two matching burgundy leather sofas at the far end of the study.

Passing the ornate desk stacked high with thick books and maps, I find my gaze searching the peculiar artifacts that decorate the office. Art hangs on nearly every wall, depicting histories unknown to this world—or at least nothing I remember from a history book. Freestanding glass cabinets house all sorts of strange things; some hold rocks, others jewels, but most display intricate weapons forged in silver and some kind of crystal.

A good ten minutes pass before a singular door, adjacent to the one I entered through, rattles open. I suck in a sharp inhale and stand to greet my gracious, yet elusive, host.

Lord Thomas Domnaill is nothing like I expected. He's younger than I imagined; at least a good six or seven years younger than his spiteful wife. He's tall, handsome in his own way, with watery blue eyes that make me oddly uncomfortable.

He smiles, outstretching a thin hand that gives off all the airs and graces of a gentleman raised in high society. Yet, for all his pleasantries, he feels cold . . . dead-eyed.

"Lady Alexandria, truly it is an honor." He slips his hand over mine and bends to offer the pretense of a kiss. I offer a wan smile and remind myself not to fidget.

"Lord Domnaill." I give a slight bow of my head because I really haven't the faintest notion if I should curtsey, or even how to curtsey, come to think of it.

"Please, call me Thomas." He grins and gestures for me to sit. "We are equals here, my dear."

"Indeed Thomas." We both sit on the comfortable sofas facing each other. "Then please, call me Lexi. I haven't been called Alexandria since kindergarten."

The startling laugh that Thomas gives leaves me a bit befuddled, and I can't quite hide my curiosity over what he found so amusing.

"It seems so surreal." His faint Irish brogue comes through in the lyrical lift to his voice. "That you, Lexi, a celestial creature of creation, would have tumbled in a sandbox with ignorant mortals in something as mundane as kindergarten."

"It may seem surreal, but I assure you, it's very much my reality," My reply comes a little more tartly than intended. I don't feel inclined to apologize. Least of all for how I was raised.

"Yes, and for that I'm deeply apologetic. That isn't what we intended for you." Thomas reclines in his chair and leers at me through pale, lifeless eyes. Before my temper can rile at his comment, he tilts his head and holds up one of his hands in a passive gesture. "But you are safe and were raised well, and I'm truly thankful for that. Agent Danu and Agent Crawford's decision to take you off our radar was surprising but not unwarranted. You have a lot of enemies."

"So you aren't mad at them?" My eyes boggle at his softer approach, his almost understanding and forgiving manner toward my parents' massive deviation from their commands.

"I'm saddened that neither of them felt they could trust me to support their plans before the elder council." Thomas crosses his left leg over his right, his gaze never leaving mine. "I could've helped keep their names untarnished; they could've moved freely with you. Heaven knows I was able to do so for Donoghue. But Marie was an impulsive woman. Once she felt something to be right, you couldn't convince her otherwise." Something makes Thomas pause, his gaze distant, soft even, and he gives a half smile. "Marie and her husband were good people. Perhaps in another time I would've called them friends. I assure you, I personally hold no condemnation toward them."

Despite the warning bells sounding in my wary heart, I bob my head and take on a pose of meekness. "You would be the first since I arrived here." I stretch then flex my fingers, doing my best to keep my true emotions hidden.

"Ah, I assume you mean my wife made her strong opinion apparent." Thomas nods, then leaning sideways to a corner table, he picks up a large silver pitcher and snatches up two crystal glasses. "I heard about the incident over dinner." He pours water into the two glasses with exaggerated slowness. The cool water creates condensation to frost the smooth crystal. Clarity sharpens my focus on the miniscule rivulets that slide down the curvature of the glass stem. Streams of muted light cascade down my arms and twine through my fingers.

I tense. He's taunting me. He knows what I'm capable of.

"It wasn't my intention to hurt her." Anger and ice splinter through my veins. I want to scream and draw that water to me. I can make him choke on it, make him drown for challenging me. It would be so easy. But it wouldn't be me. It wouldn't be human.

"It's perfectly fine, Lexi." He gives a devilish grin, but the mischief never lights his leer. Those eyes never leave mine. They watch my every reaction with veiled curiosity.

Thomas finishes pouring my glass and hands it to me. His gaze narrows expectantly. An expert poker face. "It was an accident, and my wife is a foolish woman. She doesn't know the power she's dealing with."

My eyebrows lift in mild disbelief. I don't even know what I'm dealing with, but can I convince him that I do? "And you think you know?" I ask in a quiet, controlled voice.

His grin widens into a smile that teeters on predatory. Perhaps he does. "What do you know of the Order of Kings?"

"It's a secret organization bound by ancient oaths to my people." I keep my chin high. "My father told me I would be safe here with you and the Order to protect me. My father would never lie to me."

"But he did," Thomas cruelly reminds me. I flinch, and he doesn't miss it. "You were entirely ignorant of your heritage, and this place, right up until his death. A lie he masterfully weaved just for you to swallow . . . his precious daughter."

"Are you suggesting I shouldn't trust you or the Order to protect me?" My voice is traitorously shrill. I didn't expect this, and I feel like a snared animal, helpless before a wolf.

"Lexi." Thomas breathes my name the way an exasperated teacher reprimands a dull-witted student. "The Order of Kings is a secret society of enlightened individuals who can trace their bloodlines right back to the ancient kings and chieftains of Ireland. Our people, and yours, had political and peaceful relations; we accepted their divine right to rule the supernatural and respected their existence. In return, they educated us, taught us many wondrous things, and gave us great advantage in battle. It was a perfect alliance."

"I still don't understand your point." I shuffle nervously on my seat, wishing more than ever I had my Silent Gardener to defend me. Thomas barely acknowledges my interruption with a quirked eyebrow.

"The Traitor, along with his rebels, destroyed what was left of your tribe and all that was good and noble about them. Three children of your tribe were delivered to us eighteen years ago. A royal male child, a sacred infant girl, and a refugee orphan boy with no significance other than he was half of our kind and therefore our concern." Thomas pulls an unamused scowl at the subtle mention of Killian's diminished status, and although I'm conflicted over him, I still feel protective.

"Is your longwinded speech getting to a point of some kind?" I attempt to remain unruffled and do my best impression of Killian's bold persona, but I know Thomas isn't buying it. He's too relaxed, too comfortable, and I hate it.

"You have spirit," Thomas says, his wicked smile and watery stare never losing its unnerving intent. "But you lack patience, and in this world it would serve you well to have some."

I bristle at his tone.

"You see, Lexi, the relationship between our tribes was built on a shared alliance. Everyone profited. And as much as I would love to tell you that your father's promises were true, that would be dishonest of me."

"I see." I sit up straight when the realization hits me like a sledgehammer to the chest. "So, what you mean to say is, my safety and protection here is dependent on my usefulness to you and the Order of Kings."

"Broadly speaking, yes." Thomas purses his lips, momentarily cocking his head to the side to consider something. "But, my dear girl, were you not the one to exercise your right to be treated as a ruler when you set your demands before my wife?"

"What other choice did I have?" I present the question back to him as calmly as my thundering heart and shallow breathing allow. "One of my own was accused, your men injured my guardian, and however unintentional it was, the upset was over me and my worth to you."

"My sincerest apologies for the mishandling of that situation." Thomas easily shifts in his seat to lean forward, adopting a genuine and serious pose. He holds his palms toward me in a peaceful gesture. "Margot will be reprimanded for her actions and this will not be spoken of again. You and your kind will be treated with all courtesy and respect deserved of your tribe's honorable legacy. But the point remains, you do recognize yourself as their last living leader, yes?" The smile becomes a cunning sneer. "Of course you do. It is your birthright."

"You want my allegiance, and in return I'll be granted protection?" He needs to stop skirting around the edges. I'm not a toy.

"Oh no." Thomas shakes his head utterly abashed by the mere suggestion. "My dear, we are allies. It is written in blood. The Order is duty bound to fulfill its oath to your people in their greatest need. Your survival and the survival of young Connor is our oath. Your protection will always be our highest priority."

"But?"

"But you were the last of the survivors to come of age, and now the ancient power of creation is seeking the return of its guardians to restore the balance to our worlds. This will not have escaped the Traitor's notice." Thomas's dead eyes turn jagged, and I nearly crumble under the weight of the fear such a look conveys. "For the first time in eighteen years, you, Connor, and even the half-blood were physically together, and unbeknownst to everyone, that surge of ancient energy led Dian straight to you. The Veil between our worlds is at its most volatile. The safety and blissful ignorance of the world is in great peril from the deranged madness of a fallen Celestial, fixated on ridding the world of anything less than perfection. Do you understand? The Order can protect you from our world, from the enduring evil things of the supernatural if we must, but we cannot protect you from your own. Only you can do that. Only you and your surviving kin can protect us from such evil."

I can't breathe properly. All the power has left my limbs and it takes every last ounce of strength I have not to burst into tears and flee from the room like the coward I am. Each little step I take forward in my quest for understanding seems to only intensify how astronomically ill-equipped I am. What were my parents thinking keeping this from me? What did this achieve?

I stand abruptly, though my legs quake with the effort. "If you knew the three of us coming together would have caused such a terrible outcome, why didn't you step in?" Tears try with all their might to escape, but I keep them locked behind my new and far too expressive eyes. I refuse to be crippled further by every blow each new revelation brings.

Thomas remains seated. "Because we didn't know." He remorsefully meets my shattered gaze. "Donoghue neglected to speak of your arrival, nor did he admit to harboring Killian. You see, Lexi, you weren't the only one being lied to."

"And perhaps there was good reason for that!" I shake my head in rejection of all these differing opinions. I loved my parents, and I know they cared deeply for me, no less than the professor cared for Connor. "Perhaps my parents and Professor Donoghue disagreed with your plans on how to raise us. Your treatment of Killian would have me doubting your capability."

"Maybe so." He stands and draws himself to his full height. "But we all have differing ideas on the best way to raise warriors, leaders, and effective weapons."

"Weapons?" I take a long step back. "I'm not a weapon, I'm a person. None of us are a commodity."

"Yes, but under the wrong influence, imagine how deadly you could be."

His words crawl under my skin, worming into my memories and reminding me how easy it is to see Margot as nothing but a fragile doll. I could shatter all of them with a thought. The memory is too much, and with laboring lungs, I slump back down to the couch and drop my head into my hands. It's true. This power inside of me is lethal. I can't understand it, let alone keep it in check. My emotions, my anger and grief, they would blind me to reason.

I could kill.

"Perhaps our way was harsh." Thomas's words grow soft; his palm settles on my shoulder. "Perhaps your parents felt raising you in a family manner would ground you in those desirable qualities—loyalty, righteousness, wisdom, knowledge of good and evil. I cannot say which is better, but I do know that Killian is a skillful warrior, trained to obey orders and disciplined in both self and duty. In my opinion, we raised him well, and I assume Marie would be of the opinion that she raised you well. The fact of the matter still stands, we are on the brink of war, and your kinsman is held captive by the Traitor. What do you think he will do to Connor, hmm? What will happen when he unleashes the lad's power and turns it against his own? Against you? Against innocent people?"

I can't even answer. I know my friend. I know he wouldn't hurt a soul. He'd kill himself first. But I can't allow him to do that either. I have to get to him before Dian does.

I speak through gritted teeth, well aware that I speak for Killian and Kes also. "I accept your demands. But I will not harm Connor. I'll free him, and when he is reunited with us, we will fight your war."

"That is a noble and queenly demand, but forgive me if I find it futile." Thomas snorts, leaning back to swirl the glass cradled in his palm. "If Dian hasn't already killed the boy, then it is safe to say he's lost to us. The Traitor's magic is dark and deep. An ill-equipped and ignorant youth has no chance against such evil. Besides, how exactly do you intend on fighting and freeing him? The Veil is a volatile and ever-changing matrix. It cannot be crossed without sanctified vessels, which can be anything. Even if you could cross it, the land is wild and uncharted. You wouldn't survive."

"You don't know what I'm capable of." My hard eyes never leave his. "Give me the resources, the training, and the people I need to prepare for this mission, and I swear I'll succeed."

"And if you don't?" He frowns and crosses his arms, possibly hoping to intimidate me, but I'm way beyond that now.

I shrug and copy his stance. "Then the world as we know it ends. So we better not fail, Earl of Domnaill."

"We?" His brows lower and his voice darkens.

"We are allies, the Order and my tribe, and you were all sworn by blood oath to protect Connor with your lives."

His jaw flexes at his own words being used against him. "You certainly don't shy away from a battle." His stance relaxes, but only marginally, and that unnerving grin never leaves his lips. "It seems you were created to lead."

"It's how I was raised." My words feel strong, sure, and for the first time since I met this man, I feel the power shift between us.

I'm not his puppet.

AN UNDERSTANDING

Thomas is true to his word. By the end of the week I've acquired the use of one major archive library on the ground floor. I've also managed to attain a wardrobe of better-fitting clothes. I'm much more excited about the books than the clothes. These people lack artistic flair. I miss my colorful, bohemian style. I miss cowboy boots and floppy kaftans, but at least I have clothes, as dull and dreary as they are.

This morning I attempt to wrestle into a structured, sweetheart-necked, knee-length dress of a lifeless charcoal shade. The scratchy velvet is uncomfortable next to my sensitive skin, and I loathe how the boned lining sticks into my waist. If I didn't know better, I'd guess that Margot was trying to send me subtle messages about my weight.

"Oh for goodness sake." Bryce's hands clamp around my middle to tug the dress down. "Stop fidgeting."

I smirk as she fusses and swats away the nonexistent wrinkles. I'm warming to the woman; she's more caring than I originally gave her credit for. Of course, heaven forbid I ever say that aloud. She'd be most indignant.

"What's the rush?" I yank my fingers through the coppery ends of my hair. Bryce's expression morphs into one of absolute horror as she beholds my lack of immaculate presentation skills.

She bats my hands away and procures a comb to tease out my lengthy mane. "It's a surprise."

"I'm not a child." I snap the comb from her hands. "I like my hair messy."

"You are incorrigible." She groans, but I don't miss the little upward flicker her lips make. I do believe she is starting to like me too.

"All in a day's work." I snicker and bend down to snatch up the ridiculous heeled courts she expects me to wear. Hitching them over my shoulder, I plod toward the doorway with feet unshod, another pet peeve of hers. "Come on then, surprise me."

Bryce purses her lips and shakes her head, but her eyes glitter with amusement. She knows I enjoy antagonizing her.

She thinks better of telling me to put my shoes on and strides to the door. We tread the familiar route to the library, but when my foot hits the first step of the grand staircase, I can barely contain my cry of joy.

135

"Professor!" I fly down the last few steps and throw myself at my old teacher. I note he leans quite heavily on a cane, but he reaches for me nonetheless. "You're okay." I choke back relieved sobs and squeeze his shoulders. He's the only thing I have left of my old life—the only connection I have to my parents—and just that little bit of familiarity helps the constant ache in my chest. "I thought I'd never see you again."

"Frankly, neither did I." He chuckles, but that's when I see it, the sadness in the depths of his eyes. A horrible grief and loss that I know all too well. "I thought my fate was sealed until Bryce paid me a little visit, with a pardon from a certain noble maiden of the Veil."

"Well, whoever she is, I'm mighty glad for her intervention," I joke half-heartedly.

"That pardon comes with price, Donoghue," Bryce says from a safe and respectable distance. With a patronizing smile, she gestures toward the corridor that leads to my library. "Lexi believes you to be the only one equipped to help her."

"Ack, nothing is ever for free around this place."

Professor Donoghue catches my eye with his sly retort, and I bite off a smirk. Bryce scowls, but both of us ignore the irritated clack of her heels as she leads the way to the library. I shrug when the professor peers between the pair of us.

I keep my pace to a slow amble to match the professor's exaggerated limp. "She's a bit highly strung," I whisper as we follow Bryce's echoing footsteps.

"They all are." He gestures with his cane. "Bloody agents; they are all dull-witted soldiers, if you ask me. But she isn't so bad . . . she offered me tea."

"Yeah, she's all right."

The comment earns me another chuckle from the professor and an extra loud stomp from Bryce as she crosses the threshold of the library doors.

"So what is this plan of yours, Lexi?" His tone turns serious as we both pause by the open doors.

"I am going to get Connor back."

So, it's not so much of a plan. But I figure it's a start.

Professor Donoghue initially thinks my plan—or lack of one—lunacy. He believes it to be near on an impossibility to breach the Veil. He's tried for years. But after a few minutes of raving about the danger of such a quest, he stomps to the back of a long line of dusty bookshelves and starts to raid through the drawers. Bryce and I stand in awkward silence until he returns, moments later, with leatherbound scrolls under his arm.

With exaggerated force, the good professor drops the contents down with a clatter on a table. "We'd best get started if we're to be of any help to Connor."

Initial tensions subside, and the three of us sit down together to work. The professor proceeds to study the ancient tatters of paper with an invested countenance, which is a minor improvement from his earlier frown whilst Bryce and I divulge what we know about my fledging powers.

I dust over the events of a few nights prior when I practically tore the castle apart. I'm still a little traumatized by all of it. Bryce discusses the Order's executive decision to support me in my endeavors because, after all, two surviving Celestial children are better than one.

We talk in length about the various obstacles of my naive and extremely ambitious plan. More than once, Professor Donoghue expresses his concerns over my complete ignorance. As much as that irks my fragile pride, I know he isn't wrong. I can neither fight nor control my powers, and truthfully none of us knows the exact extent of them.

But what I do know is simple—if we don't act, Connor will die. Or, worse still, Dian will return to finish what he started. I can't allow any of that to happen, and I cannot allow another soul to die for me. But as much as Professor Donoghue agrees with me when it comes to Connor, he isn't so keen on the thought of risking my life.

"What we really need is for someone to train Lexi." Bryce cuts in with her suggestion, a clear attempt to distract the professor from his ranting over how he promised my father he'd look after me.

I'm touched over his paternal-like care, but, like it or not, I'm going to have to get stronger. Strong enough to defend myself, at least. Question is, how? How am I going to learn what I truly am in the shortest amount of time possible? We have books, maps, scrolls, artifacts, but no real idea of how to put any of this knowledge into action. I'm beginning to understand the professor's despair. Maybe this is crazy.

Professor Donoghue waves his hand to dismiss Bryce's suggestion. "There are hardly any huntsmen left."

"I suppose so." Bryce sighs as she drops her chin into her hand. "Any left alive are probably unfit for service. Marie and Fred were our best, God rest their souls." Bryce catches herself at the end of her statement when I flinch. She attempts to articulate an apology, but I shake my head. I can't handle that conversation right now.

Sensing my discomfort, the professor scoffs and says, "Ronan Hunter was the best huntsmen there ever was, and you know it."

My hearing sharpens at the name Hunter . . . as does the pain in my chest.

"Ronan was a traitor," Bryce says coolly. "Or at least an embarrassment. He forfeited any honor when he fathered that bastard child."

"He has a name." Professor Donoghue raises an eyebrow and removes his spectacles. "And he is no more a child than you are, and he's no bastard either. Ronan loved his son and the boy's mother."

"It was a violation; they should never have met, let alone produced such unwanted offspring." Bryce sneers in disgust. "Their little affair could've destroyed everything. They could've caused a war."

"But they didn't." The professor's agitation is evident by how furiously he polishes the lenses of his spectacles with a handkerchief. "Honest to goodness, is love such a crime to the Order?"

"It was his oath. We all took them."

"Maybe so, but Killian is innocent of those crimes, and his treatment here has been downright cruel." The professor scowls at the desk and picks up a magnifying glass again, returning to the map. "And Thomas wonders why I never told him of his whereabouts. Humph."

Bryce inspects a broken pinky nail and tuts. "I do question a lot of your decisions of late Donoghue."

"The lad deserved a bit of attention." He frowns at my caretaker whilst I try but fail to pretend to be entirely disinterested in their argument. Instead, I stare out the windows and fidget with my locket, twisting it over and over between my fingers and thumb. Darkened clouds frame the skies, alluding to yet more rain and no hope of sunlight.

"He's a trained warrior." Bryce gives an exasperated cry, the sound drawing me back to the conversation as she jabs her finger to the desk. "As close to a human weapon as you'll ever get, and you had him stowed away in your home, working in your school, around children? He could've seriously hurt someone."

"He'd never hurt a flea. He couldn't. It isn't in him to be so ruthless," the professor says followed by as much of an exasperated groan as Bryce gave. "And I do suppose you've never witnessed the true extent of the Curse of the Ancients. His physicality was diminished beyond your comprehension, Bryce. He was as weak as a defenseless child out there, and to be absolutely frank with you, I think he preferred it that way."

"He could still use his elemental magic." She folds her arms to sulk. "You should have been more diligent."

"Without him, I wouldn't be alive today; neither would Lexi." The professor gives us both a pointed look. "He is a credit to all of us. To both his tribes. He isn't half of anything, or if he is, then he is our better half."

I swallow a hard lump in my throat and glance out the window, guilt trickling like ice through my blood. Killian didn't deserve my anger or my disregard. I should've listened. It's a courtesy he would've afforded me. Instead,

I believed strangers. I should've known what it's like to be the unwanted. He's frightened, and I slammed the door in his face.

Ugh, I feel sick.

I rise and turn toward the door. I snatch up my discarded shoes, cringing at the thought of running in heels, but it's marginally better than soaked feet. I scuttle past the professor and my caretaker, mewing out my need for a short comfort break. They don't seem to notice my departure, their argument switching to whether or not it would be wise to charge Killian with my training. Bryce is against it, and the professor thinks she's being an elitist snob . . . can't disagree with him there.

It isn't until I run the length of the castle and out into the back courtyard that I realize I haven't the faintest notion where he might be. I haven't seen him since the night I told him to leave. For all I know, he could be locked up somewhere. I cringe at the memory, my words replaying in my head and sounding even more hurtful now.

As the dark skies predicted, the first drops of energetic rain pound down on my skin until it tingles, like each little drop shocks me with a pulse of life. For a few seconds, I'm distracted by the sensation. That is, until I catch the old groundsman hurrying to get in out of the torrential downpour. If anyone would know where a gardener would be, the senior groundsman would.

"Hey!" I slosh toward him, and he recoils. "Where is Killian? Is he in the Glass House?"

He points toward the courtyard and mumbles something in a thick accent I don't quite catch before disappearing into the castle. I resist the urge to yell a parting insult at him for all the help he was, but instead I follow his noncommittal directions and make my way through the courtyard to the far gate.

Much to my surprise—and relief—I find Killian pulling the iron gates shut all by himself. It is a small mercy that I don't have go traipsing around the castle grounds in heels just to look for him. The rain I enjoy, but crippled toes, not so much.

I teeter toward him. His shirt is soaked through and sticking to him in places where he's been sweating. Hard. His punishment obviously involved hard labor. This only adds to my guilt.

He throws his weight into hauling the huge, ten-foot gates shut, and I forget my point in coming here. The cotton of his tatty shirt clings to his frame, making it easy to see the extent of his physical strength. The now unrelenting rainfall only serves to enhance the muscles of his back where they flex and tense around the sodden material. I remember when those very muscles were weak and twisted out of place, and now he seems more god than man. It's intimidating, and truthfully, he makes me nervous.

"Killian!"

He startles at my voice, his head snapping to the side, and his eyes—my Gardener's strange and emotive eyes—convey a mixture of joy marred by something sour.

"Lexi?" He steps away from the gate, and I jog toward him. "What's wrong?"

I wince in guilt. It's so typical of Killian to be concerned with my welfare first.

"Everything's good," I say when I reach his side. "I just wanted to speak with you."

His jaw flexes, and my hope for a reconciliation wanes.

"I'm busy."

He stalks toward a stack of logs, which he begins securing with watertight plastic.

"Oh, um . . . I see. Well, can I help?" I blink against the battering rain and jump to grip the other end of the ropes he uses to keep the plastic coverings in place. Gusts of wind blast through the yard, making the job of securing the plastic all the harder.

"I don't think it's appropriate for a noble lady to attend menial labor with the common slaves." He nods toward the castle. "Go inside, Lexi, before they send out their mutts to restrain me for bothering you again."

Jerking back from his cold dismissiveness, I stare down at the rope in my hands. I know he is angry, and I try to remind myself that I caused it, but doesn't he know I wouldn't let them hurt him? In frustration, I toss the rope at him, catching him across the shoulder. I instantly regret it when he snaps his gaze to mine. Those peaceful eyes darken, becoming wild and unpredictable.

"I never meant for you to get hurt!" I shout over the crashing rain and cutting wind. "But you lied, and it scared me. I'm sorry, Killian. I don't know what else to say."

It's true, I don't know what to say. But I sure won't let him intimidate me with his frosty glare.

"It's fine." He turns away and leans into the wood.

The trembling muscles in his arms look all the more threatening as his hands clamp around a log. The wood whines and crunches under the stress of his grip, and I gulp—perhaps this wasn't a good idea.

"I think we should talk," I say in a vastly more quiet and cajoling voice. "I think we need to clear this up, whatever it is, and put it behind us."

"Just leave it alone."

His fist draws so tightly around a block of wood that it shatters in his grip. He turns away from me, but I step with him.

"No." I slip in front of him, my nose practically touching his chin when I strain to meet his gaze. "Killian, I'm so sorry for the way I spoke to you. It wasn't right of me, and although I don't understand why you couldn't just tell me about your grandfather—"

"He is not my grandfather!" Killian snarls and throws the shards of wood hard against the ground. I remind myself not to recoil from him. "Dian is nothing to me, nothing to my parents, and it is only by sheer misfortune that my name is linked to his."

I raise my hands and hover them over his chest before deciding it's safe to rest my palms there. Blinking up at him, with a look that I hope conveys the depth of my sincerity, I attempt to mend what I may have inadvertently broken.

"I know that now, I just had to think about it." His labored breathing relaxes under my hands. "I had to consult my heart."

I don't lift my eyes from his chest, don't meet his gaze, for fear that he'll reject any attempt at a resolution, but he hasn't snapped my wrist off for touching him yet. I'm taking that as a good sign. After a few moments of contemplative silence, his fingers draw around both of my trembling hands. I wilt with relief when I finally chance a brief glance upward and find his eyes are so much more placid and familiar.

"I'm sorry." Killian hangs his head. "I never meant to withhold that information. I should've known how it would have looked to you. But I swear, Lexi, I swear I'd never hurt you, or your parents."

"I know. And I'm sorry for not giving you the chance to explain." I'm well aware that trust is a two-way street; both of us need to make a concerted effort here. "The thing is"—I bite my lip and attempt to articulate my next statement without sounding like a feeble-minded damsel—"I can't get Connor back without your help."

"I told you I'm with you, all the way. We'll get him back."

"It's more than that." I glance down at my feet. "I need you."

He squeezes my hands in his. "I'm here."

My lip quivers as I hold back a gigantic sob of relief. I hate it when he does that. I hate how he easily forgives, and how he looks at me like I am just little old Lexi, making her social blunders, as usual.

"Why are you crying?" Worry creases his brow, and I flit between wanting to shove him in frustration and desiring to stroke those dripping wet lengths of hair out of his eyes.

"I thought I'd ruined everything." I sniffle and scrub at my eyes, although it seems pretty useless in the streaming rain. "You mean a lot to me, Killian, even before all of this." I flash him a tiny smile and resist the urge to rub the worry lines that deepen his forehead. "I don't want to lose my Silent Gardener."

"Your what?" He pulls back and quirks an eyebrow.

I flush scarlet when I realize I've let his secret name slip from my usually guarded lips.

"Uh . . . well, um, it's just . . . you didn't speak before." I stumble for words—any words—that might save me from embarrassment. "And you were technically a gardener. It kind of stuck. It's not meant to be offensive. I thought you were, uh . . . interesting."

"You thought about me?" A half smile tugs the left side of his lip upward in a roguish, albeit bashful, grin.

"Well . . . yeah." I'm certain my cheeks are so piping hot that the raindrops are turning to steam on contact. "Didn't you, um . . . ever think about me?" I almost don't believe I've said those words out loud, and what's worse, I don't know if I want to hear his answer. "I mean, like, 'cause we were the same. With the blood and stuff?"

Killian's grin widens. He steps a little closer and catches my chin between his thumb and finger, forcing me to maintain eye contact. "You never left my thoughts," he tells me with a voice so warm, my earlier shame ebbs. His grin morphs into a chuckle. "In fact, you have a tendency of messing me up, Lexi. I didn't drop that terracotta pot because of useless hands, you know?"

I balk a little in disbelief. Feeling flustered, I duck my chin and disguise a nervous giggle with a cough. Killian senses my sudden discomfort and, being the ever-considerate gentleman that he is, wraps an arm lightly around my shoulders and walks us back toward the castle.

"Let's go inside before this storm hits." He smiles gently. "We can talk later."

"Really?"

Curse my overenthusiasm. Curse his smile and his stupid, puppy-dog eyes.

"Sure. Let's say, supper at midnight, in your fancy suite, and I'll supply the feast."

"Sounds great," I say, ignoring the shiver that runs down my spine. "We've got a lot to catch up on."

"I bet."

He deposits me in the back entrance hall and attempts to rub some heat into my shivering arms. If only he knew the tremble has nothing to do with cold and everything to do with him.

OF BROWNIES AND
BOTHERED BIRDS

I arrange the blanket on the floor of my bedroom. Then rearrange it again for good measure and scatter some cushions off the bed. It hits me that this is perhaps a bit silly, so I remove them all—blanket included.

"Don't look at me like that, Kes."

Her head is cocked to the side and she flaps her wings twice.

"You were the one that said he wasn't that bad."

She coos, sheepishly narrowing her eyes as she hops onto the fireplace mantel and wraps her clawed talons around the ticking clock. One of her sharp nails taps the glass, drawing my attention to the time. I sigh.

"Maybe he's waiting for his guards to fall asleep before he can sneak out," I say, though my stomach sinks a little. Kes throws her head back and gives a wheezy cry. I can't be sure, but I gather she might be a little cross. "He'll be here. I know he will."

Kes hisses and lops down from the fireplace, then toddles off to her designated perch by the bay window. With a flourish, she outstretches her beautiful wingspan and flutters onto the large iron perch. I give her a disgruntled snort as she flicks her wing upward and begins preening it, ignoring me as she does.

Fine, she can take an attitude if she wants.

I glance at the clock again, for the tenth time in the past two minutes. It's now twenty past midnight and still no sign of Killian. With a dejected huff, I plod to the edge of my bed and stare mournfully at the floral comforter.

Maybe he isn't coming.

I wouldn't blame him if he didn't. Even I'm embarrassed by my motor-mouth admittance to finding him interesting.

I whine out loud, then cringe at the awkward memory of my social suicide stunt. Unable to stand the horror a moment longer, I face plant into the mattress and squeak incoherently into the fabric. Kes gives a baffled chirp, which only makes me cringe further into the sheets. Can't a girl die of shame in peace?

"Uh, Lexi?"

A soft rap follows his familiar voice. Mortified, I shove off the bed and present my guest with the goofiest smile in the history of ever.

"Heeey!" I sing in much too high an octave. "I thought you'd changed your mind."

"Sorry about that." Killian winces, the faintest blush spreading delicately across his cheeks, warming the tone of his skin to a coppery bronze. "I completely misjudged the time it takes to bake brownies; in fact, I completely misjudged my ability to bake brownies. You'd think it'd be easy."

Killian tentatively holds out a tin box lined with baking paper, and before I can blink, the chocolatey aroma of fresh brownies wafts my direction. Well, there we go—in an instant, he is completely forgiven. I haven't had chocolate in weeks, and by god I miss it.

"You bake?" I pry the tin out of his hands. "How unreal are you?"

"I don't bake, that's the problem." Killian slides out of the cold bathroom and into my cozy bedroom, with its roaring fire and low-lit aesthetic.

Oh, meep, is this a date? Did I just make this a date? Do I want this to be a date?

"Well, these look pretty great." I'm almost positive my voice is verging on soprano.

"You haven't tasted them yet." He collapses on the bed, letting out a moan of pleasure—a sound that almost makes me drop the tin. "This is heaven." He stretches the full length of the bed, and his scruffy, navy tee creeps upward, revealing just enough of the curve of his hip.

I swallow reflexively and bite my lip. I shouldn't be looking . . . why am I looking?

"I will admit, it's a real comfortable bed." I set the tin of brownies down on the side table.

"Yeah, it is." Killian sighs in contentment, using his forearms to pillow behind his head. "Mind if I steal it?"

Oh, heaven help me. Why is he so ridiculously alluring? I blame this whole water and earth, natural attraction thing. Yes, that's what it is. This isn't real, this is just . . . nature.

"Yeah, it's all yours." I giggle, then resent myself for sounding so girlish and silly. I shuffle to the edge of the bed, contemplating whether to sit or not.

"Nah, that wouldn't be at all gentlemanly of me." Killian shakes his head in faux displeasure, but a mischievous look lights his greenish-gray eyes, and before I know it, his hand darts out and snatches my arm. With one sure tug, I land on the bed beside him with a graceless thud.

"I can share though," he tells me as his grin twists into a smirk. He props his elbow up to rest his head in his hand. "Lexi, are you blushing?"

"No," I say, but my cheeks burn traitorously.

He reaches forward and, with his free hand, picks up a strand of my mussed-up hair and sweeps it away from my face. His knuckles draw across my fiery cheeks. A little zing prickles over the surface of my skin and makes me tingle, makes me want to lean closer, but that seems forward, possessive even. I don't want a repeat of the Glass House.

"You are a terrible liar." Killian laughs and shakes his head, making the loose ends of his hair fall into his vibrant eyes. The earlier blush on my cheeks crawls over the rest of my skin when his laughter subsides and he looks me deep in the eye. Too deep.

"Relax, you aren't going to lose it again. Or at least I hope not. You don't feel uncharacteristically angry, do you?"

I pout. "I'm not a raging green beast, y'know? And I don't have anger issues. At least not normally."

"Perhaps it's me that brings out the inner animal." He raises his eyebrows and sits up to stare me down.

My mouth pops open to reply, but I do believe my brain might've vanished. For someone who couldn't speak and still isn't the overly talkative type, he certainly knows how to make mischief with his words.

"Just to be on the safe side, we should feed the beast." And in his unruffled manner, he slides off the bed and reaches for the tin of brownies.

His devilish grin stretches wider, the expression so infectious that I feel my own lips move quickly upward, though I try hard to prevent such a treasonous act. If he sees me smile, he will claim victory, and I just can't have that. I might've forgiven him but that doesn't mean he gets off easy. Although, showing up with brownies is a clever move. I snatch one of the delicious, squidgy squares of chocolatey goodness from the tin and shove it straight in my mouth.

The rich, gooey, slightly underbaked sponge of happiness melts on my tongue, and without thinking, I roll my eyes in utter ecstasy. This elicits a not so dignified moan of pure bliss.

Holy saint of chocolate brownies, this is good.

"That good, huh?"

I swallow, narrow my eyes, then pick another out of the tin. "Hmm, I'm not sure." I purse my lips in a show of consideration. "I might need to try another before giving my honest opinion." And with that, I snaffle the second brownie with just as much joy as the first.

"So?" he asks again, and this time I nod appreciatively, both my thumbs pointed upward to signify my approval.

Killian winks at me and takes a bite of his brownie. Wise move. I was about a second away from stealing it.

"Gods, these are good," he mumbles in agreement between mouthfuls and sinks down onto the bed again, hand clamped tight around the tin.

"Ugh . . . you have no idea." I groan and make no bones of licking my fingers clean in front of him. "Tell me the truth, did you bake these just for me?"

"Honestly?" Killian sucks in a breath through his teeth and gives a dramatic pause before answering. "Technically, I didn't bake them. Pádraig did. But I helped, and yes, they were made specifically for you."

"Ha! I knew it." I playfully punch his arm, then snatch the brownie out of his hand and gobble it before he has a chance to pry it back. Killian frowns when I lean forward again, right palm spread on the bed between us. I flash an innocent smile.

"Gotta be quicker, Hunter." I launch my left hand forward to pinch another brownie from the tin on his lap. He maneuvers the tin out of reach in one swift movement. I give a disgruntled snort at losing, but don't give up that easily, and stretch after the tin.

In a whir of movement, much, much faster than I could've anticipated, Killian swipes my right arm out from beneath me. The blow so forceful and fast that I'm left unbalanced and nose diving the bed. Except, I never collide with the mattress or Killian. Instead, before I can blink, he wraps an arm around my middle and uses his weight to flip me into the middle of the bed. I let out a little gasp when my back sinks into the soft mattress. Killian's long body traps my knees, and his hand holds my right arm captive at my side. His other hand clasps my wrist above my head.

"Don't be greedy." He flashes a rather patronizing grin on his smug face. "There is enough to share. I promise."

A shrill twittering sounds from beyond my head, the waft of air with the flapping of strong wings alerts me to Kes's timely involvement. I give my captor a wicked grin as my feathered companion hisses and snaps. That'll teach him for being so bold.

Although, I'm not exactly worried. Not once has he hurt me, not even as he holds me still. In fact, I'm quite enjoying myself. Should I be enjoying myself?

"Easy, Feathers, I'm only playing." Killian release me, rolls onto his back, and raises his hands. Kes cocks her head and glares in disbelief.

"It's okay, Kes." I crane my neck back so I can see her uneasy movements. "It's just a game. I'm not hurt."

I receive a chittering snap of disapproval before she turns on Killian and hisses at his proximity. She hops forward and pecks the hem of his tee, yanking it with obvious irritation.

"All right, all right, I get the picture." Killian slides off the bed and backs away, followed by Kes, as she quite defiantly plants herself between us. "Spoilsport." Killian sticks out his tongue at my ruffled friend.

"Kes, don't be so unsociable." I reach to stroke her silky feathers. "You know Killian would never hurt me."

She hisses again, making both Killian and I share an exasperated look. We are never going to be able to talk, or just be ourselves, with my well-intentioned guardian interpreting his every move as a threat. So, the question remains, how do we ditch the chaperone? In search for an answer, I stare pleadingly at my quick-witted Gardener. Killian takes a step back toward the bathroom, his eyes making a gentle rolling motion in the direction of our secret passageway.

That's it.

If I can distract Kes for a few minutes, then the two of us can be out that door and out of the castle before she can find us. Even in her human form, she'll never know those passageways like Killian.

"You know"—Killian steps over the threshold of the bathroom—"perhaps Kes is right. That was stupid of me. My apologies if I caused offense. I think I should go, but you keep the brownies. They're my gift."

Kes ruffles her feathers and chitters. I interpret her body language as suggesting that she agrees. She wants him to leave. I roll my eyes but catch the wink he gives.

"There was no offense taken, but I accept your apology." I bob my head, then nod toward the door. "I agree, it's probably more sensible for you to leave. Goodnight."

"Goodnight." He slips into the dark bathroom.

I wait patiently for a few minutes. Chewing on another brownie, I ponder my next actions and act very much discouraged by the events of the night. Kes flutters off to her perch and takes up her proud pose, her sharp eyes scanning the clear night sky.

My avian companion takes her protective duties seriously, and even though I insist she take her humanoid form and sleep on a proper bed, she refuses. At night, she takes to her perch and stands vigil over me whilst I sleep. Her watchful gaze searching for things unseen, looking for something amiss in the dark, and for that reason, I almost feel guilty for tricking her.

Almost.

"Hey, Kes?"

She draws her attention from the window.

"I need to brush my teeth and clean my face. I've got brownie everywhere. I'm just going to use the bathroom, okay?"

She gives a soft chirp and bob of her head before resuming her vigil. A sly smirk spreads across my face as I slide off the bed and shove my feet into moccasin slippers—not the smartest footwear, but at least it isn't raining.

Gliding across the floor, I slip into the bathroom and close the door, using the little push lock on the handle to secure it. I sneak over to the sink and turn the tap on, pretending to bash about with my toothbrush. Kes's keen ears will seek these familiar sounds. I pause for a moment, noting that the panel door on the wall is open wide enough for me to squeeze through without causing any noise. Perfect.

I slip through the gap and straight into the inviting warmth of Killian's chest. He catches me around my waist and twists us around in the cramped space. My heart seems to double in speed every time he touches me. I'm beginning to think it's nothing to do with our natural affinity and more to do with just him.

He pulls the door shut so that it makes no noise. I'm pretty certain the two of us don't take a breath. We wait in silence, listening for a tell-tale shriek of alarm from my personal bodyguard. When none comes, we know we've gotten away with it.

With a little click, the soft light of Killian's pocket torch illuminates the gloom of the passageways. I find his face only an inch or so away, both of us smiling at one another. His hand seeks mine in the dark, and I let him lace our fingers together. Then he pulls me down into the murky corridors and out into the night.

CLOSER

The Glass House is all the more enticing in the quietness of night. Inside the protective globe, in a garden that is entirely separate from the world, I happily forget the demons that hunt me. Both the honest monsters and the ones that hold me to ransom in their cold castle.

I follow Killian's footsteps where he leads me through the contained wildness. I should've guessed he'd bring me here. Our perfect little haven filled to the brim with ethereal, glowing shrubs and patches of strange yet colorful night-awakening flowers. In this hidden world, I can't deny the existence of magic. This is a place of dreams, and my childlike heart wants to call it home forever.

The massive trees that splay high and wide to the very tips of the domed glass glow subtly beneath the surface of their bark. The colors, like dancing amber veins, glow and light the garden to ward off the shadows. Patches of lilac flowers bloom over large swathes of ground, the scent heavenly, and in the presence of the glowing trees, their powdery hues glisten as if they are made of tissue paper.

Everything seems to hold energy that shines in the night; even the rocks in the streams have veins of light that illuminate this secret paradise. I can't help but compare it to my strange blood. I can't help but think that it's no mistake that everything has this familiar strain running through it. Even I'm created to match the design, and Killian too. Nothing is out of place, everything runs in unity with each other. It is perfection.

Killian leads me deeper still, farther into our Eden, where the streams weave together to create a deep pool of crystal water. The pure, colorless light of the river rocks make the reflection of the water shimmer whilst the golden embrace of the trees warms its shallow edges. This is where he finally halts. With our fingers still entwined, he pulls me down to kneel before the water's edge.

"Isn't it beautiful?" Killian whispers. His free hand hovers over the water were the lights meld together. I nod because I'm at a loss for words. My strange new eyes burn with intensity as I shift toward the water and get lost in the calming, almost sleepy essence.

I swallow reflexively and retract a little from the edge to sit back on my knees. I sigh and shake my head.

"What's wrong?" The concern in Killian's soft question draws my focus from the hypnotic movement of the water over the lights.

"Aren't you worried?" I tug my hand away from his. I draw my knees to my chest and clasp my arms protectively around them, determined to keep my freaky new powers in check. I won't humiliate myself in front of him again.

"Of what?" Killian's eyebrows draw together in confusion. Then realization dawns, and his gaze flicks between me and the water. He gives an amused chuckle and points an accusing finger at me. "You think I am frightened of you?"

"I didn't say frightened, I said worried." I retract from that finger—my ego stung a little.

"Lexi, sweetheart, you really need to get it through your pretty little head that I'm not a gardener." Killian crawls closer to me, offering me his hand again. He sighs in exasperation and rolls his eyes when I hesitate. "I am trained in several different forms of combat, I know how to handle a battle axe and any type of blade you can name. To answer your question, no, I'm not even slightly worried about your temper."

"Is all that supposed to impress me?" I ignore his outstretched hand. "I did have you pinned against a tree, and I wasn't even trying that hard."

Killian smirks, his beautiful eyes crinkling around the edges as he sits himself down directly opposite me. He plants both his scruffy boots on either side of my hips and stretches his hands forward. I tense, drawing myself tighter into a ball, and continue to shoot him a withering look.

His fingers curl around the calves of my legs. One sharp breath later, and he tugs me toward him. I yelp, throwing my hands out to catch my balance, but it's pointless. Killian is much faster than I am. The moment my arms slacken from around my knees, he lets go of my legs and catches my forearms, drawing me forward so I find myself resting on my knees, hands braced against his shoulders. He grins victoriously, his fingers still around the crooks of my elbows. I can't even say I feel anything other than the gentlest touch of his hands.

"I get it." I shove his shoulders as hard as I can, but they barely shift. "You're strong." Killian nods, his mischievous grin widening, but I refuse to be beaten that easy. "Still doesn't mean you get to manhandle me, you tree-hugging jerk."

"You started it. I didn't ask to be pinned to a tree." His innocent reminder sends a blush crawling all over my skin. He narrows his eyes and bobs his head toward the closest tree. "And, for your information, I hug trees because they are excellent friends. They don't talk back so much."

I blurt out a peal of loud laughter. I can't help it. He looks so serious and so offended.

"Jeez, Lexi . . . it's not funny. Trees need friends too."

"Oh, shut up." I snort and start swiping at the tears of glee gathering in the corners of my eyes. "You're such a dork. A stupidly strong dork who is treading on thin ice."

"Something has to break that ice eventually." The humor fades from his vibrant, green eyes, and in its place, a warmth of familiarity fills them and stills my anxieties.

I sink down to rest on the back of my knees. My hands slip from his shoulders to his chest, and I consider the hidden intent behind his words. I've been as sharp and cold as ice of late. My words, my actions, even the way I hold myself has been as unwelcoming and frosty as an artic wind. I frown, a painful ache burning in my chest. I'm not this person. I'm not that cold.

A finger curls under my chin, and I allow Killian to tilt my head up. His constant, soulful gaze never seems to waver, even when I know I've said the wrong thing, or been hurtful, or less than understanding. His heart is as patient as the earth. Figures.

"You're safe here."

I flicker my eyes away from his, not fully trusting his statement.

"Lexi," he says, but I don't look up. "Don't be frightened to be yourself. At least not here. Not with me."

"You are so kind to me." I lift a hand to pat his cheek. "I just wish I knew why."

"There doesn't have to be any reason to be kind." He covers my hand with his much larger one, holding my palm against his stubbly jaw. "What reason had you to be kind to me when I was crippled and mute?"

"It wasn't your fault that you were those things." I cringe a little at the memory. "Besides, that's what my parents taught me to do, to be kind to others, especially anyone less fortunate." I freeze and start shaking my head. "Not that you are lesser, of course. I mean. It's just you looked—"

"I was a mess, you can say it." Killian laughs and I nod in agreement, glad that I've evaded offending him yet again.

"Yeah, but so was I." I give a little shrug. "Horrible, ugly, facial disfigurement isn't exactly the most flattering."

"You weren't ugly."

Killian squeezes my hand, but I respond with a hard and disbelieving snort.

"Fine, don't believe me, but I didn't see this horrible disfigurement." An angry and forceful edge enters his tone that pulls me up. "I saw a kind, beautiful soul that saw past a curse. Even if her eyes weren't quite strong enough to know for sure."

"But who needs eyes to see when your heart can tell you all you need to know, right?" I attempt to hide the shy smile pulling on my lips.

"At last . . . she actually believes me."

"Well." I sigh and give another little shrug of my shoulders. "My parents did also raise me to be cautious of strangers, and you are pretty strange, Killian Hunter."

"Tell me something I don't know." He rolls his eyes and leans toward me. His lips level with my ear.

He noses the loose strands of my hair out of the way. I freeze, a shiver running down my spine as his hand tightens around mine. His breath sends a ticklish tingle across my ear and down my neck.

"Lexi," he whispers, and I nod. "Do you trust me?"

I nod again, not entirely sure that I do, but I am far too caught up in the thrill of this night to worry too much about it.

Killian tugs me closer to him, but his body shifts back toward the water. He glances to the undisturbed pool, then back to me. I let him draw me to the edge, confident he'll not push me further than I want to be pushed. With deliberate slowness, he holds his palm over the back of my hand, fingers stretched over mine as he guides my palm over the water. I breathe in and out, acutely aware of how easily I lost my senses before. But this time seems a little different.

I still feel excited. My stomach still turns over with anticipation, and my skin still itches to feel that tingling thrill of true power coursing through it. Yet, I don't feel out of control, or at least I don't have the desire to break the Glass House down to nothing more than rubble. A miracle in itself.

"Every elemental energy has its own attributes." Killian guides my hand over the shimmering water, making little infinity patterns with my fingertips. As he does, the water current begins to change to copy the movement. "Water is fluid, changeable. It can be peaceful and calming, or"—he jerks my hand upward, the swift movement causing the water to spike and fall like a miniature tidal wave—"it can be turbulent and unpredictable."

"A little like me then." I snicker, and Killian tries, and fails, to disguise his own laughter at my honest appraisal.

I still our hands, drawing his back. I push his palm down toward the earth beneath us. He peeks up at me as I press both our fingers into the dirt. "But what about earth. What are its attributes?"

"Strength." Killian drops his chin and struggles to find words. He's shy when the spotlight turns on him, but I'm curious now.

"I bet there's more to it than just strength."

"The earth is protective, robust, as ancient and patient as the world itself." His words are forced, his cheeks that faint bronze color, but he perseveres.

"It's quiet until provoked, but it only becomes destructive when all it protects is threatened."

"Sounds like the sort of power you would like to have on your side in a fight. Earth sounds much more useful than water."

"You might think that." Killian nudges my fingers forward until they dip in the water as it laps against the earth. "But actually"—he nods toward the pool—"water is restorative and life-giving. Without water, the earth can't yield harvest. It can't breathe or be strengthened without the energy of water."

Our fingertips barely touch, but I see the green in his eyes intensify when he focuses on our hands. That familiar tingling sensation washes over me as the slender rivulets of water crawl over our entwined fingertips. The thin, watery tracks are drawn into his palm and then directed down deep into the earth. After a few seconds, the bare earth beneath our hands blooms a patch of vibrant green clover. I gasp at the sight, my heart beating a little faster with the thrill of creating something beautiful. No . . . more than that. I did it with him. It felt strangely intimate but not wrong. In fact, it feels right.

"Water is very important. It should never be overlooked or misunderstood; it should always be respected. Revered even," Killian says, but I notice how he keeps his eyes just shy of meeting mine. Does he feel it too?

"Maybe so"—I give a shaky bob of my head as I squeeze our tangled fingers—"but what purpose would water have if it didn't have the earth?"

"I get the impression you're not talking about elemental attributes anymore," Killian says and sits up a little straighter. His earthen eyes scan the horizon for a moment before they land on me, then dance away again.

"Were we ever just talking about water and earth?" I crane my neck around to study his side profile.

Killian lowers his gaze, his mouth opening then shutting again. He wants to say something but thinks better of it. I lean in closer, wishing him to say whatever it is he chooses not to because I don't want him to stop. I could listen to him forever.

He twists to look at me, registering my proximity as our noses brush. A few strands of his hair fall against my cheek. My face flushes, and I begin to pull away, but he stops me. His callused fingers brush my cheek.

"Lexi." He breathes my name like some kind of yearning, his lips practically grazing mine as he speaks. His thumb tracing the curve of my mouth. His eyes glittering like backlit emeralds.

"Yes?"

Killian's brows knit together as he contemplates something. All I do is stare into his eyes, entirely captivated by all the colors hidden within their depths. He has such old eyes, like the soul inside has seen so much. Perhaps too much.

A second of silence passes. Then his lips carefully press against mine.

It is the sweetest and lightest kiss. It is everything and nothing.

My eyelids flutter closed as I draw both my hands up to wrap around his neck. His hand curls around my cheek. His explorative fingers working into the hair at the nape of my neck, but he pulls away, for only a brief moment, to inhale a steady breath. I nudge against his nose with mine, and he tilts his head and kisses me again. This time, I form my lips around his, feeling just the tiniest bit brave. In response, Killian deepens the kiss between us.

It all ends as sweet and innocent as it began.

I'm left dumbstruck, wondering how exactly we've found our way to this point. I can't deny I wanted his kiss. It felt right—completely right—and natural. I was more than eager to let him, more than willing to string it out a little longer. But is this wise? This doesn't feel like me. I don't do anything this reckless. What will my parents say?

A pain as sharp and real as any knife stabs through my heart. My parents are dead. They're gone, and here I am in the arms of a stranger, letting him kiss me. Letting him take my pain away. Making me forget.

I don't deserve to forget.

"I'm sorry." The apology tumbles off my lips as I shove away from him.

"What for?" The bemused look he gives me as he outstretches his hand causes my heart to jolt in guilt. But I still back away. My fingers rise to my lips where they burn.

He makes to stand. To follow me. But I turn and run, darting for the exit, praying he won't follow.

"Wait! Don't go!"

It's too late, I can't answer him. Can't look at him. I break through the hidden door of the Glass House and into the cold night air. The brisk breeze kicks up my hair and fills my lungs with a settling clarity. Tears brim at the corners of my eyes. My heart heavy with regret, mingled with guilt and a truckload of confusion.

What have I done?

PUT TO REST

I don't run toward the castle—that would be counterproductive. Instead, I run in the opposite direction. I vault a low wall, the velvet of my dress snagging on the crumbled stones.

My slippers fly off with the jump, but I don't stop. I continue to race parallel to the ancient wall, feeling the draw of a strong, salt breeze. I force my feet to fly toward something my heart comprehends but not my head. The sting of grief still clings to me like a shroud, like cobwebs sticking to my bones and making me unclean. I need to wash it away. I want to get it all away from me.

The crumbling and porous wall tapers away and the grass turns to sand between my toes. The sound of water washing across a pebbled beach is like a melody to my ears, and so I slow to a stop, breathing in the freshness of water-soaked air.

My mother brought me to water when I was little. She used to say that if we listened long enough, we'd forget all our worries. I used to believe that, but the more I stand out here, listening to the loud splashes and slaps of water against rock, I only hear her. Saltwater tears dribble down my cheeks and past my chin.

"Mother." I sob in a stupid and childish voice, hugging my arms tighter around myself. I shiver a little from the cold and step toward the water's edge, letting the waves swallow up my toes. "Mommy?" I call her again.

I haven't used such a casual term for my mother since I was little; she preferred the proper title, and I never questioned it. Now I realize it was an attempt at being formal, not getting too attached, like smothering all the little endearments would make the inevitable separation easier. It didn't. But who was to know this is how it would end? Whatever superhuman abilities I possess, I doubt they will somehow magically bring her back.

It doesn't matter. None of it does. Not anymore. I hold a hand to my chest, torn between clawing out my heart because I can't stand the festering agony or trying to hold the heaviness inside. Instead, my fingers find the metal of the locket and curl around it.

"I don't want this!" My cry is lost on the groans of frigid gales, the wind berating my hair so that it flails about in the breeze. "I'm not ready. You can't leave me here."

Nothing but the crash of the angry water against the shore replies.

I pick up a rock from the sand and toss it at the water, then another, and another, until I stagger forward and fall on my knees. I gasp as the icy water wraps itself around me. The sting of the cold cutting my breath from my lungs as I shudder and choke.

Nothing makes sense. None of this seems fair. I'm supposed to be this powerful being, yet I can't make sense of my own emotions. I can't make anything happen. I couldn't save my parents. I can't even save myself.

My fingers curl into fists around the murky sand beneath the surface. The shale cuts into my knuckles. A low, menacing hiss slithers through my teeth.

What a fine mess I've gotten myself into. Not only am I reliant on the charity of dishonest men, humans who will only protect me if I save their weak hides first, but now Killian is my only ally in this disaster, and I kissed him. I should drown myself now and save everyone from my idiocy. Only I doubt I can drown myself. I probably have magical gills that prevent me from doing something as foolish as dying from mishandling my own powers.

"Lexi!"

His voice pierces through the cutting wind, and I grind my teeth.

"What are you doing?"

I don't answer him, the anger in his voice only irritating my already frayed nerves.

"You crazy banshee. Get up!"

Killian sloshes toward me, his jeans shoved about his knees. I glare furiously at his legs. The thick, dark hairs are stuck to his skin from the swirling water, and I register, albeit a little late, that he is shivering.

I refuse to care. Refuse to cave to his demands. I bristle even more when his palm shoots into my line of vision.

"Get. Up."

He makes a disgusted sound before his two hands clamp roughly around my shoulders. With one sharp movement, he drags me upward.

"Get off me!" I flail into the water, my feet kicking in directionless patterns.

Killian continues to hoist me into his arms. He clamps my wriggling knees in place with his iron-wrought forearm. I lash out and beat his chest, but it doesn't seem to bother him in the slightest, he just turns and walks back toward the grassy bank. I don't give in though; I continue to thump him and writhe about like a suffocating fish. So much so that when we reach the bank, he drops me in a heap on the ground. I yelp in pain and grace him with a vicious glare. So much for our tender kiss. Clearly he didn't mean it that much.

"Did I not make myself clear enough?" I shuffle away from him, batting his hand out of the way when he offers it to me. "I didn't want you to follow me. I didn't ask for that kiss either. Who do you think you are?"

"Shut up, Lexi!" The fury in his voice startles me. His usually placid eyes harden as his outstretched palm curls into a fist. I panic that he's going to aim a punch at me, but instead he swings it at thin air.

"Spit your venom elsewhere but not at me. I've had enough of being your emotional punch-bag." Killian spins to face me again and points a warning finger. "You know I care for you. I wouldn't be here if I didn't. Now get up off the ground and start acting like an adult. Cut the sniveling victim act. It's disgusting. Your parents would be devastated."

I gasp in utter shock and attempt to scramble to my feet. "How dare you?" Killian goes to steady me, but I throw myself at his chest and shove him back. "You don't know me! You don't know anything about me or my parents, or how they would feel. I didn't ask you to be here. Leave if you want. I don't care!"

I know the words are lies because they sting as soon as they leave my lips. They sting more than the icy water, but they sting Killian worse. He shudders, like I've jolted him, and immediately he holds up his hands as if to surrender.

"You're right, I don't know you," Killian says, and I open my mouth to hurl more abuse, but I wasn't expecting him to agree. He looks around the ground for a moment before he kneels and picks up a sharp piece of flint. "I don't know what your favorite book is." He takes a step toward me, and I step back. "I don't know if your father played baseball with you, or if you went fishing together, or if he taught you how to tie a proper knot or something useful like a good right hook."

My brows furrow at his ridiculous ramble.

"I don't know the lullabies your mother sang to you, or if she let you sleep in her bed when you had nightmares, and I don't know what she said to stop your tears." Killian pauses, his own eyes filling with what could be tears, but he doesn't let them fall. Instead, he points to himself. "But I do know what it's like to lose that. I know what it feels like to wake up to nothing, and no one ever speaks their names again, like they were never real. So don't think for one second I can't understand your pain. I do know some things. Not everything, but I know more about you than you think I do."

"How?" I ask, and admittedly it sounds more like a weak cry for proof than the challenging growl I had intended it to be.

"I know you like to wear your hair in a messy bun because that's how your mother used to wear hers and you admired it."

I balk in disbelief. How did he know that?

"I know you drink milk by the gallon because your father said it would make you grow up strong. He used to make you believe that was true by letting you win arm-wrestling matches."

"You couldn't possibly know that." I shake my head in disbelief. "No one knows that."

"Yes, they do. You told Connor. You two sat in the campus gardens and talked about everything and nothing, but I was there. I was always right there."

My head fills with the memories. The hundreds of memories shared between Connor and me. The conversations we never thought to include him in because . . . well, he didn't have a voice. Or did we just not think. I'm such an idiot.

"I couldn't join in." He continues, maybe not noticing the guilt in my eyes. "I couldn't tell you that my mother used to trick me into eating my greens, convincing me they made me super strong. I couldn't tell you that when my father risked his life to come see me, he brought me books filled with pictures of a strange world, and he told me all kinds of stories about his people. I couldn't tell you to hold on to those stupid, senseless memories because they are the only things that remind you that love existed. That once upon a time, you mattered to someone." He pauses, his voice rough and hollowed out in pain as he points to himself. "Now I speak. Now I can tell you. And I swear it kills me that it's too late. I never wanted anyone else to suffer the way I did, least of all you."

"Oh god." I sniff back one painful sob and run my hands through the roots of my hair. "You always knew who I was, didn't you?"

"From the moment I met you." He steps right into my space.

Killian holds out his hand, drawing the sharp end of the flint across his palm to expose our beautiful blood. It drips and curves in swirls and pretty patterns of deep purple, gold, and silver.

"I know I can't replace your family, and I really don't want to." Killian's voice is so soft, so forgiving, that it only makes me sob harder. "But I care about you. I always have. And I recognize I don't know all of you yet, but I know we are the same." He wraps his bloodied palm around mine. "I know the girl who tried to save me when I cut myself, the girl who was ready to defend all my secrets before she even knew her own. I hope she knows that I meant every minute of that kiss, and if she'd let me, I would do it again. I hope she knows she doesn't have to cry alone, for she has me. And I'm never going to let her fall. Never going to let her face any of this on her own."

"Even when she punches you in the chest and acts like a deranged banshee?" I stutter through ugly tears and trembling limbs.

"Especially when she punches me and tries to drown herself in the lough." Killian chuckles, but stretches his arms open for me. A timid request for an embrace.

I stare at him for a long minute, wondering why I felt like running from him in the first place. I suppose it was panic. Panic that I'd forget my parents, panic that he'd hurt me, and panic that it wasn't safe to love anything again in case I lose it.

I draw in a settling breath and step toward him, meeting him halfway. I clasp his cut hand tightly, drawing his palm upward to place it to my lips. I kiss the healing cut. In response, Killian wraps his arms around me and holds me against the rooted warmth of him.

The wind howls and whips around us. The water crashes tumultuously, but he never moves. He's always steady, and in a tiny way, his steadiness reminds me of the security of home. I marvel at the thought for a moment. Maybe there is a greater power out there that knew my parents would be leaving me soon, and in their place, it prepared for me another companion. Of course, nothing can replace them in my heart, but my heart is wakening.

"I'm sorry, Killian," I say and rest my cheek against his shoulder as I press in closer to him. "I'm just frightened."

"I know." He tightens his grip around me. "You'd be mad if you weren't. Let me help. Please?"

"I need all the help I can get." I snivel out a pathetic little laugh but make a point of pulling away from him. "I care about you, too, and I know we are more than friends, but I don't know what that means yet. I don't want you to waste your time waiting on me to figure it out."

"And what else am I going to do with my time?" One of Killian's bushy eyebrows raises up his forehead. "Lexi, sweetheart, there is the greatest possibility that in the entirety of creation, we are the only two of our kind left. I'd happily waste the rest of eternity waiting if I thought there was even the slightest chance that you could care, even a little, for me."

"Oh," is the only thing I manage to squeak out.

I take hold of a strand of my hair and wring it nervously as I glance down at my feet. Killian stands there, patiently waiting for me to answer, but all I can do is feel my heart constrict in my chest and sense butterflies flutter in my tummy. "Well, I do care." I tug the ends of my hair. "But an eternity might be a little dramatic. I kinda meant more like a few months."

"Oh."

It's Killian's turn to blush. He takes a step back and awkwardly shoves his hands into his pockets, bouncing a little on the spot, his shoulders shoved somewhere just shy of his ears. "You know my mother always said I was prone to theatrics." He chuckles but continues to cringe. "It always sounds so much more romantic in my head than it does when I open my mouth."

"No." I reach to coil my arm around his. "It was very romantic, and I fully appreciate the thought behind it. I'm just unprepared for the grand gesture. Will we try it again, and I'll act more excited? Swoon perhaps?"

"Please, save my ego the abuse." Killian shakes his head and clamps my arm tight against his side. "I'll know for the future to prepare you for any more romantic speeches."

I giggle and rest my head on his shoulder. We turn around to walk back toward the castle, and I'm relieved that I didn't lose him—or myself—to another one of my emotional outbursts. I resolve that these ridiculous dramas will have to stop. Killian is right, my parents would be embarrassed at my selfish displays.

My parents spent their lives teaching me to survive, and thrive, no matter the circumstance. I spent my childhood learning to rebuild my life every time we moved. My parents were always preparing me for this, for a time when they couldn't protect me. So I know I have the ability to rebuild my life here. I can honor their memory by doing exactly that.

Killian and I walk the rest of the way back to the castle in companionable silence. I mull over my own thoughts, and now and again I peek up at Killian and find his lips twisted in a contented smile. That expression softens his whole countenance. Each time I glance at him, his smile stretches, and he gives my arm a little squeeze, and with each little squeeze my heart jumps. Perhaps it isn't as broken as I initially thought.

"Whoa . . . wait." Killian breaks our comfortable silence and slows the pace. I tense and slink closer into his side.

"What's wrong?" My eyes dart about the gardens trying to find the threat, but all I see is the castle walls and beyond that . . . lights?

Bright lights and the sound of car tires on gravel. My eyes lock with Killian's. It's a little too late in the night for impromptu guests to the castle.

Killian places a finger to his lips. "Follow me."

With almost noiseless movements, Killian and I creep past the walls that defend the castle courtyards toward a well-preened hedgerow that encircles the perimeter of pebbled entrance. Pausing by a shadowed portion of the dense hedges, closest to the commotion, Killian kneels down and eases his hands into the center of the bristly plant. I squat beside him and lean into the shadows his body casts. He closes his eyes for a moment in concentration, and then, as if he silently communicated orders to the shrub, its twisted branches move aside just enough for us to see through.

All I can make out are low voices and feet crunching on gravel. Then I hear it—Thomas's poised voice—and I narrow my eyes when I spy him descending the steps of his home with his sour-looking wife. Neither of them appear as though they were trailed out of bed, so I assume they were expecting the company. I look to Killian, but he doesn't sense my pleading gaze boring into the side of his head. Instead, he scrutinizes a bulky vehicle with intense curiosity.

An animalistic roar comes from a large trailer attached to a black SUV, and I flinch in fright from the sound, but Killian only leans forward, anger flashing across his features. The noise sounds again, and whatever is inside the trailer begins thrashing about. Whatever it is, it definitely isn't human, but that really doesn't bring me any comfort.

"And what exactly are we going to do with an injured water horse?" Thomas asks one of the burly men I recognize as Killian's guards. "The beasts are wild and unbiddable things, and if it's been broken by Dian's henchmen then we are only prolonging its suffering. Someone fetch me my pistol."

"Let the boy work with it."

I crane my neck when I hear the professor's familiar voice of reason in the midst of the chaos.

"Killian?" Margot gives a doubtful chortle.

"Yes, of course I mean Killian." Professor Donoghue limps into my line of vision, his face drawn. "I don't see why any more innocent blood has to be spilled." He waves his hand toward the trailer that rocks from the deranged animal inside. "Give it a chance, for pity's sake. Perhaps the lad can fix it up enough that it may be of use to us. Heaven knows we need a vessel to cross the Veil."

"You are too soft, Paul," Thomas says, then nods for the guardsman to go deal with the animal. "Very well then. Take the beast to the Glass House and go get the little bastard out of bed. He can deal with its aggression. I'm not risking losing a chunk of my arm for a lost cause."

Killian's shoulders sag at the insulting title the earl so eloquently selected for him. I figure we'll need to get back to our respective rooms before the mutts come looking for him and find him AWOL. I give his shoulder a little shake, and he turns to nod his agreement, but just as he does, I spy another car being unloaded.

Two guards haul a long, black bag from the trunk, then another. And then I understand.

Body bags.

I grip Killian's arm, digging my fingernails into his skin. He moves to draw me away from the scene, but I am glued to the spot, my fingertips brushing the metal of the locket resting above my heart.

I know it's them. I can feel it.

"Where do you want the bodies?" one of the men asks, and my stomach churns.

Bodies? They were my parents. They weren't just bodies.

"Lexi," Killian warns in a low hiss, but I can't help it. I'm already inching forward, my eyes fixated on the smaller of the two bags.

"Mother." I choke as I start to stand. "That's my mother." I turn to Killian. My eyes sting with tears. "I know it is. I have to see. I—"

"No, Lexi."

Killian scrambles after me, but he is too slow. I've already jumped the hedge before he manages to get to his feet.

I hurtle toward the shapeless bags, screaming at the two men to leave them down. I fling myself in front of the larger of the two bodies. The bigger of the two men drops his end and jumps back from my crazed advances.

"Lady Alexandria!" Margot's tone is alarmed, embarrassed even, as she marches toward me. Her husband, being the slightly wiser of the two, keeps his distance. "What on earth are you doing out at this ungodly hour?"

"My parents!" I throw my arms out wide, trying to make myself bigger—a shield. "You brought my parents' bodies home without even consulting me. You knew where they were this whole time, didn't you? When exactly was I going to be told? When you'd dispose of the evidence? Huh? Is no one going to answer me?"

"Lexi." This time it is the kindly professor, who at least has the courage to address me. He hobbles forward, leaning on his cane and wearing a look of genuine sympathy. "Lexi, I would have told you in the morning when you were awake. I know this must be a terrible shock, but—"

"But nothing!" I register that I'm trembling when Killian comes up behind me and rests his hand on my shoulders. "I should have been informed." I scan each and every one of their faces, hoping to find a shred of truth in their eyes.

"You were not told because I didn't deem it wise." Thomas surprises me as he walks forward with confidence. "You were in a very vulnerable position."

As he begins to unravel his reasoning, I stare him down, not entirely trusting him.

"And I know for a fact that the bodies of agent Danu and agent Crawford are horrifically damaged, particularly your father's. I didn't want you to bear witness to anything that would taint what memories you have."

"I still had the right to know." I remain rooted to the spot, unwilling to yield an inch, all whilst Killian tries to draw me closer to his chest. I imagine if he could shield me from the earl's advances, he would.

"My apologies." Thomas gives a slight bow of his head. "But if I'm being honest, I hadn't expected you to find out. I didn't realize you would be out in the grounds at nearly three in the morning with"—Thomas flicks his cold gaze to Killian—"*him.*" I don't like how the earl's disdainful eyes sweep over Killian and me, like he is judging us and finding us both guilty of some unspoken crime.

"I didn't realize I was supposed to inform you of how I wish to spend my time, or who I spend it with." I fire back with just as much disgust.

Thomas smirks, but I find it less of a smirk and more of a snarl when his eyes light on Killian.

"Well, it seems we both like keeping information from each other." He answers me with such venomous cruelty that it takes all my courage not to cry in front of him. "But"—he gestures around him—"I suppose it is better now that we both know our little secrets, hmm?"

I bite down hard on my tongue. Killian shifts behind me, and I know without looking that he is about a minute away from punching Thomas. I can't say I'd be annoyed if he did.

"I think we should all go inside," Professor Donoghue says in his vain attempt to break the heavy atmosphere descending between the three of us. "Lexi has been through enough." He reaches out to guide me away from the scene. "I think she needs some space to say her goodbyes and make plans to bury her parents."

"Her parents were traitors." Margot has been mostly silent in the shadow of her husband, but by the venom in her words, she's not about to let this go. "There will be no funeral or ceremony for traitors. The Order will never allow such a dishonorable act."

I am about open my mouth to scream at the foolish witch of a woman, but Killian beats me to it.

"That is not your decision." His voice is fierce, intimidating. "Lexi is one of the Ancients. If she wishes to exercise mercy in honor of this man and woman, then you should get down on your knees and thank the Creator that she would show such respect toward your feeble race."

"I would be careful who you call feeble, boy." Thomas squares his shoulders.

"Don't patronize me, Thomas." Killian snorts, amused by the threat. "We both know you need me to fight your bloody wars for you. So, with due respect, get out of her space and leave us in peace, Earl of Domnaill."

I want to kiss Killian here and now for his courage, but I refrain, considering it a little improper after our earlier agreement. Thomas's jaw flexes as he flicks an unimpressed glare between Killian and me, but he nods once and gestures for Margot to follow him back inside.

In the sudden flurry of activity, Killian and I are once again left alone, and this time I don't need to be encouraged to accept his embrace. I seek for it before he even offers.

"Thank you," I whisper as I curl into his side and let him lead me back into the castle and out of the cold. "But how much of your little speech is the truth?"

"I may have overexaggerated on your right to demand a burial," Killian admits with a sheepish grin. "But I'm not wrong when I say you have the right to exercise mercy toward members of the Order. And, Lexi, hear me good on this one point and hear me well. You certainly never have to bow to the likes of Thomas Domnaill."

The thought clangs through me. The freedom of it lifting my chin higher. No, I don't have to bow to anyone.

FINAL FAREWELLS & NEW BEGINNINGS

The earth is cold. The late November dew left a frosty dusting to the ground, yet somehow I barely feel it as I stand overlooking the Glass House. Only a black A-line dress and woven shawl cover me. Every exhale makes little clouds, which I use to keep myself focused.

Biting air rushing from the lough freezes my face into an indifferent mask. I've cried my tears in the forty-eight hours since they brought my parents' bodies. I resent shedding any more under Thomas Domnaill's scrutinizing gaze. Resent showing that burying my parents might be a task I'm incapable of. I am strong. Mother and Father made sure of it. If they thought I'd run and hide, it would break their hearts. Killian is right about that, at least.

He's here with me, in the background, giving me some distance to sort through my reckless mind as they lower my parents into the frozen ground.

I chose this spot, where earth gave way to sand, near where the water laps at the shale beach. It's in the shadow of the Glass House, yet close enough to the peaceful embrace of the water and far enough from the castle's gloom. A tiny sapling is nestled between the two graves, which I hope will one day grow and mark my parents' resting place.

If the Order had their way, both Mother and Father would be cremated and hidden away.

The Order see my parents' actions as abduction, but I know different. My mother sensed things that others didn't. Something must've been wrong for her to leave with me. She didn't trust them, and clearly, Father trusted her enough to follow.

She must've known this day would come. Known she'd lose the battle and have to hand me back. But I think—I know—she raised me well enough to smell a rat.

I have nothing to pin on the elusive Order of Kings. They've been kind to me, reverent even, but it's conditional. My access to information is limited, and none of them are forthcoming.

Maybe I'm being kept ignorant deliberately.

Perhaps that's why they treat Killian as a threat. He knows things, secrets, and he's happy to educate me.

I also suspect reinstating the professor unnerves them. He must know something about the Order, but he keeps silent. His silence kept Connor safe all these years, but with his son's life at risk, I hope he will drop his guard.

But bringing me into confidence will prove difficult. Professor Donoghue is watched persistently by Bryce, servants, and guards.

I'm going to have to get smarter. I'm fighting a bigger battle than I'd thought. I don't know friends from foes. But Father always said you can never tell.

Swells of emotion bubble in my chest. My fingers twist around the locket, which weighs heavy against my chest today.

A petite hand cautiously rests on my shoulder. Humanoid Kes stares up at me, her sharp features tight with stress.

I shake my head and offer her a small smile. My guardian hasn't left my side since I returned from my escape with Killian. I had expected her to raise the alarm and sell out Killian the moment she realized she'd been duped by us. She didn't. In fact, she was more stressed over why I just didn't tell her where we went so she might've continued her watch. Apparently if I want privacy, all I have to do is ask for it. Though it's still a baffle why she wants to keep Killian and me apart. She's admitted that she trusts him . . . maybe it's more that she doesn't trust me with him. But from the moment I returned, she's been nothing but her steady, helpful self, warding off unwanted attention during the dark hours following the discovery of my parents' bodies.

Kes gives a silent nod in the direction of the burial site.

The old groundsman and his younger companion shovel the last of the earth on the fresh mounds. They both stretch and take a step back, staring at the sparse graves. The elder jerks his chin, motioning for the younger to follow. I nod my thanks as they pass, but they keep their heads low and eyes downcast.

Only Thomas Domnaill represents the Order at this measly funeral, carrying a simple posy of flowers. Neither his unpleasant wife nor any of the guards attended to farewell their superiors. Not even Bryce.

Thomas steps forward and crouches, laying the flowers on the earth above Mother. After a pause, he removes his leather glove, presses a kiss to three fingers, and places them on the overturned dirt. The gesture strikes me as quite genuine, but Thomas Domnaill is crafty. I doubt I'll ever know his true intentions. His company deeply unnerves me. He doesn't seem safe, not like a leader should. Not like Killian.

He straightens from his crouch and pushes his long, pale hand back into his glove. With a little sigh, he turns his watery, calculative gaze on me.

"May God rest their souls," he says in a cold voice. He strides toward the castle, pausing to place a hand on my shoulder. "May they find pardon with their Creator."

I glare at him, daring him to call them sinful or traitorous. It would delight me to drop a torrent of ice water on his ignorant head.

Thomas Domnaill gives a twisted smile and walks away from the two unmarked graves. Anger swarms in the pit of my chest. I can do nothing because I need their protection. I hate myself for that.

With a pained inhale, I glance at the castle. My new, powerful eyes zero in on Lady Margot peering through a wide landing window. Human eyes would not have the strength to pick out the tiny details I now can. And I can see the wretched smirk of victory on her beautiful face—but, so can Killian.

He stands downwind of the events, neck craned toward the same window I've been studying. His filthy hands are wrapped around a shovel and his clothes threadbare; even the servants have better clothes. He spent all night digging the graves, and yet he stands taller, more honorable than any person I've met since arriving. He meets the earl's disdainful stare with a hardened expression as he strolls toward him. The look they share seems to stall the earl, but Killian's gaze drifts past Thomas and back to the castle. His nose scrunches, and he slams the shovel deep into the earth. Then he strides toward the graves.

Thomas swivels on his heels, scowling with a flash of hatred in his eyes.

Killian kneels by the graves, facing me, Thomas, and the rest of Domnaill.

I frown as Killian kicks off his boots, planting his bare feet in the ground. He burrows his hands into the earth around the roots of the sapling. Curious, I can't help but step closer, but Kes holds me back, her panicky eyes flicking toward the earl.

"How dare you?" Thomas jabs an accusatory finger, features contorted in rage.

Killian raises his head, eyes shining with flecks of earthen colors—greens, golds, browns, and grays. Utterly captivating, but no less terrifying. The muscles along his shoulders and back tremble, arms flexing in the soil. The colors in his eyes radiate through his veins, a muted glow, unlike the glaring brightness of mine.

The ground moves, rumbles beneath us. The grass shakes off its frosty dusting, standing straight. The little sapling's body stretches, growing so fast that Killian shifts back from its expanding limbs. But his hands remain firmly entangled in the earth as he watches the tree flourish.

He's growing it up, making a beautiful memorial. A statement to the Order.

My chest bursts with pride.

The yew tree reaches at least ten feet into the sky, limbs spanning many yards. Vibrant green leaves adorn the branches, despite the depths of winter. The life Killian fed the sapling is supernatural, not dictated by the seasons of man, but our immortal, everlasting seasons.

For the first time since meeting Killian, I'm oddly frightened. Not of his character, but of the amount of power he wields, kept hidden. Wild, commanding, and fierce, he rises to stand proudly before a lesser man.

The mortal flinches.

"A gift." Killian's eyes drift from Thomas to me, and he bows his head. "For my queen."

My brows furrow. Why the reverence?

Killian isn't finished. "A token, to honor the mortals who protected you." He glances at Thomas. "A statement of love and mercy for all men."

Splintering anger dances across the earl's eyes, directed at my Silent Gardener.

"Thank you, Killian. That was a very thoughtful gift," I say, calmly as I can. I'm frightened for him . . . very frightened.

"You are clever to mask it as a gift," Thomas says, but his jaw is tight. "Your belligerence offends me. Another move like that and even your queen won't be able to protect you. You're still half a man—I own that half."

Thomas storms back to the castle to hide behind his crumbling walls. Margot glares daggers from the window, and a smirk settles on my features. She straightens, then departs. That was a dubious move on Killian's part, but it made a resounding impression.

"That was too close, Killian. Far too close." Kes wrings her hands, eyes darting over Killian.

"Awk, Kes, stop twittering. It was an empty threat." Killian's eyes soften, wildness dissipating as he saunters over to us.

"You're reckless." She angles herself between us, her little chest puffing up bravely. "You'll get Lexi hurt, and I won't stand for that."

"And here I was thinking you were expressing concern for me." He winks, and Kes scowls. I roll my eyes and suppress a groan—they're as antagonistic as ever.

"I am concerned for you, you big lug." She stretches on her toes to reach Killian's chest. "But you walk yourself into trouble. You deserve everything you get, ugly brute."

"Kes." I shoot her a sidelong scowl. She twitches a little. I shake my head and turn my attention to Killian. "She's right." My voice cracks, emotion getting the better of me. "You shouldn't put yourself out on a limb. What if I can't protect you?"

"It's not your job to protect me," he says in that soft lilt. He steps closer, lifting my hand and holding it against his chest. "Besides." He squeezes my palm. "I didn't do it just for you. I did it for them too." He nods at the graves. "Stop worrying about me. Thomas won't make good on any threats yet. He needs me. The Order needs me. I'm not going anywhere."

"You'd better not." I drop my chin, lips curling upward in a small smile. "I'd miss you too much."

Killian beams at my admittance to my fledging feelings, but he doesn't draw attention to them. He only lifts my hand and presses a kiss to the inside of my palm. Warmth floods my chest at the intimate display.

"Take care, Lexi." He releases my hand. "I have to go to work."

"Yes, that is probably wise," Kes says, prodding him toward the Glass House. "Don't worry about Lexi; I'll keep careful watch over her."

Killian chuckles, making a pacifying gesture as he backs away. "Okay, Kes, I get it, I'm going." His eyes latch on to mine.

I watch him leave with a sense of longing. I miss him when he isn't around.

"My lady," Kes whispers, interrupting my thoughts. "I know you have feelings for him, and he you, but it would be wiser not to act on them."

"I don't think that's any of your business," I reply. Her observation ruffles me. In fact, I'm peeved that anyone thinks they have a say in such matters. Besides, I don't even know what's going on between Killian and me. It's hardly the business of anyone else, especially the Order.

"Begging your pardon." Kes droops her head. "You're right, it's none of my business. I only worry the Order would intervene if they knew. I wouldn't see either of you hurt."

"Why should the Order of Kings care about such trivial things?" I scoff and tighten my shawl around my shoulders, beginning the walk home.

"You are a pure celestial descendent of your people," Kes quietly reminds me, taking two strides with my every one to keep up. "Killian is a half-blood grandson of the enemy. There are laws against such things."

"Yes, I know about their laws, and ours. But this is an extreme situation." I hold my chin high. "We're talking about the extinction of an entire race. I don't think those laws still apply."

"But if Connor was returned they would."

I halt, open-mouthed. They wouldn't force Connor and me together just to keep a race genetically pure . . . would they? The notion is barbaric.

"Kes, this is senseless." I plough forward, ignoring the nausea sweeping over me. "I'm barely nineteen. I've never even considered marriage and children. It wasn't even a possibility, and Connor would feel the same way. Besides, you can't just force people together. It's ridiculous."

Kes nods and hurries to keep up.

Will I be expected, out of duty, to be a vessel to ensure my race's survival? Honorable it may be, but my parents didn't die for such a simple duty.

Flames dance around charred logs in the library fireplace as I hunch over a stack of books. Is fire my natural elemental enemy? And Connor, who has he become? What powers are hidden within him? Will I recognize my friend when I find him?

Not finding him is not an option.

I give a long sigh and gaze at the parchment before me. An old book from the archives containing some of the ancient lore of my people. Most of it seems like old wives' tales, but every so often, something rings true. It's difficult to sift truth from fables.

Professor Donoghue sits opposite me, fingers curled around a glass of whiskey. He studies his set of books with a scowl. Purplish rings circle his eyes. The darkening gloom of evening ages him more than ever.

He wasn't allowed to attend the funeral this morning. He's prohibited from doing anything unless the Order or Thomas grant it. That in itself would drive me to drink.

"Find anything useful?" I always feel I'm disturbing him when I ask infantile questions.

"Not in the slightest." He takes another long slug of his drink. "Just a pile of nonsense about the power of dolmen stones. If anyone could march up to a dolmen site and cross the matrix to the Veiled Lands, I would've done so years ago. Stupid, misinformed historians."

"So, dolmens are not a port of entry to the unseen then?" I duck my head when he glares at my stupid question. I lift my pen, flip a few pages back in my notes, and scratch out "dolmen stones" as a viable option.

"No, Lexi, the only way to cross the Veil is to have access to a key." He spins one of his books around to face me and jabs a finger at a chunk of text. I stare vacantly between him and the page, not having the foggiest of what it says.

"So where do we get a key?" I ask, imagining a nice, big, brass key opening a secret door into a new and unexplored world. But I know better than to voice that idea. Things are never that easy.

"A key can be anything." The professor throws his arms in the air. "An animal, a thing, it could be a bloody carrot for all I know."

"I highly doubt it would be a carrot." I sniff, aggravated that he doesn't take my questions seriously.

"Well, all right, it probably isn't a carrot. The point is, the objects can be anything. They just have to be blessed by Celestials and enchanted for such a purpose." He drops his head into his hands and scrubs at his tired eyes. "My only other theory is that the injured water horse could serve as a key. Those animals usually do. But if it's badly broken, I doubt it shall ever trust us enough to carry us across the divide."

"But Killian is helping him," I say, perking up. "If anyone can fix the horse, he can. I mean, if that's all it would ta—"

"It could take months before the animal is healed. If it's even capable of being healed." The professor shakes his head, lifting his spectacles from his forehead and placing them on the edge of his nose. "And that does not guarantee it will ever be tame enough to aid us. No, I'm afraid that option is a long shot."

"But it's an option," I remind him with a pointed look. "Right now, that's better than no option at all."

"I don't think my boy has months." He regards me with an expression so strained, I feel foolish for trying to comfort him.

"I'm sorry," I mumble, leaning away from the table. "I know this is equally, if not more, important to you."

"Yes, well at least you have allowed me to be a contributor." Professor Donoghue bobs his head. "I only wish I had more luck and more time."

"We'll figure it out." I give a confident nod. "In fact, I'll go speak with Killian, see what he has to say about the water horse."

"Good idea." The professor gives me a kindly but exhausted smile. He probably knows my talents are wasted in study.

I clamber off my chair and slip my arms into a heavy mohair jacket—I'm not going outside without proper attire this time. I reckon Killian's still in the Glass House; he usually stays until the last dregs of daylight disappear. Longer if weather and time permit.

I pause as a thought pops into my brain. Spinning back toward the professor, I clear my throat.

"How did Killian's father meet his mother if she was one of the Celestial? He must've known how to cross the Veil." I'm surprised I hadn't thought of this before.

"I wondered how long it would take you to ask that." Professor Donoghue sets his book down. "That, my dear, is where dolmen stones do work. One of my greatest discoveries, you know."

"Oh? I thought they weren't an option?"

"They aren't," he says with a slight chuckle. "Dolmen stones only connect to our world if a Celestial from the unseen makes it a pathway. Otherwise, it's just a cluster of useless stones."

"Wonderful." I cross my arms. "I thought I was on to something there."

"Sadly, it is much easier for your kind to find their way here than it is for us to find a way there." Professor Donoghue gives a sad shrug. "But I won't give up hope. I can't afford to. My Connor deserves no less."

"You're right." I glance out the huge bay window. "Maybe he's trying to find his way back to us. Maybe he just needs to figure out how."

"Maybe so, Lexi. Maybe so." He nods solemnly. "But until then, I'm searching for a way to reach him first."

I stomp through the thick overgrowth, clutching my mohair coat tighter. "Killian?" I whisper-shout, glancing around the nighttime glow of the Glass House's secret garden. I don't think he's here, but I'll scour the place before calling off my search.

"Killian," I hiss again, trundling across the pool from a few nights before. I pause to stare at where we'd blanketed the earth in new grass and clover. A smile tugs on my lips. I lean down and let my fingers brush the fresh growth, sensing the thrill of earth and water mingling under my touch.

Water sloshes. I retract my hand as something moves behind me.

I spin. A huge animal emerges from the shadows, looming out of the water. It's great muzzle flares, ears pinned flat against its neck.

I release a strangled cry and stagger backward. The creature rears. Stampedes toward me, its huge head swinging. An aggressive roar rumbles from deep in its chest.

I shield my face and tumble to the ground. The horse tramples its powerful legs before me, squealing the most inhuman defiance. I scramble from between his hooves and stand.

I swivel to face the infamous water horse. I've read somewhere you shouldn't show fear to animals such as this, and you certainly shouldn't run. Can't say I trust that suggestion, but the horse has four legs to my two. There isn't a hope that I'll outrun it.

Bravely, or rather stupidly, I throw my arms out at the horse. He gives a shrill whine, wild eyes rolling, and rears again, stretching to his full height.

I give a warning cry, driving him toward the water. He backs a few skittish steps.

This isn't bravado, but fear. I understand that.

"Hush, boy," I say, lowering my hands and my voice. "I won't hurt you. I'm just looking for my friend. I'll leave soon, I promise."

The water horse stills, then cranes his neck, snapping a warning with an odd nicker of discontent. His ears remain flattened, and he stamps. Otherwise, he seems marginally pacified.

"Lexi? What are you doing here?" Killian launches over a tree trunk and races to my side, angling himself between me and the distressed animal.

"I came looking for you." I throw him a disgruntled look. "To ask about the water horse. You didn't tell me you were letting him have free rein."

"I wasn't expecting a visit," he says, gracing me with a furious glower. "He could've killed you."

"Please, I doubt it's that easy to kill one of us." I roll my eyes. "Besides, he's frightened."

"Frightened is an understatement. The poor boy's traumatized." Killian's pose relaxes, and he nudges me away from the retreating water horse. "It's taken me all day just to get him used to my presence, let alone touch him. I don't know when I'll be able to check his wounds."

I peek around Killian for a better look at the kelpie. He stands at the far side of the pool, head downcast. He's strange in the muted glow of the trees and shimmering water. His body is of a great horse, but with skin like a seal; a dark blue-green. Small gills line his neck; his mane and tail resemble fins more than anything else. He's something between land and sea—I find him oddly familiar. Kindred perhaps.

He lifts his head and turns to look at me.

Tears spring to my eyes.

The right side of his regal face is mutilated. Deep cuts and claw marks run the length of his face and muzzle. A gouge marks his eye socket. With a pained grumble, he lowers his head and coughs, like something chokes him.

"Killian." I step toward him. "He's in agony. Surely we can do something."

"If I could get closer, I could apply a poultice to his eye and wrap it with soaked gauze." Killian steps with me to the water's edge. "His legs are badly burned too. I'm not sure how he's even standing. The howlers must've tortured him for hours to break him."

"Why?" I choke in anger and pity. "Why would they hurt an innocent animal?"

"Because he's a key."

"Oh." My eyes widen at the realization. They used this horse to cross through the Veil when they attacked us. I shake my head and swallow back tears. Am I really worth so much pain and destruction?

I take a few brave steps into the pool. My heart cries out for this animal sharing my water spirit. I reach my palm into the water connecting us, and the kelpie lifts his head, observing me with resigned interest.

"It's okay, buddy," I whisper, letting the water's energy radiate between us. "I'm not going to hurt you. You're safe now. I promise."

The kelpie gives a low rumble, the turquoise depths of his sound eye sparkling with intelligence. He understands me. Perhaps not my spoken word, but he understands our water connection. Curious, he stretches out his nose and snuffles the water, one flattened ear flicking forward, followed by the other. He steps toward me, one foot followed by another, and he slowly bridges the gap between us.

"Whatever you're doing, don't stop," Killian whispers, backing away. "He trusts you. I should've known he would. Keep that up. I'll be right back." Before I can protest, he darts between the trees, and I'm alone with an unpredictable, wild animal.

He stops in front of me, his cold nose pressing into my outstretched palm. His eye regards the marks glowing on my skin.

"Hey, buddy, you like that, huh?" I carefully move my fingers up his nose to stroke his silky face. He doesn't flinch, just keeps a wary eye on me. His ears twitch, but the longer I sit with him, the more he relaxes. I don't push him, I just let him sniff my face and hair.

Killian returns carrying a wooden bowl and bandages. I'm dubious about how much this will work and frightened that if we cause the kelpie pain, he'll not trust us again. I also know leaving his wounds untreated will make them worse. So, as Killian cautiously wades through the water toward us, I place both my hands on the kelpie, one on his shoulder and the other on the side of his face.

"Don't be frightened," I whisper, drawing rivulets up to embrace the hurting animal. "Killian's going to help you." I continue drawing soothing patterns over his silken skin. "You've nothing to fear, nothing at all. We'll make the pain go away." I nod to Killian when I think the kelpie is relaxed enough, then I hold my breath as he begins to inspect the wounds festering across his face.

It takes several attempts, but eventually the kelpie allows Killian to administer the medicine. Between the two of us, we manage to clean the eye socket and bandage it. The kelpie occasionally snaps or kicks at Killian if he's too bold, but I'm just relieved we can help him. It takes a few hours and a couple of breaks, but when we finish, the kelpie is sound asleep and in less pain.

Killian gives me a tired high five and offers to walk me back to the castle. I happily agree, excited to crawl into that plush, four-poster bed. So together we amble back and navigate the secret passageways to my apartment.

Kes sits on her perch keeping sentry but turns a blind eye when Killian and I enter.

I plonk myself on the edge of my bed and kick off my shoes, heaving a sigh.

Killian chuckles. "You sound worse than you look." He pulls back the bed covers, wearing a halfhearted smirk.

"Gee thanks." I slip into the inviting comfort of the bed. "I think there was a compliment in there."

"There was." He tugs the blanket under my chin. "Just a little one. Don't want to give away that I might like you or anything."

"Right." I shake my head in faux exasperation and snuggle into the downy pillow.

"Goodnight, sweetheart." Killian ruffles my hair. "You were pretty amazing tonight." His hand retracts, and he turns to leave.

I snatch his wrist. He stops and regards me cautiously, a divot forming between his brows. He opens his mouth to speak, but I cut him off.

"Stay with me." I push myself up on an elbow. "Just for a little while. I hate being on my own. And, well . . . I feel safer with you around."

Killian wars over my suggestion a moment longer than I prefer. He glances toward the secret door, then to Kes, who watches with narrowed eyes. When he looks at me, I give him the sweetest, saddest look I can muster. His shoulders sag.

"All right, but I can't stay long." He crawls over me and settles above the covers.

Kes gives a warning hiss.

He rolls his eyes. Leaning forward, he picks up a spare blanket and waves it at my companion. "Calm yourself, Feathers." He drapes the blanket over himself. "I'll keep my hands where you can see them."

I laugh, but when Killian loops an arm around my waist and draws me against his chest, it catches in my throat. The warmth of his breath brushes my shoulder. I shiver. This isn't unwelcome. This makes me feel all kinds of things. I clutch his arms and snuggle back into him.

Killian squeezes me a little tighter. His lips graze my bare shoulder. I bite my lip to prevent a smile from breaking through.

"So what's bothering you?" His husky voice is heavy with sleep.

"Nothing, and everything, I guess."

He gives a throaty chuckle. He's probably smirking at my senseless theatrics. "You spend too much time thinking." He yawns and snuggles into my hair, lips resting against my ear. "Get some sleep. Tomorrow will be better."

"You think so?" I run my fingers along the planes of his palm.

"I know so," he says without pause.

A moment of silence passes. "Thank you for today," I say. "I didn't know you were so powerful. What you did . . . that was incredible."

"There's a lot you don't know about me." He sighs tiredly. "But I think we had this conversation."

"All right, you're tired." I giggle and twist in his arms, lifting my fingers to caress his stubbly cheek. His beautiful eyes, though fatigued, glitter mischievously. Our noses practically touch.

"Sweet dreams, Lexi," Killian says firmly, then presses a warm kiss to my forehead.

"Promise you won't disappear?" I arch an eyebrow.

"I'm right here," he says, his voice a gentle croon, then cuddles me closer. "I promise I'll always be right here."

LOVERS, NOT FIGHTERS

It has been three months.

Three short months since I arrived in Ireland and was delivered to the protection of the hidden Mide Estate. Yet my arrival feels like a distant memory. So much has changed. I've changed.

I'm growing to like Mide. Ireland did feel like home, or at least the mirror of something akin to home, but I still can't shake the uneasiness in my heart. The lack of words spoken by the earl and his inner circle unnerves me. Although, my days are uneventful and filled with learning about myself and the people I once belonged to, the nights long, and they often give me far too much time to think. So I keep myself occupied. I take up Bryce's advice to explore.

I explore the old castle with its crumbling stones and dark shadows. I find nothing of interest; only boarded up rooms and dead ends. I give up trying to find things out by myself and reach out to the people.

Pádraig, the head chef and the one responsible for running the kitchens, is a pleasant older gentleman. He barely speaks English and seems to prefer to converse in Gaelic. It amuses him greatly that I often don't have the faintest idea what he says. I don't get much useful information out of him, but I do learn that he dislikes Margot just as much as I do. I often hear him hiss a few unsavory words about her when she storms through the kitchens ridiculing everything in sight. So if he doesn't like Margot, then he's certainly a man of good taste in my eyes.

There is a cluster of housemaids, two of whom I see more regularly than the others. Tess, the younger, a rosy-cheeked woman in her late twenties, has springy, blond curls that never seem to stay in place no matter how hard she tries. She's sweet but quiet. She brings me my meals throughout the day and moves about my rooms like a shadow, never disturbing anything or making her presence known. I often refer to her as "Mouse" because that is precisely what she reminds me of. Her companion, Deirdre, however, is not quite so mouselike.

Deirdre is the elder maid, who hails from Scotland, and nearly always makes her presence known. She has a laugh like a hyena's crossed with a sow, and her movements are not as graceful or unobtrusive as those of her counterpart. Deirdre is always barreling around my rooms, chattering endlessly as she works. Although she's an overbearing kind of soul, she isn't at all bad, and her gossipy nature works very much to my advantage.

Through Deirdre, I learn a lot about the earl's function and his private estate. Or, perhaps, dysfunction would be the better description.

Thomas Domnaill is allegedly the last in a long line of earls that traced their lineage straight back to the three ancient kings of Ireland. His family's a prominent and revered one, but over the years they gradually lost their weight. Thomas had been a "sickly bairn," according to Deirdre, and was never expected to survive, yet he did. Now he's the only surviving heir of his father's wasted legacy.

It appears that Thomas Senior was a neglectful man; he drank his money and ignored his duty. Never truly protected the secrets he was entrusted with. The Elder Council pumped their energy into his son, sending him away to London and Europe to learn, to train in the secrets, lore, and skills of their secret organization, but it all came a little too late.

The fall of my people and the emergence of darkness is not only felt in the Unseen. It radiates through the mortal world. Truthfully, it was the Order of Kings that lost. Dian and his followers hunted and killed many prominent members, wishing at last to cleanse the world of mortal flaw and tear the Veil between worlds. Dian's wrath fell hardest on Mide and the Domnaill clan. For they hold the treaties; it is their blood that holds claim to the last hallowed ground of the mortal world. Or so Deirdre claims.

There are more, many more elite members of the Order of the Kings. There's a hierarchy to the Order. Elite members, like Thomas and Margot, are direct descendants of royal lineage and create an inner circle of leadership with the more senior members, claiming elder status. After that there's the scholars, bloodlines linking back to druids and powerful families; these are the defenders of the laws and truths of our world. Professor Donoghue belonged to that group until recent events. Then there's huntsmen—like my parents—gifted and talented warriors from bloodlines blessed by my kin. They have enhanced abilities in combat, heightened awareness to the supernatural, and other varying gifts, but there's so few now. None reside in Mide. After that, there are guardsmen, agents like Bryce, who make up the majority of the Order and the running of it. Most of them are implanted in worldwide military, just as the elites are planted in politics, business, and various corporations that allow them to infiltrate world affairs and monitor the supernatural uninterrupted. They take oaths—blood oaths—that surrender their lives and the lives of their descendants to the Order.

All of them are scattered throughout the world, defending certain "thin places" or middle grounds to the Unseen, but apparently, Mide is sacred. A Celestial gave her life to defend it and held back the last of Dian's horde. Because of her, he can't set foot here. He can't really set foot anywhere; his power was pretty much tanked at the end of the war, and whatever that unnamed Celestial did, she closed off the Veil, keeping Dian contained for a time. A time to allow three surviving children to grow.

Dian may be limited, but he can send his minions in his place—monsters that make up myths and legends. Demons that every religion and culture only whisper about. I learned Killian has been the main reason they do not attack Mide; at least not often. It appears he's been fighting his whole life. A child warrior and a useful deterrent. But the countless disasters, murders, violent attacks, and senseless acts that plague the mortal world—the ones left forever unexplained—they are all evidence of the greatest supernatural defeat of our age. The Fall of the People of Light. And Thomas . . . well, he is a direct descendent of the king that swore in blood to defend this sacred ground, and any Celestial that should require sanctuary in it. So only he can protect the last remnant of the People of Light—Connor and me.

I'm beginning to understand now why my survival is so important. Why the Order was distressed to no end by my disappearance, and why Thomas is duty bound to retrieve Connor. Our power comes from the Veil. As we've grown, so has Dian. The Veil laws demand balance, and darkness has tipped the scale for too long now. We're the antidote. A way to bury Dian and his evil doings for good. But there has to be more.

If anything, Deirdre's stories fuel my belief that what my parents did was paramount to my survival. Something is wrong with the Order of Kings. Something unnatural, but I just can't quite figure out what. Still, I have more pressing issues to preoccupy my time. Figuring out the secrets of the elusive elite will just have to wait.

My most important task, presently, is getting to grips with my powers, and that means getting tough—not exactly something I'm good at. Bryce has insisted we get straight to work on building my physicality. She's under the assumption that if I connect with my physical strength, my abilities will simply follow. She's wrong.

I remain, forever and always, a walking disaster.

This cool February morning, I take my time lacing up my sneakers from the stone steps in the cobbled training courtyard. The place is desolate and crumbling, just like the rest of this cursed building. I blow out a grumpy sigh and shiver against the dank air. I really hate exercise.

My stomach sinks to my boots when I poke my belly through my stretchy exercise tank—the only casual clothes I'm allowed to own. I'm really not built to be a guardsman, let alone a huntsman. In fact, I will go as far as saying I'm not really built for anything remotely physical.

I loathe it all with an enduring passion.

Absently, I curl a lock of my hair that has burst free from its messy bun and silently contemplate what torture Bryce has cooked up for me today. She's sadistically fond of burpees and making me run until I think I'm going to cough up a lung. The worst and most embarrassing moment to date is when she had Kes fight me with the wooden staff thingies. I was flat on my back within a minute, crying in surrender. Even the memory makes me cringe. I really hope we can avoid combat today. If anything, I think I have proven my complete incompetence at that, although I'm aware copping out is not an option. Thomas was clear on that side of the bargain.

"You really shouldn't be sitting around."

The blunt end of something metallic prods my shoulder, upsetting my silent grumble. I yelp and skitter forward on the steps, barely avoiding face planting into the cobbles. I swivel to confront my assailant.

"Even we supernatural beings need to stretch." Killian finishes his statement with a teasing smirk as he rests a threatening battle axe across his broad, and very much bare, shoulders.

"Uhm," is my famously articulate reply. I straighten and divert my boggling eyes in any direction that is not his naked and chiseled chest. "M-morning." I awkwardly wring my hands. "W-wh-what are you doing here?"

"Same as you," he says as he lops down the steps and comes to a halt not an inch from me. "Only I get up before the crack of dawn, unlike you, lazy bones."

I frown when his fist casually punches my arm, but I keep my eyes downcast and focused on my feet. I can't deny how incredible he is. He has a body that would rival the myths of Adonis; tall, broad, but not so broad that he is disproportionate or grotesquely bulky. Killian is a perfect definition of the natural beauty of creation, forever youthful and strong.

"You all right, sweetheart?" Killian's finger curls under my downcast chin. "I thought it was my flaw to get tongue-tied and mixed up."

"No, not just you." I huff in utter defeat as he forces my eyes upward to meet his mischievous gaze. My blush intensifies, and suddenly, it isn't so cold anymore.

"I love that color on you." He grins and rubs a thumb along my cheek. I roll my eyes and attempt to bite back a telling smile of my own.

Killian has kept his promise to me, giving me all the space and time in the world, being respectful and careful in my presence. Our friendship has only blossomed, much as I knew it would, for we are definitely kindred spirits.

"I'm blushing because I'm in the presence of a half-naked Celestial man," I say and duck my chin. "You should really do the decent thing and cover up. It's not fair on the rest of us."

Killian scoffs disbelievingly. "You're too kind. Besides, it's nothing you haven't seen before."

"You're never going to let me live that down." I groan, shutting my eyes to cringe and allow my skin to bloom a very unbecoming letterbox red.

"Nope, never." He chuckles as his thumb again strokes the length of my cheek, but I don't miss how he rests it on my lower lip with just enough pressure that it pries my mouth open a fraction.

My stomach does a little somersault, and my heart skips a beat as his otherworldly gaze falls from my eyes to my lips. I knot my fingers tightly together, holding them prisoner, debating my next moves. I know what he's thinking, and I wouldn't stop him if he tried. Not this time.

Bravely, I loosen my fingers from their tight embrace of each other and slip one of my hands around Killian's wrist. I let my featherlight touch ease up his arm until I can rest my palm on the curve of his neck. My fingers rest around his nape, and I marvel, briefly, at the softness of his hair as it tangles underneath my fingertips. Killian's grin falters and fades into a look of understanding, all mischief scatters from the depths of his eyes, and in the silence of a second, he lowers his face to mine, and I strain on my tiptoes to breach the gap.

"Alexandria!"

Oh . . . brilliant timing, Bryce.

I snap my panicked eyes to Killian's to find his expression hard as nails. His jaw tightens, and he rolls his eyes skyward in a manner that suggests he would gladly hurl his terrifying axe straight at Bryce's head.

Bryce struts furiously toward us with an anxiety-ridden Kes at her heels, and before I can articulate an excuse, Killian mouths a silent apology. I blink once in confusion, but my perplexed expression is quickly replaced by horror. Killian's fingers move from my chin to sharply clamp around my neck. I gasp at the jolt but note that his grip isn't painful. The axe in his other hand expertly slides and swivels in his sure grasp. In a blink, he brings the wooden handle down on the arm I've rested against his, breaking my grip at his neck and leaving me entirely at his mercy.

I almost don't catch how he uses his grip on my neck to dictate how his body twists around mine, and before I know it, I'm pinned against his chest. His arm replaces his hand to twine around my neck, the sleek, glinting edge of the battle axe resting in threat against my heaving chest.

Someone gasps—Bryce perhaps?

But it's all a front, a deflection on Killian's part, and so I fling my arms up to pretend to tug at his grasp. Attempting to wrestle against his unmovable strength.

"And that is why you never go for the obvious attack," Killian loudly and pointedly reminds me, just for the benefit of everyone in earshot, before loosening his grip and shoving me forward with a teasing peal of laughter. He winks, and I suppress a shy smile. Our secrets remain ours, for now.

Making a show of dusting myself off and acting like I've been greatly ruffled by Killian's assault, I spin to face Bryce with arms crossed. Her eyes narrow between Killian and I, but whatever she's thinking she keeps it to herself. Instead she lifts her chin in her usual arrogant way—a gesture I've come to realize is just a mask for her insecurity—and gives me an appraising look.

"You didn't mention you were bringing company along this morning." Bryce quirks her perfectly shaped eyebrow and purses her lips. Kes peers around her, my companion barely reaching her shoulder as she shoots Killian an exasperated look.

"I'm not keeping company." Killian snorts, and I watch in mild irritation as he flips Kes an inconspicuous rude finger. She hisses and he smirks.

"Killian was here training before I arrived, so he very kindly agreed to show me some moves." I'm hoping to distract from the immature antics of the supposed wise and supernatural remnants of my ancient clan of legend.

I twist around to frown at Killian but find he is waggling his eyebrows suggestively, no doubt amused by my choice of words. I resist burying my face in my hands as my smug Gardener settles himself down on the stone steps and fishes an apple out of his trouser pocket. He bites into the hard flesh and crunches through his breakfast with no account for manners, clearly making his point to Bryce. He won't be moved.

"How thoughtful of him." Bryce scrunches up her nose at Killian, who graces her with an innocent look that would be incredibly endearing, except for his hamster cheeks and gnashed-apple smile.

I choke off a chuckle when my assigned babysitter glares between us. It probably isn't wise to make any more enemies, specifically ones that can exact grueling forms of punishment in the disguised form of exercise.

"Well, I suppose it would do no harm for Killian to be here," Bryce says, though by the strain in her features it pains her to admit it. "It would probably do you some good to watch him fight. Would you be so obliging, Killian?"

"I ain't fighting you, sunshine." Killian casually examines his apple.

"And why not? Is it because I'm a woman?" Bryce sounds offended, but in fairness, I wouldn't want to be pitted against Killian, regardless of having combat training or not.

"No, I'd happily take any opportunity to kick you sideways till Sunday, guardsman, but it's the principle." Killian lounges back, resting his elbows on the steps as he points a finger between Bryce and me. "You are sworn to protect Lexi by order of the treaty between our people. I can't hurt you."

"And what makes you so sure you would even hurt me?" Bryce is practically spitting at this point, her temper exacerbated by Killian's self-assured posture. We all know he's right, including Bryce.

"Oh, let me fight him." Kes launches out from behind Bryce, her small, bony fist shaking in threat. "I'd love a fair crack at bringing him down a peg or two."

"You never give up, do you?" Killian groans at Kes as she shifts into a challenging stance.

"You worried I'll bruise your pride again, Hunter?"

"The last time we fought I was fifteen and you cheated." He jabs an accusatory finger.

I cover my mouth to hide my sniggering. This is a lot of fun, and more importantly, it gets me out of doing anything remotely physical.

"This is ridiculous." Bryce glares heavenward, then clicks her fingers impatiently at Kes. I don't know how happy I am about her ordering my friend around. "Go call in Agent O'Neill and Agent Rea. Perhaps those opponents will satisfy your ego-fueled needs."

"Splendid." Killian springs to his feet, tossing his apple core aside. "I owe Guard Mutts One and Two a fist to the face."

"Killian," I cry out, involuntarily, for I don't like the idea of him getting hurt just to teach me something. "You don't have to fight anyone for me."

"I know I don't, but I will, gladly." He speaks with a strange tone, his gaze weighted and expressive, like he isn't only referring to this battle or these opponents.

Of course he'd fight for me. I just don't know when I'm going to ever feel I deserve it.

Killian waves off my concerns with a breezy and unconcerned grin as he saunters out into the open courtyard and begins stretching. Bryce orders me to the sidelines to watch. Kes returns within a few moments with the two guardsmen I recognize as Killian's personal bodyguards, who suddenly don't appear so sanguine about their latest command. I pretend not to be a teeny bit gleeful about that.

My un-feathered companion joins me moments later with orders to enlighten me to the ensuing battle. She sits with her knees drawn to her chest and her chin resting on the bony caps. I always take these opportunities to observe the strangely beautiful tribal tattoos that pattern her skin. The whirls and swirls give her tiny frame a kind of fierceness that makes me believe she is a force to be reckoned with, yet her beaming smile and happy countenance are a sharp contrast. Looks can be so deceiving.

"Combat is fairly straightforward." Kes interrupts my internal musings as she points toward Killian and his challengers. "Killian is tough. He'll use strength to his advantage. But little guys like us, well, we have to rely on speed. Agent Rea is fast. Watch how he attempts to outmaneuver Killian. I tell you now, he'll still be standing when O'Neill is flat on his back. If he's smart, he'll keep Killian on his toes until he tires out, hopefully get him some lucky shots."

I cringe at her animated description, inwardly wondering what happens when you're neither strong nor fast.

"Truthfully though"—Kes sighs, oblivious to my panic—"they don't stand a chance. Killian will destroy them. Poor fellows."

"You seem pretty confident about his abilities for someone who was goading him earlier." I can't help how my eyes are drawn to Killian's powerful back, the defined muscles quivering in anticipation of the fight, and I'm suddenly overwhelmed with the desire to touch them, to feel the power in him. I swallow and divert my traitorous gaze. If I don't catch myself, I'll give us both away.

"His father was one of the greatest huntsmen that ever lived. Some say he rivaled the great legends of Cú Chulainn," Kes says in a quiet, almost reverential voice, then ducks her head to tell the rest. "We shouldn't speak of Ronan; the Order wouldn't like it. But Lexi, Ronan was just a man. Killian isn't. That should count for something."

I stare at Kes for a long moment until she looks away. Her sharp eyes return to the brawl as she begins to describe the various moves and techniques employed by the challengers. But I can't follow her. My mind swirls around her revelation of Killian, and as I watch him fight so effortlessly, new feelings blossom in the pit of my chest.

Pride. Desire. Longing.

The fatal mix of emotions stops me from concentrating on the technique of the skill he employs just for my benefit. Instead, I watch him with a sense of possession. He is strong, powerful, possibly even revered, and at the very least acknowledged for the capacity for greatness that he could achieve. And he kissed me.

My heart stutters.

I flinch in my seat when, as Kes predicted, Agent Rea gets a few lucky digs in. I try to catch my breath and still my twitching, but each time Killian masterfully executes a well-timed kick or perfect wrestle, I practically shout with pleasure. I know Kes senses my preoccupation, and I'm acutely aware that Bryce watches my every move, but I'm hoping it comes across more as interest than anything else.

When the brawl ends with Killian artfully dodging a swing by Rea and winning by a kick that nearly rends the poor man's jaw from his body, Bryce orders me up and into the center of the courtyard. Kes, of course, follows whilst Killian backs off, his body glistening with a slight sheen of perspiration. But apart from this outward evidence of exertion, he looks barely fazed.

"All right now, Lexi, let's see what you learned." Bryce gives another irritating snap of her fingers.

"You want me to fight like that?" I didn't realize there would be a test at the end of the demo. Someone should've warned me.

"I want you to at least try to emulate what you've witnessed," Bryce says, entirely unconcerned with the wide-eyed look of fear I'm desperately throwing at her. "Kes will lead the fight, and you will defend yourself. Do you understand?"

"Yes." No.

I groan as Kes takes up her challenging stance in front of me, a teasing glint in her eye. She knows I wasn't listening to her earlier descriptions. Ugh. Why am I such a harebrained, hormone-driven artist?

"I'll take the moves slow," Kes says, but I highly doubt that'll make a massive difference. I'm doomed.

Bryce gives the nod, and Kes lunges forward. I yelp and skitter backward a few steps. I thought she said she would take it slow. Liar.

Her wiry arm flings out, and I just about block it with my own forearm, wincing at the pain. I don't see her knee as she wedges it in my gut. I cough and stagger. Kes springs back, her little feet still dancing on the spot, and suddenly I remember what she said about using speed to her advantage.

"Come on, Lexi." Killian's emotive cheer has me momentarily distracted as I glance toward the sound of his voice. "Use your head."

Use my head? Literally or figuratively? I don't have time to contemplate his meaning when Kes assaults me again. This time she takes a few jabs, which I dodge, but her high kick connects with the side of my head, and the blow sends me flailing toward the ground.

"Ow." I whine into the cold stone, then stretch my jaw until it clicks back into place. That is going to hurt tonight.

Bryce groans from the side lines. "You're not even trying."

I grind my teeth at her comment. I am trying, but this is the farthest thing from what I am. I'm an art loving, tree hugging, book reading, animal loving, girly girl. Is that such a crime? Can't I just be terrible at fighting? Not all of my ancestors were fighters, and since when did being strong equate to being physical? Isn't the mind the strongest weapon?

Wait. Mind . . . head . . . use my head.

Killian, you genius.

Slowly, I draw myself back to my feet and take my defensive pose. Clenching my jaw tight, I focus on Kes as she bobs about in front of me. I sense what she is—flesh, bone, blood, and water. A thrill of power runs down my spine as my opponent dances toward me.

I duck and dive her blows. I've got to get her close. I have to get a hold of her. My strength isn't in offensive skills, I'm all about self-preservation, and the only way I can exploit my powers is to put myself in imminent danger.

Kes catches me around the back of my knees, and I drop to the ground. In the same second, she reaches to wrap her arms around my neck, and when she does, I grip her head tightly between my hands. A wave of anger wells up in me, my temper flares at being so humiliated, and for the briefest second, I forget this is only a game and that I'm fighting a friend.

That is all the moment I need.

I feel the water boil with my fury. I draw it to me, pulling it into my attacker's lungs, letting them drown on their fatal mistake.

Kes begins to choke, her grip loosening. I use her momentary weakness to my advantage. A sharp twist and our positions reverse. Now I hold her in an unyielding grapple. She gasps for air, her lungs gurgling.

"S-s-st-op." She pulls at my arm encircling her neck. "L-L-Lexi . . . I can't . . ." She draws a crackling breath.

What am I doing? She's dying.

"Lexi, stop. Let go." Killian's voice is close, but I struggle to rein myself back, the power too alluring, too easy to manipulate.

But this is my friend.

An earsplitting crack echoes the courtyard as a bony elbow implants itself directly between my eyes. With a terrible crunching sound, black speckles burst across my vision.

I fall, my back hitting the ground with a solid thump. A horrible metallic glob slides down my throat.

"Ouch." My vision remains fuzzy, and I blink a few times to see straight, but at least I no longer feel murderous.

Killian kneels by my side. "Good gods, Kes, you broke her nose." An awful pressure presses against my poor crushed nose. A wave of sickness follows, and I groan.

"I didn't mean to." Her voice is hoarse and scratchy but no less panicked. "I didn't know how else to stop her."

"She would've stopped."

"You don't know that," Bryce's voice sounds in the distance. "Good lord, Thomas is going to have my guts for garters. Is the damage repairable?"

"He should." Killian says gruffly, and I wince. "This was your stupid idea. She isn't a pawn, Bryce, she's a powerful being. You can't predict what she'll do, and you shouldn't provoke her."

"Your opinion wasn't solicited, Killian. I asked was the damage repairable."

"Of course it is, but that isn't the point."

Strong arms encircle me, and I'm hauled upward.

"Where are you taking her?" Bryce calls after us.

"Away from you," Killian says, more to himself, before loudly replying, "to fix the damage. We'll be in the kitchens. You don't have to send spies."

The process for resetting my nose is something I've committed to the deepest, darkest crevices of my mind. I swear a blue streak when Killian crunches the bone into place. I honestly think I saw the light at the end of the tunnel during those brief moments of agony.

Kes stays for a little bit, and Killian checks her lungs. I apologize profusely through pathetic sobbing. She keeps mewing that it's fine and that there's nothing to forgive, but I still feel terrible. I should've taken her beating like a normal person.

Eventually Killian tells her to leave so he can clean me up, but I know he's just sick of listening to us. I make a concerted effort not to sniffle in his presence. But when he dabs my nose with the rolled-up gauze, I crack and warble out my pitiful cries. I'm such a wuss. Killian doesn't respond to my cries. He's contemplative, distracted even. He only frowns at my theatrics and waits until I stop squirming before he continues the cleanup.

I sit in relative silence, my heels tapping out the passing minutes whilst Killian mixes something to bring down the inflammation and reduce the pain.

"Drink this." He hands me a cup with a warm, tea-like substance inside. I dubiously sniff it but receive a warning look. I take a tentative sip.

Ugh. It's vile.

"Are you mab ad me?" I ask, after a few more beats of silence.

Killian stills his cleaning and glances over his shoulder. He is a kind man for not laughing at my ridiculous voice.

"No." He reaches for a cloth to dry his hands. "I'm angry for you."

I stroke the edges of my china teacup thoughtfully. "I jub thoob dat mabbe my lil' stunph upseb you."

He scoffs and comes to stand in front of me. "Hardly." His warm palms resting on my knees, he gently massages them.

"I didna meb to hurb her," I say, aware I sound like a kindergartener with a head cold.

"I know you didn't." A tell-tale smirk pulls at his lips. "And Kes knows that too. No one is angry at what you did. In fact, I think we are suitably impressed."

"Oh-day." I sigh and nod my head pitifully.

"Now, drink your tea and try to put this out of your head." His hands leave my knees to rest on my shoulders. "You did really well today, and if you'd been given half a chance, I know you would've controlled yourself. You're strong, but not every power needs to be beaten out of us."

"Wub you meb?" I pull a quizzical frown, or as much of a frown as my nose allows.

"I don't agree with what they did today." Killian tucks loose curls behind my ears. "You have this beautiful, rejuvenating, healing power within you, and all these idiots want to do is turn you into a weapon. Not everyone's calling is to be a warrior."

"Bub you're goob." I make fists with my hands to signify I mean he is a good fighter.

"Just because I fight doesn't mean I want to." Killian strokes my face ever so gently, his eyes scrutinizing the bruising. "I don't like to hurt things. It doesn't feel right. I fight because I must, but I love to heal things, to make things grow, to be useful. And I think"—he looks me dead in the eye—"well, I think you're the same."

I give him a goofy grin, breathing heavily through my mouth, and nod in agreement. At this point Killian does laugh, his eyes crinkling at the corners.

"You are too adorable." He leans in to press a warm kiss to my forehead. I wilt with gooey happiness, and this only seems to amuse him more, but I don't mind—his smile is exactly the medicine I need right now.

"Web will I beeb bebber?"

"Soon." Killian gives my shoulder a reassuring squeeze. "I'll take the taping off tomorrow morning and check it, but I reckon you'll sound more like yourself by this evening."

"Goob."

"Yes, goob." Killian sniggers at my frown and captures my face in his hands again before I can reply. "And if I'm satisfied your nose isn't completely misshapen. Perhaps then you would like to join me for a picnic? As a thank you for saving your nose?"

"You meeb like a dabe?"

A faint blush tinges Killian's cheeks. "Yeah, like a date. If you're comfortable with that terminology," he says as casually as he can, but I see the brightness spark in the depths of his eyes. I couldn't refuse him, even if I wanted to.

"Oh-day," I eventually say with a lopsided grin.

KELPIES LIKE SUGAR TOO

It is becoming an increasingly common occurrence that I should find myself waiting in the cold for a certain Silent Gardener to drag his lazy butt my direction. Honestly, the guy has impeccable timing when it comes to life-or-death situations, but on any other occasion he appears to take his sweet time.

The Glass House is its usual peaceful self in the early afternoon haze. The only sound being Sebastian—the name I picked for the kelpie—as he munches through a bag of fresh seaweed.

Sebastian is a difficult individual for everyone but me. Our natural elemental affinity means he's most relaxed in my company, and therefore I take on most to do with his care. Killian has taught me most of the basics, and thus far Sebastian and I are learning to survive pretty well in our new home. Scars and all.

As if in agreement with my thoughts, Sebastian lifts his head and turns it awkwardly to the side, nickering gently. His membranous mane runs razor-sharp down the length of his long neck, but the flimsy skin trembles when he shakes his head, the green and purple veins catching the light. His good eye bright, alert, and mischievous. When he isn't in pain or feeling a little homesick, he tends to be a handful. Always sneaking up behind me and using his great big head to shove me over a tree root. I think he likes to pretend it's because he can't see properly, but there's that familiar glint in his eye that makes me think otherwise. He's such a cheeky chap.

Sebastian dunks his head downward to snuffle through the rest of his meal, evidently growing bored with my company. Really, what the heck is keeping Killian? He said be ready for one o'clock. He is at least twenty minutes late for our date.

Sitting with my hands shoved into tight fists in the pockets of a mauve mac, I debate the various outcomes that this new little situation might bring. Instinctively, I fluff my hair around my face. I've expertly parted it to the side so that a decent proportion of hair smooths over my embarrassing infliction. A trick I'm well used to employing. Although, I do feel a little silly. It is only a bruise. Killian's been privy to my lack of beauty before, so why should I feel insecure now?

Probably because I hadn't realized what a tall drink of water he is. And probably because—celestial transcendence aside—I'm still awkward and prone to overreact. I suppose I hope that Killian finds my lack of skill and poise attractive. It bodes well for me that I'm the last girl alive in our race. Thank the Creator for endangered-species lists.

I give a little piglet snort at my own stupid joke, then cringe. Ugh, so not a sexy sound. I bury my head in my lap and cover my head with hands. This is going to be a looong date.

"Sleeping already? I'm not that late, am I?"

I sit up straight and paint a ridiculously happy smile on my face at the sound of Killian's voice. It's my hope that it will help me exude an aura of faux calm, but I think I just look deranged. Even Sebastian cocks his head to the side and looks a tad perplexed. No turning back now. Here goes nothing.

"No, I was just . . . rest-ing." I sound the word out, internally screaming at the sickly sweet sound of my voice.

What am I doing? Trying to impress him by being the embodiment of Stepford. Yeesh, it's a bit late for girly-girl manners now.

"Uh huh." Killian arcs a disbelieving eyebrow. "Well, once you stop having a complete mental breakdown about socializing with me over cheese and crackers"—Drat, he sees right through my act—"I would very much like to get this show on the road, before Margot realizes I'm skiving off from varnishing her garden furniture."

"Margot has you varnishing tables and chairs now?" I ask the obvious question, but mostly out of utter astonishment at how much the Countess really does look down her too-thin nose at him.

"Oh yeah." Killian shrugs with his sly smirk playing on the corner of his mouth. "Apparently it keeps me out of trouble."

"Then she seriously underestimates your ability to get into trouble." I snort back more undignified laughter.

"You aren't exactly a goody-two-shoes either." Killian nods his head to indicate my healing nose.

"Yeah, well, they started it." I lift my hand to obscure the yellowish bruises.

"I completely agree." Killian winks, a gesture that makes me flush a little. "But I do love a girl with a little bit of an attitude problem. Makes things interesting."

My shy grin, saved only for him, creeps across my face. I look away for the briefest second to gather myself, but it is in that brief second that Sebastian decides to make his presence known.

"Oh for the love of all that's sacred, Bash, get your nose out of my lunch."

Sebastian, with his permanently crooked head, is speedily investigating the contents of our lunch and is not in any way perturbed when Killian swats at him. Giving up on shooing the curious kelpie away, he moves the basket to his other arm, but Sebastian follows. This time his nose picks up the scent of something that must be hidden in his clothing.

"Ack, get off, you overgrown donkey." But Sebastian carries on nibbling Killian's hoodie pocket before excitedly shoving his nose straight into the gray fleece lining. "Sebastian. Cut it out . . . argh!"

Sebastian knocks Killian straight to the ground in his zealous body search. I jolt forward in kinks of laughter.

"Get him off." Killian huffs as the kelpie removes his snout from the pocket and snorts rather indignantly before shoving his nose straight into my friend's crotch.

I gasp through my breathless laughter and clamp my hand over my eyes. I swipe my free hand out to roughly shove Sebastian off a very violated Killian.

"Stop laughing." Killian grunts through gritted teeth, a real sound of terror in his voice when I hear Sebastian chomp excitedly at air. "Good gods . . . please . . . Get. Him. Off."

"I'm trying." I giggle and stagger around Sebastian's uninjured side, still keeping one hand over my eyes, every so often peeping through my fingers, but when I look, I only laugh all the more. "You must have something in the pocket of your jeans that he likes." I really don't need to look to know the daggers Killian is mentally throwing at me. "Seriously, give him whatever it is or you'll lose whatever it is you'd like to keep."

"Oh, shut up, Lexi!"

Laughing rather girlishly at Killian's predicament, I chance a peek. Sebastian has him pinned flat against the ground with his full body search. Killian shuffles back on his elbows trying to use a raised knee to angle Sebastian's snout away from anything south of his naval. He grouches and pants as he tries to stick his hand into the pocket of his jeans, which are a smidgen too small and a little too revealing.

After a few more minutes of cursing on Killian's part, snuffling on Sebastian's, and yet more disabling laughter from me, my delighted kelpie lets out a shriek when Killian produces a small paper bag. However, no sooner has my frazzled friend procured the desired item and managed to haul himself onto his knees, than Sebastian misinterprets his skewed depth perception and head butts Killian straight in the groin. The little bag is tossed in the air, revealing it to be filled with sugar cubes. Sebastian follows his prize without an ounce of concern.

"I hate your bloody water horse," Killian seethes into the earth in a voice barely above a gravelly whimper.

I slump on the ground beside my dear friend and weakly pat his back. A pathetic attempt at sympathy. My laughter doesn't help Killian's bruised pride, but for all his embarrassment, I find it quite endearing. Such a brilliant start.

We walk hand in hand for what seems like forever, until the shadow of Domnaill Castle is barely a speck in the distance. I don't complain. I like the easygoing, silent companionship that Killian's presence brings me. It is a relaxing and enjoyable activity, but when my stomach starts to growl, Killian pulls me up onto the grassy bank overlooking the beach and lays out our picnic.

It is a simple feast—fruit, cheeses, and a variety of crackers. Killian has the foresight to make up flasks of warm tea. The sea breeze isn't terribly warming, and the hot drinks are a welcome respite.

"Who keeps sugar cubes in the pocket of their jeans?" I point my flask of unsweetened tea at Killian who lies full-stretch on his side, partially propped up on his elbow.

"I told you, I was running late trying to dodge Margot, and I forgot the sugar, so I just threw some in a bag and shoved them in my pocket." He drags a hand down his face in exasperation. "I blame you anyway." He picks up another grape and tosses it in his mouth to chew in an indignant manner.

"Me? How is it my fault?"

"Because you like sugar in your tea, and if I'd known you were perfectly capable of drinking it without sweetness, I would've never been assaulted by your kelpie." He points an accusing finger toward the shale shoreline where Sebastian is frolicking along the water's edge with not a care in the world.

I grin at the happy image, ignoring Killian's huffy tone because I'm so pleased at Sebastian's improvements. We never thought we'd get him out of the Glass House, let alone see him playing in the water. He seems to trust me, and our little bond appears to give him much needed confidence. Killian says it's because I'm the guardian over the waters of the earth, so anything that is naturally of the water will submit to me. But I like to think it's because Bash and I understand each other. We both got washed up on this strange island, sporting our injuries and missing our homes. Sometimes, when Killian isn't around, I find myself telling Sebastian all about my life before that fateful storm. I like to think he listens in silent understanding. I also like to think it helps us both to know we're not alone, but then again, I might just be talking to a mythical horse.

Killian's amused laughter breaks my trance, and I start when his wide palm waves in front of my face. "Daydreaming again, sweetheart?"

I blink, glancing around to find him sitting upright on the tartan rug. His smile so widespread that it makes the corners of his eyes crinkle.

"Yes?" I pretend to be most unamused with his interruption.

Killian catches a strand of hair that has blown across my face from the sea breeze and places it behind my ear. "I was just wondering what you're thinking. You spend so much time in your head that I'm intrigued. It must be a fascinating place to be."

"No, actually I think you'll find it's quite the opposite." I sigh, twisting on my side to better face him. "I'm sorry, Killian, I know I've the tendency to space out. I promise you've got my undivided attention, starting right now . . . What were we talking about?"

"About a disobedient kelpie and mostly the weather." Killian gives a pointed look and I grimace.

"Hmmm." I make a show of tapping my chin with my forefinger. "Well, what else could we possibly talk about? You already know so much about me, like my sugar-tolerance levels, but what about you? What does Killian Hunter like to do when he isn't 'skiving off' from work, or training shirtless in courtyards, or helping resettle a long-lost Celestial queen?"

Killian scratches the back of his neck then shrugs. "Gee, I mean that really does fill up my calendar, especially looking out for the new girl. She's a handful." Killian takes one look at my scowl then blows out a sigh before lying back on the rug and using his arms to pillow his head. "Gardening. I like gardening. And herbalism."

"Wow, I would never have guessed." I raise an eyebrow. "See, this is why we only talk about the weather; you can't keep conversations going with one-word answers."

"It was technically two answers."

"Killian."

"Okay, I get it, you want me to talk about me."

I give him a pointed look and he sighs. Not in a frustrated manner, more like a sound of defeat.

"I'm not that interesting," he says. "Apart from what I am and my usefulness as a fighter, I don't have that much to say."

"I don't buy that for a second." I prod his shoulder and narrow my eyes. "You saw the Veiled Lands. You grew up there, or at least you were more than a baby before you came here. The things you must remember, the world you must've seen? I mean, you cannot think that isn't interesting."

"When you put it like that, I guess it does sound interesting." Killian chuckles, but his eyes mist over for a second, like his memory takes him somewhere beyond any place I can follow. I feel a pang of jealousy for his memories. He knows of my true home and I know nothing of it. That isn't fair.

"The problem is, no one around here likes to talk about my home." He crosses one leg over the other and stares up into the overcast sky. "They don't understand; it's too hard for them. I guess I don't think to recall it in conversation anymore."

"Well," I say as I lie down on the rug, curling closer to him and resting my head in the crook of my arm. "I'm interested. I want to know about home."

"You called it home. You've never mentioned it like that before." A look of genuine surprise crosses his features that makes me grin. I knew he'd like that.

"I guess I like the idea of having a home. I never really had one, so, you know the old saying: You always want what you can't have." I give a nonchalant shrug.

Killian scrambles onto his side to face me with wide, expressive eyes. "But you will have it," he says, in a way that almost sounds like a promise. "Your home isn't here, not among mortals or a dimmed world that is practically a shadow of the beauty of the Veiled Lands."

"Tell me about it." I push him, absently stretching out my fingers to play with the frayed sleeves of his tattered hoodie. Killian catches my straying fingertips with his own. The sensitive pads of our fingers touching, barely connecting, but the energy between the gap is tangible.

"Things shrivel and age here," Killian begins, his eyes remaining locked on our splayed fingers as they test the forces between us. "But in our home, nothing ever fades. Nothing loses its beauty. There are no barren winters or parched summers. Only times of harvest or times of rest, where time is perpetual and irrelevant to life. Everything has a cycle, a time and season, but nothing rots or ages. Even the creatures who do not possess immortality always maintain their beauty, and when it is time for them to enter the Great Sleep, they return to the earth or the sky or the water or fire that bore them. It is—was—a balanced plane of existence."

"Was?" I croak the barely audible question. My eyes are wide and wonder-filled. I don't want him to stop. "What happened?" I dive into the depths of Killian's earthen eyes, conjuring an imaginary world beyond the realms of reason. It's like my perfect childhood daydream.

"The great disruption happened." Killian pauses, the shadows on his face darkening. "Dian's insanity happened." He hisses the name with venom but his eyes droop in sadness. Even my heart aches at the thought of the ruination of such a wonderful place.

"What did he do?"

My fingers retract from his and tighten around the rug in anxiety. When Killian looks up at me, I see utter despair in his eyes. The type of horror you know leaves a deep scar in the mind of an innocent who saw too much evil.

"He betrayed our king." Killian draws a deep inhale through his nose before he continues. "I don't remember how the king was murdered. I just remember that it was unexpected and that the ensuing war was more like an extermination. We never lived with our people, my mother and I. Our home was in the great forests. I only remember her lifting me from my sleep when the war reached us. I vaguely remember an acrid smell of burning fumes in the air. Everything was dark and there were terrible cries and ear-splitting howls in the night. The last I ever saw of my forest home was it burning to the ground from the confines of a small boat on a blood-stained river."

I can't speak for a long time. I can only keep Killian's gaze locked with my own as I try to convey some type of empathy. My mind briefly wanders back to the night I lost my parents and how, on a much smaller scale, it mimicked Killian's own memories. I can only imagine how much worse it is for him, how truly terrifying it must've been for a child. Even the thought makes the hairs on the back of my neck stand on end.

It's entirely natural for me to outstretch my hand and twine my fingers with his again. Killian accepts the gesture and tugs my hand closer to his lips, his thumb gently rubbing a pattern on the back of my hand. His smile is understanding.

"It was a long time ago," he says before skimming his lips across my hand. "You don't have to worry about me."

"I wasn't." The comment only a half-truth as I let him pull me closer. "I was only thinking how strong you are to have survived all of that."

"I had a brave mother. And she had a lot of friends to call upon to keep us safe."

"I wish I could've known her." An image of a formidable forest enchantress with kind eyes of green and hazel fills my wild imagination.

"She would have liked you." Killian chuckles as he inches closer and begins to play with a thick strand of my wind-tangled hair. "I think she would have adored your talents. She would have wanted to teach you so much. You would've given her hope."

"Hope?" My voice grows light as Killian's fingertips untangle from my hair and begin trailing gentle patterns up my arm, making me shiver.

"Yes, hope," he says as the green hue in his eyes intensifies. A quirk I have become accustomed to when we are close. "Hope of a return to our innocence, before the corruption of power and darkness, like starting over afresh."

"Like cleansing water," I whisper, because I feel something more than just attraction or flirtation from his words.

That same drawing motion from our first time in the Glass House pulls at something within me, like how the tides pull and push the shore. I feel each breath he takes in, and how they flow almost instantaneously from my every exhale. I taste the water vapor in the air between us, and it excites me.

My hand stretches out to press against his chest. The thrill of his heartbeat jolting under my fingertips, like I've shocked it. With that small gesture, I find Killian's lips pressed against mine.

For a moment I'm disoriented. My mind registers both my physical senses and the desires of my superlunary essence all at once. It's a little harder than I imagined to separate the two, for they understand this situation very differently. However, it takes only the feeling of Killian's fingers knotting in the hair at the back of my neck and his low, gravelly groan to remind me of exactly what I want to do next.

I lift my hand from his chest and encircle it around his neck and jaw, marveling a little at how easy this is, and how it really wasn't worth all the worrying. Without letting him pull away from our kiss, I boldly give his neck a little tug, hinting at him not to back down.

The air crackles between us.

Then, with more confidence than I knew I had, I force his lips apart and let him deepen the kiss.

I can't remember to breathe as he explores every curve of my lips. Killian's touch is so gentle yet so demanding that it is quite hard to think in straight lines. His palm gently cups my face, his fingertips brushing my flushed cheek.

Tiring of the gap between us, Killian lets his hand slide down the column of my neck to rest on my chest, his thumb pressed neatly in the center of my throat. The lengths of his fingers curl around my neck, encouraging me forward. All the while our lips never part, perhaps only for breath, but I would be lying if I tried to recount otherwise.

I haven't the faintest clue how we will ever stop. I had daydreams of kissing handsome princes as a little girl, but I always knew they were dreams. No one would kiss a girl with a monster's face, and yet, here I am.

It's nice.

My soft giggle parts our explorative kiss. Killian doesn't seem at all upset; instead, I feel his smirk through our parting lips. My eyelashes flutter open. His soulful eyes with their vibrant green depths peer into mine with a look between amusement and satisfaction. I give a tiny, breathless gasp. Reflected in his eyes is the soft shimmering of the strange, vein-like patterns that tattoo my body. I glance warily at the fading marks on my hand and flush in embarrassment. Killian shakes his head, a reminder not to look away. He gently draws our foreheads together and offers me a smile. That smile is so encouraging, so warm and accepting, that I don't feel so freakish when he looks at me like that. Like I'm not the monster I feel I am.

We don't speak. What is there to say? I'm far too giddy to make up a coherent statement, and anything else would ruin the moment. So we gaze at one another, totally lost in the moment, until that moment is shattered. Shattered by long, slimy seaweed dropped unceremoniously on our heads.

INTO THE DEEP

"Sebastian!" We shriek in unison, leaping apart and wrestling out of the tangled, smelly mess.

Sebastian nickers and tosses his head, the sound like laughter, like he might have planned this. I peel a clump of seaweed from my shoulders and glare at my kelpie.

"You." Killian jabs a fistful of seaweed at Sebastian and clambers to his feet. "You're more trouble than you're worth, you little weed."

Sebastian clops behind me, head downcast.

"He didn't mean any harm." I offer a defeated sigh. When Sebastian holds his head in that awkward position, giving me that sad little look, I have to protect him. He's playing on my weaknesses. I'm being manipulated, but I don't care. He deserves the attention.

"Oh, so you're on his side now." Killian scoffs with a teasing smirk.

"Of course," I say, and reach up to scratch behind Sebastian's ear. "He only wanted a little attention. Didn't you, gorgeous boy?"

Sebastian misjudges the distance between us and bashes me with his head. I cringe but say nothing. After all, it isn't his fault, and I'm used to his inept moments. I find his clumsiness rather relatable. Bruises fade and being a one-eyed bandit comes with a few limitations.

I do remember those days. Vividly.

"You're spoiled." Killian forcibly tosses the remaining ·seaweed at Sebastian. "You'll ruin him, Lexi."

Offended, my kelpie flattens his ears and snaps at Killian's hand, just missing the skin. The pair engage in a stare off. Sebastian's head is cocked to the side as he eyes Killian. I muffle my snigger and slide between the pair.

"Now, now, no fighting." I glance between them. "Or neither of you will be getting any attention."

"Is that a threat you intend on keeping?" Killian quirks his eyebrow.

I grin. "Perhaps."

"That's a shame. I really enjoyed those attentions." Killian shrugs and begins backing away. "But if you don't want me anymore, I can go."

I narrow my eyes. "You wouldn't."

Killian turns on his heel to walk toward the beach. I expect him to turn back, but he doesn't. Maybe he thinks I'm serious. No, that's silly . . . isn't it? I better not chance it. I don't want to live without those aforementioned attentions.

"Wait," I say, charging after him. Behind me, Sebastian gives an aggravated harrumph but trails after us. I suppose he only tolerates Killian because of me. In fact, Sebastian probably puts up with a lot of things because he loves when I praise and coddle him. Hmm, I really do spoil him.

Reaching Killian, I slow down, pull a mischievous grin, then jump and throw my weight against his back. He grunts, barely twitching a muscle, and instead of stumbling, as I'd hoped, he catches my thighs as they lock around his waist. I scramble to grip his shoulders with a huff, disappointed at how little impact my bulldozing made.

"You tired of walking or something, milady?"

I grumble. "I was trying to capture you."

He gives me a slight boost to rest comfortably against his back. "Ooh . . . yeah, I didn't get that." He shakes his head.

I scowl, shoving his head forward with my palm. That achieves nothing. "I could capture you if I wanted." I pout and rest my chin in the crook of Killian's left shoulder. He isn't putting me down. He's making a point. I lost.

"Nothing good ever comes of capturing living things," he says, voice losing all of its lightness.

I'm becoming accustomed to his strange mannerisms, like how his playfulness can ebb away to quiet seriousness in a heartbeat.

"Do you feel captured?" My lips brush the edge of his ear. I try not to let his body's obvious shudder distract me.

He turns to gaze upon the water without answering. The murky depths create a mist, billowing rolls of hazy cloud that shroud the Western horizon. It's like we're living under a smokescreen dome, caught between two worlds, with little indication of which is real and which isn't.

Killian rolls his shoulders and punctuates the silence with a sigh. "I don't feel captured. I feel . . ." He pauses, carefully choosing his words. "Obstructed."

I frown. He never quite responds how I imagine he should.

"I feel that I don't have all the facts." The skin around his eyes crinkles as he squints. "I feel like the truth is kept from us, because if we knew the truth, we'd be truly free to decide our fates. That's something I believe the Order doesn't want."

"So, technically like being captured then," I point out a little more peevishly than I'd intended, which earns me an aggrieved huff.

"No, being captured implies an amount of restraint." He twists his neck to look at me, our foreheads touching. That friendly smirk plays on his lips.

"We aren't being kept here against our will, but somehow I think that's worse." His brows furrow, and he ducks his chin. "Ack, I make no sense."

"Hey, your Irish-ness is showing again," I say in a timid attempt to disperse the tension. "Your accent is coming back."

"Great, something else for you to tease." He grins, and I can't help but kiss his reddened cheek. I'm proud of myself for lifting his mood, and slightly smug that I affect him so.

I nuzzle his ear again. "For the record, I don't think you're senseless. I think that you think too deeply, and the rest of us can't keep up."

"In other words, I'm the oddball." He laughs, and I nod—his words, not mine.

I loosen my legs from his waist and drop to the wet sand, the tide lapping at our toes, but I don't unwind my arms, not wanting our loose embrace to end. Much to my delight, he wraps an arm around my waist and cuddles me close, a warm reprieve from the chilly breeze biting at our skin. I nuzzle against his chest, taking a moment to grin happily to myself, then tilt my chin back to gaze into his wild eyes. "But you're my oddball."

Killian grins back, flushing darker than I did, then pulls me closer and buries his face against the crown of my head and kisses me there. "You're too sweet for your own good," he says, though it sounds more like a growl against my ear, but his little warning only reaffirms how much he enjoyed my comment. I do love making him uncomfortable. He really can't handle it, and it's amusing.

I let my fingertips rest on his shoulder, playing with the flimsy fabric of his worn hoodie. Frowning, I worry at the poverty he lives in. There shouldn't be such a marked difference between us. It doesn't make any sense. Killian is right, the Order is too secretive, and their prejudices too obscure. But what choice do we have but to make use of their hospitality? It's a cruel world out there, but I can't imagine a world filled with howlers and nightmarish devils is any safer. I can't decide which to trust, so, in lieu of an actual plan, I'll stick with what I understand.

Right now, I understand Killian. I can't imagine why, but he's steadfast, and presently that is much more appealing than sneaky, unpredictable, and often cruel-mouthed mortals.

My Silent Gardener doesn't speak much, just keeps me wrapped in a comforting embrace. I try to silence my overactive mind. I don't want to ruin this day with my chattering and suspicious thoughts. I want to be in the moment, present and alive.

I close my eyes and lean back, secure in the knowledge that Killian's grip is sure, and breathe in the salty sea air.

It feels good . . . feels right.

When I open my eyes again, I find him staring at me curiously with a wicked grin. I narrow my eyes. "You wouldn't dare let go."

He begins to chuckle and shake his head. I'm relieved, until hooves splash in the water behind me.

There's a nicker, a few chomps, and the rip of fabric at my pants waistband.

I squeak and scramble forward, but Killian—the traitor—steps back, leaving me to my fate.

"Sebastian!" I grapple at Killian's shirt. He backs off, saving himself.

My kelpie whinnies cheerfully as he drags me into the water by his teeth, entirely delighted with himself. I frantically try to remain upright, sloshing backward until I'm hip-deep in the freezing water.

Killian retreats to the safety of the shale banks, laughing uproariously at my predicament—jerk.

"I told you, you'll spoil him," Killian manages to say between laughter.

"Shut up, Killian," I slap the water, trying to bat the stupid water horse away.

But Sebastian doesn't fear my anger, and with one rough snag, the entire seat of my pants rips.

Wonderful.

I gasp and hunch in the water, trying to save my dignity. "You are a brute, Bash! You hear me?"

Sebastian throws his head in the air, letting out his delighted bray. It reminds me of gloating laughter, although it's hard to tell with Killian's barbaric, Neanderthal chortle echoing around the whole bay. "You two are scoundrels," I say, the words escaping like hiss from behind my clenched teeth as I vainly attempt to secure my sodden pants. Thank god my underwear is intact. "I swear, I nearly think you planned this."

Killian ceases his ridiculous laughter, but the wicked expression never leaves his eyes. Rather, the grin on his smug face intensifies. "Isn't fun to be caught in a compromising condition, is it?"

I flash Killian an inappropriate finger. So ladylike.

"Oh, ouch, you wound me." He begins chortling again.

Defeated, I sink farther into the water to obscure myself behind my delighted kelpie. Sebastian slooshes his front legs side to side and nudges my chest, not bothered by my glowering. I shove his snout away, but this makes him more determined to gain my attention. He bobs his head and grunts, pawing the sandy lough bed.

What does he want me to do? Build sandcastles?

He throws his head around toward his back, and I narrowly avoid his neck clipping my shoulder. I follow his frantic repetitions until realization dawns.

He wants me to get on his back.

A thrill of excitement runs up my spine. With itching fingers, I reach for Sebastian's smooth neck.

An awakening, feral instinct guides me, with the greatest of ease, onto Sebastian's back. The powerful water energy courses between us, mingling with jittery excitement. Wildness surges through my veins as my kelpie turns to face the open water. I inhale the wet air, and my lungs burn with an all-consuming need. I need to be as free as the water beneath me. I must be free of this restrictive skin.

I need to be free.

"Lexi."

The glorious sound of crashing waves and the water's gurgling swirl drowns Killian's warning.

I don't listen.

I won't listen.

Sebastian launches against the rolling waves. I marvel at how the water crashes against us, how each pound is like being shocked with paddles. Someone is calling for me, trying to pull me back to land, back to restriction and dulled senses. I happily ignore them.

The kelpie launches into a strange gait, swimming, no more ground beneath his feet. With the next wave, my comrade releases a high-pitched keen and crashes into the sea foam.

We dive into the water, like a rock shattering glass, and we separate. My fingers slip from Sebastian's silken skin. Thousands of tiny, shimmering bubbles rise between us. Their heavenly glow chases the darkness from the murky water until it gleams, clear and unpolluted. My eyes follow the source of the glow to my arm, where light bursts from my veins. The bubbles are my flesh, consumed by my own light.

I gasp, but I have no voice, and breathing water causes me no pain. I should be frightened, but I feel only relief. Like I've been holding my breath for a long time, and now I can breathe.

With one more churn of the waves above my head, I close my fleshly eyes and let the current roll me away.

It's like letting go of heavy weights I didn't realize I was carrying. One moment I am a solid thing with limbs and skin holding me in, and the next there's only my mind, or at least the sensation of awareness. Instead of disappearing, as I thought I would, I find I am the water, the very essence of it. I feel strong, unhindered. Neither blind nor deaf. The earth grumbles below, echoing through me. I hear the air above, how it tickles and dances over my surface. I hear the longing call of the land, its distant voice the only thing enough to remind me of what I left behind.

The whole expanse of water is my vision, the dark depths and the wavering light of the shallows. I see the animals hiding in the coral, seaweed, and rocks. I sense their cold blood and how their lives are tied to the water's energy. My energy.

For a time—uncountable, because I don't have need to measure it—I simply exist, stretching and filling up the whole of the lough. Finding mouths of rivers that feed into it, and where it joins the ocean. I could continue to follow the currents, travel farther, go beyond just this little place, but as my essence touches the very bottom of the lough and roams over the surface, I become aware of something new. Not earth, or rock, or anything natural. It's crystal. Strange crystal; not an element of this world.

A wide basin of crystal stretches for miles under the surface of the lough. Intrigue draws me deeper. I reach into the gloom, my free form dancing over the jagged, crystalline basin. Like a fogged mirror. I settle over its blinding surface, searching for a reflection, only to catch a glimpse of a fish swimming on the other side.

This is no mirror. It's a window to another world.

My world? The matrix between us and them?

A doorway to the Veiled Lands?

The waters beyond that crystal basin sing to me like a siren call. I want to flee into that place, into that powerful current. I test the surface, searching for a crack or chink in its armor to slip through, but there is none.

The key . . . I need that key.

Frustrated, I retreat from the depths, returning to the pull of land. To find a key, I must return to a solid form, and I'm not thrilled about that. The thought of dragging that heavy weight of skin and bone and blood around me like shackles is repulsive. Freedom is this place. Freedom from rules and demands. Freedom to be who and what I am without being answerable to men.

Freedom from memories.

Those memories pull at the corners of my awareness, and with those memories of that fleshly form—that girl—comes emotion. Powerful emotions that slam some sense into me. I won't have any freedom if I don't go back. Others will lose their freedom if I don't pull myself together. I have a purpose, and it is more than this.

Whatever I am in this moment, this power is entirely selfish and seductive. I don't have control of myself, and I'm horrified at how easily I let it rule me. How I let myself forget everything. Forget the fact innocent lives depend on me. Forget Killian and Connor. Instead, I'm happy to squander away in the oceans and ignore it all, and that makes me far worse than Thomas, or Margot, maybe even worse than Dian.

With that jolt, I reach for the land, but I don't know how to put myself back into skin. Don't know how to contain all of myself. So I do the only thing I can think of and rush all of myself to embrace the shallows of the lough.

My essence swells and rolls around the shore, embracing the rocks and solid earthy things, but nothing helps. Nothing feels like me, or like it might trigger something in me.

Except—*there*—the sturdy legs of my kelpie as he swims in the shallow water. I visualize myself clambering onto his back, but only manage to roll waves over his body. Sebastian is too much a part of my elemental spirit, sharing my desire for the freedom of water. That will never ground my wild spirit.

Am I stuck this way? Panic—a very real emotion—has me throwing myself at the shore, over rocks, and stretching out for something solid, like if I stretch far enough those little ripples of water and seafoam will form into fingers and hands. But they don't.

How will I be of any use to Connor in this fine state? How will I prove I'm alive and able to think for myself? The Domnaills will assume me dead. They'll retreat into their castle and leave Connor to his fate, and probably blame Killian for my disappearance.

Killian.

I can't leave him behind. I won't let him take the brunt of their anger or be the scapegoat for their failures. I won't abandon him, just like he'll never abandon me. He's probably there now, scouring the shallows, frantic, thinking I've drowned.

Yes. Of course Killian will be looking for me. I switch my focus to him and sense out his earthy essence. He stands like an anchor, chest deep in the murky water, a few meters from the shore, with hands outstretched. He's real. He's skin and blood and bone. His familiar essence matching something in mine and crying out for me. That vibration I can match, and I follow the sensation, like how great tree roots draw the water toward them.

I embrace the tips of his fingers and mine begin returning. The glow surrounding my flowing movements concentrates, forming solid lines. I stretch at the annoyance of being restrained to rigid patterns. The little bubbles of foam decorate my light and encase it, creating my skin, forcing my senses back into dulled and narrow channels. My heart gives a solid thump. My lungs heave, craving oxygen. Blood flows through my veins.

My head breaks the surface, and I gulp frantic breaths as my feet dig into the lough bed. I have a body again. I release a delirious peal of laughter, squeezing Killian's palm.

"Lexi . . ." He runs a shaky hand through his hair. "Thank the Creator you're okay." His relieved expression morphs into anger. "You don't go swimming with kelpies. They're unpredictable, and you just . . . ugh. You're mad . . . clean off your rocker." He stabs a finger at a sheepish Sebastian, who swims toward us carrying my blouse and my locket between his teeth.

My locket. I slam a hand to my chest—my very bare chest.

In the haze of realizing I am me again and the delirium that it causes, it takes me a little longer than it should to realize my skin has returned but not my clothes, and I feel it all at once—shame. Yes, I recognize that very human emotion as it crawls over my exposed skin.

I yelp. Drop Killian's hand and sink back in the water, covering my chest. I sincerely hope he's too busy ranting to notice that under the murky water, I'm wearing nothing but my birthday suit. Ugh . . . can immortals die of embarrassment?

Five seconds ago, I'd little concept of nakedness. That incredible and wild being, whoever she was, has retreated as swiftly as she appeared, and I've none of her bravado.

"Lexi, what on earth? Stop goofing around, this isn't funny."

Killian steps toward me. I cover my chest with one arm and hold up the other.

"Don't you dare come any closer." I attempt to look intimidating. "And keep your eyeballs skyward . . . I'll gouge them out if you sneak a peek."

Killian's eyes bore into mine.

"I mean it, Hunter . . . eyes up!"

Killian clears his throat as a faint blush blooms across his cheeks. He ducks his head, pulling a bashful smirk.

"I said look up!" My body vibrates in indignation. Why do these things insist on happening to me?

"All right." Killian throws his hands in the air, tossing his head back to plant his gaze skyward.

Sebastian's agonizingly slow approach brings him close enough for me to tear the ruined blouse from his teeth.

"Lexi?" Killian asks casually, keeping his gaze fixed high. "Did you . . . are you . . ."

"Naked!" I wrestle the cream blouse around my chest, "Yes, Killian, I am naked. Now shut up."

"I didn't say anything." He shrugs, his grin widening on his ridiculously handsome face.

"Your thoughts were loud enough." When he begins sniggering, I jab a finger at him. "Oh grow up. Do something useful . . . instead of giggling like a schoolboy."

"So it's okay to hang around my neck when I've nothing but a towel protecting my dignity, but despicable for me to find this slightly amusing?" He glances down at me and waggles his eyebrows.

I recoil. "That's completely different."

"No, it isn't." He chuckles, wading away to put an acceptable distance between us. When he reaches the shore, he pauses. "Get out of the water."

"No way. You leave, and then I'll get out."

He goes to the banks and grabs the tartan blanket we used as our picnic rug. Returns to the water's edge and unfurls the edges, holding it out to me. "Get out of the water. I swear I won't look." Killian shakes the blanket at me. "Come on, it's getting cold."

"I don't trust you." I try to hide behind Sebastian. He gives a low rumble and shoves me toward the shore with his nose——traitor.

"Don't be ridiculous." Killian shakes his head. "I gave you my word, now stop being a drama queen and get out of the water."

"No." I dig my heels into the sand as Sebastian continues shoving me forward.

"Lexi?" Killian uses his exasperated warning voice. That tone probably means he isn't against stooping to forceful measures. I wince at the idea of walking home in a sodden blanket, should he decide to return and drag me out, wet blanket and all.

"Fine"—I point to the blanket—"but drop that rug on the ground and turn around. I'm capable of sorting myself, thanks very much."

Killian raises his eyebrows but drops the blanket and turns around. He folds his arms and stands rigid. I wait to make sure he won't change his mind, then creep out of the water.

The minute I reach solid ground, I snatch the rug and wrap myself, glad that it's dry. Then I stomp to my Silent Gardener and prod his thigh with my knee.

He drops his arms and looks at me with an amused, expectant expression. I drop my gaze and kick the sand with my bare toes. "Thanks."

Killian cups his ear. "Sorry, what was that? I didn't quite catch you."

I roll my eyes and reply louder, "I said thanks."

"For?"

I resist the urge to knee him in the groin. "For keeping your word." I'll never live this down.

He gives a broad smile. "I told you I would. When are you going to start trusting me?" He wraps one arm around my back and another behind the crook of my knees, then lifts me into his arms.

"I can walk, you know." I clutch the blanket in the right places.

"You're shivering, you've lost your shoes, and a brisk breeze is picking up." Killian starts back toward the castle. "So unless you want the soles of your feet sliced to bits whilst a wind whips that blanket back, you'll shut up and let me carry you."

"Fine," I say, snuggling against the damp heat of his chest. "But my inner feminist loathes this damsel-in-distress treatment."

"The metrosexual man in me fully supports your right to feminism," Killian says with a tinge of sarcasm. "But due to societal injustice, he still feels obliged to rescue ungrateful damsels. Even when they imply he's dishonorable and unable to control his caveman desires."

I open my mouth, but only a disgruntled squeak escapes. Killian grins, so I do the only thing I can. Closing my eyes, I toss my nose in the air.

"Good. I'm glad we understand each other." I wait, expecting a saracastic retort. When he says nothing, I peek up at him. "But the mortified woman in me is grateful for the sensitive handling of her bruised pride."

Killian's grin broadens until sunlight flashes on his pearly teeth, but keeps his gaze fixed ahead. Probably making sure we don't get caught. I give a dejected sigh.

His warm palms squeeze, holding me a little closer.

The gesture makes my heart soar.

OBSTRUCTION

There is something reassuring about the warm, crackling fire and the dusty tiled fireplace. I like the smell of the burning tinder and the entrancing color. I'm grateful for the heat and the light it omits to chase away the cold shadows of my empty room. It warms me. Makes me feel human again. If human is a word I can use.

Sighing contentedly, I link my fingers and stretch them above my head, enjoying the sensation of freeing the tension from my spine and neck. Since returning to this restrictive form, I've never felt so many knots and kinks in my muscles. Mother would've been telling me off if she were here. She'd be grumbling about my posture, saying that I'd regret my slouching. I give a nostalgic smile and touch my locket, which is safely back around my neck. Bash returned it, along with my tattered blouse, but he'd refused to surrender his freedom, and to my knowledge, he's still given Killian the slip.

Shrugging, I return my attention to the array of scraps of paper, pencils, and even a lump of coal I smashed up to use to darken the lines of my drawings. Running a sooty index finger over the page closest to me, I study my crude sketch, trying to remember the shape of the crystal basin. I'm positive it reminds me of a glass ceiling, but it has sharp, geometric edges, not completely smooth.

It's not like I had human perception of touch in that moment, but with what understanding of feeling I did have, I am of the conclusion that the Veil is not a flimsy, ghostly matrix. From what I can tell, it's an impenetrable wall of otherworldly, elemental rock that's as clear as crystal but as tough as diamonds.

The floorboards give an almost inaudible creak. I snap my head up and suppress a knowing grin. I don't need to look to know who it is.

"Don't you ever knock?" I flick my eyes from the fire as I direct my question to the intruder standing in my lounge doorway.

"You're getting quick." Killian leans back against the wall, crossing his arms about his chest and placing one leg over the other. "I think it's safe to say you're settling into your skin."

"Ha!" I snort and pat the ground beside me by the fire. "Only my essence doesn't want to stay in my skin."

Killian winces sympathetically as he crosses the room to flop down beside me. His sincere expression a contrast to the glinting humor in his softened moss-green eyes. I hold his gaze, though my cheeks flush with heat at the mortifying memory of this afternoon's antics. He's a wise man for biting his tongue and not saying any more on the subject.

"We'll iron out the technicalities eventually." He bumps his shoulder with mine. I drop my head to rest against his chest, shaking it a little, too embarrassed to look him in the eye.

"You're so adorable when you're too bashful to speak." Killian slips his hand through the wild mass of my hair to cradle my neck. I give a muffled sigh of contentment as his thumb gently works the skin between my neck and shoulder—a particularly tense spot.

"So," he says, a smile in his voice. "What's got you so stressed, sweetheart?"

"Ugh, I hate that pet name." I slip my chin up to rest against his shoulder, leveling him with my best frown. Killian just grins, silently not apologizing as his free hand rummages through the paper in front of us.

I lay my head against his shoulder. I don't think my heart is ready to fall that deep yet, but when he looks at me like that, when he calls me his sweetheart, it seems my heart does what it wants. Still, we don't have the time to be selfish.

"I saw something when I was in the water . . . or was the water." I cringe and run a hand nervously through the ends of my hair. "I think . . . well, I think it's the Veil."

I snatch up the scrap of paper closest to me and hold it under his gaze. He tentatively takes it from me, his eyes narrowing, their color darkening as he scrutinizes my drawing. I monitor his expression carefully, trying to ascertain if this is new to him or if he has knowledge of something like this.

"It felt like a mirror, y'know, only a mirror that reflected back a different world." I flutter my dusty fingers over the page, pointing to the rugged edges and naturally shaped curves. "Umm . . . well I think that's what it would feel like . . . but it isn't something flimsy, nor is it invisible. It's right here. Right beneath us."

Killian doesn't answer, he just continues to study my rough sketches and draws in unsteady breaths. His full lips slightly parted.

"So, w-what do you think?" I shuffle around to sit opposite him, looking expectantly at him, hoping he'll confirm it for me.

"Lexi . . ." Killian breathes out my name, his eyes flickering to mine as he drops the page. He reaches for me. Both his hands clamp around my cheeks.

The intensity of the emotion in his eyes stuns me to silence. I didn't expect this reaction. Did I miss something?

"You saw this?" He asks as he rolls onto his knees to push himself closer to me.

His eyes never leave mine. The wildness of his gaze so unnerving yet not exactly unwelcome. I give a jerky nod and swallow, unsure of what to make of the quivering in the pit of my stomach.

"Eighteen years these idiots have been looking for the Veil. Twelve of those years I have spent looking for a doorway, praying the Creator would give me eyes to see, that I wouldn't be blind like my father's people."

Killian's ramble is a little hard to follow, but I smile when he outright laughs, albeit a little deliriously, and runs his thumbs under my eyes. "It was you, Lexi," he says. "It was you all along."

"I don't quite follow." I frown and tilt my head to the side. I really have missed something.

"You have seeing eyes," he says in a voice soaked in awestruck reverence that I don't think I deserve.

"Oh, I'm sure every Celestial has that ability." I dismiss his comment with a shrug, but he doesn't relent, he just sits back on his knees and continues to stare me out. "Besides," I say, untangling his hands from my face. "It was by complete chance that I discovered this. No one knew I was going to turn into a spray of sea foam. And technically—*technically*—if it weren't for Sebastian wanting to go for a swim, we wouldn't have known about the crystal basin at all."

"Okay, I accept that coincidence." Killian pokes me with his finger. "But only you have the ability to surrender completely to your elemental power like that. Therefore, Lexi, only you have the ability to see the Veil."

"Fair point." I blow out a defeated sigh. "But seeing it doesn't exactly fix the problem, does it? How do we get through it?"

"Maybe you can get through it." Killian waves his hands to gesture at all of me with a perplexed frown. "Your other form is obviously very . . . fluid?"

"Fluid? Really?" I raise an unimpressed eyebrow and he cringes.

"You know what I mean." He shuffles awkwardly. "You could move through rock, right?"

"Porous rock, yeah. I mean, it's theoretically possible." I lift up one of my sketches. "But the basin didn't feel porous. It is literally impossible to pass. I wanted to figure it out, but I can't. This is what's stressing me out."

"We'll figure it out." Killian rests his hand on mine. "You've found it, Lexi. You've found a way in, now all we gotta do is find the way to open it."

I know he is trying to remind me of the positive, but it really doesn't feel like a victory. It feels like I fell flat before the finishing line. It feels like a failure. Still, Killian is looking at me with so much hope and adoration that I don't feel like raining on his parade.

"I know, you're right." I lift his palm to my lips and nuzzle into the comforting warmth there. "Thank you."

"Maybe the professor will know," Killian says, cupping that palm around my cheek and reaching out with his other hand to pull me onto his lap. I oblige because I could really do with a cuddle. It has been one heck of a trying day.

"I'll take it to him in the morning. Hopefully he can shed some light on it or find a book that can." I study the scraps of paper littered about the floor, still vainly trying to connect the dots to something I feel like I'm missing.

"Good idea." Killian's lips brushing the crown of my head as I snuggle closer, enjoying the protective embrace.

"Did you manage to catch Sebastian?" I ask, attempting to steer the conversation into more comfortable waters.

"Yeah, he was knocking around outside the castle, waiting for you, no doubt." Killian shakes his head. "I offered him a sugar cube and suddenly all past grievances were forgotten. I'm going to regret saying this, but that clumsy doofus is growing on me."

"He does have a certain charm." I grin and lean back in Killian's arms to meet his gaze. "And he can't help that he's clumsy. He's half blind, you know. Don't be so hard on him."

"I find his clumsiness endearing . . . mostly." He tightens his grip around me. "A bit like a certain other half-blind girl I used to know."

Killian tugs me down farther so he can hover his face above mine. I give a shrill little laugh as his nose bumps mine, then wriggle one of my hands free to tangle around his hair, clutching his face closer. "Used to know?" I keep my tone light, pretending that the quiver in the pit of my stomach hasn't intensified to the point where I might just tremble.

"Well, she's not blind anymore." Killian's lips brush over mine teasingly.

"Aw, that is a shame. I suppose she's lost her endearing appeal." I give a faux little pout, and he graces me with an achingly sweet smile. I feel that traitorous tremble run down my spine.

"No, it's better." Killian lowers his lips again, but this time bypasses my eager mouth and touches them lightly to the base of my jaw, where my neck meets my ear. I hold my breath.

"She can see me now," he whispers, brazenly continuing to kiss along my jaw. His strong, callused fingertips, skimming over the skin of my neck, tracing a tell-tale pattern on my skin.

I swallow.

There is a heartbeat of complete silence. The only sound being the crackle of the fire as it sparks in the air between us. I should probably think this through. I should be logical and not rush into anything. My parents would warn me to be cautious with my heart. Yet, being cautious never led me to anything good. Breaking the rules, trusting my instincts led me to Killian, and in that short space of time I've discovered more about myself than eighteen years of being cautious could ever show me. So, I throw caution to the wind.

My lips force themselves onto his, and I claw him closer. A tingle of excitement runs across my skin.

Killian gives a shocked gasp. His hands, which were momentarily frozen to the spot, come alive and grapple around my hair. His fingers twining into the loose ends that have tumbled from my messy bun, and with only a little bit of friction, he tears the tie out. Grasping substantial fistfuls, he eagerly kisses me back.

That familiar energy between us ignites and begins to pull. With every breath I exhale, Killian pulls in. Each touch between us roots me to myself, giving me form, making me feel like a whole thing.

Between breathless kisses, Killian shifts. His hands clamping around my legs and twisting them around his waist. I like this new position. It feels more intimate, but not close enough. I don't want any space between us. I want to feel more of him. I want to wrap around him.

I sink to the floor. Tightening my knees around Killian's waist, I force him to follow. He moans—a thrilling sound—as his weight settles on top of me.

"Lexi," Killian gasps between a rough kiss. "We should stop, I don't know if—" He struggles to pull away from me but stops as my hands slide under his threadbare shirt. His warm skin shivers against my cooler touch.

He sighs, dipping his mouth to the crook of my exposed neck, trailing a string of kisses along my collarbone. I bite my lip and arch my back. His hand slips over the curve of my thigh and winds around my waist. His fingers brush my hip through the silk of my wrap dress.

"You don't know if . . . what?" I mumble against his ear, my palms flattening against his shoulders as I push him tighter against me. His teeth graze a sensitive spot just above my collarbone, and I let out a surprised yelp. I didn't know these feelings could exist, that just a touch could make me react so passionately. I want more.

"I don't know if this is right." Killian groans weakly as he finds my lips again and draws another deep and lavish kiss. He breaks it again to speak. "This energy, I can't control it."

I silence him with a kiss, but he wrestles his mouth from mine.

"It's wonderful," I say, and another intoxicating pulse radiates between us.

"It is." Killian nods in agreement through another heated kiss. His hands still roaming in directionless patterns over my body, like he isn't quite sure what to do with them. He groans in defeat when I let my fingers run the length of his stomach.

"Lexi, sweetheart, focus for a second . . . you're killing me." He tries a more pleading approach.

"I'm just a teeny bit stronger than you when it comes to this, aren't I?" I give a wicked grin.

Killian's only retort is a huff. He leans down to kiss me in a much more controlled manner. "Shut up, Lexi."

I laugh, but remove my hands from under his shirt. "Okay, I'm behaving myself." Wrapping my arms around his neck, I use one hand to take a firm grip of my other wrist. "See, I'm keeping my hands to myself."

"And I'm bitterly disappointed about it." He sighs, but relaxes against me, his now vibrant eyes shining with a mixture of ecstasy and mischievousness. "But I don't believe either of us are the type to hit anything above second base on a first date."

"True." I acknowledge his statement with an obvious blush.

"Maybe I need a safe word or something."

I scowl, tugging a strand of his hair.

"Ow . . . I'm kidding!"

"Not at all funny."

"You know that was funny." He sniggers and begins poking my sides until I have to squirm to defend myself.

"Stop it, you fiend!" I slap his shoulders but laugh despite myself. "I'm not all to blame. You didn't exactly stop me. And you're supposed to be the more educated one when it comes to all this energy stuff."

"Educated, yes." Killian confirms with a nod as he pins me down again and rests his forehead against mine, his smile turning gentle and a blush warming his cheeks. "But this, and how you make me feel . . . well, I'm just as much a novice as you are."

"See, now that doesn't help." I caress his cheek, smiling at the heat his flushed skin gives off. "That shy little admission is only encouraging this bad behavior. You're going to have to lock that down."

"Hmm, well then, it's a good job I know how to handle your little penchant for troublemaking." Killian says playfully as he lets our lips meet again. This kiss is a little more chaste, definitely more calming than the others.

"You're not helping," I say in sing-song voice in the pause between the kiss.

"It's okay." He chuckles quietly. "I trust you not to take advantage."

I scoff at the ludicrous statement, and Killian winks before returning to our kiss. Unfortunately though, he is right. I don't know what I'm doing. All these feelings, all this energy, it easily controls me, and that in itself could make me so very vulnerable.

This is a sobering thought. However, for the moment, I let it slip into the background. I want to enjoy a rare and stolen moment of happiness in Killian's arms. We both deserve it.

A faint click disturbs our peace.

The hinges of my apartment door groan as it swings open. Killian breaks our quiet embrace, his head snapping toward the door, his frame rigid with stress.

There, in the silhouette of the doorway, stands Thomas Domnaill.

GIVE IT UP

The earl's hard, ice-like eyes splinter on Killian and I entangled on the floor in a position that neither of us can explain away as a mere accident. I freeze under the furious judgment of his glare.

Killian immediately straightens, attempting to take a defensive pose over me. Like a coward, I cringe behind him.

"What in the name of all that is holy is going on here?"

"Nothing that concerns you." Killian's low and cold tone leeches any warmth left from the room.

"Oh, you think not?" The earl sneers, a dark sneer that sends a thrill of fear through me. I reach for Killian's arm, concerned for him.

"He is innocent!" I cry and scramble to my knees. I try to put myself between them. "I asked him to come here, I consented. He isn't breaking any laws, Thomas."

"I'm afraid he is." Thomas's cold eyes turn their full force on me. "You both have."

"What?" I balk and look to Killian with a horrified expression.

"She hasn't done anything." Killian's eyes never leave mine.

"Guards!" The earl's fury surfaces from beneath his usually indifferent mask.

A second later, my room fills with four guardsmen. With a flick of the earl's hand, I'm wrenched from the ground by my hair.

"She's innocent!" Killian launches for me, but two of the other guards wrestle him back. "Have you lost your mind!" He turns his betrayed eyes on our so-called ally and defender.

"Gag him and take him to my study." Thomas sighs in exasperation, though his stern and merciless gaze never leaves mine. "As for Lady Alexandria, if she cares for her friend here like her noble display suggests, she'll come willingly and give you no trouble."

"And what makes you so sure I will," I say with sharpness, despite the warning in my gut to keep my mouth shut.

"Because if you don't, I'll make him suffer."

I glare at the reflection of my two guards in Thomas's highly polished desk.

Bryce is one of them. I don't recall the name of her companion, but both wear matching expressionless masks.

They flank me as I sit on this opulent—admittedly rather hard—timber chair like a badly behaved school child. I shift uncomfortably, wondering what's taking this earl so long to grace me with his presence and enlighten me as to what law I've broken.

Last time I checked, I'm entitled to kiss whomever I please. What century is this? I suspect Celestial guardian queens have to do a little more than kissing to repopulate their teetering-on-extinction race.

Is this some kind of sick, twisted universe joke? If it is, then it's inherently not funny.

Bryce clears her throat and touches my shoulder. I overdramatize my flinch from her palm, acting like the touch repulses me, and she at least has the common decency to cringe. I twist my neck around to scowl in her direction, successfully making her squirm with guilt. Good.

"Lexi." Her voice is soothing, more a plea than anything else. "Please restrain your temper. Don't make this worse." She pauses, looking away at the sound of numerous footsteps clattering from beyond the door. "Especially for him."

A knot of anxiety twists in my gut. Only for that reason do I suppress the urge to thrash my way out of this rotten tomb of a castle.

As expected, the door bangs open with intimidating force. I watch in wide-eyed horror as Killian's favored guards drag him in. They toss him on the floor before us, standing back to smile smugly at their handiwork.

"Killian." I lurch forward, but the hefty guardsman that joined Bryce smacks his two hands on my shoulders and shoves me back on my chair.

I can take him. I can easily render this fragile human useless and pathetic in front of me, choking on his own spit, but that would make me no better than these brutes. Just because I've the ability to be dangerous doesn't mean I should exercise it. Killian taught me that.

He kneels on the ground in front of me. His clothes—literally the only things he owns—ripped and tattered. I know by his scruffy appearance, flushed cheeks, and drawn expression that he has taken yet another beating from these ruthless men. But I also know a lot more.

I know that he could kill them with the slightest of movements. I've felt the strength radiate from his essence. I've seen the speed at which he moves, and how fighting is as easy as breathing to him. Still, he restrains himself with these people—humans. He wouldn't hurt someone lesser in strength, for that isn't right. He can suffer silently through a beating because he'll heal in a matter of hours, but if he turns his wrath on them, they'll never walk again.

Killian's self-discipline is inspiring. His understanding of right and wrong surpasses even mine. I trust his reactions. So when his steady, green gaze lifts to hold me in his sight, and I see the reassurance in his eyes, the calm in their depths, I don't fight. I'll stay quiet for him. These mortals are not our enemies.

At least not yet. I'm just dying for Thomas to give me a reason to hurt him.

Speaking of the devil himself, Thomas saunters in behind the guards, carrying a hefty briefcase. He stops and regards Killian with a disgusted snort before clicking his fingers impatiently.

"Get up, boy. You're not nursing any injury. Honestly, anyone would be foolish to think a couple of trained guardsmen could finish you off."

Tweedledee and Tweedledum share mildly offended looks whilst Killian betrays the slightest smirk. Rolling his eyes, he gracefully comes to stand, and with a little tug, he breaks the thick electrical cord used to restrain his wrists.

"Aw jeez, thanks, Thomas." Killian unravels the cord from about his wrists and gives his captors a bored glance. "I was having fun messing with these guys."

"Oh, do be quiet, Killian," Thomas groans in irritation as he points to a visibly stressed Bryce. "I told you to keep Alexandria monitored at all times. Was I not clear enough?"

"Sir, I—" Bryce begins but receives a withering look for attempting to speak.

"Why do I need to be so heavily monitored?" I glare at my host as I place a hand over my assigned guardian's wrist. "Bryce does a wonderful job. What happened tonight has nothing to do with her negligence."

"It's okay, Lexi, it's not your fault," Bryce says, but cringes and drops her head when Thomas glares her back into silent submission.

"On the contrary, Agent Bryce, it is Alexandria's fault. She abused your trust by bringing Killian into her rooms," Thomas says tartly as he sits down on his leather office chair and clasps his hands in front of him. "Don't play innocent, Alexandria. I'm not your parent. I have no inclination to give you a lecture on propriety. But you're breaking a serious law, and it's my duty to uphold the law."

I bang my fist in exasperation on his desk. "What law prohibits a friendship between me and my own kind?" My eyes light with fury at the ridiculous secrecy of this Order and their rules.

"He is not your kind!" Thomas snarls and points his finger at Killian. "He is an abomination, a damned creature; neither of heaven or hell, nor mortal or Celestial."

The tension in the room is almost tangible. Even Bryce swallows a hard lump, her downcast eyelashes dampening in sympathy over such harsh words.

I twist in my seat to regard Killian, but he only stares at a point in the distance, acting like the earl's insults fell on deaf ears. But I know by the twitch of his jaw and the flex of his fist that he heard everything.

"Everyone is dismissed, except Alexandria and Killian," Thomas says in a quiet but commanding tone as he reclines back on his chair. The nameless guardsman that came with Bryce makes an unsure-sounding hum, but Thomas shakes his head and adds, "I'll be fine. I have leverage."

I narrow my eyes at his comment. What could he possibly have as a leverage against Killian and me?

The room empties swiftly. Killian remains standing poker-straight in the far corner whilst I sink deeper into my chair. I don't like any of this, none of it seems right, but I feel a lot more nervous now that we're alone with this psycho. I don't trust anyone who can appear so genteel but feel so menacing. Unfortunately, Thomas Domnaill rocks that particular shade with far too much ease.

Thomas picks up his briefcase and silently begins working the lock. I take the moment's reprieve to glance to Killian, hoping to gain some reassurance from him, but I find his eyes trained on the case. His stare is both wide and fearful. I cringe deeper into my chair.

This isn't good.

"Do you know what kills one of your kind, Alexandria?" The earl's smooth voice melts, distracting me from the deadness in his watery eyes, as he pulls out an object draped in crushed velvet from the battered case.

"Howlers?" I say timidly. "Um . . . other Celestials who, um . . . go bad?"

"Technically, yes." Thomas strolls around the desk. He grips the edge of my seat, then roughly turns it so I face Killian. "Perhaps I didn't word that question appropriately; what would your enemy use to kill you, Alexandria? What weapons, precisely?"

"Thomas." Killian's voice is thick with emotion, his hand outstretching in warning, his eyes filled with fear as he steps toward us. "Think about this. She's royalty . . . you can't—"

Thomas rips the velvet from the object in his hands to reveal a strange, gleaming dagger with a blade that looks like crystal. The light casts a sheen across its edges, highlighting the keen sharpness of the blade. The hilt is made mostly of the same element, only veins of silver and gold wrap around it for what I assume is decorative effect.

It is beautiful. Breathtakingly beautiful. Dangerously beautiful.

I swallow reflexively as he holds the exposed blade an inch from my heaving chest. My eyes widen in recognition.

I was cut once before by a howler's blade, and I would've died if it weren't for Killian. But I thought my pain was brought on by poison, not the weapon itself.

"You offend me, Killian." Thomas feigns hurt as he glances apologetically to me. "Lady Alexandria is an honored guest and ambassador; she has the right to safe asylum. You, on the other hand, do not."

I gasp an almost audible "no" as Thomas points the blade at Killian. It's shimmering edge rests just shy of the cleft of his chin.

"Am I not a hunter by name," Killian says through gritted teeth. His head jerked back ever so slightly, hands raised in innocence. "Am I not bound in service to the Order by my father's blood?"

"Regrettably, yes you are." Thomas retracts the dagger. "But you're only allowed to live by the mercy of the select of the Elder Council. We don't kill those of our own blood, nor do we harm a Celestial, lest we break the ancient oaths and unleash Armageddon on our race."

Thomas breathes in deep as if to compose himself. He takes a short moment to glance between the two of us, then continues his deranged rant.

"Laws are part of how we function; we take them very seriously. Blood oaths protect us, and we uphold them tirelessly." He smooths his tweed jacket and gives an exasperated sigh. "They're not senseless laws, they're there to protect us, to ensure the progression and continued relations between our realms and people."

"So enlighten me to these laws," I say, and my fingers tighten around the wooden arms of the chair. "And explain to me how I'm breaking them."

"You already know most of them, Alexandria, whether consciously or not." Thomas shakes his head and runs a hand through his hair. "Don't you read? I thought this was why we allowed Donoghue to return, so you would be taught."

"I must've dozed off during that lecture. Sometimes I get a little tired trying to figure out your Order's problems." I shoot him a purposefully snarky sneer. "Learning the laws comes secondary to saving your hides from an imminent attack from Dian, right?"

"Ugh." Thomas rolls his eyes and waves his hands in the air dismissively. "I haven't the patience for teenagers. Must you all be so . . . difficult."

"Well, I lost my parents, my home, my life, and got dragged across the ocean to take on your problems"—I fold my arms about my chest and raise an eyebrow—"then you subtly threaten me with a weapon. I think I have an excuse to be a tad bit difficult. Now, enlighten me to these laws, my lord."

Thomas lifts an eyebrow straight back but gives a nonchalant shrug. He holds the dagger behind his back and bounces on the balls of his feet for a few seconds, then stops and raises his chin.

"There are a number of laws, most of them only pertaining to mortals and entirely exempting of your kind. But the three most sacred are thus: a Celestial shall never harm a mortal, nor a mortal a Celestial; the secrets of the Celestial will never be spread to the rest of our race; and above all, there shall never be relations between our races that could result in the bearing of offspring. Such mixing of blood is forbidden. It's not right before the eyes of the Creator."

"Yet, it's obviously an invalid law." I scrunch my nose in confusion as I gesture to Killian. "Killian's parents were able to conceive and raise him. Clearly my kind were more lenient on that law. And if it's such an abomination then how is it even possible for there to be a mixing of blood? If the Creator sees it as so repulsive, we would be designed to repel each other."

"It was not always so." Thomas sighs in exasperation, as if he's explaining to a dull-witted child for the tenth time. "In the ancient days, in the times of our ancestors, the Celestials had many sons and daughters to mortals, but these children were gifted, stronger than men but lesser than gods. Some became corrupt, their weaker hearts lusting for power, and men feared extinction. We reached out to the rulers of your kind and they in turn saw the danger. The law was made, and a cull of the abominations took place. It was a terrible black mark in both our histories. None wish to relive it, and the law was not broken for centuries until Ronan Hunter's transgression."

"Do you ever get tired of beating me with that old stick?" Killian slowly shakes his head side to side.

Thomas strides the distance between them. "If you were beaten a little more, perhaps you would learn gratitude."

"I am grateful." Killian rises to his full height, matching Thomas's threatening stance. "I'm grateful every day that my father was nothing like you, you cowardly, lying fool—"

The moment I see the glint of the crystal dagger, I leap from the chair and cross the room in a few short strides, arms raised to halt Thomas. But, before I can reach them, Thomas's hand drives straight into Killian's hip. The sickening sound of flesh slicing apart pulls me up short.

Killian fights the urge to buckle under the blow. A muted hiss escapes his lips. His face contorts in pain. The affable Earl of Domnaill claws his long fingers around Killian's throat. They tighten and constrict as he holds my dearest friend in my line of view. His other hand removes the blade and aims it at his chin. His cold and calculative gaze turns on me.

"I realize that I never clarified your answer to my question, Alexandria. How rude of me." Thomas breathes heavily as he continues to squeeze Killian's throat, my friend's obvious pain distracting me more than it should. "The

Blades of Illumination are the only weapons formed by your people that have the ability to incapacitate—or kill—one of their own."

He stretches the handsome dagger toward me. It's blade drips in beautiful, shimmering blood. Blood that's no different from mine.

"The High King of the Ancients gifted our Order with a small number of these weapons from his own armory." Thomas admires the deadly weapon. "A means by which we men can defend ourselves from the darkness of your kind, the corrupt, and the abominations."

Killian gives a guttural whine, and I realize then that Thomas has taken his thumb and pushed it into the wound. The pressure makes Killian fall to one knee. I take another frantic step forward, hands fluttering uselessly.

"Please . . . stop . . . Thomas, don't hurt him." My trembling voice betrays my fear. "There has been no law broken, I promise you that. I promise he's innocent."

"He's not innocent." Thomas sneers into Killian's face, his wiry fingers tightening around his chin, ensuring he can look nowhere but into his own ruthless eyes. "He's an abomination. Nothing but bad luck follows this mutant. Misfortune and death—he reeks of it. Good people die around this mongrel, isn't that right, Killian? Your mother, your father, even Holly. All dead because of you."

"You bastard." Killian wrestles to free his jaw from the earl's hand.

I see his temper breaking at Thomas's goading. I watch the muscles of his back ripple and tremor, a slight sheen of sweat dampening his brow, and the shaking in his legs convince me that he is prepared to fight.

But this is precisely what Thomas wants him to do. He wants Killian to lose his control. He wants an excuse to use against him. To justify his mistreatment of an innocent and kind soul. I can't let that happen.

"Regardless of how you see him"—I clamp my hands tight in front of me, my face drawn into a pleading expression—"I need him. We need him. You must believe me that he is innocent of that crime, and I can assure you I will not break it or allow anyone under my rule to be found breaking it. If it is the law, then it must be honored."

Thomas twists his head to regard me for a second. He weighs my statement with careful consideration before nodding. Pursing his lips, he turns back around and kneels in front of where Killian rests on his knees. Lifting the dagger, he rests the sharp, glittering edge against Killian's inner thigh. Killian breathes in a long, slow breath.

"You are fortunate to be so useful," Thomas whispers into Killian's ear. "I may not be able to kill you, but I'm warning you now, Killian. You even think of touching her again and this pretty knife will aim a little higher." The earl finishes the threat with a sadistic sneer. As he stands, he lifts his palm and swings it hard. The blow collides across Killian's cheek.

My heart turns to lead in my chest to see Killian hang his head in such depravity. He doesn't even try to look at me but keeps his gaze downcast and cowers in on himself. He's so far folded over that the long tails of his hair nearly touch the ground.

Thomas walks back to his desk and plucks a handkerchief from his pocket. With care, he cleans the blade and returns it to the briefcase before gesturing for me to sit again. I hesitate, my full attention on Killian as I stubbornly stand by him.

"He is a runt that should've been drowned at birth." Thomas exhales loudly as he flounces down onto his own chair. "If his mother had been mortal, we would've left him to die. He's nothing but a commonplace slave. You cannot sacrifice your purity for the likes of him."

"He is my—" I pause, choking on the different words that float in my mind, for he is much more than a friend. "Killian is dear to me," I say, keeping my protective stance over him. "He'll never be a slave, but what has my purity got to do with you or anyone else for that matter?"

Thomas drops his head into his hands, groans, then leans forward to press a few buttons on the ancient phone on his desk. I hear the few trills before Bryce's voice answers.

"Send guardsmen for the boy," Thomas says into the receiver. "And lock him in his cellar. He won't be any problem tonight." He pauses, then pinches the bridge of his nose. "Lexi is capable of seeing herself to her own chambers. She is a respected guest." He slams the phone down with an irritated thump.

Thomas lowers the hand from his face, rising off his chair to lean his weight through his clenched hands onto the desk, and speaks slowly, glaring at me through darkened eyes. "I'm going to be blunt with you." He pauses to glance between the pair of us. "You're female, Lexi. Your protection is only to ensure one cause. A noble cause, indeed, but your only purpose is to bear Connor's children. You're a vessel, nothing more or less. There can never be any question over the purity of your offspring's blood. The continuation of your monarchy depends on it."

The room starts to spin, and I feel a little sick. I catch the back of my chair and cling to it like it's all that's keeping me upright.

I belong to Connor? I've already been selected for him, to pop out his babies like some kind of graceless sow? No. I can't think like that. My parents didn't risk their lives on such a commonplace purpose. I won't believe it. I won't condemn my life to servitude for the sake of a monarchy.

A second later, the guardsmen arrive to whisk Killian away. I cringe as they drag his listless body and shove him out the door. I try to catch his attention, even just to share a reassuring look, but he doesn't lift his head. My heart crumbles in my chest.

"Alexandria, we need to discuss something." Thomas says, and I give a nervous flinch before turning to face him, aware that I'm very much alone. There is no one left to protect me from his madness.

"My intentions for coming to your room tonight were of a much more important and, I had hoped, optimistic nature." Thomas's voice morphs into his genteel lilt. I shudder at the switch. "I really am sorry for having to be so forward with my handling of the situation, but now we all know where we stand, yes?"

I nod, keeping my eyes downcast and fixed on my fidgeting thumbs.

"Good." Thomas sounds pleased with himself. "Now, moving on, I have exciting news."

I feel like this my cue to lift my head and at least give him some eye contact.

"The Elder Council has decreed a summit to take place three weeks from today, right here in Mide."

Thomas crows in delight. I resist the urge to wretch, and instead give a serene smile of fake approval.

"There will be a grand banquet on the first night, in which you shall be officially presented as rightful heir. It's our hope that we can work together to see your rule restored, and of course, Connor's safe retrieval."

"Seems about time that I should meet these elusive nobles." I'm barely able to restrain the sarcasm in my voice. "Perhaps with some combined knowledge we might be able to get the help we need to save Connor . . . my lord and king."

"Yes, indeed." Thomas's eyes spark at my usage of Connor's official titles. "You know, I am impressed by your capacity to rationalize this tremendously difficult situation, Lexi. You made the right decision today regarding Killian. It's regrettable, but we often must make personal sacrifices for the greater good."

I bristle at the comment but force my head to bob once in agreement.

"I also trust that you'll know the right thing to do for everyone, exactly as a young monarch should," he says rather pointedly. Is that a threat?

I lick my lips and give a reassuring grin as I move to stand. Thomas rises with me and offers his hand. I stare at it. The conflicting feelings of venomous hatred and troubling fear swirl in the pit of my stomach, but I keep it all locked behind a blank mask. Thomas takes up my hand and mimics a kiss.

"Lady Alexandria." He bows his head. "It has been a pleasure, as always."

"Yes." I barely get my voice above a strangled whisper as I retract my hand. "Well, it has been . . . educative."

I rip back from his uncomfortable presence and run from the room. I find Bryce waiting just outside the door with Kes. Both of them wear expressions of deep remorse. I breeze past, unable to speak, and throw my hand to shade the tears as they make salty tracks down my face.

"Lexi?" Kes calls and bolts after me. "Please, wait, this is my fault. I should've been with you."

"Just stop." I spin on my heels and plant my palm in her face. "Just leave me be."

Mercifully, they do just that.

Killian's room is dark by the time I find my way there using the old passageways. There isn't even a light or a fire, but I do catch the fading, flickering light of the washroom. I follow my gut and pray he'll be better dressed this time.

I tiptoe into the large, tiled room, noting first that there are many shower cubicles that run down both sides of the wall, and a center unit of hand basins with cracked mirrors. It's a dingy and aged place, but at one time I imagine it was bustling with talented huntsmen. I imagine the banter and the sounds of brotherhood bouncing off the walls, and, absently, I wonder if my own father stood by one of these sinks to shave in the early mornings. Did he know Ronan? Did they speak of secrets in hushed voices, like Killian and I do? But all I hear is the lonely drip of a leaky tap and the quiet, restrained sniff of someone holding back painful emotion.

"Killian," I whisper as I crouch on the ground and crawl toward his dull silhouette, obscured by the sink pipes in the middle aisle. "I ripped up some fabric strips from a towel, in case you're still bleeding. Here." I stretch out the material to him.

He pauses a moment before he leans forward and takes the bundle from me. I note the redness of his eyes and the dampness of his cheeks. He's been crying, but I don't draw attention to it. Instead, I curl up close to him and rest my hands on his injured hip.

"Does it hurt?"

Killian's head rests against the pipes, his gaze not meeting mine, as he swallows and shakes his head. A lie.

"Well, here. Let me help you get this mess cleaned up." I rip the torn fabric of his pants further, revealing the gore and congealing blood that ooze from the wound. I lift a clean scrap of towel and get some fresh water from the leaky tap above me before returning to dab the wound.

"It'll probably need stitches," Killian says, still avoiding my eye. "Although, I do wonder if they provide needle and thread to runts and mongrels."

"Don't say that." I reach for him, my fingers twisting into his tangled hair. "Don't ever let me hear you say that about yourself. You're not those things."

A weighted pause hangs between us before Killian sighs. This breaks the ridiculous stand-off between us, and he reaches to cradle my cheek in his palm.

"And you are far more than just a vessel," he says in a thick and heavy voice. I duck my chin, quickly soaking more water from the basin.

I wring the water onto the gash, hoping the force of it will wash away the rest of the blood. Placing my fingertips on the surface of his skin, I massage and manipulate the flesh around the wound. Predictably, I sense that familiar current swell between us. I bite my tongue and bury the frustration.

I cannot understand these laws. How can something that feels this natural be so wrong? As if to answer my question, the remaining water droplets on Killian's skin draw toward my fingertips. The light in my veins builds and gleams through the skin of my hands, running up the length of my forearm. The water pools around the stretch of torn flesh where my fingers rest. An idea strikes me.

Water cleanses. It renews. And in Killian's case, it certainly increases his vitality and strength. Perhaps if I focus hard enough, if I channel the harmonious energy between us, then maybe—just maybe—I can heal his wound.

I focus on that.

I force the light in my veins to radiate down into Killian's, mixing our essences. I feel that pulse between us and willfully imagine it focusing around his wound, trying to envision it healing as I do. Within moments, the flesh begins to knit itself.

My eyes widen in shock at my own ability. But I can't break focus now. Planting my palms over the wound, I hold it closed, forcing all my thoughts into it, feeling the energy between us begin to draw in a useful direction. When I remove my hands, the only thing left of the wound is a fading vein of light.

A smile tugs at his lips as he pulls me toward him. "You're infinitely more than a vessel." The look of awe on his face I know matches mine, but I grip his wrists and pull away.

"I can't, Killian," I whisper, the thought of refusing his touch or kiss causing me a great deal more hurt than I'd like to admit. "I won't risk getting you hurt like this again. I won't gamble with your life. You're far too important to me."

"It's my life," Killian says, but I hear the struggle in his voice as he works to suppress the emotion. "Don't try to protect me. Don't . . . god, Lexi, please don't give up everything because some man tells you it's the law."

"I'm not giving up." I clutch his hands in mine and squeeze them, sniffling back a sob of my own. "I'm never giving up. Not on you, or us, or the hope of it, but—"

"But what?" Killian shakes his head, his eyes squeezing shut. One lone tear breaks for freedom. "We're so close, we could leave. I bet that stupid kelpie would even help us figure out how to cross the Veil. He'd do anything for you. Gods, I'd do anything for you. Just don't say but."

"Killian, the Elder Council has ordered a summit to take place here in Mide three weeks from now." I rush through my words, hoping that if I do, it'll be like ripping off a Band-Aid—painful but over quickly. "I have to be in attendance. I'm the ambassador. I'm what they need to see. There will be distinguished people with information, secrets, things we can use. I have to prepare for it, and I won't be able to focus if I think for a second Thomas Domnaill is going to use you against me."

"I don't care." Killian tries to grip my hands, but I pull away and lurch to my feet.

"But I care," I say as firmly as my trembling voice allows. "I care for you too much to see you treated so cruelly again. You sit this one out, Killian. You lay low and we avoid being seen together. We can't give them any excuse to hurt either of us again, or to goad you into doing something that I know isn't you."

"So, what? I just forget you until you think it's safe?"

I flinch at the iciness of his tone.

"Newsflash, sweetheart, we are never going to be safe. You can't redeem me, at least not in their eyes."

"I can try."

The words leave my lips without due consideration. The pain creeps across Killian's face like I've just stabbed him all over again.

"No . . ." I try to retract the words but with no notion of how I can. "I don't mean it that way. I don't care how they see you, or us . . . I meant—"

"Get out." Killian's voice is dead. Void of any feeling. His chin drops to his chest.

"Killian, you know I'm trying to do the right thing."

Fresh tears spill from my eyes when he doesn't look at me.

He exhales a hefty sigh. "I know what you're trying to do," he says, again in that hollow voice. "You don't have to explain yourself to me, my queen. Your commands are final. But, if you don't mind, could you just leave?"

"Killian—"

"Lexi, please just go." His eyes teem with unshed tears, and the pain of today's events rest heavier on him. He looks much too old.

I nod and suck back a few sharp sobs as I turn to leave. I never meant to hurt him, but I don't think there was any way I could avoid causing him pain.
None of this was meant to happen. We weren't meant to fall in love.
I knew this would hurt like hell.

THE KEY

The blades of drying grass sting as they stick into my knees. It's been unseasonably warm these past few weeks. The ground drying up, the plants parched, wilting in the weariness of their ebbing energy. The grass, in particular, feels rigid and uninviting. I can't help but liken its unwelcoming nature to another thorny, earthbound spirit.

Killian still isn't speaking.

Not that there is anything new about this. He's hardly a chatterbox. But I'm beginning to learn his moodiness is as constant as the earth below me.

I'm exasperated with him. I've apologized, but silence is his weapon of choice, and he's pretty talented at wielding it. Still, I don't have time to argue with him. There's so much more at stake than just us. Doesn't he know I'm trying to protect him too?

I tilt my head back to squint at the afternoon sun streaming through the canopy of the tree that marks my parents' grave. A tree he grew for them. For me.

Ugh . . . this would be so much easier if I could just hate him.

Rolling my eyes, I flop back against the ground and let my fingers clasp around my locket. "This would be a great time for one of our heart-to-hearts, Mother." My free hand tenses around the earth. "And Father, a little pep talk right now would not be entirely unhelpful."

Only silence answers.

"The elders and the other attendees have been arriving all day. The feast is tonight. Margot made me an actual formal gown." I frown at the thought of trying to navigate stairs in a fancy dress. "They're going to dress me up like a peacock. It's like my version of hell . . . No, hell would be a holiday retreat compared to this."

More silence.

I chew my lip. The banquet is the least of my worries. It actually feels kinda frivolous to be concerned about frocks and dancing when Connor is out there. The Veil is beneath me, and I'm still no closer to discovering a key.

"I was supposed to figure this out." I roll onto my belly and tug the locket over my head, turning it over in my fingers. "I don't think Thomas believes me when I tell him you guys never told me anything. Honestly, everyone acts like I know something I don't. Sometimes I wish you had left me clues. Some regressed memories, or a manual, or . . . something."

That empty silence fills the long pause.

I take a deep breath, studying the locket clasp, then gently pop it open to reveal the two fading photographs of my deceased parents.

I always need a moment before I look at their pictures. It's irrational, but sometimes I catch myself trying to recall the exact shade of Mother's eyes, or the placement of Father's laugh lines. I'm frightened I'll forget them. Or that I'll open the locket and find they've disappeared. Mercifully, every time I do open it, they're there, smiling out at me, reminding me that at least some of my memories are real.

I run my thumb over the picture of my father on the left and smile fondly at his cheesy grin, recalling his obnoxious laughter. I hesitantly glide my eyes right. Looking at Mother's is the hardest. Perhaps it's the innocence in her eyes. Of course, when I was blind, I thought the addition of the pictures was kind of useless, but now I understand. They always knew I'd be able to appreciate this one day.

I swallow the lump in my throat and press the pad of my index finger against the raised card of the photograph, noticing that it doesn't fit properly. The slight curve in the image irritates me more and more every time I look at it. I sit up, my lips pursed, and work at the delicate edges, trying to smooth the paper back into place.

There's something solid behind the image, and not the curved hollow metal of a locket.

With patience, I use my nails to pick away one of the edges of the photograph. It comes loose after some delicate and well-timed effort. I gingerly slide out the image of my mother and slip it in against my father's.

My brows furrow in confusion. My thumb brushes the gold filigree that encases clear crystal. I never thought of taking the locket apart. Father told me to be careful because it was antique, and I always did what I was told. But this isn't just antique.

This is an artifact.

My mind runs ahead of itself, presenting me with the image of the underwater crystal basin. Then back to the beautiful, warped crystal stone encased in the golden threads of my locket, like a mirror image. Like . . . like a map of the basin.

So they did leave me something. A map. I had it the whole time. This is . . . This is . . . I know what this is. It has to be . . . right?

A key.

But how does it fit? Where does it fit?

I wrack my brain thinking of every crevice and dip in the ethereal crystal basin. I don't remember any keyhole, but then again, a chink in its armor would be counterproductive. Maybe the locket creates a hole to pass through. I just have to get close enough and be in a physical enough form to test my theory.

I lurch to my feet and clutch the key tight to my chest, my eyes darting to the shadow of Domnaill Castle, watching the busy comings and goings of its new guests. Stoic, serious, evasive people. Strangers to me. Suddenly I'm not so inclined to tell them of my new discovery. Not until they give me reason to. The elders want to have their secrets, the council wants to be elusive, and Thomas wants to use leverage to control me and my people. Well, I think I've just secured my own leverage.

Glancing back at the great tree, I smile, my eyes welling up a little. Pressing a kiss to my palm, I kneel to place it against the earth.

"Thank you," I say, in hope, to the sleeping souls of my parents. "You taught me well. I know what to do now." And with that, I slip the locket back over my head and confidently make my way back to the castle.

Domnaill Castle has never looked so clean and bright. Everything has been polished to within an inch of its life, including myself. Every effort has been made to bring some light and cheer to the dark shadows of this crumbling skeleton. I have to profess, Margot and the servants did a marvelous job.

Fires burn in nearly all of the grand fireplaces in the communal rooms. Carefully positioned candelabras warm the dull corners, and all the furniture is turned out so that it looks its best. Even the floors and walls sparkle, and every spare space is decorated with beautiful spring flowers, garlands, or greens. There's no need to guess who created those works of art. But my Silent Gardener is nowhere to be found.

Leaning over the top of the servants' stairs bannister, I let my manicured fingernails dig into the wood. The balls of my feet burn already. These shoes are torture devices. I watch with wide-eyed panic, waiting for Kes to come scurrying up and give me my cue.

Thomas wants to make my presence a spectacle. I'm going to make a surprise entrance, because apparently some of the Order don't believe he found me. I didn't like to remind them that they didn't. The howlers did. They just benefited from that unfortunate turn of events.

Sucking in my bottom lip, I groan. I swivel on my ridiculously heeled—and slippery—courts, and tentatively skid to the corner of the hallway where an old, dusty mirror hangs. Glancing at my reflection, I wince. The beautiful lady in the mirror, though graceful and courtly, is not me. I press my fingers along the thin pins in my hair, where Margot has tightly braided it then scooped it into a severe yet elegant bun. It will never last the night. Balling my hands into fists, I clamped them at my sides, determined not to scratch my head senseless. It will only ruin all the hours of effort Margot put in to achieve this polished look.

Truthfully, Margot has been much kinder lately than I expected. I assume she knows of the altercation between myself, Thomas, and Killian a few weeks previous. She didn't directly broach the subject, but she seemed pensive, sad even, as she diligently worked on my appearance. At some point between the braiding and the bun-wrapping, she stopped, placed a wobbly and uncertain hand on my shoulder, and told me to remember that I am a queen in my own right. I understand the meaning behind her well-intentioned words, and for Margot, it really is a big deal, but it feels wrong to my wild heart. I'm not sure how I'll ever escape the duty placed on my shoulders. Or if I can ever escape the desires of my heart. It seems altogether strange not to be so congruent with myself.

A foot on the stairs alerts me to the approach of another. I run my hand over the tight, corset bodice of my dress. The grayish-blue of the organza fabric disguising the boned, body-forming, under-frame beneath that sucks me in right to the tops of my hips. The rest of the dress fans out like waves breaking on the beach. Of all the fakery plastered on my skin and hair tonight, this dress is the only thing I love, even if I occasionally struggle to breathe.

More footsteps . . . heavier . . . not Kes. I turn slowly, swallowing, expecting to see Thomas. Or worse, some strange elder come to gawk at the wild bird in her pretty cage.

A large, tanned hand appears around the staircase newel post. I know that hand. That warm skin. I don't blink in case my mind is playing tricks on me. I want the moment to last, real or not.

"Lexi," Killian whispers, peering around the post. His eyes as deep and earthy as I remember them. No hint of the anger and betrayal that hardened them before.

"W-What are you doing here?" My jaw tenses and shoulders inch higher with stress when I realize how dangerous this could be for him.

"Escorting the princess to her ball. Why else would I be dressed like a penguin?" He gestures to himself as he clears the landing and steps toward me.

My eyes rake over him, and I resist the urge to laugh at the comparison. He looks like no penguin I ever saw. He doesn't even compare with the patrol of penguins waddling around the banquet hall downstairs. Then again, he's the son of a huntsman and a Celestial woodland Druidess. He could never conform to stuffy clothes. It just wouldn't suit him.

"First off," I say, running my thumb and forefinger up the seam of his open shirt that reveals a little too much of his broad chest for a fancy dinner party. "A bow tie is kind of essential for a tux, and you seem to have forgotten yours."

"I couldn't find a shirt that fits." He gives a guilty shrug, catching my wrist in his hand. "And I don't own any ties. I'm going for the relaxed, casual look. Frankly, you're lucky that Pádraig's nephew's dinner jacket fits me."

"Wow. Pádraig's nephew must be a beefcake," I say with notable appreciation. "Dang, I've got to meet him."

"Dorian's happily married," Killian says with a pointed look as he steps in closer to me, his head tilted toward mine. Our noses brush.

"Typical." I sigh but feel my lips twist into a smirk. "Guess I'll have to settle."

"If that dress wasn't so ridiculously tight, I'd make you suffer for that comment." He cuts off my snigger with the pressure of his lips against mine.

I practically inhale him. My hands sliding up his shoulder and clasping him around the neck, drawing him close. His fingers curling around my cheek, his other hand lightly settling on the pronounced curve of my waist. He gives the softest groan as our foreheads meet. The longer tails of his hair fall forward from their slicked-back style to tickle my chin. I smile despite myself.

"I'm sorry," he whispers in the breaths between our kisses.

I shake my head and draw his chin upward when he pulls his gaze away from me to his feet. I can't bear the sadness surrounding him. I won't be the one to make him feel unworthy.

"You don't need to apologize. But I do."

"No you don't." Killian frowns and takes my wrists in his hands again, pulling them away from his face. "I don't blame you for drawing your conclusions, for trying to protect me. I figure I'd probably try to do the same if the shoe was on the other foot. But I'm not backing down, Lexi. I'm not letting you go without a fight. Accept it."

"You'll get yourself killed!" I whisper-shout in my panic. My eyes trying to express a level of anxiety that I'm beginning to think Killian doesn't ever feel.

"Then at least I'll die fighting for something I actually believe in." He smiles and I groan, letting my head hit his chest with a muted thud.

"I won't let them hurt you," I say against his skin. "And I know I should keep away from you so they can't, but I don't know how to do that, Killian. I don't want to do that."

"Then don't."

Killian suggests the idea so flippantly that I have to pull away to ensure he receives the full brunt of my disbelieving glare. Is he really that unconcerned?

Killian's eyes darken, the green in them burning intensely, and with one easy movement, he steps forward, forcing me back, straight into the wall behind. His body presses hard against mine. His fingers twist into mine as he pins them to either side of my head, our foreheads pushing together like magnets.

I open my mouth and our lips brush. I breathe, and my chest presses against his. My heart hammers in time with his. Our energies flare between us. The silvery veins beneath my skin start to illuminate, that euphoric sensation of wild freedom pulsing through every inch of me so that when our eyes meet, Killian's shine with such vibrancy. He grins in a feral way. He isn't trying to hold back this time. The wildness in him is because of me.

"Tell me this feels wrong." He almost growls the words, his breathing labored. "Tell me this means nothing."

"Don't goad me," I say, but my fingernails dig into the backs of his hands as I strain forward. The spike of energy between us switches the balance of power, and Killian trembles a little. His eyes squeezing shut for a second. His expression twisting into something between pleasure and pain.

I kiss him, hard, until the weight of him against me is more to do with the exertion of energy between us. I kiss him until his head lolls against my neck and he inhales my scent in short, shallow breaths.

"Of course this means everything," I say in the quietness, my lips nuzzling into the crook of his neck. "This is right. But everything about this place and these people feels wrong."

"We'll find a way out." Killian draws back, his hands now resting on my waist, like he isn't prepared to let go. "We'll rewrite the laws if we have to."

"Killian." I reach to press a hand to his cheek, my heart swelling at the excitement of what I have to tell him. Maybe we can rewrite the laws. Or at least escape them. "Killian, I have to tell you something. I—"

"My lady?"

I twitch at Kes's voice, turning immediately to the sound. And when I spy Bryce, I'm about ready to push Killian away from me when he gives me a lopsided grin that tells me he knows something I don't.

"I might've had a little help coming to the conclusions I did." He jerks his chin to Bryce, who blushes and ducks her head.

"I never did like those stupid laws anyway." She tugs at the black sleeve of her satin dress.

Kes beams at Bryce, looking quite out of place in her short, floaty number.

"And Kes believed that you would be much more amicable if you and Killian made up."

"I did," she says, but then scurries toward the staircase. "However, you don't have much time, Lady Lexi. Earl Domnaill is about to make your introduction."

I take a deep breath and glance between the three of them, a thought crossing my mind.

"Where is Professor Donoghue?" I ask Bryce directly.

"He wasn't invited." She crosses her arms and raises her chin defiantly. "So, naturally, I invited him as my plus one."

I grin wickedly. "You sneaky, brilliant agent."

"It's my job." She bobs her head toward the stairs. "He's waiting at the bottom. With his injuries, he wasn't interested in climbing six flights of stairs, so when you're ready, Alexandria . . . " Bryce holds out her hand, gesturing for me to descend the steps.

I turn to Killian, and without a word, he grips my hand tightly in his. I take a settling breath, and his thumb massages the skin of my palm, another soothing gesture. I glance upward to meet his softened gaze.

"They're not going to like us entering together," I whisper, my eyes rolling toward Bryce and Kes. "Probably even more than me entering with these guys."

"A whole room of ignorant sheep staring uncomfortably at us?" Killian gives a faux gasp. "Imagine that. It's not like we experienced that every day for the majority of our lives."

"Touché."

He chuckles. "Hey, I'm up for it if you are." He nudges my shoulder, and I grin widely at the thought of the drama I'm about to cause.

"Besides, I'm really doing them a favor. 'Cause let's be honest, Lexi. You tend to make something explode at every social gathering you attend."

"He has a point," Bryce says from the corner before I can open my mouth to respond. Kes snickers gleefully from halfway down the stairs, and I suppress the urge to pout. I'm clearly outnumbered on this point.

"And how exactly are you doing them a favor?" I raise an eyebrow.

Killian grins, then leans in to my ear, gently kissing me there. The gesture makes me melt into a giggling mess, the tension built before ebbing away, and I relax against his shoulder.

The boy has a point.

THE ELDERS

Silence is not quiet. It's deafening.

At least that's how it feels stepping over the threshold onto the landing of the grand staircase that leads to the banquet hall.

I've never in my life felt the weight of so many judgmental, appraising eyes upon me. I've known my fair share of weighted glares, but nothing could've prepared me for this.

I flex my fingers around Killian's. He glances downward, just enough for me to meet his gaze but not enough to suggest we are communing. I feel Kes's petite palm on my shoulder, a little gesture to let me know she has my back. I don't look, but I assume she's squashed between Professor Donoghue's stouter frame and Bryce, both of whom stand tightly behind Killian and me.

The professor's walking cane taps in irritation every few seconds and he harrumphs. "Lively bunch."

Bryce tuts, Kes giggles, and Killian's pose shifts defensively. I only stare, my eyes roaming the crowd, noting how much smaller it is than what I'd expected. I'd mentally prepared myself for something grander.

The faces are nondescript, nothing exceptional about anyone, but I do notice there is a definite class difference. The aristocracy are easy to distinguish. Well dressed, poised, often overweight or too skinny to suggest they work in physical jobs. The guardsmen are even easier to spot. Poorer clothes and constantly in work mode, weaving between the small gathering and guarding exits. They watch us, as they always do, trying to determine if we're a threat. But the elite watch us with thinly veiled judgment.

The elders, however, may as well wear a neon sign.

A small pocket of intimidating people sits at a large round table at the head of the hall. All of them inconspicuously guarded, but they watch and calculate as sharply as any well-trained grunt. Thomas and Margot sit amidst them, or, I should say, Thomas stands, gesturing to me, his expression strained and flustered. I guess he wasn't expecting me to enter with my own entourage. Probably thinks I'd be easier to control and manipulate if I'd arrived alone, without backup. Silly little man.

I take a deliberate step forward, letting go of Killian's hand. The stress rolling off him is palpable. He doesn't like the idea of me descending into a lion's den without him, but he also isn't stupid enough to try and stop me. There is a game to be played tonight, and we all have our parts.

The audible clack of my heels on the marble floor leading to the staircase is testament to the quiet in the room. I twist the fingers of my right hand through the organza of my gown in an attempt to fidget nervously without looking obvious. My left hand trembles a little as I set it on the cool marble of the ornate newel post at the top of the stairs.

I keep my chin high as I descend the steps, looking down on them as they peer up at me. When my feet touch the floor at the bottom, I carefully fold my hands in front of me, still watching them, still noticing their varying reactions.

Some step back. Others lean in curiously. But most gawk. Exactly how I imagined they would.

"If you're expecting me to do tricks, I'm afraid I'm not very good at those," I say, glancing around at the faces closest to me. A teasing smile spreads across my face at the horrified expressions shared. "Yes"—I hold out my arms, palms up and exposed—"it's ordinary skin mostly, but sometimes it glows. No, I don't bite, pretty sure I'm not rabid, and up until about six months ago, the only weapon I could wield was a butter knife. So you can all just relax." I drop my arms at my sides. "Jeez, I thought this was supposed to be a party."

"Ah . . ." Thomas claps his hands together, giving a strained chuckle. "Lady Alexandria was raised in America. The culture seems to have rubbed off." His face flushes in anger. His cold eyes spring to mine.

A warning.

"Yes, beautiful country," I say in a whimsical manner as I gesture for my entourage to follow me. "I honestly miss it. Perhaps I'll be able to visit someday, or do I need permission from the Elder Council for that? Is there a special Celestial visa waiver scheme?"

A rumble of nervous laughter vibrates through the crowd. Thomas's expression turns thunderous, Margot downs her entire wine glass in a second, and Bryce gives strangled wails as she approaches behind me. It amuses me that Professor Donoghue is the one openly cackling, not in the least bit concerned.

"Lady Alexandria." Thomas puts emphasis on my name, and my smile only sweetens as I bat my eyelashes. "This is Lord Callaghan, Master of the Order of the Kings, our esteemed leader."

A distinguished gentleman dressed in all black with silver hair leans back in his dining chair and tilts his head in acknowledgement. Truthfully, I wouldn't have picked him out as the leader. I had imagined someone more pompous, someone with a formidable presence, but he is utterly simplistic. His clothes are pristine, clean lines, and expensive but not showy. His dark eyes are like coal, slightly sunken with age, but it would be hard to place exactly how old he is. He's oddly familiar yet a complete stranger all at once. I get the impression he likes to remain inconspicuous. An elusive shadow in the world.

I don't like it.

Don't trust it.

"Interesting," Callaghan says more to himself than to me as his dark eyes sweep my frame. I cringe, my confidence waning under his calculative, almost predatory leer.

A shadow appears over mine. A comforting breath warms my shoulder. I nearly wilt with relief but resist the urge to sink back into Killian. He's just making a point. He's my subject, my guard. He's doing his duty, but I don't need to look at him to know the threatening stare he is eyeballing Callaghan with. I smirk at the thought. But this is my show, this the part I have to play, and I can't be intimidated so easily.

"It's interesting to finally meet you too, Lord Callaghan." I lift my brows and nod around the table. "I was nearly inclined to think that this elusive council didn't exist. What with all the secrets and hushed conversations."

Thomas gives a cough that sounds more like a threat.

Callaghan chuckles, but the mirth doesn't reach his eyes.

"My apologies," Thomas says pleadingly as he leans across the table to his superior. "She is ignorant. Her childhood guardians chose to keep her in the dark. She doesn't mean—"

Callaghan raises a thin hand to silence the earl, who instantly stops his whining and drops to his chair. I note the shame in his features and how he doesn't dare lift his eyes from the table. It would appear I'm dealing with a shark if the big fish in this pond is silenced with only a gesture.

Great.

"I see you have no trouble expressing yourself, Alexandria." Callaghan's voice is gravelly. He stands gracefully to his feet and smooths his jacket. A cold smile slides across his ageless face. My brow furrows. Something feels off about him. What is it?

"I have found that if I don't ask questions, I don't get answers." I lift my chin high and keep my gaze unreadable.

"Indeed, wise girl." Callaghan grins and glances around me to scrutinize my little crew of misfits. "Wiser even than I expected, arriving with her own retinue, like a queen. It seems I'm mistaken."

"Mistaken?" I try not to sound too surprised or like I'm more ignorant than I want to be.

"I was led to believe I was coming here to meet a gormless youth, but it seems that information was misleading," Callaghan says, his eyes flashing accusingly to Thomas. "There is an intelligent adult in our midst. A beautiful, articulate woman. A born leader, no doubt."

"A leader, yes," I answer, but my eyes flash with indignant fire. "But I'm no mere woman."

"Indeed, indeed, my mistake." He continues to chuckle as though his comment was an innocent slip of cultural misunderstanding. I doubt very much someone like him would make such a faux pas. He is insulting me in the way politicians do—with manipulated words.

"Come, let us eat together." Callaghan gestures for me to take my seat with them. "I'm certain I speak for all my associates when I say that we are captivated by your tale, Alexandria—the Lost Light of the Ancients."

I don't understand. I didn't realize my story had a title in these parts, like I'm some kind of whispered legend. Still, I don't want any of them to know that I'm missing a sizable chunk of my own personal puzzle.

"Of course, but we'll need four more places for my compatriots." I don't ask for their permission. I figure queens shouldn't ask for anything. And I must've figured right, because with a nod from Callaghan, servants rush to rearrange the table.

We are seated, and the rest of the guests, who've been standing patiently through the whole exchange, take this as the silent command to return to their tables. With a short speech, Thomas advises us all that dinner is ready.

With a flourish, every servant that I know to exist in Domnaill appears, and the banquet is served like a well-oiled machine of impeccable precision. A feat achievable by only one overbearing task master, Lady Margot. The way she scrutinizes each tiny detail, I fear for the life of any servant that so much as drops a piece of lettuce.

I'm relieved to be snugly slotted between Bryce and Professor Donoghue. Kes sits by his right and Killian to Bryce's left. I'm thankful for the round table, for at least making eye contact with Killian is much easier, and there is nothing more interesting than watching him conduct himself in a group of people who probably want him dead.

I don't recall the names of the eight elders at our table as they introduce themselves. My nerves make it too difficult to concentrate. But I do notice that most of them avoid eye contact with Killian, except Lord Mackey, who offers him a friendly greeting. Though, Lord Mackey is hard to miss and is the only name I remember, purely because he sticks out like a sore thumb decorated in the Jamaican colors—his homeland. He's a bright and charismatic man, and before the main meal is served, he has proudly regaled me of the tales of his Irish blood and his ancestors never-ending loyalty to the Order. He's amused that I'm so surprised to learn of the large percentage of Irish descendants in Jamaica, and enjoys educating me. I like him the most, possibly because he's the most talkative of the group.

His breezy nature seems to ease the tension from the table, and more conversations emerge between the guests as the wine consumption increases. Killian and I share a look when we register that the elders are now getting bolder. They start to glance Killian's way and whisper between themselves.

"Is this the half-breed?" an oddly masculine lady who has been side-eyeing Killian for the past ten minutes asks Lord Mackey. In response, he lowers his fork to nod in the most conspicuous way.

"Should he even be allowed in public?" the middle-aged woman continues, alternating between appalled glances directed at Killian and nervous fidgeting with her napkin.

"He's doing no harm." Lord Mackey waves a dismissive hand toward Killian, who straightens in his seat and peers curiously at the whispering duo.

I debate intervening, but a warning tap of the professor's finger to my wrist changes my mind. I glance to my teacher who gives a subtle roll of his eyes toward the unfolding situation.

"I'm not a half-breed." Killian directs his soft-spoken statement to the woman. She flushes purple.

"Pardon? Are you addressing me?"

"Yes." Killian takes an elegant sip from his wine glass. "You were discussing me."

"I-I . . . well, this is ridiculous." She flusters even more, her skin glowing like a shiny berry. I barely contain my giggle.

"I just thought you should know that I'm not a half-breed." Killian shrugs and continues cutting his portion of beef, pausing to glance up at the hassled woman again. "I'm dual heritage actually. I was born to a Woodland Druidess, in my homeland, therefore I'm fully Celestial." He pauses and smiles at Lord Mackey, who shrinks into his chair. "And like Lord Mackey's ancestors, I have a mortal, Irish father, therefore I'm fully of the world of men."

"Forgive me, but I don't see the similarity," the woman says indigently. "Lord Mackey is an honorable, law-abiding elder of the Council. Your father was a traitor."

"Apologies, that was not my meaning." Killian exhales slowly, stopping to lower his utensils to the plate. "I meant only that Lord Mackey's Irish ancestors mixed with native Jamaicans. He is dual heritage. Not a half-breed. I believe it would be considered racist to suggest such a thing."

A gobsmacked silence descends on the table, and I almost burst into applause. The triumphant grin plastered over my face is not lost on my wonderful Silent Gardener. He ducks his chin to hide a bashful smirk when his gaze meets mine for a brief second.

Callaghan's emotionless voice shatters the awkward tension at the table, but he never lifts his eyes from his dinner.

"Domnaill."

My head snaps to the earl, who glares viciously at Killian.

"Killian." Thomas's jaw flexes. "I see you've finished your meal. The domestic staff will be needing assistance carrying the logs for the fires. See yourself out."

I open my mouth to shout my injustice, but the professor beats me to it.

"He has barely touched his food." His elbow sticks into my side. "Let the lad eat something, for pity's sake. I'm sure there's no harm done, and it's an absolute shame to waste a good cut of beef."

"Professor Donoghue, I quite forgot who you were for a moment." Callaghan's coal eyes flit to my friend. "I don't recall you were invited this evening."

Bryce shifts in her seat beside me. "I-I invited him, my lord,"

"Ah, I see." Callaghan nods in understanding and sweetly adds, "Well, that was not your place, so perhaps both the good professor and the mongrel can see themselves out, yes?"

"Excuse me, but these are my compatriots." I direct my statement clearly to the Master of the Order with all the courage I can muster. "You may not dismiss them."

Callaghan picks up his napkin and dabs his lips before tossing it on his empty plate and leaning forward to rest his chin on his interlocked fingers. His lips twist into a crooked smile.

"They are both men of my Order. You do not have the power to command them, Alexandria, not here at least. . . . They leave."

"Killian is my subject and the professor is my teacher. I require him for advisory purposes." Though I don't relent, every fiber of my being is screaming at me not to anger this man, at least not until I know the full extent of the power he wields. "And with all due respect, Killian is my appointed guard. You wouldn't leave a lady unprotected."

"You have my word that you are perfectly safe in the care of my guardsmen." Callaghan nods to the Professor. "And there is no one more educated at this table than I. You needn't fret, Alexandria, you are well cared for."

"I have no doubt." I smile in the most genuine way I can, given the circumstances. "But it would make me more at ease with familiar faces. I'm sure you understand this can all be a little overwhelming for me."

Callaghan glowers at my defiance, his jaw clenching and unclenching, but I refuse to be intimidated. I remind myself that I can probably kill him with ease, and that his attempt at forcing power over me is his show of control. But he knows what I am capable of.

I assume he's carefully weighing up his options. Still, this could backfire. In fact, I'm more than positive that it will. But I have my key, and once we survive this evening, I'm getting these guys out of this backward prison.

Professor Donoghue interrupts the stare off between me and Callaghan. "It's quite all right, Lady Lexi." He rises from is his chair and places a comforting hand on my shoulder. "I'm a bit tired anyway. This knee is playing me up. Perhaps Killian could help an injured veteran back to his quarters."

"It would be a pleasure," Killian says with a bright smile, then stands and circles the table. I stare up at him pleadingly, but he remains expressionless, so I try not to show my utter devastation at my defeat.

"Good choice," Callaghan says into his wine glass, his dark eyes never leaving mine, and for the first time tonight, I feel completely at his mercy.

How will I ever survive this?

HURRICANE

The rest of dinner is a silent affair. No one at my table dares speak. Not to me, and not to each other. Not even Lord Mackey attempts to break the heavy atmosphere. For the most part I just push food around my plate, too nervous to eat. Loss of appetite is a sure sign that I'm upset, for I never turn my nose up at cake, and specifically not chocolate fudge cake.

No one comments on my lack of enthusiasm. Only Bryce stares, a worry line creasing her forehead. Kes covers for me by shoveling my portions onto her plate when no one is looking. For such a tiny thing, she sure can pack away obscene amounts of food.

The conversation that follows the meal is clipped and shallow. I answer the questions directed to me regarding my upbringing as vaguely as possible, and, similarly, Callaghan and the elders don't discuss any business. If I ask anything remotely related to the Order and its history, it is dismissed with a chortle, and I'm reminded that tonight is for festivities.

I'm relieved when the small orchestra sets up for the evening's entertainment. At least with the music filling the silences, I can avoid awkward conversations. It doesn't take long for the invitations to dance to come my way. I get away with politely declining most of them, using the excuse that I can't dance, which isn't a lie. The only dancing I know is the dorky side-to-side waddle, because being half blind and entirely uncoordinated kind of ruled me out of all dancing activities in the past. Still, I know when Thomas Domnaill asks, I'm not allowed to say no.

Reluctantly, I let the young earl lead me from the safety of my seat to the center of the floor. I pale when the crowd recedes to create a circle of curious observers. The orchestra begins its tune, a melody that demands a waltz. A dance I knew my parents to enjoy after a few drinks on a summer evening.

"Just follow my lead, Alexandria, and try not to catch your shoes on your dress."

Thomas sighs in exasperation as I clumsily stagger out of time to his fluid steps.

"I'm so very sorry that I disappoint you."

I regret the comment when he gives my fingers a sharp squeeze.

"Manners," he says, giving me a dismissive once over. I scowl.

We circle the floor once before the other couples begin to join us. I suppose it's because my skills are too painful to watch. Probably even more painful for Thomas, considering I crunch his toes regularly. I can't say that I am too concerned about that.

"I thought I made myself clear," Thomas says through a painted smile.

"About what?" An equally false grin pins to my face. "You're always sharing your very vivid points of view."

A sharp heel to my foot.

"Killian." He spits the name through a tight, crazed smile.

I grunt and stumble for the next few steps.

"I have not the slightest clue what you are suggesting." I hiss the statement through gritted teeth, ignoring the pain in my foot. "He can protect me. It's his job. I thought you'd approve."

"I don't." Thomas's grip verges on painful. "And don't think it has gone unnoticed. If you thought my threat was weak, I can assure you Callaghan will do much worse. He is practically looking for an excuse."

"So why are you warning me?" I raise an eyebrow. "Don't you want Killian out of your hair?"

"He's a cumbersome burden, I'll not deny it." His nose crinkles. "But he is an invaluable asset to all of us, and he fights better when he isn't maimed, so don't risk losing such an effective weapon over lustful desires."

"Stop it." I land my foot against his a little harder than I intend. "Stop talking about him like he's a commodity."

"To a true leader, everyone is a commodity," Thomas says, deciding to ignore my jab at his foot. "People have their uses, and when used correctly, they keep us in power. But add feelings into the mix and you're giving your enemies all the ammunition they need to kill you."

"You are a reptile." I sneer in disgust, attempting to end the dance with a firm shrug, but Thomas keeps a tight grip.

"I'm not your enemy, Lexi."

His purposeful use of my preferred name disarms me for a second. I stare at him in silent confusion.

"Keep your heart guarded. Trust me when I say Callaghan will exploit any weakness he finds."

"What are you saying? That the elders are not to be trusted?" My stomach knots in panic as I glance around the room looking for an exit.

"You are a foreign queen in a strange court," Thomas says in a quiet voice. "You should never trust a soul. No one is on your side. Remember that."

With that, Thomas lets go of my hands, and I take a step back, my heart hammering in my chest. I turn back to watch the elders sitting at their table.

All scrutinizing me, judging me, working out my every weakness. My lungs struggle, and I sway a little on my feet.

"Are you well?" His voice could be mistaken for concern, but heck, how can I be sure now?

"Y-Yes." I grasp my forehead and take in a deep breath. "Just . . . excuse me a minute. I need to get some air."

"Certainly." Thomas nods in agreement and steps aside so I can slide past him and make for an unattended exit.

I throw myself into a flat sprint, making for the nearest stairs. The balls of my feet feel like they've burst into flame by the time I reach the top of the staircase on the third-floor landing. There's a balcony through a set of oak doors at the bottom of the left wing. Breathless and limping, I charge for the door and burst into the cool, night air.

With an angry growl, I wrestle with the zipper at the back of my dress, cursing loudly when it won't budge. I gasp in raspy breaths and contemplate the idiocy of wearing a bloody bodice when my ribcage feels like it's about to collapse.

When I can't get the dress unclasped, I give a defeated shriek and kick the nearest plant pot. Predictably, my heels send me off balance. Instead of the satisfying crack of terracotta, I totter backward. I yelp and brace myself to hit the ground.

But secure arms snake around my waist before I do.

"What did that shrub ever do to you?" Killian asks as he sets me back on my feet.

"It's not the shrub!"

He visibly winces at my shrill tone.

"It's these stupid heels, it's this ridiculous zipper!" I claw at the back of my dress. "I'm wearing a bodice, Killian. I can't breathe. My hair hurts because there are a zillion pins holding it to my skull. I am in pain!"

"But you look hot, if that's any consolation." Killian offers a delayed flash of appreciative grin.

I feel my bottom lip tremble, mostly at how sweet that was of him to say. But also because I really can't feel my toes anymore.

"Calm down. Sit before you fall . . . again."

Killian guides me to sit on the ledge. I plonk myself down with an audible huff, blinking up at Killian with pathetic, teary eyes. He drops to his knees and fishes around at the hem of my skirt. I give a shocked gasp when his strong hand clamps around my ankle and yanks it out from under the swathes of fabric.

"Jeez, no wonder you're in pain." He points to the offensive skyscraper heels. "These things could skewer a wild boar. I've knives less threatening than the points on these things."

He works to undo the buckles and slips the slinky torture devices from my feet. I nearly groan in ecstasy when he rubs the cramps running along the soles of my feet. I whine loudly and throw my forearm over my eyes.

"Killian . . . I think I love you right now."

It takes me about a nano second to realize what I've said, and even less time to wish I could somehow jam the words back into my mouth. Killian's silence is the stark reminder that I've just massively screwed up. So much for Thomas's warning. I think my common sense disengaged the moment he called me hot.

"Uh . . ." I sit bolt upright. "That um . . . that was, uh . . . I mean, I loved what you were doing . . . with the rubbing." I slap my hands over my mouth and watch in horror as Killian flushes pink.

I drop my hands in my lap in defeat. "I'm a disaster. I'll stop talking. In fact, I'll just go."

"Lexi, just wait," Killian says as I squirm, trying to free my ankles.

I get all the more flustered when his hands run up my legs and rest against my knees, gently parting them enough so he can push his torso closer to me. His face tilts into mine. I wriggle and flush, my lips parting to argue a point, but they quickly shut when his fingers wind around my neck.

"Shut up for, like, a minute."

A mischievous glint sparks in his eyes. Before I can protest further, he kisses me.

I can't quite help myself as I melt into his embrace, completely forgetting my earlier embarrassment. I relish in how Killian's hands run a little more aggressively over my back, his body pressing against mine and stretching a little taller. He pulls me close, forcing my hips apart, and invades more of my space.

Those explorative hands find the hidden zipper. With a sharp tug, he pulls the zip halfway down my back, exposing the tightly laced bodice. With much too clumsy fingers—too strong and too large to be delicate—he gives the fabric a yank. Relief—and air—rips through my lungs.

I don't want to know how he did that so easily. I don't even think I care. The sound of the tension in the fabric, the boldness of his fingers touching the little bits of skin exposed through the lace, and the recklessness of our kiss are enough to wipe my memory of any warning ever issued by the Order.

Killian is mine. They can't have him. I want him.

I wrap my arms possessively around his neck, attempting to keep my balance, only a little concerned that I'm on a ledge three stories up. Killian's hands slide to the crooks of my knees, and with one demanding heave he pulls me forward, forcing me to wrap my legs around his waist. Without breaking the onslaught of feverish kisses, he stands, with me in his arms, and steps back from the perilous drop. It's both thrilling and slightly disconcerting to feel how easily he can hold me without even breaking a sweat.

"I'm not sure I want to ask how you know your way around ladies' dresses." I giggle and steal another satisfying kiss, knotting my fingers through his silky hair, grumbling a little when he gently sets my feet back on solid ground.

"Not the first time I've cut someone out of restrictive clothing." Killian gives a lopsided grin. "Although it's usually under different circumstances."

My brow furrows as I peer up into his earthen eyes, noticing the way the different shades of green and gray glitter when the moonlight shines on him. It's rather enthralling. I'm so envious of his eyes. No one has ever had such pretty eyes.

"The women's guard armor seems to include a lot of tight leather bodices." Killian shrugs, and I almost admit to having lost track of our conversation, but that would be rude, so I just nod.

"Tends to be the first thing that needs to go when they're injured."

"Has there been much need for your healing skills over the years?" I attempt to do the mental math, trying to figure out how old he must've been when he left Domnaill.

"Yes, but they had more need of my fighting. There used to be a lot more guards, even a few huntsmen, but the only ones left work with Callaghan now." His startling eyes fix on something unseen in the distance as he sifts through unpleasant memories. "But there was about a decade of fighting after we came. Surviving rebels of Dian's legions still had access points throughout this world, but mostly here and Europe—that's Callaghan's territory."

"Access points?" My brows lift and Killian must read the question in my mind before I can fully formulate it.

"Men were helping Dian. There was just as much corruption and rebellion within the Order of Kings as there was among our own people."

"Men were helping Dian and his zealots cross the Veil? Knowing he was evil? Knowing he hates mortals?" I can't quite fathom what type of person might sell out their own race.

His shoulders sag and he shakes his head. "Dian promised them immortality. A seat at the table of the gods."

"Can he do that?"

"No." Killian gives a hard laugh. "Only the Creator gives and takes life. But clearly Dian gave a convincing sales pitch."

"What happened? I mean with Dian's followers and the traitors who were conspiring with him? And the fighting, is it still happening?" I haven't witnessed any violence since the night of the howlers. And I can't help but remind myself of Thomas's parting comment about not trusting anyone. It wouldn't be a stretch to imagine Dian might yet still have sympathizers within the world of men.

"There still is the odd unwanted arrival. Rogue creatures from Dian's perverted court terrorizing humans if they can. Carrying out reconnaissance, most likely looking for signs of you."

I swallow a hard lump that sticks in my throat—they got Connor.

"Callaghan and his huntsmen led a bloody cleansing of anyone they even had a suspicion of corroborating with Dian or his sympathizers. If there are still traitors, they'd be well hidden."

Killian angles his chin and offers a tiny smile, and I realize I'd gone quite still.

"Domnaill is safe, Lexi. Though a lot people died defending it over the years, it still is considered a sanctuary. Dian and his minions haven't breached this place in some years. I've made sure of it." He chuckles at the confused frown I pull and gives a nonchalant shrug. "I guess the older I got, the less inclined enemies were to attack. I've been Thomas's deterrent since I was twelve."

"Twelve?" I gape in shock, unnerved at how easy he smiles through the painful memories.

He slides one hand around my waist and the other though my fingers. Without much effort he begins to sway me in time to the music seeping up from the banquet below.

"I killed my first howler when I was nine," Killian says, like he's referring to something as mundane as catching a fish. "Decapitated one of my grandfather's henchmen when I was eleven. After that, the fighting eased off, but there were still the injured. My mother taught me never to turn away a wounded huntsman. That's how my parents met, you know."

"Funny." I smirk as I'm gracefully spun in a small circle. "It was you who was sporting the injury when we first met."

"Maybe I was trying to get your attention." Killian grins and spins me back against his chest a little tighter. "Seemed to work for my dad."

I let out a peal of delighted laughter at the thought. He always manages to chase my fears away. Still, something bothers me. "Was Holly one of the guards that died?"

Ever since Thomas dropped the name into the list of people Killian loved, I've been morbidly curious. Curious, and extremely jealous, over any female that had my Silent Gardener's attention before I did.

"Holly? How'd you . . ." A look of recognition passes over his face. "Oh. Thomas." Killian scowls, stilling our little dance for a moment. I gather by the darkened look in his eyes that this is a sore point of discussion.

"I'm sorry." I give an uneasy shrug. "She must've meant a lot to you. I didn't mean to bring it up."

"She did." Something suspiciously like tears gathers in his eyes, but his pride would never allow them to fall. Instead, he shakes his head and gives a fond smile. "I guess you could say she was my first love."

"Oh." I drop my gaze, bitterly disappointed that I wouldn't be his first. Maybe that's why he didn't say it back when I mistakenly blithered out the words. Maybe he still loves her. The thought crushes me.

"What's wrong? Did I say something?" The concern in his voice is evident.

"No, no, of course not." I shake my head, trying to dislodge the image of some powerful, athletic huntress play wrestling with my Silent Gardener. "I just didn't know you had a . . . well, someone before me."

The long pause of silence unnerves me. I dare a peek up.

"What?" I bristle at the amused look on his stupid face.

"You think Holly was a lover of mine?"

"That's what you said." An uncomfortable heat creeps up my neck.

"Lexi, sweetheart." Killian chuckles. "Holly was my dog . . . well, technically she was a phoxen."

"A what?" I balk, a full blown, beaming blush colors my entire face as Killian continues to snicker at my expense.

"A phoxen. They are an indigenous hound-type creature that live in the woods of our homeland. Something between a fox and a wolf; beautiful creatures and extremely loyal. My mother gave me Holly as a pup to raise. She came with me, but she was killed seven years ago. Her dying was part of the reason I ran."

"Oh. I'm so sorry, Killian, that was really petty of me."

"On the contrary. I quite enjoyed the show of jealousy." He gives a bold laugh but has the sense to duck when I threaten to smack the side of his head.

"Holly seems like a very human name. You can see where I might have been confused."

"I can, but honestly, I think you need to know." Killian pauses to smile down at me, the humor fading to something a little more serious, something a little warmer. "I think I might be a little bit in love with you right now too."

I can't say anything. I just stare, swallowing the dryness from my throat.

Is this right? Should I be risking his life like this? They'll kill him for this, but I can't deny these feelings. This desire to be near him.

Oh, curse my conflicted and traitorous heart!

"Killian, I . . ." I'm not entirely sure what I'm going to say, but I know he sees the endless anxiety rolling like storm clouds in the back of my mind.

He rests his forehead to mine and presses his thumb to my lips. "Don't say it out loud," he whispers. "You don't have to say a thing. It's only for us, only between us."

I inhale sharply. It feels like relief to keep this secret, but the injustice of never being able to enjoy it hurts like a knife. I drop my head against Killian's chest and nod in agreement. His strong arms wrap around my shoulders and the heat of him chases away the chill in the lonely night air.

I absently wonder how Killian's parents endured the long years of separation—it must've been worth it. Love must be worth the fight. At least this is a type of warfare I might be good at.

With the mention of Killian's mother, I imagine that enchanted woodland across the Veil, and that jolts my memory—my locket! Our key, and potentially our ticket out of here. My heart leaps for joy in my chest. This news will bring him so much happiness. Excitedly, I lean back in his arms, parting my lips to speak as I fish around my neck to grip the chain of my locket.

A frigid burst of wind whips across the balcony. The gust so strong that it pushes me forward and into Killian's chest. I hear him curse in surprise, and he grips me a little tighter. I frown in confusion, unsure of the strange turn in the weather.

Wait . . . *No.*

Carried on that strange gust of wind comes a sickening crack. Loud enough that it echoes around the estate and drowns the music.

A blinding streak of lightning sends a tremor of fear up my spine. I spin into the direction of the terrible gale. My eyes widen in horror as the dark clouds roll over the water. The irony that it should happen now, like they heard Killian speaking and decided to make good on his challenge.

Another frightening brattle of thunder. An unmistakable howl on the wind follows.

"No!" I cry in terror, throwing my hands to my ears. My legs buckle beneath me and my knees hit the hard stone.

Killian pulls me around the waist. "Get up . . . now!"

"It's them." I sob as the howls intensify. The screams of the guests filter up from the party below.

"Don't listen to the noise, just listen to me." Killian forces me up.

The sound of glass shattering makes my heart stutter. My eyes wheel out over the grounds. A flash of orange and gold bursts from the destroyed domed roof of the Glass House. I reach out and cling to Killian's hand, blinking a hundred times, but not once being able to make the image disappear.

"It's a portal!" Killian shouts to me against the wind and the blood-curdling howls that grow closer with every passing second.

"They're in the Glass House." I stagger forward. "S-Sebastian . . . my Sebastian."

I glance back in devastation, finding Killian's hand outstretched, ready to pull me away.

"Lexi, get back!"

He reaches me just as a formless shroud blows past. The rasping howl it makes as its shadow billows around me leaves me immobilized. The image of the ghoulish demon that held me in its deathly grip floods my memory, and I choke on the fear.

Another high-pitched wail sends a deafening ring through my ears, and I shut my eyes. But the sound is more frantic than menacing. Another whoosh of movement sends the shadow away from me.

The light of the moon reaches behind my lidded eyes. Forcing myself to find some courage, I open them.

Killian's body is smashed against the stone ground. The black demon struggling against him where he holds it in a chokehold. Those strong fingers gouge into the roof of the creature's mouth, his other hand pulling apart its wide and howling jaw.

With an angry shriek, he snaps the howler's head from its chin.

Tossing the blackened body away, Killian rolls to his feet, breathing heavily. His own face and arms are splattered with strange tar-like blood, his fingers still curled around the skull of his kill.

I cringe into the ledge, watching him toss the head into the night air. He stalks toward me, eyes wild. I don't struggle when he grips me around the shoulders and drags me from the ground, pushing me back into the castle at speed.

Killian bars the balcony door behind us, but I doubt the wooden door will keep them out for long. He turns me to face him, his free hand roughly yanking my face to the side, his eyes raking over me for injury. He trembles with a wild rage that I don't recognize.

"I-I'm not hurt." I quiver, then cringe at the smell of the putrid blood still clinging to his skin. His stance relaxes, humanity returning to his feral gaze. His grip on my shoulder loosens.

The screams of our guests bounce up the staircases along with echoing shouts and confused commands of the guardsmen. Both of us snap our heads to the chaos. I automatically step closer to him, feeling a lot safer with him than with them.

"You need to get to safety," Killian says, voice guttural and raw.

"So do you." I dig my fingers into his arm. "I'm not leaving you."

Killian looks at me with an expression warring between comforting and fierce. He only manages a brief smile. The little bit of warmth in his eyes vanishes the moment Thomas's voice echoes from the top of the stairs. His hand tightens around my shoulder and he marches straight toward the frantic earl.

"Thank god." Thomas practically wilts in relief when he spies me, but his eyes narrow on a blood-stained Killian.

"I swear to the Creator, if any harm comes to her, I'll rip your lungs out through your throat, Domnaill!" Killian tosses me against Thomas.

"It's my duty," Thomas says, but I note how he cowers ever so slightly from Killian's advance. "Just as it is yours to fight. Get out there!"

"Wait, no!" I wrestle with the earl's feeble grip. "You can't send him out there. Killian, don't you dare walk away from me."

My shrieking falls on deaf ears as my Silent Gardener backs away. He moves for the stairs. His eyes the only thing betraying his conflict when he glances back one last time. There's a world of unspoken words behind those eyes and in that brief second before he disappears down the staircase, I can sense all of them. He'd not leave me if he had a choice. He'd take me and run right now, but he can't . . . his life belongs to them.

I struggle with Thomas so much that he has to use both arms to keep me in place. "It's his duty, Alexandria. His life is forfeit for the survival of us all."

"Oh, shut up, you pompous jerk!" I elbow him hard in the ribs, marginally loosening his grip. "Killian!" I bolt for the stairs, Thomas scrambling after me.

I take the steps two at time, the skirts of my dress hoisted high to give my legs more freedom. I bulldoze past startled guests and guardsmen clambering the stairs. Thomas is yelling for them to stop me. Hands grab at me, but I duck and shove my way free, continuing to shriek for Killian. Hoping he'll hear me. That he'll stop.

When I hit the last staircase, the one leading into the main hall, it's crammed with guests and servants all rushing and pushing in every direction. Guardsmen are trying to direct, yelling commands, and every so often the lights flicker or cut out entirely and the howls of those monsters rattle through the castle. They're trying to get inside.

I frantically try to use the vantage point of the top of the stairs. "Killian!" My voice rips through several octaves, the sound enough to draw the attention of a few guardsmen.

One of them, the one closest to the bottom of the stairs, shouts and waves at me. I can see he is already wounded. Blood gushes down the side of his face from a blow to the head. At first I think he's dazed, but when he has my attention, he jabs a blood-soaked hand toward the main doors of the castle at the far end of the hall. To a figure who is redirecting fearful guests and shouting commands at guardsmen to bring anything forward that will barricade the door.

Killian.

I shove my way down the last flight of steps. Shrieking for him not to go out there. To wait.

His back straightens and he swivels to face me head on. The look in his eyes. The panic warring with the anger stays me a moment. He shakes his head in warning and someone hands him off a glinting weapon—an axe with a crystal blade. He throws out his hand—a sign for me not to come any farther.

"Don't leave me!" I screech over the din. Someone else's arms find me. More sets of faces, more bodies holding me back. "Killian!" But before I can shout another word, he moves beyond the threshold of those doors and they bang shut. He disappears from my sight.

The panic that fills me sends my head spinning. They don't understand, these people. They don't know what happens when the howlers come.

My father went into the night and never came back.

They don't understand. Those monsters are back to finish what they started.

They'll kill him.

They'll kill anyone who stands between them and me.

OUT OF THE ASHES

Everyone and everything pushes me. I try to push back, but more hands shove at my body, more heavy shoes crunch my toes, and more fingers nip and pull at my dress and snag my hair.

It's chaos.

All screams fade into the demented howls of those monstrous creatures. I know they're in the castle. I hear the frantic cries of confused people right before their pitiful wails turn into gargles of floundering life. I smell the metallic tang of mortal blood. It's horrifying. It's everything my nightmares have been made of for months, but this time I can't wake up.

They've come for me. To take me to Dian so I can be slaughtered for a people I never knew. None of it's fair. The injustice of it all turns my guts to ash.

The crowd keeps pulling me along, like a directionless current. My coherent thoughts abandon me to my nightmares. I know I can do better. Fight this somehow, think around the problem and make an attempt to escape, even force myself to take a stand. But every time I try, a spine-tingling howl splits the night and I crumple in cowardice. I keep moving forward, pulled by the crowd, until my bare toes touch the cold stone of narrow steps.

It's then that I register how significantly thinned out the crowd of escapees has become. In panic, I look for someone familiar and find Margot's severe bun and spidery limbs tottering ahead. Her ruby-painted talons scrape the rock of the exposed brick of the cellars, and every so often, she flicks a terrified gaze over her shoulder, tears seeping down her cheeks. Guardsmen flank us, along with some other nobles, but I can't see Bryce or even Kes.

We are in the upper cellars just off from the hallways that lead to the kitchens. Rows and rows of vintage wines and kegs of whiskey fill the room with a heady scent that quells the more distinct aroma of blood and smoke.

"Where are you taking me?" I ask the man whose gloved hand snares my forearm. He pauses to glance at me with a bemused expression, his footsteps slowing as I dig my heels in.

"A safe passage through the foundations of the castle. Come now, miss." The guard hauls at my arm, but I resist.

"Where is my guardian? Where is Agent Bryce?" I search the panic-stricken faces that pass me in the hurry to escape. "And Kes. She's small. She could easily be missed."

"I don't know." The man huffs, his thick accent unfamiliar. "I'm stationed in Jamaica with Elder Lord Mackey. I don't know those people. You have to come, miss. Now."

"We can't!" I reach around to pull his shoulder. "We can't leave them. They're under my protection. I have to help." His deep, dark eyes—so very different than the pale and listless gaze of the servants that inhabit Domnaill— roam over me.

"They're probably dead." Fear from the depths of his soul bubbles up into his eyes. "And we'll be too if you don't move."

"Alexandria!" Margot's voice sounds like shattering glass. "Alexandria, you come now. Kes and Bryce have orders to protect you. You must let them do their job."

"They aren't protecting me!" I screech and shove away from the guardsman, jabbing a warning finger at Margot. "They're dying for me."

And with that, I take off at a sprint, ignoring Margot's screams for someone to catch me. I narrowly duck the arms that reach for me and hurtle out of the cellars. I haven't the faintest clue what I'll do or even how to defend myself, but I can't just cower in the dark and let innocent people die.

I'm not like this Order. I don't count my life above others, and I really don't care if they think I'm some goddess incarnate. No one needs to sacrifice themselves for me. That's supposed to be my job, so I'd better woman up and fulfill my stupid ancient destiny.

I am not afraid. I am not afraid. I am n—

"Lexi! You're going the wrong way."

The professor's breathless shout catches my attention. I pause near the tight corner of the cellar entrance that I was dragged around only moments ago. Professor Donoghue ambles down the hallway toward me, huffing and puffing with exertion as his cane thuds against the ground with every other step.

"I have to get Bryce and Kes." I want more than anything to throttle the next person that tries to prohibit me from finding my friends.

"I know," he says when we finally meet. "But you're still going the wrong way." The professor pats my shoulder and points to one of the tiny, offset doorways that lead to what I always assumed to be servant quarters or storage rooms. He hobbles determinedly toward it. He isn't following the crowd. With piqued interest, I scurry after him, confident that wherever he's going, it'll be better than hiding with Margot in the bowels of a crumbling ruin.

"Quick, down here." Professor Donoghue beckons as he pulls back a wall. Not a wall. A hidden door?

I tentatively tiptoe forward and peek into the gloom. I don't know this part of the secret passageways, but it's narrow, cleaner than the others. The professor grimaces apologetically and nods again toward the tight space.

"Follow the path. You'll come to a locked, wrought-iron door." He digs in his pocket. "Inside is my hoard of artifacts."

I arch an eyebrow.

"Things I don't want getting into the wrong hands. Things I've kept secret for decades." He shoves something cold and metallic into my hands. "Here."

"Professor?" I examine the hefty iron key in my palm. "Who knew of this?"

"Very few. Trusted servants mostly, and the boy." His expression remains somber.

I suppose he means Killian, and I guess I shouldn't be angry that he didn't tell me about it. Killian keeps his word; it's an irritatingly great quality of his.

"Don't be angry at him." Professor Donoghue sighs, reading my peeved expression. "He's a good lad, and he begged me more than once to let you see the place. Except, you and I both know you weren't ready for it. But it seems we've run out of time . . . again."

"Wait, I don't understand. What's down there?"

"There's a chest, a big chest, you can't miss it." The professor animatedly motions the length and breadth of this chest. "The key is under a loose tile by the hearth. Open it and you'll find a broken spear wrapped in velvet. Be careful. It's still sharp and wrapped in barb."

"Okay . . ." I nod, mentally recapping the commands in my head. "Then what?"

"Get it to Killian. He'll know what to do." Professor Donoghue pats my shoulder.

"Aren't you coming?"

My stomach sinks when he shakes his head. Margot's demanding shrieks for my return bounce up the corridor, and the sound of heavy boots beat off the tiles.

"Go on, Lexi. There's a hatch out into the courtyard from the cellar. You've got this. Drown the gits. They'll not know what hit them."

Another shriek from Margot, and I'm sliding into the dark passageway, my hand reaching behind me to grip the professor's in solidarity. He gives my knuckles a firm squeeze and smiles.

"Help Bryce and Kes."

He nods once then slams the door shut, leaving me alone in the dark. Nothing but a stone wall behind me and complete uncertainty before me.

Come on, Lexi. Woman up. People are counting on you.

I am not afraid.

I let my sight adjust to the dark. My palms spread across the damp walls, and I edge forward. Water trickles along in a trench on the left side of the passageway, part of the damp stone chiseled away to create a narrow drainage. I assume this far down in the castle, flooding can be expected. I make a silent call for strength, and in answer, the little rivulets draw toward me. But there's more. I already feel the water undulate and seek for me when I call for it. The water in the pipes, the water under the earth, even as far as the lough. I can sense its rage, but I hold it at bay. I breathe in and out, and use the edge of that rage to hone my focus.

I focus on staying in my skin, although, having skin that glimmers works in my favor. The dark shadows recede as I light my own path through the gloom. Water droplets seep upward, soaking the stonework and drawing into my fingertips where they claw the slimy bricks. I keep going forward though because I must, and because there really is no going back.

Chaos rumbles above me. The howlers' moans cause my chest to constrict, but I hold to that focus. That edge of power in my veins. The wind roars noisily through this tiny tunnel, and with it, the sounds of screams and the smell of blood and ash.

Reaching the iron gate, I collapse against it in relief. I search for the lock, giving a tiny sigh, when my fingertips embrace the keyhole. I shove the key into the lock, crank it open, then dash inside.

I stumble over a table and land in a heap on the floor. I hiss and push myself up, pulling the lengths of my dress out of the way to reveal bloodied knees and skinned shins.

Great . . . well, that'll ruin the only pretty dress I've ever owned.

Peering around the dusty space—a glorified storage closet—I spy the empty fireplace and limp toward it. With trembling hands, I sweep away the gathered ash and dust, looking for a loosened tile.

Nothing moves.

I slap the smooth orange tiles with frantic force. My impatience is rewarded when an edge rattles free. The hole just large enough for me to wriggle my fingers through and feel the serrated edge of a smaller key.

"Yes." I hold the delicate edge of the small key up in the air like a trophy.

I hobble in circles on shaky legs, frantically looking for a chest, but everything is covered in lengths of gray sheets. Lots and lots of sheets, draped over everything. I rip the fabric away, searching for this unmissable chest, but mostly just finding books and drawers stuffed with maps and parchments.

A length of gray sheet spills over a low unit littered in papers. I grab those loose papers in tight fists and draw in ragged breathes—why is this so difficult?

Another howl punctuates the night, and in my fright, I scramble. Fear mixed with temper flares, and I fling the sheet from the unit, papers and all. But as the leaves flutter to my feet, I notice that the low unit is carved in ornate patterns—in swirls and veins of silver and gold that remind me of my blood. Of course.

My eyes zero in on the tiny black lock.

Hands tremble as I kneel by the lock. I drop the key a few times in my anxiety, but I eventually click it into place, and the mechanism chinks open. With a hefty grunt I flip the lid and lean in. A length of something sharp lies twisted up in royal blue fabric. When Professor Donoghue described a broken spear, I expected something small, but this is at least half my size. Carefully, and with no small amount of awe, I pick up the artifact and hold it firmly in both hands.

I look around. There's the hatch that the professor mentioned in the ceiling on the far side of the room. I ease toward it, hands still trembling. I've got to get this to Killian. Once we've stopped this terror, we can run away. I've spent my life running from them. What's one more escape?

Laying the wrapped spear at my feet, I fumble with the bolt that secures the hatch. It loosens enough for me to stretch up against it, and with a grunt, I push it open. The wind rattles above my head, whipping my hair across my eyes. A howl catches on the air and a gust of wind sends the doors crashing down against their own hinges. The force shatters the wood. With a gasp, I throw my arms above my head.

A hollow face with yellow eyes hovers above. I see it though the gaps in my fingers.

The second of silence that passes between the creature and me turns everything to ice. Even the blood in my veins freezes when it captures me in its deathly stare. I cower away from its ghostly descent. Its specter body collapsing on me like a dark wind. Its clawed, skeletal hands aim for my exposed throat. A dusty, raspy, lingering yowl wheezes through shadowy lungs.

Talons scratch my skin. A cold thumb embeds the delicate flesh at the center of my throat. The gesture so assured, nothing but a choked sob escapes me. I shut my eyes. Its rasping breath skitters across my skin. Undiluted fear steals away any edge of power I thought I had.

Poor little child of light. Still weak as a feather.

My eyes fly open.

That voice. It scrapes across the inside of my skull.

"You!" I shove my palm against the creature's bony chest. "It was you."

It remembers?

The thing sounds amused.

More yowls echo above.

"You killed my parents." The edge of my power returns with a razor focus.

I claw into the howler's chest cavity, feeling a dull thread of life through wasted bones. The shadows of others begin to circle, blocking out any light from the moon. Darkness traps me, except for the burning yellow eyes that sear into my memory. The demon that cut my arm and stole my innocence. The thing that haunts the crevices of my dreams. The monster that lurks behind my eyelids.

The wrath that brews and spits from the depths of my essence spikes and flows through my veins. The tremendous, ethereal glimmer of my skin shines into the dark shadows as I push against the oppression. My thoughts focus with intense ferocity on the thick sludge that oozes through this demon's body. It's blood, after all, because all things need blood to live.

The howler's hissing laughter begins to fade, and in its place, a choking sound emerges. A wicked, feline smile splits my face. The howler's eyes narrow, its drawn mask of a face turns ashen, its slit-like mouth stretches wide in a silent shadow of wails. Faint gurgles and pops sound in its lungs. Dark blood oozes from its nose and eye sockets.

It takes only seconds to suffocate it. The gathering horde above us shriek and swamp the little trapdoor. Their boney talons scratching the stone and wood. But I'm not afraid anymore.

I am strong.

The howler disintegrates into dust. The heavy material of its clothing collapses against me. With its dying wheeze, its comrades let out vengeful cries.

Every inch of me burns with light against the darkness. Face turned upward, eyes wide open and awake, I cast the material aside, pick up the spear, and rise out of the ash.

They swoop and duck, their claws grab for me as they screech out their horrifying calls. But I don't cower. Not this time.

The rush of water thrums in time with my pulse. I draw every source I can sense to myself. From the pipes, from the drain, from the damp air and the earth outside. The leash I've held on myself to keep the rage in check breaks. It takes no time for all that water to answer the call of my essence, like the being within me was waiting on it—waiting on me to embrace her.

Streams of captured water circles my physical form, blending with my essence and catching in the turbine of wind created in the howlers' frenzy.

My fury births a hurricane that feeds my strength. They won't know what hit them.

With a deafening shriek of my own, I force the whirlwind of water upward and out from around me. The roaring sound of the funnel explodes up and out of the little hatch, taking each and every howler with it, until their screams are nothing but drowned mews.

I can sense their blood. It takes only moments and I have all their lives held in my mind. No longer do I need to touch them. The first howler was enough. I know what I'm doing now. I can taste their essence. With sharpened focus, I turn my thoughts to their dwindling life force and begin to pick them off, drowning them one by one.

I emerge from the hatch, drenched, my once pinned hair free and cascading down my back in slick tendrils. The cold blue light of my essence bathes the courtyard and illuminates the drowned bodies of misshapen howlers that lie strewn on the stones. Those still alive wail and groan as they pull themselves along the ground. Those that drowned disintegrate into dust that catches on the breeze and blows out into the night.

Something claws the tail of my skirts. I glance downward to find a howler pulling at my hems, its mouth twisted in a grimace, its dulled eyes filled with pleading. I lift my bare foot and press it down against the creature's shoulders, watching how it crumbles under such a gentle shove. Its skeletal arms reach to shield itself from the brightness of my incensed gaze.

I pause. There's something broken about the demon. Something empty, like it has lost all ability to wield fear. Or perhaps fear has lost all power over me. Why should I kill it? Why shouldn't it live with the same fear I carried for far too long. I'll let it go.

A warning for Dian—I am awake.

He should've left me sleeping.

"Go," I command the sniveling creature as it crawls away from me. "Return to the shadows where you belong. You won't haunt this place or these people any longer."

I watch the creature crawl away from me, slinking over the ground like a snake.

In the distance, great plumes of smoke rise from the Glass House. It appears the fire has been extinguished, and there's no activity in that direction. In fact, things sound eerily quiet. I take a tight grip of the spear and follow a trail of acrid fumes to the entrance of the castle. This was the last place I saw Killian. I can try to trace him from this point.

The great courtyard is awash with bodies and a line of fire that cuts a path across the open doors of the castle. The flames spark and crackle, dancing dangerously close to the wood but never igniting it. Strange?

My heart hammers as I move cautiously through the injured and dead. I check each face, searching for familiarity, praying I don't find any. I'm not sure whether to be relieved or distressed that Killian isn't here. The less helpful part of my mind reminds me that the Glass House is probably the first place he went, and by the looks of it, that battle didn't last long. I hesitate, contemplating that I should listen to my gut and go straight to the Glass House. I make to turn, but a familiar body sprawled over the fountain catches my attention.

I gasp and drop the spear. "Thomas."

Yanking my skirts up, I run for the fountain and note, with anxiety, that the stone edge around his body is reduced to rubble. He must've been thrown. Cautiously, I kneel and ease his face away from the water, whispering a silent prayer that he hasn't drowned. As fortune would have it, his arm protected him from inhaling any of the water. Still, drowning might've been a better way to go. His injuries are brutal.

With care, I shift him to the ground, trying to avoid the nasty burns on his face and head. The mess of wounds bleed relentlessly, and I'm not sure if he's lost his right eye or not. I rip a length of my dress and press it against his head. I give him a quick glance over and decide that there are far too many injuries, and I'm not qualified to know which need attention first. I'm almost certain by the way they're angled that his legs are broken—maybe his pelvis too—and a worrying pop sounds every time he inhales. Killian would know what to do; he'd know how to help him. Though, considering the abuse, would he help him? Knowing Killian, he would. He wouldn't think twice about saving this idiot's life, and truthfully, I'm not exactly comfortable with letting him die either. He's been a real jerk, but he's our jerk. At least we know where we stand with Thomas Domnaill, unlike his superiors . . . who don't seem to be among the fatalities.

"Ugh. Fine." I rip more lengths of dress to replace the now blood-soaked rag. "It's really messed up when you, Earl of Domnaill, turn out to be the noblest lord in the Order."

Thomas gives a weak cough, and his left eye flutters. I nearly cry with relief.

"Yeah, I'm talking to you." I sniff back ridiculous tears. It's been a bad day when I'm crying over Domnaill. "Please don't die just to spite me. It's not classy, and Margot looks hideous in black."

A smile tugs at the edge of his lips. I might be wrong, but I think he chuckles.

"Yes!" I cry in triumph. "Stay with me. I'm going to get help. You'll be fine." I push more fabric against the ugly wound on his face before jumping to my feet. I'll call for help; the howlers have been subdued. I have time at least.

I spring up the steps toward the castle entrance, then stop dead when the fiery barricade running in front of the doors appears to blow up at my approach. With a shocked gasp, I scramble back a few steps, my arm raised to protect my face against the heat.

How'd it do that?

Stepping forward again, I ready myself to leap through a small gap in the flames, but a blast of heat again knocks me back. The force sends me flailing down the stone steps, and I land face first on the cobbles.

A spasm of pain runs down my back when I push up onto my forearms. Ignoring the twinge, I twist back around and blink up at the flames.

Not flames. A whole body of moving flame that springs down the steps toward me.

With a panicked cry, I attempt to crawl away, but barely manage to get onto my knees when the intense heat engulfs me. I raise an arm in defense and use my free hand to search the earth for the feel of water—anything to quell the heat—but fire licks around my arm instead. The long spidery flames curl around my wrist. Pain shoots up my forearm. I grit my teeth to stop the cry.

The scorch is short-lived, and to my astonishment, the fire recedes to reveal a smooth, perfect arm. That's not possible. They'd have to be Celestial. They'd have to be—

The flames lessen, then die away, until a creature emerges. No, a man. A man so dazzling I have to look away to ease the scalding of my eyes.

"Lexi."

The man's warm and crackling voice sounds so utterly familiar that I can't breathe for the pain and joy it brings. Slowly, and with deliberate caution, I open my eyes and lower my raised arm. I'm too frightened to let myself hope.

But there he is.

A man with golden hair that glitters like the sun at noon. A man with eyes as blue as a summer's day that glint mischievously where they flash over me with recognition. He smiles—a smile I'd know anywhere.

Connor.

REIGN OF FIRE

"Connor?"

His smile stretches but appears tainted. Manic. I'm unable to marry the image of this tall athletic man—who stands on lean and muscular legs—with the golden boy in the wheelchair. Then again, I'm sure he thinks the same of me. But he's here. He came back.

My dear friend stands before me in all his Celestial glory wearing nothing but tight leather pants that are apparently pretty flame-retardant. But I suppose they'd need to be, considering his essence.

So . . . fire, huh? Should've seen that one coming.

"H-How?" I begin, still shaking my head. "What are you doing here?"

"I came for you." He walks toward me. His smile shifts toward menacing. My stomach flips.

He reaches me, and in a single, sudden movement, his fingers grab and tighten around my arm. I swallow nervously, twisting away from him, my gaze sweeping out across the carnage of the courtyard. Beyond it, to the great pillars of smoke that continue to rise from the Glass House.

"Connor." I shiver, and glance back at him. Dark shadows pass over his eyes when I speak. "D-Did you do this?"

"Yes," he says with such pride, and I recoil, the horror in my expression far too obvious.

"I punished them . . . for you . . . Are you pleased?"

"Pleased?" I balk. Bile rises in my throat, confirming the ugliest truth; this is not Connor. At least not the Connor I know. "Why would I be pleased? These were innocent people."

Connor's face contorts between confusion and rage. The burning in his eyes intensifies until I feel heat radiate through his palm and into my arm. I cringe in defense. My veins glow and glitter, the cool light rushing to the source of discomfort. Fury burns in his gaze. I duck my chin in fright.

"He told me you'd say that. He said they would corrupt you . . . make you weak. But He'll fix you. And they will pay."

"Who are you talking about?"

I whimper as Connor yanks my arm upward, dragging my body straight off the ground. A sliver of agonizing heat scorches my wrist and fingers. "Please, Connor." My shoulder gives a worrying crack. "You're hurting me."

He stops to regard me with furrowed brows, those wonderfully high-set cheekbones appearing sharper and more severe than I remember. His eyes more sunken, ringed in purple, hinting at the weeks without rest. There's a madness to him and it terrifies me to the core.

"Pain is necessary."

Another shot of fire strikes through his palms and down my arm. I wince, biting my lip to curtail the scream of pain, but my body is quick to repel the flame.

"You'll come back with me now. He will fix this."

He's too strong. Too unhinged. I can't fight this. I'll be sensible, wise in my words. Perhaps I can appeal to his conscience. Surely he can't have forgotten us. I won't believe that he's that lost.

"Connor." I paint a smile on my lips and breathe through the pain. "I'm so happy to see you. We've missed you so much. Killian and I—"

"Killian?"

Connor's eyes widen and his grip loosens enough for me to wriggle my hand free. I clutch my weakened arm to my chest and nod in encouragement, being careful not to make any jerky movements. I don't trust that he won't attempt to knock me out if I try to make a run for it.

"Yes, Killian's here too, and he's just like us." I take a tentative step back. "Oh, Connor, he's missed you so much. He hasn't stopped trying to think of ways to rescue you. Come. We'll find him and—"

Connor's hand clamps around my windpipe. In panic I throw my arms to his wrist and claw uselessly at the skin. I strain my head upright and fight to draw in a breath.

"Where is Aimrid's misshapen monster?" Connor's question comes out like a monstrous growl. My eyes pop at the bloodlust in the depths of his glare. "I'll tear his head from his shoulders and present it to our king. A trophy."

I don't need to be told who has twisted Connor's mind against the man he used to consider a brother. There's only one name I can think of. One thing so filled with hate toward Killian that he'd have a bounty on his head.

"Where is the whore's runt?"

Those cruel words sound even more awful spoken in Connor's voice. Of course, even if I knew, I wouldn't answer him, but my stubborn silence gains me an impatient throttle.

I shake my head and brace my juddering bones.

"Tell me!"

When I shake my head again, he draws his hand back as if to strike. Instinctively, I cringe, eyes closed in expectation of the blow.

"Last chance."

I refuse to open my eyes.

"Where is he?"

"Right in front of you, you ignorant bastard."

My eyes fly open at the sound of him. Killian. He's alive.

"Take your hands off her, Connor." His voice dips to a deathly decibel. "I won't ask twice."

Connor yanks me closer by the neck, and I groan at the rough movement, my spine protesting the misalignment.

"She's mine." His manic possessiveness makes me ill with stomach-twisting fear. "She belongs to me." He sneers, almost gloating. He flings me around so fast I stumble, but with unnatural speed he clamps me against his chest with his forearm. "She isn't going anywhere but with me."

"Lexi belongs to no one, save her Creator. As we all do. Though I doubt my grandfather spoke much of that, hmm, Connor?"

I make out Killian's approaching silhouette against the smoke and fire. His stance predatory and wild. Like a lion, he circles us, eyes constantly flickering, calculating every possible attack.

"Dian speaks for the Creator," Connor says, but his voice sounds garbled, and he twitches and fidgets. His breathing's all wrong, like he isn't really present. And he could snap my neck with just an accidental jerk.

I am not afraid. I am not afraid.

"Does he now?" Killian's laughter startles me, and I watch in nervous anticipation as he plays with the axe in his right hand, testing it. His eyes flash over Connor with a crippling authority. "Mark my words, little brother. Dian will answer to mine . . . Let the girl go!"

Connor gasps in anger. "Blasphemous heathen!" In his shock he forgets himself and loosens his grip on me. I duck straight out of his arms and make a hasty sideways scramble. The moment I'm safely out of Connor's hands, Killian's stance shifts to one prepped for attack.

"You dare threaten the Divine One?"

"You sound like a madman." Killian's voice is tainted with slight mockery as he shifts a little to the right, predicting Connor's favored side. "A zealot. What has he done to you?"

"He freed me."

Connor screams in defiance, and I jump clean out of my skin. He lunges at Killian, teeth barred, eyes gleaming. I barely have time to draw a breath, to warn Killian, but there's no need. He is poised and ready. His immoveable strength takes the full brunt of Connor's attack.

I use the distraction to lunge for the spear abandoned near Thomas and the fountain. Grabbing it, I roll to my knees and turn my attention back to the fight.

Connor blocks a blow, the fire spreading down his arms and burning Killian on contact. Killian only hisses, then draws back and squarely head-butts his little brother. The forceful crack sends a shudder up my spine and a pain through my temple.

That had to hurt.

Connor's neck snaps back, his eyes wide and dazed. He lands on the ground with a colossal thud. Blood spurts from his nostrils like water escaping a faucet.

Killian doesn't waste a second. He picks up his axe and sprints to my side. Dropping to one knee, his fingers brush my neck. He swallows back an angry curse. I give a weak smile, pushing his fingers aside, trying to convince him—and myself—that I'm fine.

"That won't keep him down long." Killian pulls me upright with him. "You need to get far away from here."

"No, wait." I dig in my heels and struggle against Killian's push. "Professor Donoghue told me to get this to you. He said you'd know what to do."

Killian's eyes fly to the object in my hands, his fingers deftly pulling back the velvet. He glances away to the Glass House, then back to Connor, who rolls about the grass, gripping his nose. I know that look in Killian's eyes. Hope. It gives me a good dose of desperately needed courage.

Killian groans. A look of complete indecision flashes over his green eyes. "I shouldn't be trusting you with this."

"Thanks for the vote of confidence," I say, bristling a little at the lack of faith.

He has the audacity to roll his eyes, but takes the hand I have wrapped around the spear shaft and tugs it and me toward him.

"Do you see the smoke?" He twists toward the Glass House and gestures with a jerk of his chin to the glaringly obvious plumes of thick smoke. I tut, and he gives me a gentle dig in the ribs with his free hand before continuing to draw his index finger down toward the smashed dome. "It's a portal, Lexi, held open by sorcery on the other side. You have to destroy the physical anchor to break the connection."

"With the spear?" I unwind the velvet and take a firm grip of the severed shaft, boldly setting my shoulders straight and preparing to run.

Killian's hand tightens around mine, staying me. His gaze is saturated with anxiety, but behind him, Connor has found his feet again, and he staggers around on shaky legs, shrieking curses and probably looking for a weapon of some description.

"It's the Spear of Lugh. The spearhead can't shatter. It'll decimate any element, be it magic or not." Killian glances nervously back to Connor. "Go, Lexi. I'll keep him busy. Just break the connection and be careful."

"You just worry about yourself." I nod toward the raging bull that takes the form of Connor.

He swivels to face us, eyes wild, blood streaking his nose and mouth and dripping down his chin. Ripples of flame already race across the breadth of his shoulders.

Killian's jaw clenches. He slides in front of me, obscuring me from Connor's view. I throw myself headlong into a sprint. Scorching heat blazes across the length of my back, along with an animalistic growl.

I squeeze my eyes shut and push on harder, forcing my feet to fly against the tremoring earth.

FORCES OF NATURE

The thick, pungent air seeps through the suffocating atmosphere of the Glass House. It burns my lungs and stings my eyes. I rip more lengths of my dress to cover my mouth and nose against the brunt of the fumes.

Wading through the scorched and wilting overgrowth is made worse by the ashen smog and lingering heat. I can scarcely contain my anger at the haphazard path Connor has taken through our beloved Eden. The dying trees and wounded ground, with scorched remains of vegetation, seem more harrowing than anything I've ever seen. Life coursed through this little paradise only hours ago, flowing like blood in healthy veins. Now it barely has the strength to give off a flicker of light.

How could someone not see such beauty? How could any soul justify this destruction? Connor is insane, blind with rage, and drunk on power to be so murderous. If he were in his right mind, he would never—could never—be so evil.

My directionless wandering in this haunting, ash-strewn snow globe costs valuable time. I'm acutely aware that not so far away, a crazed battle is in full swing. Eventually though, my toes squelch through mud, and in a few more steps, water trickles over my feet.

Picking up the tattered tails of my dress, I pad along the cloudy water and follow its trail back to the source—the center of the Glass House.

I freeze. The barest hint of a gasp scrapes past my lips.

Dropping the spear, I spring over strewn boulders. The muddied path is too slippery, and I slide to my knees and skid the rest of the way to the shattered cauldron. My hands flutter toward the water, darkened and made ugly by the smoke. The once massive marble basin lies shattered. The whole side of it crumbling away so that it gushes streams of putrid water.

I pick up broken pieces of the basin and cradle them to my chest, wondering if it can be mended, or if somehow I can stem the flow of the magical spring beneath. Assuming there's more damage, I pull myself up on the larger stones that were once the cauldron's base. The water bleeds a river over my shoulders and runs down my back in angry swathes as I clamber up the moss-slick boulders. Reaching the top, I grip one hand to the smashed edges and lean into vast basin, my other outstretched into the dark. I search for the real damage, leaning deeper, skin glittering light against the dark hollow.

There's no bottom to the cauldron. I frown and retract my hand a little, my grip slipping on the smooth onyx edges.

Something is wrong . . . very wrong.

Moving my hand across the waters near the edge, I bring the rivulets toward my skin like a magnet. I take a firmer grip of the edge, and attempt to peer closer, this time letting my whole arm submerge.

A surge and a roar bubbles up from the deep. With an almighty force, the water spews up and out of the basin like a tremendous geyser. I fly backward and hit the ground face first, swallowing a mouthful of mud mid-scream.

Dolmen stones. The cauldron sits on dolmen stones.

Groaning and coughing up a lungful of muck, I slither onto all fours then slop through the mud looking for my discarded spear. I'm not exactly sure how to break the connection with a bottomless portal, but I may think of something quick. That explosion is bound to catch Connor's attention, and I'm royally screwed if he shows up.

Think Lexi . . . think, think, think . . .

The wall of water continues to roar with relentless force behind me. A growling wind bounces up from the depths of the portal, rushing outward in all directions and reminding me of the time I don't have. I slide through the soupy puddles on hands and knees searching for the spear, but I only seem to be scraping mud, my arms and legs slathered in it. I growl and slap the earth in frustration. This is stupid. I'm stupid for thinking I could do this alone. I don't know what I'm doing.

"Lexi?"

That voice that calls me through the smog and deafening wind . . . I know it.

It's impossible. It can't be. "Mother?" I abandon the search and stagger to my feet, muck-stained hands outstretched into the darkness, tears breaking free as I inhale broken gasps.

"Lexi?"

"I'm here!" I spin in frantic circles through the mud, desperately trying to find her in the darkness. The niggling cry in the back of mind warns that this can't be real. She's dead. I watched them stick a blade through her like she was made of hot butter. But I can hear her so clearly. Maybe she is on the other side. Maybe she's alive. Maybe she's helping me.

With wide eyes, I turn back to the portal, my bare toes catching the end of something. I glance down and see the spear. Brows furrowing, I bend to pick it up. I have to do something. I have to break the portal, but—

"Lexi, help me."

In the instant her voice reaches my ears, I leave the spear. I can't ignore that voice. Thoughtlessly, I chase the earth beneath me and race straight for the portal. It's her, I know it's her. She's alive!

But my mother's voice turns to callous laughter when I reach the basin's edge. A cold stab of ice runs through my veins.

A trick.

A horrible trick, and I'm so weak, I fell for it.

The terrific wind changes direction and flies straight back into the Glass House, barreling toward me. It collides with my unprepared body. With a shriek, I attempt to defend myself against the strength of its assault, but it's too much for me.

Buckling under the force, I find that the wind takes a heavy form that solidly embraces me. I grunt, my fists balling around the oilskin fabric of a battered jacket, but I can't quite get enough force to push my assailant off. We both slam to the ground, air huffing out my lungs.

"Silly girl," she says in a feminine and accented voice. In her feathery husk, she giggles playfully. I yelp as her knees dig into my thighs, pinning me to the ground. Something sharp presses against my neck.

"Didn't your mother teach you not to wander the woods alone? Lest the bitter fairies steal you away? *Teeheeheehee*. Silly, pretty thing . . . she smells like the sea."

The demented creature runs her silk-covered nose along my jaw, and I cringe. She clutches a handful of my hair, pausing to inhale the scent. I twist my head around, struggling with her weight on top of me. She's deceptively heavy for such a slight thing.

Narrowing my eyes, I try to decipher something about her, anything, but she's covered from head-to-toe in black. The only thing visible is a pair of almond eyes with irises shining like obsidian stone. Those dark eyes brighten with recognition when she uses her knife to cut a lock of my hair. I growl in defiance, but she continues to giggle, her knife finding a new threatening point at my ribcage.

She lowers herself closer. Her cloth-covered nose an inch from mine.

"Oh, you've been a naughty little queen." She tuts, then giggles dementedly again. Her long nails dig into my chin, tapping out a rhythm. "You smell like sea and earth. *Teeheeheehee*. Oooh, that's not allowed. No, no, no. Bad queenie."

Before I can speak, she slaps her palm over my mouth and shakes her head. She sits up straight, and I watch in utter terror as she removes her hand to make a shushing gesture with one long finger.

With a devilish grin, she runs the sparkling edge of her knife over her exposed palm, drawing a thin line of blood—blood like mine.

There are more?

She rips something from a leather bag tied at her side, then empties the chalky substance on her palm and scrunches my lock of hair between her hands with a bit of mud from the ground. She mutters incomprehensible words, her eyes dancing wickedly, and before I can react, she lunges for me. Slaps her hands to my face, then pushes me hard against the mud.

She lowers her face close to the side of mine. "On hallowed ground no more to be, so blind thy eyes and punish thee."

At the utterance of her taunting verse, pain rages through my skull and rips a blood-curdling scream from my lips. I wriggle and squirm as spikes of what feels like electricity rage across my face and into my left eye. The demented woman cackles and lowers her lips to my ear again.

"Bear thy curse far from home, where thy light dare ne'er to roam."

The pain intensifies. My eye almost bursts from its socket. My skin burns and stings like a thousand knives score it at once, as though acid crawls along in my veins instead of blood. I scream and thrash against this crazed witch. Every ounce of my strength focuses on getting her off me. Her laughter is frightening against the howl of the wind, but I fight back. The fingers of my left hand creep through the mud until they grip the hilt of her discarded knife.

There is a shrill keen on the air, the sound enough of a distraction that this nutcase takes her heathen hands off me. She moves back, and I use the opportunity to get the knife firmly in my grasp. With a determined huff, I shove the blade into her hip. Her horrified gasp is followed by a slap that snaps my neck to the side, but a scream on the wind sends a sadistic sneer across my lips.

The woman screeches and hisses as Kes valiantly swoops to my aid. Her sharp talons slice into my captor's skin. She yowls and rolls off me. I crawl onto all fours. But when I try to open my eyes only broken darkness and confusing shapes are in my vision.

"My eyes!" I claw my face, feeling the familiar scars of horrid, welted skin.

How? It's not possible.

I throw my fists into the soft mud and scream. I thought I was free of this. I thought no one could saddle me with these weaknesses again so long as I stayed here. Who is this woman?

Glass shatters and the roar of flames halts my anger from spiraling. I jerk my head to the side. Connor must've breached the Glass House, and Killian along with him. I struggle to my feet, trying vainly to remind my ears that they can sense just as much as my eyes ever could. I didn't need my sight to survive before. I sure don't need it now.

To my left, Kes still wrestles with the witch. Straight ahead I hear the unmistakable cries, thuds, and grunts of combat. It's getting closer. To my right, the portal still howls, the deafening reminder of its continued existence.

I have to break that connection. I can still do it, blind or not. I'm not broken.

Blocking out the carnage, I retrace my steps in my mind. I turn to face the cauldron, then estimate the distance by the proximity of the noisy clamor coming from its depths. I step back three strides and feel the soupy puddles beneath my toes. Lowering into a crouch, I pat the ground with spanned fingers, shuffling back until I find the indentations of my knees from before. Hands outstretched to the side, I bite my lip in dire concentration, practically willing the spear to still be where I last saw it.

Come on . . . please be here.

I prick a finger on one of the jagged barbs. With a cry of relief, I snatch up the shaft in my palm and bolt toward the basin.

Hauling myself up the slippery steps, and throwing my legs over the side, I slide closer to the gargling portal. The water is rising again. I hear it on the wind as it whips up. But I won't let it rise, not a second time.

Lifting the spear above my head, I hear my name being cried from many directions—either in threat or warning. But it doesn't matter.

For the portal to close, Dagda's cauldron must be broken. This will mean the end of Eden, but what else can I do? There are far too many innocent lives at risk.

I smash the point of the spear into the edge of the basin.

The stone gives a thundering crack. The vibrations fly up my arms and into my very bones, making my whole frame shudder violently. The screaming wind begins to suck downward, like a vacuum, and with one last shriek of determination, I throw my weight against the shaft of the spear, wedging it deep into the cracked rock.

The bowl of the basin creaks and groans as it gives way. The spring of water spews from beneath it and covers me in a fountain of water. I gasp at the relief. The coolness chasing away the acid in my veins, the stinging from skin, and bathing my blinded eyes.

Like a miracle, my vision returns, though still slightly clouded and weak. But it's there. My indignation flares. The witch's spell is only a pretense of my curse, just like her voice was a mock of my mother's. I let myself become disabled by an illusion.

The dolmen stones the cauldron sat on sway and shatter under the weight of the cleaved basin. I withdraw the spear and kick away from the basin, letting the force of the break and the flow of the current wash me away from the yawning portal.

I heave myself up off the waterlogged ground, listening as the wind is sucked down through the portal. It'll close soon, and innocent lives will be safe. In the midst of the carnage, I turn to glare defiantly at the witch cloaked in black. In her cowardice, she springs across the strewn rocks and dives into the failing portal. She never looks back, gone like a shadow.

Kes hisses and screeches, flying to perch on the broken ridge of the basin, just above my head. Her beautiful tawny wings stretch, the two of us blocking Connor's last route of escape.

He's only a handful of feet away, his eyes dancing with rage. He keeps Killian in a head lock, then tosses him to the ground. Killian lands hard on his hands and knees. Blood and sweat run down his trembling arms, and his back boughs.

Flames race dangerously across Connor's skin. His gaze sweeps over me in threat, like my fate will be similar if I don't step aside.

But I'm not afraid anymore. I've been disillusioned, lied to and tricked too much to care over a threat. I bare my teeth at him. I've power too.

The remaining water from the spring already twists and shapes around me, rolling down against the ground like a tidal wall. Connor will have to pass through me to risk his escape, and he knows better. I'll quench that uncontrollable fire of his and not think twice about it.

It's Killian I fear for, his body a ragged picture of lacerations and horrendous burns. I know he can heal just as fast as I can, but those injuries slow him down. Blood and mucus splatters from his cracked lips. His breath sounds like it's being sucked through the bones of a corpse. But his eyes still shine, though he struggles to lift his head.

"Connor." He coughs, a horrible chest-crackling sound that makes me wince. More blood spews from his lips. Somehow, he finds the strength to stand and face Connor.

"Little brother . . . don't . . . run."

"I'm not your brother!" Connor turns the full brunt of his fist into Killian's stomach.

The flames that dance across Connor's fist leave another vicious burn through the tattered remains of Killian's shirt. His knees hit the ground so hard, the whole earth shudders. Gripping his hair, Connor yanks his head back, then draws back another fist.

My hands fly to my mouth to muffle a cry. The fear in my voice is tangible, for Connor lowers his hand and turns to stare quizzically between us. Killian's shoulders rise and fall with tremors as he chokes on the blood congealing in this throat. Every second wasted is drowning him. I don't know if even our supernatural bodies can survive suffocation.

Connor seethes in sudden realization. "You have feelings for him?"

"Connor." I step toward him. "Killian is your family. You called him brother, remember? Remember the college, and the gardens, and your dad?" I say, hoping the memories will trigger his conscience.

"Shut up! You speak lies!" Connor yanks Killian off the ground, then throws his head hard against the rocks. The sickening crack is enough to make me abandon my post. I dart across the ground to throw myself over Killian's body.

"So, this is your choice. You're throwing your lot in with this ill-reared mutt." Connor spits, his shadow stretching over us. Flames ripple around him, making his silhouette taller and broader than it truly is.

I run my fingers through Killian's sweat-soaked hair. A gash splits his forehead and blood pours over his left eye. But still he grips my elbows and gently pushes me aside, shifting in front of me. Still determined to defend me. I refuse to cower behind him. Instead, I shoulder his weight against mine.

"You're more pathetic than I thought." Connor laughs, a cruel sound. "But, no matter, you'll still be coming with me. Perhaps our Master will keep you for his entertainment."

Connor's hands claw into my scalp to yank me away. He sneers as he smacks Killian aside, but the blow doesn't connect. Killian's hand encases Connor's fist and squeezes it until I hear the bones crunch. Connor gasps and drops his hold on me, and I slip to the ground with a thud. Killian pushes himself to his feet and continues to squeeze that mangled hand until Connor whines and buckles beneath him.

"I've tried not to hurt you," Killian says, his voice rough through ragged breaths. He towers over Connor, purposefully twisting his hand, more bones cracking. "But I cannot, will not, allow you to go back to that demented demon"—he heaves in a shuddering breath—"and watch him destroy what's left of my family."

Connor grinds his teeth in frustration, but his attention is split, for the portal is nearly closed and the vacuum of wind ebbs. He doesn't have time to argue with us, and if we can contain him just a little longer, then we've got him.

"I'm not"—Connor's teeth grind beneath the force of Killian's strength—"the family"—he huffs out a painful breath, then lifts his chin and flashes a sneer at Killian—"of some common whore's offspring."

The insult earns Connor a firm crack to the jaw. The force sends him sprawling out on the ground, his broken arm limp and at a wrong angle. I use the moment of distraction to slip back toward the cauldron and block his escape. But before I get even two steps away, Connor laughs, a ghoulish sound that sends a thrill of fear up my spine.

"You shouldn't have let go, you stupid brute."

Killian glances down at his hands, realizing that he's been duped. I try to cry out, to warn him, but before I can, Connor lunges forward, striking out at Killian's throat. His fingers curl around Killian's thick neck, but it's not the power in his grip that worries me, it's the scorching energy that radiates from his touch.

I watch on, completely helpless, as Connor burns Killian from the inside out. Killian gasps, but only a hollow sound escape him. His veins burn through his skin until they start to turn an ashen gray.

"Connor!" I call the wall of water toward me. The waves crash over my limbs. That wild power runs in tandem with my essence, making it unstoppable.

Connor loosens his grip on Killian and lets him fall. He turns toward me, eyes shining with wicked intent. But the look disappears as he beholds me in all my feral wonder.

With an animalistic cry I throw all my strength toward him. A wall of water crashes over me and barrels straight into Connor. The sound of hissing and popping where cold water collides with flame is utterly satisfying, not least because Connor yowls in agony at his defeat. But a tsunami of water isn't enough to take him out. Not completely.

Connor emerges from the water, thrashing and snarling, his fire extinguished, his crazed mind inflamed. He charges for me. I brace for the impact, rallying that wall of water again, but at the last moment, Connor side steps me and dives for the portal.

I lunge sideways after him, trying to grab his arm, but his speed is inhuman. He disappears into the last of the wind funnel as the portal draws in its last breath. Nothing but eerie silence follows. I stare down into the still, dark waters of the broken cauldron.

I've lost Connor.

My Salvation

"Lexi?" Kes's cry is quivering and devastated in the gloom. "Lexi, come quick, please. It's . . . it's Killian."

I look back to where Killian lies and blink a few times, trying to process everything. Between the fog of smoke and ash, Kes—back in her humanoid form—hunches over Killian's still body a few feet away. He's flat on his back, eyes closed. Blood oozes from various wounds and his skin is drained of any warmth. The metallic stench of burning flesh and blood saturates the already pungent air. Little fires continue to fizzle and die out around his splayed body.

Kes holds fingers to his wrist, her face tight and sharp, eyes darting up and down his body. He doesn't move. I expect Killian to get up, but no matter how many times I blink, he doesn't move. Kes drops her fingers from his wrist and clamps her hands over her mouth, suffocating another cry.

I ghost the short distance from the broken cauldron steps to where he lies on the parched earth. It's the only patch of ground not sodden wet, and I gather, albeit a little slower than I should, that Connor's scorching flame radiated through Killian's entire essence, impacting even the earth beneath him.

I drop to my knees, heavier than intended, and reach for his hand. Shaking my head, I bite back tears, because how stupid am I? How does an earthbound spirit survive the destruction of fire?

"Kes?" I splutter out a few useless and desperate tears that catch in my throat as my fingers slide through Killian's. They don't flex around mine. They don't even flicker. "Kes, what's wrong with him? He'll wake up, right?"

Kes shuffles her feet a little tighter to herself, inching her knees so close to her chest that I'm not sure how she remains balanced. She peers forlornly up at me from behind her knobby joints. Tears stream down her filthy cheeks. I swallow, but the horrible lump in my throat doesn't shift.

I scrutinize every inch of him for movement, looking for any twitch of a muscle, a quirk of his lips, a flicker beneath his bruised and blood-caked eyelids. But there's nothing.

"Kes, he's not . . ." I suck back an ugly sob. We lock gazes, and her lips part to offer some entirely pointless condolence. "No . . . no, he's not . . ." I shake my head in rejection. Kes recoils as I lean over Killian's body and grab his face in my muddy hands.

"Lexi." Kes rests a palm on my arm, but I ignore her, because she's wrong.

"He's okay," I whisper, but it's a broken thing. I hoist my tattered skirts to my hips and straddle him. Gripping the blood-stained collar of his destroyed shirt, I rip open the fabric. Both Kes and I inhale in tandem. For a moment I look away. The burns are the stuff of nightmares.

Kes launches to her feet. "W-What are you going to do?" She sniffles and begins to pace in nervous circles.

"I don't know." I attempt to find some unmarred skin around his neck. I search for a pulse, but the stench of burning skin is too disturbing. "Just get help, Kes. Fly back to the castle and find someone who can help us . . . and hurry."

Her light feet create barely a whisper of sound as she darts into the smoky darkness.

"Come on, Killian. I know you're still there. Stop fooling around." I can't decide if my passive aggression is useful, but it keeps me sane to talk to him like he can hear me.

I duck my cheek to his nose. Is he breathing? I can't tell. I tip his head back and stick my two fingers into his mouth. Maybe there's blood clogging his airways.

Nope, clear.

"Breathe, you stupid, overgrown tree! If you think you're getting a kiss of life outta me for this, you're sadly mistaken."

Tears continue to drip down my chin. I glance about helplessly, wracking my brain for an idea. I turn my attention back to Killian. Take hold of his shoulders, and slide down his body so I can rest my ear against his wounded chest. I pray for a heartbeat. For a moment, there's nothing but eerie stillness, so I squeeze my fingers tighter against his skin, searching for the energy that weaves between us.

"Please, Killian, don't be gone." My lips move just enough to make my pleading audible. "Please?" I squeeze my eyes shut, my nose scrunching tightly, and fight against the pain crumbling through my chest.

And then, something flickers between us. The echo of a familiar vibration, a pulse of energy. My eyes fly open, my breath catches in my lungs. His fingers curl.

A hollow rasp of air . . . and another.

He's breathing!

Killian gives a weak moan, the faintest of sounds, almost undetectable, but I hear it. Shooting upright, I slip off him and hurry to sit by his head, lifting him to rest on my lap. My teardrops fall forcefully against his stained cheeks, and when one bounces off his closed eyelid, I see them flutter.

"Killian?" I run my trembling fingers through the matted lengths of his hair. "Killian, I'm right here. Kes has gone for help."

His lips part as if to say something, but to my horror, his face contorts into an agonizing grimace. His shoulders tense, inching upward, and his body curves and shudders. One of his knees bends as he squirms. I try to hold on to him, attempt to soothe him with reassuring whispers, but when my palm brushes his forehead, I'm scalded by the heat of his skin.

He's still burning.

Killian lets out a guttural cry. An animalistic sound that comes from deep inside. The pain makes his body twist and contort until he rolls onto his side, his head slipping from my lap. I weave my arms around his chest to steady him, but the heat is unbearable. I retract my hands, leaving him to writhe helplessly in the dirt, delirious and screaming in pain as he claws at his already wounded skin.

"Killian!" I cry in desperation, his yowls torturing me.

I don't know what to do.

"Killian, hold on." I crouch above him, but he's lost in the pain, and when his terrified gaze meets mine for a brief second, my courage crumbles. The vibrancy in his eyes has faded. The beautiful earthy greens have turned to an ashen gray, except for the burning golden veins that scorch across the whites of his eyes. Connor's last parting gift, to burn him from the inside out, to trap him in his own personal furnace. Only a monster could do this.

Launching to my feet, I tangle my fingers through my hair and cover my ears to muffle Killian's cries. I have to think. I can't just watch him suffer. There must be a way to ease the pain.

If I can cool him down, slowly, carefully, from the inside out, maybe that will buy his body enough time. Time for its self-healing to kick in. But how? I can't just dump water on him. The shock alone could kill him. No, I have to think of something else.

Wait.

I dart toward the basin, stooping to pick up a curved broken corner. I use it to catch enough of the clean water, still bleeding from the mouth of the cracked cauldron, then slip across the muddy ground. I slide to my knees behind Killian, and, using an opportune moment between thrashes, catch his collar and pull him toward me, leveraging his weight against my chest. His head lolls back onto my shoulder. I loop one of my legs over his thigh to ease his violent jerking.

"Shhh, it's all right. I've got you." I dribble the contents of the makeshift bowl over his neck and down his chest. The water pools around my arm that lies flat against his torso. Predictably, Killian cries out in shock, his body arching as if to reject the pain, but it fades quickly.

I let my quirky skin do its job. The water pulls toward my glimmering veins. The cool rivulets soak through his skin where I press my palms to his body. After a few minutes, his thrashing stills and his breathing becomes less erratic. I want to sing out in relief, but it's premature to think he's out of the woods. I grip the rest of the bowl in my hands and carefully pour the last of the water over his head. His skin sizzles where the cold liquid runs over inflamed skin.

"See, that feels better." I run my fingers through his scalp, then press my palm to his forehead and watch the water work its way into him again. "You're cooling down," I say, then wince at the sound of the hollow rasps of breath that scrape through his lungs.

"L-Lexi," Killian says between labored gasps for air.

"Yes, I'm here." I cup his face, ducking to press my lips to his temple. "I've got you."

"G-Get . . ." Killian's fingers curl around the crook of my elbow, his voice weak and feathery as he strains in my arms. "Get more . . . water."

"Is it working?"

He gives one jerky bob of his head, and I twist my head away, calculating the distance between us and the feeble spring of water. Little dribbles from a broken piece of ceramic tile aren't going to save him. I have to get him to the water. I can transfer so much more energy to him if I can just drag him the distance.

I nod. "Okay, we'll get more." I push myself onto my knees, then circle my arms under his and brace myself with bare feet into the earth.

I attempt one solid pull, huffing as I do, but Killian lets out an agonized groan. I try again and again, making little progress. His entire body tenses and shakes with each of my attempts. I can't do this. He's too heavy. And when the wound on his stomach stretches and begins pouring blood, I fall to my knees and abandon my mission.

"I-I can't." Killian sighs weakly, his eyes rolling back in his head a little, and I worry that I'm losing him again.

I pound my fist into the ground. "Yes, you can. We just need help." I glare out into the dark. "And it's coming. Just try for me, Killian, please." But he doesn't respond, and my heart sinks to the pit of my stomach.

I clutch his head in my hands, feeling the heat rise through my palms, and growl out a wretched sob that rises from the pit of my chest. There's nothing I can do, and the guilt of that kills me. No one is coming for us. No one is going to save him. Every one of them will celebrate his death, and it won't matter that he has saved them countless time before.

I hate this world. I hate them. I hate them all.

"Please, help us," I say toward the ground, hearing nothing but silence in return and hating it even more than I hate them. "Help us!" I shout into the gloom, but only my own voice echoes back. The indignation swells in that wild part of myself. "If we mean something to this world, if he means anything to you, then help us."

The strange ring to my voice clamors through the Glass House, shattering the quiet eeriness, but still, nothing returns. Only ashes float by, coating us in a gray shroud. I lower my chin to my chest, sobbing pitifully as I stroke Killian's face. My tears roll off my chin and drip onto his muddied cheek. I'm a fool to think anyone listens, even a Creator. No one would venture into this hell. There's nothing good or decent here—only monsters,

A rustle of leaves, and I lean protectively over Killian. A soft thud follows, and I peer into the dark. Listen for an attacker. Perhaps a howler, now trapped in our world, waiting for its opportunity to pounce. I flex my fists. My jaw clenches and my nostrils flare in anticipation of a fight. My teeth grind together. I pull in a steadying breath. On the release, I let that untamed thing inside me writhe and rise to the surface.

A soft nicker and another gentle thud breaks the building fury. Everything inside me quells in relief. My muscles slacken, and I outstretch my hand toward my frightened kelpie.

"Sebastian."

Happy tears spring anew within my tired eyes. I don't know if my beautiful water horse knows how miraculous his presence is. He clops out from the brittle brush. His coat has a dusting of soot, and he's a bit nervous, but for the most part, he looks entirely unharmed.

"Bash, quick, I need your help."

He trots up to me, head held curiously to the side, and observes Killian.

"Yes, yes, it's Killian. We need to get him to the spring."

Sebastian snorts and bobs his head before dropping down onto his front legs. I take that as permission and don't waste a second hauling Killian up to drape him over Bash's back. The movements cause him to cry out, but he doesn't fight against us.

Once we reach the cleaved cauldron, Sebastian lies down, allowing me to slip Killian into the water. I work quickly now. We've wasted too much time.

Yanking off Killian's shoes, I submerge his bare feet in the water, making sure that they're grounded in the earth. I can only assume that too much of my essence would be equally as damaging. It's all a careful balance. I just have to get it right. And I can. I know I can.

I remove the rest of his tattered shirt and let his back sink into the cool water. He groans a little, and squirms in pain, but he's conscious enough to know it isn't going to last. Then, with my one palm still supporting his neck, I stretch out over the top of him, free hand splayed against his wounded abdomen, and rest my forehead on his chest. I focus every thought toward him. I feel the essence of the water run through my colorful veins, creating the same beautiful patterns through him, until it cleanses and feeds his spirit.

That natural energy between us begins to build. His strength returns, his heart beats with vigor in his chest, and when I look up, the vibrancy in his beautiful eyes has returned.

Killian blinks a few times, and when his eyes focus on mine, he smiles. I burst into ugly tears.

His hand cradles my cheek, his brows pull downward in a baffled expression. The look is so adorable that I splutter out a giggle. Crushing my nose against his, I kiss him, and I don't care if it hurts. I'm just so relieved to feel the coolness of his lips against mine.

"Hi." Killian's half-hearted greeting is more of a croak than actual words. His thumb brushes my cheek. Exhaustion is evident in his eyes, pain is written on his face, but still, he smiles for me.

"Hey," I say, and kiss him again, this time with a bit more tenderness.

Our names echo from outside the Glass House, and I sit up in time to see Kes flutter down to perch on the strewn boulders that were once the dolmen circle. She gives a screech, then coos at both of us before tilting her head. I recognize Bryce's frantic wailing and Professor Donoghue's more controlled calls from just beyond the Glass House.

"We're in here!" I shout and help Killian onto Sebastian's back. "We're coming!"

Holding a steadying hand to my Silent Gardener so he can sit on Sebastian's back, properly this time, I urge my intuitive kelpie forward and nod for Kes to hitch a ride. She obliges, perching on Bash's rump, even outstretching a protective wing to cover Killian's exposed skin. The sight brings yet more tears to my stinging eyes, happy ones this time. At least we're safe for the time being.

As we limp along, I ponder my understanding of safety. I study the rampant chaos left behind and puzzle over how perfectly timed all of this was. None of this seems right; something is very wrong. I become increasingly suspicious until realizations dawns.

There's a wolf among us.

36

ALWAYS

The water in the washrooms connected to Killian's dorm is lukewarm at best, but it's a welcome reprieve to wash away the stench and hideousness of tonight. It's only been an hour, maybe two, but it feels like years.

Some of the castle is still smoldering—the banquet hall and a few of the upper rooms—but most of it remains unscathed, albeit trashed. Yet somehow this only heightens my suspicions. I didn't see a single survivor on our return, only bodies of fallen guardsmen, servants, and a few civilians I assume were either fleeing servants or aristocrats of the Order. Although, half the time their bodies were so mangled it was hard to be sure what they were.

Bryce ordered us to stay hidden down in the old guardsmen dormitories, at least until she can make sense of the destruction. She knows the secret passageways continue under the castle and lead to the military base. Survivors will be there, along with any remaining guardsmen. I told her about Thomas, and that the last time I saw him he was in the courtyard. She thanked me and left in minutes of us reaching the groundmen's entrances. I sent Sebastian with her, reckoning he'd be able to carry any injured. Right now, the only thing I'm certain of is that my friends and I are alive—and that's enough.

Scrunching the coarse towel through my cleaned-to-within-an-inch-of-its-life hair, I pause to stare into the steamed mirror above the sink. It isn't a pretty sight. In fact, I'd probably go so far as to say I look better with the gruesome birthmarks and funky eye.

The purple rings around my eyes hint at my exhaustion whilst the pounding in my head suggests that sleep is the last thing I'll get any time soon. That niggling voice of suspicion still rings in my ears—something was amiss.

I pad to the threshold of the communal washroom. Kes keeps sentry outside the bathroom door, her sharp, golden eyes flickering in agitation, her incredible hearing picking up even the slightest of noises. She glances at me and gives a sympathetic grimace. She pats my arm in reassurance, but we both know things don't look good.

"Ah, there you are. How's the head?" The professor's bland voice reminds me to keep focused. It isn't the time to start processing events yet.

"Like a woodpecker has taken up residence in my cranium," I say, massaging my scalp. "How's Killian?"

"Alive." He fidgets with the rolled-up ends of his shirtsleeves. I note the bloodstains on his cuffs and swallow uncomfortably. The sound makes the professor cease his frowning, along with his silent debate. He glances my direction and offers a sad smile. "He's fine; already on the mend, but he's very weak. Best to let him rest."

I nod in agreement, craning my neck a little to make out Killian's shape on his rickety bed. He looks so pale, much too pale, and visibly shivering.

"He's cold," I say and hug myself a little tighter. "Maybe I was too rough? Maybe I just made him worse. Do you think I could've made him worse?"

"No, no, absolutely not. Your quick thinking bought him valuable time." Professor Donoghue clasps my shoulder and gives it a little shake. "He'll be okay. His body is just in shock."

"I should find some more of those herbs he uses to make medicines."

"You'll do no such thing. You'll stay here and keep out of view." Professor Donoghue tuts and reaches for his cane. "Besides, it's me that owes the lad, not you."

I tilt my head in confusion, unsure of exactly what he means, but I don't get to voice the question before the answer hits me.

"Connor didn't mean to do any of this." I hold out my arm to stay the professor. "He's not well. He's been brainwashed. You know he'd never hurt anyone, especially not Killian, if he were in his right mind. He's a good man, professor. This isn't your fault."

Professor Donoghue swallows one of those sticky lumps from his throat. I see the tears rim his eyes, but he slips his thumb and index finger under his spectacles to rub the evidence away. With a watery smile, he pats my cheek and gives an unconvincing nod of his head.

"Thank you. I appreciate your kindness." He sucks back a shaky breath and straightens his shoulders. "But he's my boy, despite what the Order would say, and I wasn't there for him when he needed me most."

I open my mouth to rush to his defense, to rebuke such nonsensical notions, but he just gives a hard chuckle.

"It's my guilt, Lexi." His feet drag heavily against the floor. "I'll get the herbs, if there are any left. Just you stay put. Besides, he doesn't stop asking for you." He nods back in the direction of Killian and gives me a half-hearted wink as he shuffles though the door, gesturing for Kes to follow. "Kes, be a darling and come with me. I'd feel better if there were trustworthy eyes and ears in the corridors. You never know who's lurking."

Kes reluctantly follows Professor Donoghue out the door but she doesn't argue with his logic. I almost feel guiltier than I did a moment ago. The professor isn't stupid; he knows what's going on between Killian and me. I'd expected that out of everyone, Connor's father would be the most offended by my blatant disregard of the rules. Yet here he is, sneakily giving me some time alone with Killian. I guess there is humanity and compassion within the Order, which only fuels my belief that Connor can be redeemed.

More than ever, I contemplate the Order. Who they are and why my parents absconded from the ranks, taking me with them. And what does the professor know? There is corruption here, but who's behind it, I've no idea. This place is dripping with secrets.

Pondering these worrying details, I glance back to Killian and resolve that tonight is not the night to bring such things up. Instead, I tiptoe to his bedside and kneel carefully by his head, trying my level best not to wake him.

He stirs. I should've known that wouldn't be successful. Killian can hear a pin drop in the middle of a thunderstorm.

"Hey." I smile and run my fingers through the roots of his hair.

"You're okay." His tattered voice a mixture of relief and pain. He attempts to push himself up on his elbows, but I grip his shoulders and ease him back against the pillows.

"I'm okay." I nod. "But you aren't, so lie down before I get in trouble for undoing all of Professor Donoghue's good work."

He scowls unhappily at my fussing. "I've had worse." His hand outstretches to my throat, and I swallow as his fingers trace the red marks. His eyes narrow and his tone turns accusatory. "You're not okay."

"Don't make a fuss; we heal fast." I catch his fingers in mine and draw his hand up to rest against my lips, giving him enough of a pleading look until he relents with a disgruntled sigh. "Can I get you anything?"

"A baseball bat and the coordinates to Connor's exact location."

Killian seethes and glares at the ceiling. I suck in my bottom lip in anxiety, although after a moment of tense silence, he twists his head on the pillow to regard me.

"Boy is clean out of his mind if he thinks he can put a hand on you . . . or anyone else. I think he needs a little bit of tough, brotherly guidance."

I try to restrain the nervous laughter that bubbles up in my chest. When he gives me a quizzical look, I shake my head and lean down to kiss his brow. It hurts my heart to know that I didn't stop Connor from escaping. If he were here, Killian would still be fighting to get him to see sense. He'd still call him brother, and he'd still love him, regardless of the hurt caused. Killian's too good for this place. He can't stay here.

"Killian." I press my forehead against his. "I've something to tell you, but only if you're up for the chat."

"I've waited two agonizing hours to hear your voice." He runs his nose along the length of mine, but I see how heavy his eyelids are as they droop, and his thick voice—though incredibly attractive—reveals how tired he is.

I debate against telling him nothing and letting him sleep, but his hands run up the lengths of my bare arms and I'm persuaded otherwise. Killian pushes his head back against his pillows for a second. His soft, colorful eyes narrow. His thick brows scrunch so close together they almost meet in the middle.

"You're freezing," he accuses, and I shrug.

"It's fine, I'll grab a blanket." I wave off his concerns and attempt to step away.

"Yeah, not happening." Killian's hand clamps around my arms. He guides me down beside him, then shuffles back on the bed, using his other hand to lift the blanket a little. I bristle, but he just rolls his eyes. "Oh please, don't flatter yourself. I'm practically channeling a furnace here. Honey, this is a purely selfish motive."

"Yeah, selfish." I snort, but the inviting waft of heat is too much to resist, so I carefully slip underneath the covers and nestle my cheek against the pillow, facing him.

The warmth practically makes me purr with delight, but try as I might, the tight space makes it impossible for me not to find Killian's skin. I only register that he isn't wearing much when my icy toes scrape along his bare legs. I instantly recoil and shuffle to the edge of the bed. With an audible chuckle, he loops his arms around me and draws me against him, his hot skin shivering and dimpling when it comes in contact with the cold of mine.

"I'm trying not to hurt you." I lie to deflect from my blushing, and wince when my fingers brush against his bandaged abdomen.

"No, you're panicking in case the professor forgot to leave me decent." He lifts both brows, and I drop my chin in embarrassment. I note that he is indeed wearing what I hope to be loose-fitting boxers.

Killian shifts a little closer to me. The knuckle of his index finger rests under my chin, forcing me to look up. His grin is filled with roguish amusement. To make a point, I tangle my legs with his. His ticklish hairs make me giggle, but that schoolgirl façade ends when my hip chaffs over the wound dressings on his knees and thigh. I swallow and drop my chin again, but Killian clamps my leg in place before I can recoil.

"Lexi." He says my name with a weary sigh. "I have five broken ribs, a dodgy left lung, and I feel like I drank a tank of acid. You're entirely assured that I only want a hug, and a gentle one at that."

I give a sad chuckle, rolling my eyes when I realize he thinks I'm being coy. I blow out a sigh and loosely wrap my arms around him. I nestle my cool forehead into the crook of his neck and press my body as carefully as I can against his.

"I apologize. I just don't want you getting any ideas." My whispery voice sends a reflexive shiver through his spine. "I'm a good girl, you know."

Killian chuckles and tightens his grip on me. "You're alive and here; that's all I want." He cuts off a yawn with a weary sigh. "So what did you want to chat about?"

"It can wait until you've rested a bit." I pull away from our embrace and clutch his face in my hands. "I'm worried about you."

"Shhh." Killian waves his hand dismissively, though his eyelids seem to have drooped even further. "I want to hear this; it'll distract me."

"If you're sure."

He nods, and I run my fingers through his scalp again, marveling at the handsome pink tinge of his warmed skin, and how that flushed look doesn't detract from his appeal. In fact, it increases it, tenfold.

"I discovered something just before the party," I begin, trying hard to keep my attention off his parted lips. I imagine softly tugging on that full bottom lip. Hmm. Perhaps it's Killian who should be nervous of me.

"Mmhmm." His eyelids fluttering open again.

"I think I found a key. To get through the Veil. I can finally take you home." I can't help the excited edge to my voice, but I'm a little deflated when Killian's reply is a barely audible mutter. I consider shaking him awake, but then his eyelashes bat open again.

"Did I just dream this conversation?" Killian asks, his gaze a little vague and unfocused. "Did you just say something about a key and home?"

"Yes." I clutch his shoulders excitedly as he pushes himself up onto his elbows. "It's my locket." I fish it out from around my neck and pop the catch to show him the intricate internal mechanism. "I think my parents knew. I think they kept this for me. Safely around my neck all along." I help Killian to sit up to inspect the key. "I think if I bring this to the crystal basin, or dome, or whatever, that it might activate a gateway. We can go back."

Killian doesn't speak for the longest moment. He turns the locket over in his hands, carefully inspecting every inch until he presses it back into my palm. He folds his large hands around mine and holds them tight in place. He studies them and rubs his thumbs along the skin. Then, slowly, he lifts his somber gaze to meet mine. The depth of his emotion is staggering.

"I knew you'd find a way." He squeezes my hand. "I trust you, Lexi. I'll follow your intuition . . . Take me home."

"I will." I nod and lean forward until our foreheads touch. "Just promise me one thing."

"Anything."

"No matter what happens, no matter what we face, stay with me."

"Always."

ESCAPE

I wake to the sound of birds chirping and the gray light of early dawn creating shafts of cold color through the small basement windows. I bury my eyes into the warmth of Killian's bare shoulder, inhaling his muskier, unwashed scent, and decide it isn't all that bad.

His chest rises and falls in a perfect, easy rhythm. He acknowledges my movement with a soft grunt, but he doesn't wake completely. I estimate by the dim light and crashing crescendo of the dawn symphony that it's very early, and we haven't been asleep that long.

We fell asleep to our talk of escape plans. Killian feels the key will activate just by my presence and proximity to the Veil, however, I'm a little more dubious. Although, there's nothing we can do whilst Killian remains weak and the Order in chaos. Just up and leaving would be far too suspicious. We need to know more about what happened before we execute any plans.

Wrestling free of Killian's arm, I make it to the edge of the bed to sit. I stretch out my sore limbs and crack my stiff neck. It's apparent that not even supernatural Celestials are exempt from post-fight fatigue. I braid my hair over my shoulder and stuff my feet into Killian's much-too-large sneakers.

Glancing back at my sleeping champion, I can't help the warmth that blooms in my chest. He's so excruciatingly handsome in the cold light. It makes his russet skin luminous and pale, highlighting every little dip and crevice in his muscular body. Still, his body is a sculpted kind of perfection, wrought from hard labor and a tough life. Yet, for all that ruggedness, there's such a sweet softness about him. An innocence I feel compelled to protect.

I know that in Killian's heart, if he had a choice, he would never fight. He fights because he has to, and when he does, he's ruthless. I'm a teeny bit frightened of that side of him. His wildness is unpredictable. It makes him relentless, and I wonder . . . If I hadn't been there to stop Connor, would Killian have carried on until he was nothing but ashes? That willful determination makes my stomach churn. I fear for him.

The rattle of the door handle makes me suck in a sharp breath. It seems I'm still running high off the adrenaline from last night, but my panic is unnecessary.

Kes's head peeks through the narrow gap.

"I thought I heard you up." She grins and angles her little body toward me. "I was wondering if we should try to find some food."

"That would be wonderful."

The pantry seems relatively untouched, if a little messy, and I'm able to find a stale loaf perfect for toasting. The same, however, cannot be said of the kitchens. Most of the main kitchen is ransacked. Knives splayed everywhere, along with other sharp tools, and there's traces of blood still left on the tiled floors.

"Maybe you should go wait by the basement stairs," Kes says, warily glancing around, listening for noises I'd never detect. "I'll check the fridge for butter."

I nod and drift out into the hallway and toward the staircase, not feeling inclined to argue. By the looks of this carnage, it isn't a stretch to imagine something to be hiding here. I'm not thrilled to be so exposed right now, especially with so many unanswered questions. But as I wait for Kes at the top of the stairs, I spy a dazed servant scuttle down the far end of the hallway.

"Tess!"

Her springy curls bounce as she jumps in surprise.

"Lady Alexandria! How?" She fidgets with her skirt, her eyes darting nervously around the room. "Where have you been? We thought we'd lost you." I know her to be a scatty girl, but there's something about her jerky movements that rouses my suspicion.

"Recovering." Not a lie exactly, but something warns me to keep the details of my location vague. "Where have you been? Is everyone okay? Pádraig? Deirdre?"

"I'm not sure, my lady." Her eyes well and she clutches a fist to her mouth, muffling her sobs. "Some of us made it to the military base. Most are still there, and the injured too. I was sent out with some of the uninjured to find food."

I nod, picking up distant voices on the grounds or in the higher levels. Only a few though—how depleted are the Order's numbers.

"Do you know how the earl is, and the elders?"

"You mean you haven't heard?" Tess balks, her little hands lifting to her rosy cheeks. "Thomas Domnaill is dying. Lord Callaghan has taken control of the estate and handed all assets to his daughter."

"His daughter?"

"Lady Margot, ma'am. Didn't you know that?" Tess is really squirming on the spot now.

"No," I say, more bitterly than intended. "No one informed me that Margot was Callaghan's daughter, not even Thomas. Why exactly is that knowledge secret?"

"I-I don't know, ma'am." Tess holds her hands up, her eyes flashing around the room as I take a rather threatening step forward. I'm getting sick of being drip-fed information.

"Tess, you seem nervous. What's happening out there?" I gesture outside, toward what I remember to be the general direction of the military base. "Why do you seem surprised to see me? And for the love of god, why are you twitching when I look at you?"

The girl literally breaks down in a flood of tears. Taking a few quick strides toward her, I reach for her arm and gently squeeze. This only makes her worse. She drops her head in her hands and continues yowling.

"What is it? You can tell me. I swear I won't get you in trouble." I smooth my hand over her hunched shoulders, deciding to try a less intimidating approach.

"They tell lies," Tess splutters into her hands. "The Elder Council. The earl knew that, but he was controlled by his wife. He's a captive here. We all are, ma'am."

"I-I don't understand. What happened to Thomas? Tess, please." I give her a gentle shake, enough so that she's forced to look at me. "Are we in trouble? Tell me now so I can help."

"I don't know." She shakes her head and wipes the tears from her eyes. "All I know is that one minute the physician said Thomas was going to be okay, and the next, Callaghan announced he was close to death. But I can't find out any more. I can't even get near him. No one can. Not even his own servants. He was brought into the military base, and Callaghan has had him on strict watch."

"I can." I spring toward the basement stairs. "I'm the superior here. Callaghan will let me see, or at least grant me answers. Come on. You can fill me in on the story as we go."

"No!" Tess grabs my arm, and the alarm in her voice makes me glance back in confusion. "No, you c-can't. You have to leave here. You need to get out before—" Tess's eyes widen at the sound of footsteps.

"Tess?" I tug her arm. "Tess, before what? What's happening?"

"He said you'd been killed," she says, spewing the words so fast that I barely process them. "Callaghan said that the lad—the half-breed—killed you because he summoned a portal from his Glass House to the other side to allow Dian to return, and you stopped him."

"That's a lie. Killian saved us. He nearly died trying to protect us. I was with him."

"I know." She continues to sob and clings to my hand, her teeth biting down on her bottom lip. "The half-breed is kind; he helped me get medicine to my mammy, special herbs from his Glass House. I know he isn't bad. He wouldn't kill nobody, least of all you. He loves you, miss, but Callaghan will kill him. And you if you don't leave."

"His name is Killian, not half-breed." I frown, throwing my hand to my brow as I try to conceive any possible explanation as to why Callaghan would fabricate such a lie. But before I can make any sense of it, another more harrowing thought occurs. "Where are Professor Donoghue and Agent Bryce? Is Callaghan looking for Killian?"

Tess stares at me, mouth agape, her features paling considerably. She shakes her head side to side. "I don't know. He never mentioned what happened to the ha—to Killian. Everyone assumes he's with Dian now. And I-I never saw Bryce or the Professor. They weren't in the room when Callaghan addressed us."

"When did he address you?" I say, shaking her arms a little too violently. Killian has been alone for several minutes. In his rooms, where they will look first.

"About thirty minutes ago. Maybe less."

I can't go looking for my friends. If I'm spotted, they'll kill me. But I can save Kes and Killian. Turning on my heels I make a frantic dash back to the kitchen.

"Kes, where are you?" I slide in behind a counter, in case I find some ill-tempered guard. "Kes, we gotta go . . . now."

"Hang on, I'm looking for jam." I follow the sound of her cranky mutter and find her in an opened cupboard. I spring for the cupboard and yank her up by the arm.

"Forget the jam. Run. Now."

Catching on to the panic in my voice, and the wild look of terror, Kes drops the various jars in her hands and follows me toward the stairs at a flat-out sprint. I barrel past Tess, pausing only briefly to bellow commands at her to find either the Professor or Bryce and to ensure the three of them escape.

I fill Kes in on my findings as we run, keeping everything short and sweet. I know by the absolute horrified expression on her pointy, little face that she's just as surprised as I am.

We slam through Killian's door, panting. I shout his name and rush to the bed but find it empty.

"Kes!"

She rushes to my side, her shrill gasp making my heart plummet to the pit of my stomach.

"Kes, he isn't here."

"I'll check the bathroom," she says, but returns only a minute later with a much more anxious expression. "He's not there."

"No. Oh god, no." I stick my fingers through the roots of my hair. Tears brim my eyes, and my throat burns painfully as I try to swallow away the awful bile. I should never have left him.

A creak of the wood sends Kes into a spin, and she knocks me sideways. Her hands fly to her hip to procure a deadly looking knife. I blink a few times in my confusion, realizing I'm sprawled on Killian's unmade bed with Kes crouched in front of me, snarling at the threatening sound.

A creak sounds again.

"Show yourself!" Despite her small stature, that voice is menacing. But the creak is followed by shuffling footsteps and the familiar muted thud of the end of a cane against stone floor.

"Professor!" I practically knock him sideways as I leap from the bed and slam into his unsuspecting arms. "I thought you were dead."

"I assume you've heard the latest news then." The professor pats my back before gingerly detangling us.

"Yeah, I'm a walking miracle, being allegedly murdered and all." I frown and lean around him. "Killian isn't here. Is he with you?"

"Yes, he's with Bryce out in one of the fuel sheds. She's crafty, that one. Was two steps ahead of Callaghan." By the mention of his name, the professor's features harden. "She's got you both some clothes." He pushes me in the direction of the hidden door in the wall. "He told us about the key. It seems fortune is with us for the moment."

"Not for long," I say as we step into the dank, drippy passageway. "It was the maid, Tess, who told me the story. I sent her looking for you and Bryce to pass on a message. I doubt it will take long for her questioning to rouse suspicion."

"Oh Lexi." The Professor groans. "You should've just stayed put. Bryce and I are old hands at this business. We know how to get around unseen."

"Yes, well, it was nice of you both to keep me in the loop," I say, my temper flaring at the amount of lies I've been force fed and accepted due to absolute ignorance. I don't know whether to throttle the professor or let it go, because, honestly, what's one more crazy lie in my disillusioned life?

"Lexi." The Professor's tone is cajoling as he slides in front of me, preventing me from continuing my aggressive march. "If you knew the things we did, it would put you in peril. We just wanted you to focus on you, find your feet, learn the extent of your talents, and besides, all we had were theories and suggestions. Nothing is ever spoken aloud in Domnaill, as I'm sure you are well aware. It's our job to guard the secrets and keep you safe."

"And what about Killian?" I prod his shoulder. "How much does he know? And when were you going to mention that Callaghan wanted us dead?"

"For goodness sake, Lexi, Killian's survival is just as important to us as yours. If he knows any more than you it's because he's smart, like his father." Professor Donoghue grabs my arm and marches me onward, motioning for a silent and entirely panicked Kes to keep up. "The Order has been choking on its corruption for years. The Hunter family, your parents, myself, and a handful of other loyal members have been trying to find the root of the poison for over a decade. I suspected Callaghan, as did your mother, but Thomas wouldn't believe the head of our Order to be the culprit. Alas, the man is paying with his life for his blindness."

"What's corrupting them?" I wince in shock as we rip out into the glare of sunlight.

"If we knew that, we'd be in a better position." The professor gives me a pointed look. "Although, I'd assume it has something to do with a contract with Dian, but that, Lexi, will be up to you to find out."

With his hand still clamped to my arm, he hurries us along as fast as his injury allows. Whilst in the open, we're at risk, but we keep to the shadows of the old outbuildings until we reach one at the far end of the back courtyard used by the groundskeepers and servants. The professor gives the door of a stone building two swift knocks.

The sound of a rusted bar scrapes open and ensures the end of our chat. I'm shoved into the tiny space. It takes me a moment to adjust to the darkness again, but when I do, I find the professor hunched by a filthy window on the far end of the glorified stone shed. He uses a pile of chopped logs to rest against, keeping a keen eye on the scaly glass.

To his right rests Killian, dressed in sturdy-looking leather pants, like the kind Connor wore, though he wears a simple black tee that doesn't hide his injuries. He leans on his axe, sitting in an uncomfortable crouched position with his head bowed. I'm about to disturb him when I register that he's praying.

"Lexi." Bryce loops an arm around my middle and draws me into an impromptu hug. The gesture so foreign that it takes me a moment to return it.

The sound rouses Killian from his devotions, and he straightens, his glinting eyes the only thing lighting this dusty room. He smiles, and I smile back, no words needed to express the genuine relief we both share at seeing each other again.

"I've got you some clothes." Bryce sniffs, rubbing the back of her hand across her nose—she's been crying. "They are as close to the apparel of your homeland as I could possibly make them. Leather trousers, sturdy and tight, but I'm afraid all I have is a green blouse for you to wear and some old steel-cap boots."

"They're perfect." I bundle the clothes into my arms whilst she and Kes make the boys turn away so I can change.

"How's the fit?" Bryce asks as I waddle out between them when I'm done.

"A little snug." I poke my hips, frowning at the little roll of excess of skin it causes over the top of the tightly buttoned pants.

"You're lovely." Killian offers me his compliments from the far end of the room, a tinge of pink coloring his cheeks as he ducks his head. I practically beam in response.

"Yes, yes, she's always lovely," Kes crows from the door, her shoulders inching to somewhere near her ears. "But how exactly is this going to work? Are we swimming? Because I'm not a duck."

"Relax, Feathers." Killian limps toward the door. "It's just a little water."

"It's a lot of water." She crosses her arms, her face turning redder by the second. "Like a whole lough full of water. We could drown."

"Fine." Killian waves his hand toward the castle. "Stay here and get turned into Easter lunch."

"Oh good grief, would the both of you shut up?" I stamp my foot for added affect, which seems to gain their attention. "No one is going to drown, and this is going to work, okay? And Killian, stop threatening her. She's too skinny to make a decent roast."

Kes practically spits feathers whilst we all chuckle in unison, our little joke enough to calm the brewing tension. Still, I don't know if this will work any more than Kes does. I can't promise they won't drown. But what choice do we have?

BREAKING POINT

The cold, restless waters of the lough crash against the shoreline, and the wind pummels the sand. It whips it up and scatters debris across the beach. It's not a day for swimming.

Sebastian whinnies at my side. His hoof digs into the sand, ploughing it over on itself. I move my palm in soothing motions across his neck and watch the horizon.

I contemplate everything in my vision for just a second longer and cradle the locket in my other hand. If this works, then by tonight, the world I know will be nothing but a memory.

Behind me, Bryce and the professor say their hurried goodbyes. They have a friend and ally on the outpost who's waiting to get them out. They only have minutes left to get on the road. I don't know what will happen to Tess. I can only pray she's wise enough to stay safe.

"Ready when you are." Kes's lyrical voice makes me smile.

I tilt my head back to watch her struggle to get atop Bash. He uses his muzzle to give her butt a little extra nudge, and with a huff, she manages to wriggle onto his back. Killian's laughter makes me turn to find him and my guardians watching Kes's spectacle. The smiles on their faces something I try to commit to memory forever. I don't know if I'll ever see them again.

I can't help the tear that slips free as I accept a parting embrace from both Bryce and the professor. Bryce sobs openly. Professor Donoghue wraps an arm loosely around her shoulder in an awkward attempt to console her.

"I knew you liked me." I grin as she kisses my cheek.

"You grew on me . . . both of you." She sniffs and attempts to dab her eyes again. "I'm useless at goodbyes. Here." She pushes two items wrapped in cloth toward Killian and me.

The one she hands to Killian I recognize as the broken spearhead, but the smaller one, I don't recognize. Carefully, I receive the gift and unwrap it to expose a fine long knife with a bone handle. The blade is thin and deadly sharp, made with that same crystal as the other illuminated blades, and of course, beautifully decorated in fine golds and silvers, similar to its kin. I'm intimidated by it but grateful, nonetheless. I'm certain that where we're going, I'll be in dire need of it.

"Thank you," I say in awe, wrapping it up again to place in the leather satchel Killian has given me. It's allegedly watertight and holds the last of his herbs, tools, and some useful medicines. All things we'll need for our journey.

"I was going to give it to you when you started improving in training, but I'd be waiting another decade if I did." Bryce chuckles halfheartedly. I giggle and nod in agreement because she isn't wrong. "Killian, make sure you teach her how to use that thing."

"I will." He takes my hand in his, squeezing it. "We'd better leave now."

One last time, I look up to the horizon and spy my parents' tree, its branches blowing in the strong wind, and I take a little courage that they'll always be here. When my vision cuts across the hilly dunes I see the silhouettes of men in the distance. Callaghan's men.

"Yeah, we need to go." I nod, throwing myself into one last hug with the professor. "What if this doesn't work?" I whisper, terrified of the thought of what will befall all of us if I fail.

"It'll work." He holds tight for just a second more.

"How do you know?"

"Because you're Fred and Marie's daughter, that's why." He roughly pushes me away and points to the roaring waves. "They believed in you, Lexi. They raised you for this. Now just you believe in them."

I give a jerky, but resolute head bob and clutch the locket around my neck.

I am not afraid.

Turning on my heels, I sprint for the water, sloshing in until the waves knock my feet from below me, but it doesn't frighten me. I'm the water and I'm the sea. It can't overcome me.

My gaze roams until I spy Sebastian treading water in the distance, both Killian and Kes safely on his back, and with that comfort, I dive into the deep. The cold, icy current feels like a thousand pinpricks on my skin, but instead of pain, I feel exhilaration.

My skin begins to illuminate. My true self wanting to be free of all its restrictions. I rein myself in, for I can't lose focus now, and I must be in physical form to operate the locket. So, much to the annoyance of my wild spirit, I dive down into the dark.

The crystal network appears not long into my descent, but after several minutes, my lungs burn. The physical need to breathe is forefront in my mind, but I push on, determined to reach the basin.

I struggle with the locket around my neck, slipping it off. Light bursts through my skin. I only have seconds to remain in this form before self-preservation kicks in and I surrender to my true self. I can't fail now. I'm too close. Gritting my teeth in sheer determination, I focus on the center of mirrored crystal, seeing the navy waters reflected from the other side.

I'm nearly there. I can feel it. Every part of my being is tingling.

Opening the locket, I hold it out to the crystal wall, but nothing happens. I gulp in a mouthful of salt water. My body convulses.

Nothing happens.

I throw myself at the beautiful, mirrored matrix, thrashing my hands. I hold the locket, pressed on my palm, against it. Still nothing.

My eyesight dims and my palms slip from the crystal. The water caresses my senses as my skin dissolves in a whirlpool of dancing bubbles. I can't hold on. I don't know what else to do.

My head falls back in bitter disappointment. The water takes my weight and draws me away from the Veil. I try to focus all my energy on my palm, determined to hold form, to stay in my skin. With whatever strength is left of my corporeal self, I channel it into my hand and slam it against the crystal. My eyes shut, and I pray with everything I have. The Veil must fall away before I lose myself.

I just want to save them.

Please, let me save them.

Epilogue

KILLIAN

Something is wrong.

I wish I could say I'm just the eternal pessimist, but when it comes to Lexi, it's definitely more of an acute intuition. She's been down there too long. Far too long. So long that I consider abandoning the kelpie and diving in after her. The only thing that prevents me from doing such a thing is the idiotic, overgrown chicken I need to restrain. Kes lasted all of about ten seconds before she burst into a bloody plume of feathers and manic screeching.

"Awk, shut up, Kes, you're frightening the kelpie." I crush her against my chest. She glares indignantly and pecks my arm. "I swear to everything in the heavens, you dull duck, I'll turn you into a feathered boa if you draw blood."

She screeches again but doesn't bite. Wise.

Sebastian snorts and lets out an anxious whinny before sticking his head back into the stormy waves. Bash is just as intuitive about Lexi as I am, if not more so. I know he senses something is off.

Another wave crashes against us, nearly knocking me straight off Sebastian's back and into the murky water. This time, however, as I splutter and cough against Bash's neck, a strong light cuts through the swell. A light that intensifies and grows, spreading wide and far until it rings us in.

Both Kes and I peer at each other and then the strange disc of light. A dull crack sounds from somewhere deep down. Kes hisses and scrambles until she perches herself on my head. Her stupidly large wings flap so much that she smacks me around the face. I grip her by one of her legs and yank her down, squashing her against my chest again.

"You'll thank me later," I say over her screams of protest.

Another deep rumble makes the water ripple back with a terrifying force. Sebastian rears and thrashes. His cries sounding excited, almost anticipatory. Not frightened.

"She did it." I grab Kes around the wings and give her a shake. "Lexi did it." I get an obligatory snap at a finger for my enthusiasm.

The celebrations are cut short. The waters beneath us surge and draw downward, forming a whirlpool. Abandoning any more excitable fist pumps, I flatten myself to Bash and grip his neck. I ignore—as well as any living thing with ears can—the inhuman squealing of one petrified bird.

"Here we go!" I shout over the din, just for Kes's benefit, feeling the kelpie's powerful muscles surge and pulse as he prepares to dive. I take a deep breath before cutting off Kes's warbling with a hand around her beak.

In a moment, everything turns to inky dark. I remember a passage through black waters. It feels so long ago. Another time. I'm not even sure if I made it up to comfort myself.

I squint through the water, the sensation like needles, but I need to find her. I need to make sure she'll make it through, but all I see is the beautiful expanse of shimmering crystal as we approach a narrow crack in its defenses. The chink is so small, but we fit. I still close my eyes. I don't know why. I guess fear is easier to overcome if you don't look it dead in the eye.

The icy air bites my skin when we break the water's surface.

Everything is dark.

It's night, and the clouds are thick and rumbling with thunder. Rain pelts down hard on the story sea. It doesn't take long for the strong waves to separate all of us from each other.

I swim in frantic circles, searching for Lexi, looking for land. I inhale again and dive below the surface, hands outstretched, waiting for her to hold them, praying that she'll find me. But I can't stay down long enough. My lungs too scorched and my muscles too weak to push against the current.

I'm not losing her. Not when we've gotten this far.

One last time I sink below the surface. One last time I hold out my hand.

Fingertips brush mine. I grasp at them, but they slip. I call out, saltwater filling my lungs and choking me. I don't care.

The waves crash and the current spins her away.

In the dark waters between us, there's a glint of her copper hair and the soft glow of her alabaster skin.

Then she's gone.

And I'm alone in the black.

To be continued . . .

Lexi's Research Notes

abominations An ancient slur given to half-blooded beings who were a result of the mixing of humans and Celestials. In ancient days, these half-beings were numerous, and they overpowered men. As punishment for defying the balance of life, the Great Cull rendered the race almost nonexistent. Since that time, relations that may result in a half-being are strictly prohibited and an offense punishable by death. There is only one recorded surviving abomination—Killian. His life is forfeit and belongs to the service of the Order of Kings.

Airmid (AERah va): Airmid defied her father's cruel ways and stood with her king and the People of Light in defense of mortal men and the Veil. She hid a secret from both her people and her father—she had fallen in love with one of the mortal's huntsmen and given birth to a son. Killian. She gave her life to defend Mide, and for her sacrifice, the Order of Kings honored her plea to protect and preserve Killian's life.

Celestials: Supernatural entities. An encompassing term for the race of peoples classified as deities, angelic, faerie, sidhe—all terms pertaining to beings with powers, abilities, and features beyond the natural/visible world. Celestials possess elemental magic conjured from the creation of the world itself and are considered guardians of creation, the balance of the universe, and architects of the Veil. There are only two known pure Celestials left alive—me and Connor.

Dian: The Traitor. He was the god of healing. He murdered his son in a fit of jealous rage and was eventually driven mad by power and greed and became convinced mortals were the true cause of the pain in this world. He channelled an ancient evil to give himself the strength and abilities to destroy the Veil and purge the physical earth of the "stain of mortality" and build it anew.

~~**dolmen stones:**~~ Dolmen stones appear all throughout the ancient world. In some mythology, they are considered the doorways between worlds. ~~Key?~~

kelpie: An amphibian-equestrian creature indigenous to the Veil lands. They are comprised of a horse's body but have the skin of a seal, webbed hooves, gills, and fin-like mane and tail.

Mide: Within this mortal earth, there is the existence of middle grounds—planes of existence between worlds. These are pockets of the earth that were blessed by Celestials in the ancient days. They remain sanctuaries for Celestials and mortals alike. Many of the Order of Kings inhabit and protect these grounds from the malevolent forces seeping out of the Veil. Presently, all are secured by the Order. The largest and most hallowed is Mide.

Order of Kings: An ancient order of mortals illuminated to the secrets of the Celestial and supernatural worlds. They are descended from the oldest kings and ruling clans of ancient Ireland. In modern times, due to globalization, immigration, displacement, and a violent history, branches of the Order exist around the world in every culture and religion. They are bound by ancestral blood oaths to defend and keep hidden the truths of creation. They follow a strict hierarchy as follows:

elders: The highest position within the Order is an elder seat. It is a small inner circle of the most elite members of upstanding moral and enlightened backgrounds, usually representing the various branches of their global network. The elders will vote on a ruling overseer who presides over the entire Order of Kings. Presently, that title is held by Lord Christopher Callaghan IV. He comes from a tangled line of Irish earldom, royalty, and European aristocracy.

elites: Elite members of the Order make up the ruling class. Most are from aristocratic lineage or they have been elevated from lower ranks. They carry out and oversee most of the executive decision-making from the elders. They blend into world governments, business, and various humanitarian pursuits to prevent supernatural exposure to the masses.

scholars: Scholars are the descendants of the druids and spiritual leaders of the ancient world. In modern times, they are the professors, teachers, and interpreters of the ancient texts. Many truths have been lost to time, war, and translation, and these members devote their lives to the preservation of ancient secrets.

huntsmen: These are the elite military branch of the Order. Their ancestry is believed to be tied to great warriors of old, blessed by the Celestials for their courage, cunning, and valor in battle. Those identified as huntsmen (or huntswomen) usually begin their paths as guardsmen, but through experience, testing, and observation, they are identified as having keener senses, physicality, and intuition above and beyond regular soldiers. Huntsmen are a dying breed among the Order. Many were wiped out in the war, and those left dwindle in number either due to age or gruesome death at the hands of wicked Celestials.

guardsmen: The majority of the Order's military branch are guardsmen. They can trace their ancestry to the same aristocratic bloodlines as the elites, but that tie is weak in comparison. Still, if a guardsman role exists among a family, it is considered a high honor. Many guardsmen are implanted within world military specialist branches, global intelligence agencies, and secret services. Their duty is to carry out orders and to pinpoint and eradicate rogue supernatural agents that manage to escape the Veil.

spiorad na spéire: An identified supernatural race of avian shapeshifters. Considered lower in magical ability to Celestials, but a subbranch of the same supernatural peoples.

the Veil: The supernatural matrix that blankets the entire physical earth, separating the celestial unseen from the mortal seen. Cited appearances indicate a crystallized mirror-like substance that cannot be passed through without access to a key—a blessed, celestial vessel or item that can allow safe passage between worlds. There are no known keys in existence.

Veiled Lands: The collective name given the supernatural lands beyond the Veil, inhabited by Celestials. Presently, the Veiled Lands remain under the control of dark and malevolent forces who answer to the Traitor. The Veil itself is the only entity preventing those forces from spilling into the mortal world.

ACKNOWLEDGEMENTS

Firstly, there is no greater gratitude I hold in my heart than for the spirit and heartbeat of my homeland. The woodlands steeped in mystery. The Atlantic coast, where the skies crackle with authority and the waves break the shore with a resounding majesty—a siren call to my soul. The emerald fields and stone circles. The ancient trees I've rested under. Thank you for giving me what no human soul could—a profound closeness to the Father, Spirit, the Creator, in which all things are from, through, and to.

Thank you to my mother for never allowing me to quit. For the nights and days spent loving me back together, reminding me of my strength, for always believing in me and this story—even when I couldn't. To Dad and my sunshine little brother, who rarely read a darn thing I write but somehow have full faith in everything I do, I love you.

To my "fellowship of fans" and Lord of the Rings friends all around (middle)earth—*look* what all your love and encouragement created! None of this would have been possible without each of you. Team Smirkwood rides again. And, of course, to Paul and Janine, the dearest of dear friends. Your love, support, spiritual guidance, two a.m. chats, and open-door policy kept me sane throughout this process. Remember when we sat around that table in your old kitchen and decided to make our dreams reality? We did it.

Eva Marie Everson—my American writing sister with an Irish soul and the "mother of God"—it could only have been divine intervention that crossed our paths. My life has been amazing since you entered it. And no acknowledgement would be complete without mentioning my heroic literary agent, Cyle Young—thank you for believing in this queen of fanfic and for continuing to represent me even after I nearly drove us off that cliff. Also, appreciation for Hope Bolinger, who read *so* many first chapters—a true legend. Eternal gratitude to Ramona Pope Richards and Iron Stream Media for believing in me and this story. And to Jessica R. Everson, the best editor deserved of a sainthood—thank you for making this process a breeze, polishing *Tempest* until she shone, and for being as passionate about this story as I am.

Finally, a simple thank you to my Granda Jack and Nana for all the books, fireside stories, and endless fairy tales. I wish I could ask you to "tell it again" just one more time.